THE
ROOKIE

ANA SHAY

PROLOGUE

AUSTIN

"Damn you, Griss," I curse under my breath as the cold air of the basement billows around my face. Shunting my shoulders, I do my best to wiggle out of the rope, but the chair restraints are too strong, and they hold me in place. Well, great. I'm officially stuck.

Come on, A. It's just a little food after the game.

My best friend Matt Grissom's words echo in my brain as a taunting reminder of my naivety.

We're just celebrating your call up. How many more chances are we going to have to do this once you're in the Big Leagues?

I bite down hard on my tongue. I should have known better. This is Griss we're talking about. The biggest goofball I know. If I hadn't had those two extra shots of tequila, I'd probably be wrapped in my bathrobe, getting ready for bed right about now. But nope. I'm the idiot that trusted my blabbermouth friend with my biggest secret. Ever since he found out, he's come up with new and innovative ways to throw that little tidbit in my face. Granted, never in my wildest dreams did I expect that a couple of shots of tequila would lead to this. No, Griss really outdid himself this time. Being tied up in a club basement with a woman dressed as a cat, staring at me like I'm warm milk is not how I'd ever planned on celebrating my call up.

"I still can't figure out why Matt is so worried about you?" Her eyes roam my thighs, stopping at my crotch, and she licks her lips, taking a step closer in her sky-high leather boots. I lift my knees as my only form of defense because there's nothing else I can do tied in this position. "You're puuurfect." She slinks toward me with all the elegance of a feline, and if I wasn't so frightened about what she was about to do, I'd be impressed with her commitment to the role.

I pull harder at the restraints, sweat prickling at the back of my neck because all I can concentrate on is the steady scratch of the whip dragging across the floor while her tail bobs in the air. Speaking of, how is it attached to her? It's not part of the suit, and it looks like it's coming out of her... Oh wait. Is *that* why she's slinking? Is she trying to keep it in place? Doesn't it hurt to walk?!

"I've got some big plans for you tonight, Austin."

Swallowing, I drop my gaze to the floor, hoping that this is some kind of crazy fever dream and I'm going to wake up at any moment. Who knows, I could be into this kind of thing, but Caterina (yes, her real name) is not the girl I'm going to find that out with. How much did Griss pay her to do this because this whole scenario is beyond embarrassing?

Her bodysuit squeaks with every slink, which would be funny if I wasn't genuinely concerned for my safety. Are those nipple clamps hanging over there? What's the third clamp for? My nipples tighten at the thought, and I hear her mewl in appreciation. Thank God I still have my jeans on, which is more than I can say for my shredded shirt beside the chair. Unfortunately for me, that was clawed off the minute I was locked in here.

She steps closer.

Lets out a little purr.

Closer still.

Time is running out. She's going to flog me with that leather thing if I'm not careful.

Closer again.

Was that a *meow* I just heard?

Too close.

This is all Griss's fault, and I plan on tearing him a new one once I get out of here... *If* I get out of here. I'm NEVER accepting an invite from him again. I will also NEVER believe him when he tells me the bathroom is down a long flight of stairs in the dark cellar. Why was I so trusting of that man? He gets yelled at regularly for wearing his hat to the side because he believes it brings him good luck. The guy doesn't have a clue, and when you follow clueless people, you end up in shitty situations.

Her stiletto heels touch the tips of my sneakers, and she pokes her tongue out, licking at the corners of her lips. My fists clench, my whole body freezes in anticipation of the hit. She lifts the whip, and I grimace. She's ready for this, and there's a serious possibility I might wet myself.

"Armadillo!" I screech at the top of my lungs. A high-pitched wail comes after, and it's only after it echoes through the room for a second that I realize it's coming out of my mouth. With my eyes still closed, I wait for the pain of the whip, but nothing happens. So I open one eye, gulping when I see her frown. Even through her full-face black leather mask, there's obvious disappointment across her features. The whip in her right-hand skirts across the tiles of the room, and my balls shrivel a little, but I have hope that this might be the end.

"Armadillo?" She repeats, her shoulders slumping. "Really?"

I nod over-enthusiastically, like one of my bobble heads glued to the back of the car when it goes uphill.

"Matt said you were inexperienced, but I didn't realize you weren't into flogging. We can try something else if you'd like?" She gestures to the table full of brightly colored things. Dildos? Butt plugs? Vibrators? I have no idea what any of them are. All I know is, I won't find out tonight.

"I'm good," I screech out, sounding like a fourteen-year-old boy. Who knows? My balls have gone so far up my crotch, there's a very real possibility that I have reversed puberty.

Swallowing hard, I pull at the restraints. "It's just that I've got to be up early for a day game tomorrow. If I'm late, I might miss my opportunity to be called up," I lie, but I have no other option. That whip is still swaying at her side, taunting me with its presence. My balls will never recover from this.

Thankfully, she takes it easy on me and unlocks the handcuffs. I bolt out of the seat, swerving around her because I'm certain she'll try to claw at my chest, and I'd rather not have cat scratches to explain in the locker room.

"Thanks for everything," I call out, my voice echoing through the makeshift, cat-themed dungeon she created. Shaking my head, I laugh at my stupidity. The place is called *Cat's Kitty Palace*. Why on earth did I think this was a cat café before I walked in?

"Don't be a stranger," she drawls out, loud enough for a few of the patrons by the basement door to hear. I slam it shut just as quickly as I opened it and focus all my attention on the floor.

Let the walk of shame begin.

I can feel the heavy glares of the other patrons as I walk past. Could this be worse than Cersei's naked walk of shame? Definitely. All of these men know exactly what goes on down there, and they're judging me. I would be too if I were them. I'm hot and flustered, and the fact that I'm

"Idiot," I mumble under my breath, still a little salty over the shit he put me through yesterday. I haven't spoken to him since because my brain is still deciding if killing him is worth the guilt of rendering his daughter fatherless. So far, my heart had won out, because his daughter, Rhode, has a mean fastball, and I'd rather not die because I got hit with a baseball one too many times. But that doesn't mean her father is off the hook. He will pay.

I kick up a little more dust, watching the batter prepare himself. Tom gives him no time to relax, throwing the ball at ninety-eight miles an hour straight down the middle.

Strike three.

The crowd cheer in our small ten-thousand capacity stadium as I take one last look at the half-filled seats, offering a wave to those who stayed until the end as I jog back to the dugout. It feels strange thinking that this might be the last time I play on this field for the year, maybe even ever if I perform well enough for the Catfish. But that's a big *if* and I don't want to get ahead of myself. A call up is just that. A call up. I could be sent back down at any time. Just like last year.

As I stand in the dugout, removing my gloves and hat, Griss slaps my shoulder. "Hey man. Why have you been ignoring my messages?"

I groan, glaring at his wide smile and big brown eyes. As much as he tries to hide it, there's always a look of mischief glimmering across his face, and it's unsettling for a guy like me. Stone cold, I say, "As if you have to actually ask."

Pushing his hand off my shoulder, I shove my gloves in the cubby behind the benches and head down the dugout, ignoring him.

"Come on." He throws his arms out to the side, full on grinning at my embarrassment now. "You can't be mad at me for that, can you?"

I glare over my shoulder, doing everything I can to remain angry. Griss has a way of making you easily forget why you're annoyed, but his charm won't work today. "I can."

"But Caterina is so nice. I thought she'd take it easy on you. Especially considering your... *condition*." He wiggles his eyebrows, air quoting.

Okay, now he's made me mad. "You *told* her?" I turn around, stalking back toward Griss and push him hard on the shoulders. He stumbles back, frowning, because he knows not to make me angry. I may be a nice guy, but when I'm pushed, I will use my force.

"No. Of course I didn't tell her. Do you really think I'd want to get whooped in the ass by you?" He dusts off his jersey, looking at me with his signature smile. "I don't want your little secret getting out just as much as you. But I may have mentioned that you might need a little guidance to figure out what feels good." I hate the way he emphasizes the last word, pretty much confirming that he told her everything about me.

I take in a long, drawn-out breath. *Don't kill him. Think of Rhode. She deserves better.* I hardly get embarrassed by things, but this is the only exception because it's just so hard to explain. And personal. Way more personal than I should have ever gotten with Griss.

Griss takes a tentative step toward me, raising his hands and bowing his head in defeat. "Fine. I get it. I crossed the line. I'm sorry."

I laugh bitterly. "Crossed the line? Griss, you left me handcuffed in a sex dungeon with a cat dominatrix. You were so far from the line; it was in a different state."

"Handcuffed?" I nod. "Dominatrix?" Another nod. He lets out a low, hesitant chuckle. "Well, when you put it like that, it kind of does sound like one of those *Saw* movie scenarios," He barks out with a laugh because he thinks he's so funny. "At least you survived without having to cut any of your limbs off."

"Barely," I mumble, shivering over the thought of her finding me, and that whip tickling against my thighs again.

Nodding, he lowers his head to talk to me. "It's okay, I get it. You aren't expected to drive a Ferrari when you've just passed your test. We need to start a little slower," he whispers, looking around the empty dugout as though someone might be listening in. We've been out here so long, everyone's already in the locker room, and no one cares to eavesdrop, anyway.

Pointing between us, I try to make my next sentence extremely clear. "*We* don't need to do anything. I don't want your help."

Griss masks his frown well, but I can tell he's taken aback by the way he steps aside. "If you didn't want my help, then why'd you tell me in the first place?"

"It was a mistake."

"You know, trying to use a vacuum as a sex toy is a mistake." He looks at me pointedly, and I don't want to know if he's speaking from experience. "Staying a virgin until you're twenty-one seems downright intentional." And there we have it. He just had to come out and say it, didn't he? I've never had sex and I'm the idiot that told my loud-mouth best friend a secret that was better off left in the high school locker room than out in a bar. Now, that little tidbit comes back to haunt me every time I look at Griss and he gives me that knowing smile.

"It's not."

"You sure? Because you went through high school, and college, and you've been in the minor leagues for three years, yet you've not even gotten close to tasting any pus-"

"Keep it down," I grit.

"Ah, yes, I forgot. You're a baseball machine, and if a small white ball isn't hurtling its way to you at one hundred miles per hour, you aren't interested." He juts his chin out, mulling over his own words. "You know, maybe one day, there will be acceptance for your love of the batting cages. Until then, I hope you clean up after you've finished hitting, because I bet it can get messy."

"When exactly did you expect me to lose it? When I went to prom? Because I didn't go, remember? I left high school at sixteen to get better at bats in college. Once I was there, it's not like anyone on campus would risk their reputation by sleeping with a minor, so I just accepted that my social life had to take a back seat."

"All I'm hearing is that you had the opportunity to bang older college girls, and you didn't take it. But guess what?" He wraps his arm around my neck, directing me to look at the other side of the stadium where the Macon Minnow fans await. "You've now got the opportunity to bang any of these baseball loving girls and every single one of them would happily take the risk of being the first person you jump in bed with. So really, the question is, are you going to take the chance with one of them? Or are you just going to keep painting those little statues in your mom's basement?"

"I only paint miniature Warhammer's to reduce my stress."

"Really? Because I can think of some better ways to reduce your stress, and they're right over there." He tips his cap toward the fans again.

"That's not happening anytime soon." There's nothing left to say on the matter, but I can see it in Griss's tight jaw. He's somehow found a new angle to take, and yet another way to bring it up during inappropriate conversations.

"No. I think I get it." Narrowing his eyes, he studies me for a few seconds before asking, "Is it because you like them older, but once those girls in college turned you down, you lost your confidence?" Okay, so maybe there's a little truth in liking a more… refined woman, but I'm not about to admit to Griss that he might have gotten something right. I don't know what it is about an older woman, but girls my age have always seemed a little superficial. No one has ever really understood why I'd spend so much time focusing on baseball when I could be hanging out with girls, and I'm fine with that. Not that I'd ever say it out loud, but it's why I'm already here, about to be living my dream with the Carolina Catfish.

"You know?" Griss wags his finger at me, getting my attention. "You should have gone for someone in the faculty." He grabs my cheek, pinching it. "They would have been much more susceptible to your big baby face." I brush his hand off me, walking away because I have nothing to contribute to this conversation. Unfortunately for me, Griss is a persistent fucker, and he's hot on my heels. "You know, in my experience, I've always found faculty members give the best head."

Lifting my chin to the sky, I roll my eyes, wondering why I said hello to him on my first day in the minors to begin with. He'd been on the team several years at that point and was eating the biggest donut I'd ever seen. He looked like a fun guy, but I should have taken it as a hint that no one was eating the donut with him. He's more interested in building a following than playing baseball. "How is it that I know your daughter, I've met your baby mama, and I bunk with you during the season, yet I'm still able to learn something new about you every day?"

He grins, holding his hands out like he's starring in *The Greatest Showman* and looks around at his imaginary audience. "What can I say? I'm a pretty fascinating guy? But anyway. Enough about me. Have you picked your victim - I mean woman - that will finally take you past third base?" He looks up wistfully, clutching his hands together like he's a teenager in love.

Silence.

I don't dignify that with an answer, and my curiosity piques when I can't hear him shuffling behind me because, usually, my non-answer would warrant a long, drawn-out response. I hazard a look over my shoulder to see he's stopped in his tracks. Brows furrowed and mouth gaped open, he asks, "You *have* been to third base, right?"

Raising a brow, I genuinely ask, "What constitutes third base to you?"

Griss groans and rests his forehead against my arm, gently knocking his head against me like I'm a wall. "The fact that you have to ask that

"Greg won't be back, but there are plenty of viable options to take his place in the league. They could just buy another third basemen tomorrow, and I'd be back in Triple A next week."

Griss whistles. "This is the Carolina Catfish we're talking about, right? The team isn't exactly known for paying for talent when their farm system is stacked. They aren't going to buy anyone when they have you waiting in the wings. The good news is with healing time and recovery factored in, Greg isn't likely to play until post season. That leaves you as their only option as their starter because they're cheap."

"Maybe. But this is baseball. If my first few games suck, things could change dramatically. Who knows? I could be traded to the Atlanta Armadillos next week." I give him a tentative smile, trying not to sound too superstitious, but it's my first time starting in The Show, and I'm seriously nervous that I'll fuck it up before I even step foot on the diamond, and going to the Armadillos would be a nightmare.

"Please, spare me the pity party. They wouldn't trade their number one prospect to their number one rival. It makes no sense." He flicks my head, then taps his own. "Get your head on straight and think about the most important thing."

"You're right. Playing the game."

Spinning on his heel, he growls, and looks up in the air in disgust. "And this is why you'll be a virgin when I ask you again in ten years from now, my friend."

Honestly, I've never met anyone so invested in my sex life. Even *I* don't care as much. Ignoring him, I walk to the showers, but Griss has other ideas. He grabs at the collar of my jersey, holding me back. "And where do you think you're going?"

"To shower. I've just played a three-hour game in ninety-degree heat. I smell like an old, shared gym sock, and I'd like to change that before going home with you." I look him up and down, stopping at his noticeable pit stains. "You should consider it too."

He rolls his eyes and looks at me as though I've missed the point again. Apparently, I have. "And that's just another reason why you've still got that big, fat V Card. Women don't want a clean ball player that smells of fresh shower gel. They want a man that's been out in the blistering sun, smelling of sweat, dirt, and grass." As I look at him with disbelief, he shrugs his shoulder. "It's pheromones, I don't make the rules. I just follow them."

"On that note. I'm going to shower."

He grunts his disapproval, slowly letting go of my shirt. "Fine. Well, I'm not going out there without you, so I'll have to take a shower as well. Meet you in the gift shop for the signing later."

Shaking my head, I say, "See you in a minute."

Holding back a laugh, I grab one of the fluffy white towels on the side. Griss starts to sing *Like a virgin* loud enough for me to hear in the stall across the room. Idealistic fool. It doesn't matter how I smell or what pheromones I exude, it's not like I'm going to meet my dream girl today, anyway.

CHAPTER TWO
MIA

Unknown: Ignoring me will only make me angry, Mia.

I toss my phone into my bag, ignoring his message because worrying about it will get me nowhere except another potential restraining order. Besides, after three years of these texts, I've come to realize they come in waves. They'll stop for a few weeks once he gets his money and just when it gets to the end of the month, bam, another one comes through. The pattern is exhausting, but at least I know not to react.

As I weave through the gift shop, I pass the tackiest memorabilia I've ever seen. Hats with fins, fishing poles in the shape of baseball bats and fish mitts. Apparently, if the Macon Minnows can stick a fish on it, they will and then they'll jack up the price for the pleasure.

But I stop looking at the cheap merchandise when I see Jett and my heart immediately sinks to my stomach. Sweet Jett is tugging at a Carolina Catfish jersey, looking at it longingly because he thinks I can't see him. I just know he wants it, but he'll never ask me for it. He never does. He knows money is tight even without knowing everything I'm throwing at Simon just to keep him at bay.

"Hey, J. What are you looking at?" I ask, squashing the Minnows hat on top of his thick black hair. His thumb rubs against the 'A' stitched across the 'Adams' jersey in admiration. Plain gray with red lettering. It does look like a nice jersey. So nice, that I'm currently wearing an 'Adams' jersey myself. Austin Adams has been Jett's favorite player since he was promoted to the Triple A Minnows three years ago, and surprisingly, Austin's stats were the only way to get him talking after the accident. I took him to a game when things got particularly tough and that was the start of our new relationship. With every Macon Minnows win, Jett talked more and slowly came out of his depression. Its why no matter what, I try to make sure there's enough money at the end of the month to go to at least one game.

Still looking at the shirt, he says, "It's just an Austin Adams jersey."

The $29.99 tag flashes at me. Taunting me like those Jimmy Choos I've always wanted but can never afford. Not that what I want matters. What matters is that Jett wants this jersey, and I want to give that boy everything he deserves… I just can't. Not on my teacher's salary. Especially when it's just me, and his father is such a pariah to this family.

I offer him a weak smile, hoping he doesn't see the sadness behind it. "Aren't you already wearing his shirt?" I lean back, looking at the bold green letters. "Do you really need another one?"

"Probably not," he resigns, and my heart slowly makes its way back to my chest. At least that means I won't get a text from my bank warning me about being in my overdraft. "It's just that this is his Carolina Catfish jersey, and it's his first year fully starting in the big leagues." I wanted to roll my eyes so badly, because, of course, his favorite player would be moving to the big leagues after a short stint there last year. I can barely afford the Macon Minnow tickets, but now if I want to see Jett smile, I'm going to have to somehow find a way to pay for MLB tickets for the pleasure.

Jett drops the fabric, looking at it like a long-lost love. It's the same look my sister Hailey used to give me when she saw me playing with a new toy I'd get for my birthday. She always hated sharing with me, but was loyal to a fault, and here I am, being just as loyal. Guilt scrambles my stomach when I think of her. Jett never asks me for anything. He's got a baseball scholarship with the best high school in the state starting next year, and he keeps out of trouble. Only talks with intention and is a good kid that works hard to get good grades. He's trying his hardest to make his dreams come true, even in these circumstances, and all I can do is admire him… and maybe buy him a jersey or two. After all, there's no one out there who deserves this more.

I just wish I had the funds. Maybe if I started that OnlyFans account like Charlie, my teaching assistant suggested last week, I'd be in a better position than this. No one would have to know about it and I could put any extra money in my savings. Although is there a market for women over thirty to strip naked? Aren't they all looking for girls in their twenties with fast metabolisms and the ability to do their makeup with their eyes closed? Not that I would start with nudes immediately. I'd only dip my toe in the water, so to speak. I hear several people have made fortunes just selling pictures of their feet, and the ladies at the nail bar I used to go to told me I had soft, supple heels, so it feels like the perfect fit.

But then all my thoughts come tumbling down when I look at Jett who's already dealt with so much adversity these last few years. The idea of one of his friends printing my OnlyFans feet pictures and throwing them around his new school is too much. I can't put him through hell because his dad is blackmailing me.

"It's his first year in the big leagues, huh?" I silently tut the roof of my mouth because I can feel myself caving in. It is a nice jersey, and Austin Adams seems to be a good role model. Clean cut and determined. If I can keep Jett focused on succeeding in baseball, then he might have his own way out of this hell without me.

Jett nods enthusiastically. "Yeah, he's making his debut on Monday when they play the Atlanta Armadillos." His voice goes up five octaves with enthusiasm and it's then I feel the last brick of the wall I'd built up crumble to dust.

I guess I could bite the bullet and go into my overdraft for three days. It's not like my credit score is incredible, anyway. Besides, it would be worth it to see Jett smile.

"Okay," I sigh, pulling out my purse, ready for the inevitable bank message I'm going to receive. My thumbs already itching to swipe it away, because the quicker I do that, the quicker I'll be able to forget about it. Just as I hand Jett my card, some guy clears his throat behind, and I snatch it back instinctively.

"Excuse me." I see a thick finger tap on Jett's shoulder and my body immediately goes into fight or flight.

No. No. No.

He's not getting him. I'll claw his eyes out and go to jail before I let him get anywhere near Jett.

I clutch Jett's other shoulder before I see who it is. "I couldn't help but notice that you're wearing my jersey." My shoulders slump because even though it's a familiar voice. It's not the one I was expecting to hear. Night after night, interview after interview, Jett watches this man religiously, and it almost feels like I know him. He lets out a low whistle. "How'd you get my first-year jersey for the Minnows?"

When I turn to look at him, I nearly trip on my feet.

Austin Adams looks… different. Certainly not what I was expecting in real life. After watching him with Jett on the field for the last three years, I was fully expecting to see a cute guy with a baby face, but nothing compares to the presence he commands standing in front of me.

Tall with a light dusting of stubble, he oozes man, and don't get me started on those quads. Thick with three c's, Austin Adams is stacked everywhere, and I'm finding it hard to look anywhere but the fabric of his jeans because I didn't know they made ones that could fit thighs as big as his. They have to be custom. There's no way anyone else has that thigh to waist ratio.

Stop staring, Mia.

Was that Jett? Nope. Thankfully, it wasn't a thirteen-year-old telling me to stop salivating over his favorite baseball player. It was just my own mind trying to save myself from the embarrassment of ogling over a guy that views me as a baseball mom with high-waisted jeans and a cross-body bag to match. Thank goodness I left that fishy fanny pack Jett bought me at home.

I blink a few times, lifting my gaze to the man in front of me, and do everything in my power to not think about his legs, or his bulking chest, for that matter. It's hard, though (no pun intended). They're right there and are so big that it's taking up my entire view. I bet he could just throw me up in the air like it's nothing if he wanted to. I'd definitely let him try. Naked.

Where the hell did that thought come from?

Jett tugs his jersey, making sure there are no creases as he looks up at Austin with a beaming smile. "I had it made your first season, sir. I knew it wouldn't take long for you to get into the Big Leagues."

He laughs at the compliment, waving Jett off. "Don't call me sir."

But what if I want to?

Cringing, I screw my eyes shut. Oh, dear lord. Please, please, please tell me I didn't say that out loud. I take my time to open one eye. A tiny amount of relief courses through my veins because neither one of them is looking at me like I've lost my mind, so I can only hope that was yet another misplaced thought.

"Well, then I think you're the only person who has this jersey. I didn't exactly sell many when I started."

Jett shakes his head, pointing his thumb in my direction. "There's two here." Austin takes a second to look at me, and his easy smile fades into something that resembles a frown before he diverts his attention back to Jett. Well, that was rude. I get it, I'm not the kid, but he could have at least given me a smile, a wave, anything other than that. "And I bet we aren't the only ones. You've been throwing bullets from third since you were brought up."

And that comment has me looking at Austin's arms. Thick. Just like everything else about him. Thick neck, thick thighs. There is nothing small about this man. Well, at least nothing I can see.

Stop it, Mia.

The guy is like, what? Nineteen? And you're staring at him like you want your own personal Magic Mike show? He is not here for you. He barely noticed you existed, and this is Jett's dream, not yours.

"I can't wait to watch you play for the Catfish next week."

And my heart immediately warms at Jett. That smile. It's all I wanted to see today, and I finally got it. "Well, I hope I live up to your expectations."

"You will."

Austin smiles. "Do you play?"

Jett nods. "Yeah. I move between Catcher and Third Base at the moment. Haven't figured out which one suits me best yet."

I laugh, accidentally drawing attention to myself. "He's being modest. Jett has a scholarship to Charlotte High's baseball program next year."

Austin's eyebrows raise, his attention solely focused on Jett. "Wow. You know I went there?" Jett nods proudly. "What's your name, kid? I'll make sure to look out for you in the next couple of years. Bet you'll be playing me in no time."

"Michael James, but I go by Jett because it's my mom's nickname for me."

"Okay, Jett James," He smirks, liking how that sounds. "It's been a pleasure to meet you." Austin turns on his heel, but something stops him from moving away. Instead, he points at Jett to get his attention. "You know what? We're in town the weekend after next. I can get you a couple of tickets if you'd like?"

Jett screeches out a "Yes," before I've been able to register it. The entire store turns to look at him, but he doesn't notice. Not even the large camera to the side of them, blocking my view.

"Great. Where are your parents? I'll get their number so I can arrange the tickets." He looks around, not even bothering to give me eye-contact even though we literally just met a minute ago. He clearly knows I'm standing here, and now he's trying to pretend that I don't exist.

Wow. What a complete dick.

I clear my throat, standing up a little taller, and that draws Austin's attention. His eyes grow wide, and he visibly swallows. "Oh wait, you're Jett's *mom*?" The last word rolls off his tongue with what feels like disgust. "I thought -" He trails off like he doesn't know what to say, but it's probably best he says nothing because he'll only make it worse. He just made me feel old. Really, really old, and to be honest, I don't know what he could say that would make this whole encounter between us better.

So, just like that, the mood dies, and an awkward silence ensues. But I can't be angry, for Jett's sake, so I try to be civil.

"I'm Mia." I hold my hand out, trying not to dwell on the subject. When his large paw accepts mine, it's clammy and loose. Not what I expected from a guy like him. "It's nice to meet you." Though, I'm not sure how true that statement is, considering he's giving me the stink eye. "Jett has been a huge fan of yours for years," I say, trying to salvage this encounter for Jett's sake, hoping that Austin gets the hint and does the same.

Austin's smile slants, and he rubs the back of his neck. "I got that." He clears his throat, the sweat now visibly dripping down his forehead. Did the guy eat some chili peppers or something? "Hotdogs."

I lift my brow, confused. "Hotdogs?"

"Uh, yeah." Crinkling his eyes shut, he shakes his head, laughing nervously. "Do you like hotdogs?"

Is that a euphemism or is this all a joke? All I know is that the longer I stay in his presence, the more annoyed he makes me.

He laughs with that same hesitant energy as before. "I'm sorry. Don't know what came over me." He's a fumbling mess and if we weren't in front of Jett, I might throw a glass of water in his face to calm him down.

"Is everything okay?" I ask.

"You'll have to excuse my friend." Matt Grissom, another ball player that Jett likes to talk about, pulls Austin into a choke hold and rubs his knuckles into his friend's ball cap. "He's a little nervous because he's going to the Bigs next week."

"So I've heard."

"That's a big deal around these parts." I lift my brows, feigning interest. "And well, there's also the fact that you're a MILF and it's throwing him off his game." He offers me a teasing smile until Austin pushes him off angrily.

"Griss! Stop," Austin hisses, his face reddening.

"What's a MILF?" Jett asks, and I'm more horrified than I've ever been in his thirteen years of life. MILF? Really? I may have been fawning all over this frat boy a minute ago, but being objectified by him is out of the question. He's looking to be objectified with his tight pants and muscular legs. I, on the other hand, have minimal makeup and have fully covered my DD breasts. So how dare they talk about me like this in front of Jett?

"I'm sorry. This is why I usually do meet and greets alone," Austin mutters, refusing to make eye contact with me.

Turning to Jett, I grab his hand. "It means nothing, J." Even as I say it, I know he doesn't believe me, and the kid's thirteen. I'm sure he's just feigning ignorance for my sake. Standing up a little straighter, I look at my wrist, which is noticeably absent of a watch, and then between the players and Jett. "Is that the time? You know what? We've been here a little too long. We should probably head home. Got a lot of stuff to do." Nothing comes to mind, but anything is better than standing here, forcing through this awkward conversation. Jett's had his moment. He's spoken to his favorite player, so I can go to sleep tonight, happy knowing that I didn't have to go into my overdraft for some cocky nineteen-year-old.

"What have we got to do?" Jett asks suspiciously, and my face flames because both ball players are still watching me with interest. Can't blame them. Watching me fumble my words around a teenager is pretty ridiculous.

"It's secret stuff that I'll tell you about in the car." Grabbing his hand more forcefully, I'm stopped from walking because Jett digs his heels into the carpet of the gift shop.

"What about the tickets?" He looks at Austin longingly.

Damn it. I was hoping he'd forget about that.

Austin scratches the back of his head, clearing his throat again as he steps forward. Is he really going to try to salvage this because nothing will make this better. "I guess if you give me your number." He swallows thickly, and Matt barks out a laugh, shaking his head. Still. They are still making fun of me. "I can text you about it?" Austin rolls on the back of his heels, smiling at me anxiously.

I snort because you've got to be kidding me? He wants my number after that MILF comment? This has to be a joke, right? I'm being set up. It's the only explanation that makes sense.

"Austin," I say smoothly. "Would you mind talking with me in private for a second?" With pursed lips, he nods. Again, a little too over enthusiastically like a Labrador. Rolling my eyes unimpressed, I look at Jett for a quick second. "Jett, would you mind going to the Christmas ornaments and finding one for your grandparents? I'll meet you there in a minute."

He shuffles on his feet, but nevertheless drawls out a reluctant, "Sure thing."

Turning on his heel, he takes his time walking away, probably hoping I'll start my tirade so he can listen in. Not going to happen.

"Wait." Austin clears his throat, standing straighter. "Before you go, can I sign your shirt?"

Is this guy gunning for ballplayer of the year or something?

Jett's face lights up *again* as he trots to his favorite player, which acts as another reminder of how much this whole thing means to him. Anger rifles through me because I have a sneaking suspicion that this is all a joke to Austin, and I don't like it. Not one bit.

Jett turns around, flaunting Austin's last name on the back, and Austin chuckles, signing it. Once he's flourished the last 'S' of his name, I push him aside and look directly at Jett.

Craning my neck toward the Christmas stuff, I say, "I'll see you in a second, Jett." There's enough intention in my voice for him to get it. I need a minute. All he does is tip his chin and walk straight to the fishy ornaments.

"Do you want Austin to sign yours, too?" Matt asks, his smile still wide and sarcastic. Austin brings his fisted hand to his mouth, apparently choking on the suggestion, but when he catches my eye, a slow smirk

When Jett looks back at the ornaments, I focus my attention to Austin, tilting my head to the side. "So you're serious? If I give you my number, you'll give him tickets?"

He nods, pushing out his tongue and wetting his lips. "And my jersey."

"Why?"

"Why what?"

"Why are you being so nice to us?"

He shrugs, and I notice a slight pink tinge across his cheeks. "You want the honest answer?"

"Wouldn't have asked if I didn't."

He lets out a hesitant groan, looking to the side before bringing his gaze back to me. "My mom always taught me to appreciate the fans that support me. Before this year, I'd only ever seen a handful of people in my jersey, and most of them were related to me. Never have I seen a fan in my first year Minnows one, let alone two. This is my way of saying thank you for the support, but if you'd rather I give the tickets to someone else -"

"No. No. That's not it." Wincing, I start to feel a little bad because maybe I judged this situation a little too hastily. My rock-hard exterior is slowly cracking at the potential of accepting something from someone. "It's just that you can't say incredible things like that to Jett if you have no intention of keeping your promises."

He stares at me, the intensity clear in his features. "You don't have to worry about that with me." He closes his eyes, looking slightly pained, or maybe he's just awkward. "I know we got off on the wrong foot, but I'm not that guy. I eat, sleep and drink baseball. That's the only thing I live for, and seeing someone who has the same passion for the game makes me want to help. I'm a man of integrity. I always keep my promises, especially ones with kids." He raises his hand, gesturing behind me.

I look over my shoulder at Jett, who's smiling proudly, showing some other fans the back of his shirt. My heart fills with joy because I haven't seen him smile so brightly in a long time. He looks so much like my sister, it's crazy. I've missed seeing that, and as much as I hate to admit it, the hotshot in front of me is the main reason I'm getting to see it.

"Fine. We would love to accept your offer of tickets." Turning back to him, I whisper a reluctant, "Thank you."

"No problem. It's nothing." He waves me off, chuckling in the process, and I'm surprised at how warm it is. Is there more to this frat boy than meets the eye?

"It's not nothing. Thank you." I don't know what comes over me, but I somehow find myself hugging Austin. I feel him freeze, probably just as shocked as I am. He doesn't stop me, though, and rests his hands on my arms. I'm guessing because his mother taught him well. It's only when I unclench my fists that I realize I'm holding onto him like he's my only lifeline. "Jett doesn't have many positive male influences in his life, so having one of his favorite players show him the kindness you are means more than you know." The words come out muffled because I'm against his chest, with little motivation to move. It's so strong and wide, and he smells so good, and I've got to stop these thoughts right now because they aren't appropriate.

"Honestly, I get it. When I was Jett's age, I got to play catch with my favorite ballplayer, Mitch Lowe. It was everything to me back then, and only solidified that I would do anything for the game." I'm taken aback by his moment of honesty as I stand, still wrapped in his corded muscles. Instead of looking at me, he glances over my shoulder and he whispers, "Now, if you don't mind giving me your number, I'll make sure to let you know about the tickets."

And that's my cue to back down. "Yes, of course. Sorry." As I settle on my feet, I realize somehow Austin's hands have dropped to my hips, and I think he does too. He doesn't immediately move them, just looks at me with a hesitant glare. Something passes between us, but I'm not sure what.

I smile coyly at him, but back away, growing some sense. He's probably a decade younger than me, and he said it himself, I'm just the MILF of his biggest fan. He only wants to give Jett tickets. That's it. I need to stop reading all those romance novels that would have me believe a guy like him would be interested in a train wreck like me.

He pulls his phone out of his pocket, offering it to me, and I quickly type my number in before handing it back and giving him a curt smile. "Thank you." It's awkward and stilted, and I suddenly feel like we're in a business deal that's reached an impasse.

"Anytime," he says, just as stilted. "Hopefully, I'll see you guys in a couple of weeks."

Why did a thrill of excitement run through me when he said that?

I nod, worried that my voice has suddenly disappeared. Turning on my heel, I walk away and see that Jett's been watching us with curiosity.

29

I wonder if he saw the hug. I'll need to come up with an explanation for the long talk in the car, that's for sure.

Either way, I make a mental note to look up Austin's age when I get home because there's no way I can be crushing on an arrogant frat boy that's only nineteen.

21. CHAPTER THREE

AUSTIN

"Do you like hotdogs?" Griss asks, mimicking my skittish voice from earlier. "I can't believe you asked that." I don't respond because I'm too busy watching Mia's ass as she walks out of the gift shop with Jett. Mia and Jett. *Mia and Jett.* What just happened? I feel like I've been punched in the gut three times over and can't get my head on straight. But that's apparently what a girl like Mia does to me, because this has never happened before. Her touch is like a slap in the face with a wet fish. A dunk in the ocean on New Year's Day. It's hard-hitting and hard to handle.

With deep green eyes and long dark hair, she was like my fantasy come to life. Worse still, she was wearing my jersey. *My* name was emblazoned on her back, and I could only think that this was some kind of sign. Mia's something else, that's for sure, and for the first time in my life, a chance meeting with a woman wasn't enough.

I wanted to know more. I *needed* to know more. Everything about her.

"Hotdogs?" Griss stresses again, shaking my shoulders while he barely stops himself from laughing. At least someone is getting entertainment over my embarrassment.

Swallowing all the pride I have left; I drop my head and close my eyes. "I know. You don't have to remind me. It was stupid." I remember so clearly that at that point, I was so stunned by Mia's beauty, my tongue felt too fat for my mouth. Words were spilling out without my consent. I couldn't talk, and was hardly holding myself together, especially when

31

she started narrowing her eyes at me. "I was trying to invite them to the Fishbowl Bar so they could have dinner with us." Even as I said it, I realized how delusional I sounded. "They have those awesome fish dogs I wanted to suggest they try."

"Seriously?" I nod, and that sets Griss off again. Barking out a laugh loud enough for the entire gift shop to hear. Thankfully, after signing a few more hats, the place had cleared out. "Please stop talking. This whole encounter is getting more embarrassing by the minute. I get that you're new to all of this, but did you really think she'd want to spend more time with you after you made fun of the fact that she was a *mom?*"

My stomach bottoms out because that's the part I feel the worst about. She completely misread my intentions. She thought I was making fun of her when in actual fact, I was stunned by her beauty. It's not her fault she couldn't tell the difference. She's probably never been around a guy with as little game as me. I had no idea what to say, let alone how to act in front of a woman I'm interested in. "I wasn't making fun of her at all."

"No?" Griss raises a brow in disbelief. "Wait a minute. Do you *like* her?" I don't respond because I'm sure the tinge of red blowing up my face gives it away. Why does it feel difficult to admit? And why does it feel wrong? "Please don't tell me that's why you went over to the kid in the first place? Because you wanted to hit on his mom?" He raises his brows in disbelief. I've seen him do worse, so I don't know why he's suddenly acting all high and mighty. "You really do like them older, don't you?" He laughs, shucking his chin.

"That's not the reason I went over. He was wearing my jersey, so I thought it would be nice to meet him. I only saw her after he introduced me."

And that was it. That was the moment that it all changed.

Griss grins, patting me hard on the shoulder. "You know what? I get it. She's hot as sin and was wearing your jersey. It's almost like she was made for you." Studying me, he adds, "It also makes sense that you'd look for a woman like her. Just a smidge old enough that you could consider her a motherly figure. Maybe she's someone that can teach you how to be a man."

"Mother figure is the last thing on my mind when I look at her." I'm baffled because nothing like this has ever happened to me before. It's like one look at Mia, and everything left my mind, replaced with inappropriate thoughts I couldn't bring up. Unfortunately those thoughts were bringing another thing up in locations wholly inappropriate for the gift shop. My dick. Because I couldn't stop thinking things like, *I wonder what perfume she's wearing. Does she laugh when she's kissed at the nape of her neck? Would she cry out in pain or pleasure if I bit down on that plump bottom lip of hers?* "I initially thought she was his sister when he pointed her out because she doesn't look old enough to have a kid his age."

Griss wags a finger at me. "This is your problem and why you need to have sex asap. You're right, if everyone waited as long as you to grope for trout, she'd be too young. But a lot of us experiment before we're forty, and sometimes experimenting can lead to long-term consequences."

Why did I feel like I was in high school having the sex talk with our Sex Ed teacher all over again?

I open my locker directly in front of his face, hoping that's enough to rid myself of Griss's less than helpful insight. Unfortunately for me, he's like an annoying gnat that won't go away, no matter how hard I try to swat him.

His hands clutch at the edges of the locker, and he pokes his eyes from behind, raising his eyebrows quickly. You'd never guess he was nearing thirty with the way he acts.

"Will you stop reminding me about how badly I screwed it up? I get it. I embarrassed myself and she'll never look at me as more than a cocky ballplayer. But you weren't exactly helping the situation. You called her a MILF in front of her kid."

He shrugs with no ounce of remorse on his face. "I call it like I see it. Girl was hot, and you were getting tongue-tied." Griss whistles, letting it roll into a laugh. "But thanks for confirming what I knew all along. You *like* her," he teases, like we're still in grade school. "I knew it. Your face went this funny green color, and I swear if I hadn't had intervened, you would have thrown up all over her shoes." He points, nodding to himself. "It's the same look I had when I asked Laura McConnell to prom Junior Year of High School. Sweaty palms, sweaty forehead, sweaty balls. My whole body didn't stop sweating until she said yes. Which she did, of course."

"Has anyone ever told you that you talk a lot of crap?"

"Has anyone ever told you your boner is on show?" I immediately look down, covering myself, but when I see nothing, I look back at him, annoyed. "Made you look. Anyway, I believe the MILF thing worked in your favor. Did you get her number when she dragged you away?"

I glance down at the blank screen on my cell phone, remembering her slender fingers wrapped around it. Never did I think someone typing on a phone could get me hard, but it did. Her hands were so dainty and small, with short, squared off nails that had my mind racing about things far from wholesome. "Yeah, I did," sounding just as surprised as I felt. Granted, I didn't get it without a few threats thrown in, but by some miracle she gave me her number, which means there's potential I'll see her again, especially if she takes me up on my ticket offer.

"See. After all that, she was still willing to give you her number." He clicks his fingers and shakes his head. "Damn. She must have a thing for over-developed calves."

I roll my eyes and get my stuff out of the locker as quickly as possible before leaving for the day. Griss stays stuck to my side, skipping beside me like he's my shadow. It's the way it's been between us since I joined the Minnows.

"Hey, don't walk away so fast. I'm just celebrating my little Austin growing up. My boy's about to go to the Big Leagues and there's potential he'll finally realize that sliding into a beautiful woman is just as good as sliding home."

And with that comment, I've never looked forward to the big leagues more. Not listening to Griss talking shit all the time will make concentrating on what's important a lot easier.

"You've got it wrong. She didn't give me her number because she wanted to date me."

He frowns as his shoulders slump in disappointment. "I should have known. I could tell you were striking out when I walked past. That's why I interrupted. I thought I might salvage a pathetic tabloid story about how the Carolina Catfish's newest rookie threw up on a fan. Although, the pictures would have made a great meme."

"I promised her son tickets to the game." I interrupt his babbling because I've been here before. If you don't stop him, he'll go on and on and on.

"And?" He raises his brow, waiting for me to elaborate, but to be honest, I have nothing to add since it all seems fairly self-explanatory. "Why are you looking so sad about that? Another game would be the perfect opportunity for you to offer her another, ahem, hotdog."

"How many times do I have to tell you? She doesn't want my hotdog."

"That's because she hasn't sampled it. No one has. I'm sure once someone gets a taste, they'll want more. Especially since it's tacoed between two giant pieces of thigh meat."

"Are we going?" I gesture to the keys clinking in his hand. My regret heightening with every tingle because it's like a reminder that I can't get away from him even if I wanted to. I live with him, I play ball with him, I technically shower with him, and I know him well enough to know that he's not going to let this go for a long time.

"All you need to do is make sure she knows there's a sample up for grabs."

Seriously, how did I put up with this guy as my best friend for so long? He's infuriating. "Griss. I am not putting the moves on Jett's mom," I grit out. As beautiful as I think Mia is, she's got a life outside of that five-minute meeting, and has probably already forgotten about the bumbling ballplayer who couldn't stop looking at her. Yet Griss and I haven't stopped talking about her since. Jett has a father. One I assume Mia still sees, even though she wasn't wearing a ring. He could be her long-term boyfriend, her fiancée, anything. He's also probably some stand-up guy that works in a skyscraper downtown for a living, crunching numbers and getting paid for sitting on his butt all day. She'd have no interest in a twenty-one-year-old rookie that's trying to earn a few dollars on a baseball field.

"Jett's mom? Are you on first-name terms with her kid now? How long were you speaking to them before I saved you from embarrassment? Do I need to warn Rhode that her uncle is getting a new nephew to hang out with?"

I whack the side of his head. "Griss. What doesn't seem to register through your thick skull is that Mia has a kid to take care of. She has a family, and probably a husband in the best neighborhood Macon can buy. I only got her number because she wants me to get her tickets to games. That's it. There's nothing else there." Nothing on her side, at least.

He narrows his eyes. "How do you know she has a husband and this idyllic home life? Did you see a ring on her finger?"

"No." And I looked, and it's not something I'm ashamed to admit.

"Then why do you think she's with someone?" he presses.

"Oh, I don't know," I say sarcastically. "Maybe it has something to do with the teenage boy smiling next to her."

Griss shrugs. "That means nothing. I also have a teen and my only attachment is to her. Not her mama." He may say that, but I know he'd get back with Selena if she ever showed an ounce of interest in him. But in my situation, he had a point. I'm being irrational and overthinking this whole encounter, which is something I never do. But why bother getting my hopes up over a woman that I'll probably never see again, let alone date? Especially if she has a husband. Besides these obvious obstacles, there are other things that factor in as well. Things I never really thought about until I noticed the sprinkle of freckles dusted over her nose.

"This situation is completely different."

"Why?" He asks, feigning ignorance. As I look at him, I realize my biggest mistake was starting this conversation with him in the first place.

"You know why," I say with a warning. "Even if she doesn't have a husband, boyfriend, partner, whatever." I shake my head, barely able to get the words out. "She's obviously had sex. Enough of it that she has a trophy to show for it."

"You did not just call her kid a trophy, did you?" I stay silent because I know it was an asshole thing to say, and I was pushing my own insecurities onto her, but I needed to get Griss on the same page. There is no Austin and Mia story left to write about. Griss is waiting for a surprise epilogue, but that isn't going to happen. This is it. In fact, if I were a betting man, I'd say I have more chance of going on a second date with Caterina from the cat café than I do with Mia. "Oh, man. There I was wondering how you managed to keep your V-Card with all these gorgeous women around you, and the answer has been staring me in the face the whole time."

Stopping in front of Griss's car, I glare at him. "What are you talking about?"

He may be a couple of inches shorter than me, but he steps forward, meeting me, chest to chest, daring me to question him. "You're scared."

I pause, staring him down as I study his face. Full of bravado and a little amusement, he knows I have no idea how to respond.

"I'm *not* scared."

"Mhm. Then you should know that it only takes one time to have a kid. I'm the living example of it. And if Rhode's my trophy after one night of the most amazing sex of my life, then I've already won the World Series baby."

"I don't know whether to be disgusted or sentimental about that."

He shrugs. "Be both. But the point I'm trying to make is that you don't know the circumstances surrounding her son, who she had at least a decade ago. What if she swore off sex after the first time because it was with some calve-less clown, and now all she wants is a Quad God to dominate her life? You're the best man for the job, Quadfather."

"That's unlikely."

"Where's your hope and optimism?" Griss squeezes my shoulders as though it's going to squeeze some of that optimism into me. "You're a huge hunk of man meat. Any woman would be lucky to be thrown around the bedroom by you, even if you accidentally throw them in the wrong direction."

I roll away from him, opening the car door and as I drop into the seat I say, "I knew I shouldn't have tried to have a serious conversation with you. It's like talking to a brick wall."

Just as I shut the car door, Griss sings, "Better than you having the same old conversation in your head."

By the time he makes it to the other side of the car, I've checked my phone three times for a potential message or missed call from her. Pathetic really, considering *she* gave me *her* number. I didn't give her mine.

"Are you going to text her tonight?" He asks, turning on the ignition.

"Why would I do that when she wants tickets to a Catfish game from me?"

"Because you want to slot your ticket in her?"

Of course he went there. I drop my head to the back of the seat, focusing on the streetlights as he drives us to the house we share with two other teammates, Jason and Travis. I can't even talk to them about it because they have enough of their own shit going on without having to deal with sex questions from a rookie.

"Seriously, though. If she really hated you, she wouldn't give you her number. You have a chance, and the only way you're going to find out if she's interested in more than tickets is by asking. That's how this works. You text. She texts back. You find out more about her and then decide if dating is something you want to do. Simple. You've just got to start."

"What would I even say to her? I know nothing about her except that her son loves baseball."

"Ask her if she likes to handle balls too," He jokes. This time with less veracity than before because I pin him with a glare. "I'm not trying to pester, I just know a little more about a situation like this. You should text her."

37

"Not pestering? Please. You live for meddling in other people's business."

"Okay, so maybe I might be trying to pester a little bit, but let's be serious here. If you're too afraid of people who have experience in the bedroom, then it's going to be pretty tough to find someone to have sex with." I grimace. "Let's face it. You're twenty-one, turning twenty-two in a couple of months, and you aren't getting any younger. Unless you're planning on saving yourself for marriage, which is entirely your perogative, you need to think about what you want. And from the looks of it, you want Mia."

"That may be, but I can't have her."

I sink into the chair, groaning like I'm a deflating balloon because he's right. I know he's right, but I hate admitting it. Mia has somehow slithered under my skin in our five-minute meeting, and I know I won't stop thinking about it until I've confirmed she isn't interested in a guy like me.

As I close my eyes, memories of her arms wrapped around me come thick and fast. It's weird. I've hugged fans before, but never *ever* have I thought about grabbing said fan's ass. It was like my body was already comfortable with her, and wanted to do what came naturally.

"You don't know if you don't try. When you're lying in your cold, lonely single bed tonight with me in the room next to you, just think about how much better life would be if the nice, warm, maybe naked body of Mia was there with you instead."

"There wouldn't be any room if she was lying in the bed next to me," I joke. The minor leagues may pay for our housing, but it's not exactly luxurious. Our three-bedroom apartment is just about big enough for the four of us, with me in the smallest bedroom and a single bed that barely houses my shoulders. But it's private and I've never invited a woman back, so I can't complain. "Besides, you're also forgetting that it's me you're talking to. I don't exactly have any game. I couldn't get her even if she was interested."

"You still haven't figured it out yet, have you, A?" He looks at me, baffled, and I shake my head slowly. "That's the beauty of looking the way you do in baseball pants. You don't need game. Just talk to her like you do the rest of us. You're a fun guy when you're not all pent up and sexless. I'm sure she'll see that if you don't overthink it."

Don't overthink it? Is thinking about it at all overthinking it?

"Whatever. I need to stop talking about this. I feel like I'm losing brain cells with every passing comment because nothing's going to happen."

"That's because you *are* losing brain cells." Griss's mouth falls flat as he stares at me intently. "The reality of the situation is that we're all dying, so you might as well make the most of your time here and ask the girl out."

I look at him. He looks at me.

Was that supposed to be a joke?

That's not how Griss usually responds. His beady eyes watch me, and after a few seconds of silence, I realize he's serious. "How very... macabre of you."

"Just text her tonight. You won't regret it."

I nod giving him a small smile with no intention of taking his advice, but at least that shuts him up.

***

"Damn you, Griss," I whisper to myself in the dark. He just had to meddle and put ideas in my head, didn't he? I'm staring at the ceiling while the spring of my single bed spears me in the back. Griss and Travis are talking about the Catfish game tonight, which I can hear through the thin walls, and for the first time in my life, I realize that the game isn't enough for me. I'm going to the Big Leagues next week, which means an immediate pay rise and relocation to a central Charlotte hotel. I've spent the last seven years focused on making my dream a reality, and now that I'm on the precipice of it coming true, it doesn't feel like enough.

I want more.

When my phone buzzes, there's an unwarranted level of excitement because I already know it's not Mia. Or any other woman that might be interested in me, for that matter.

Mom: Good game, Honey. Did you get home safe?

I inwardly laugh, because, of course it's my mom. She and my sister, Annie, are the only two women that I get texts from these days.

Austin: Thanks mom. Home safe. Talk tomorrow.

I drop the phone beside me and stare ahead. The pristine ceiling is marred by one long crack running down the middle, which has never really bothered me before, but tonight, it kind of feels like it represents me. It's got everything going for it except this one fatal crack that will eventually rock its foundations, making the whole apartment block come tumbling down. Griss is right, I might be over thinking this a little.

But it's easy to do when you're alone in your bedroom with no prospect of that changing in the foreseeable future.

As much as I love my mom, texting her is just a reminder of how lonely I am. It's not her I want to be texting right now. I want to take Griss's advice and text Mia, but after the way everything went down, I'm certain the only thing she wants from me is tickets to the Catfish game. Who can blame her? She's potentially a married woman with a kid. Not to mention I'm going to the Big Leagues, which means I have to prove myself constantly, especially when Greg gets back to full health. Thinking about anything other than baseball could be catastrophic to my career, but I can't stop myself.

Closing my eyes, I try to imagine facing some of the Atlanta pitchers in a last-ditch attempt to think of anything other than Mia's eyes. Green with specs of gold that could only be seen if you looked at her close enough. The light dusting of freckles smattered across her face suggested that she couldn't be *that* much older than me. Maybe five or six years? If I'm honest with myself, she could be twenty years older, and I'd still get a boner because she was just that hot.

When she hugged me, it didn't *feel* like she hated me, and the only hesitation she had about giving me her number was that she thought I was playing some game with Griss. What if I've read the situation wrong and there is something else going on? I won't know until I text, and if I know her relationship status, it might make it easier to stop thinking about her.

I snatch my phone from beside me and before I have time to think better of the situation; I type out a text and send it to her.

Austin: Hey Mia. Sorry about how things went down. Hopefully I can make it up to you and we can start fresh.

Not even a beat later, there's a message from Mia.

Mia: If you message me again, I can guarantee you, I will flambé your balls and serve them to your dogs. Leave me alone or I will report you to the police for stalking.

Shit.

I drop the phone immediately because what the fuck did I just read? That was a very visceral reaction to a very tame message. Had I sent her something in my sleep on the way home without realizing?

I pick up the phone again just to confirm that was the first message I sent. Albeit, I probably should have worded it differently and signed my name at the end, but I wasn't thinking straight. I just wanted to get a message to her.

I re-read it, and now I'm starting to think I'm not the one that sounds crazy because what the fuck kind of threat is that? She can't think it's me, surely? I know we got off on the wrong foot, but flambéing my balls seems a little extreme considering she still wants tickets.

I scratch a hand across my face. Do I risk messaging her again? I want to. Griss would want me too as well, but how can I salvage this?

You're a fun guy when you're not all pent up and sexless.

Like the devil on my shoulder, Griss's words repeat in my head again. I'm a fun guy. I have a severe lack of banter, but maybe if I think of her as one of the guys, I'll be able to be 'fun.'

I type out the message, figuring that I've already embarrassed myself twice for her. What's another time?

Austin: Well, okay. Thought you wanted those Catfish tickets, but I'd rather not have my balls doused in brandy and set alight for your pleasure. Also, I don't have any dogs, so who are you going to feed my tasty, flambéd balls to? If you still want the tickets, I could give your number to Matt Grissom or someone in head office to deal with it.

I'm not sure how aggressive that sounds. I was just trying to be funny, but reading it back, I sound like a dick. When the bubbles appear, its almost like a douse of cold water and I relax.

Mia: Is this Austin?
Austin: Yeah. Guess I should have introduced myself, but I was too intrigued by your threats. Flambéing balls? Who hurt you?
Mia: I'm sorry. I thought you were some other guy and may have overreacted.

Some other guy?

So that confirms I'm not the only one interested in her. Not surprised. Mia's hot as hell, but the question still stands. Is the other guy her partner that she's having an argument with, or a creeper. Both I'd like to strangle, but I'd have more reason to do it against the latter.

Mia: Thank you for the ticket offer again. I promise I won't flambé your balls because Jett would never speak to me again.

Interesting. She double-texted. If Griss were here, he'd be telling me that means she wants to double bone, but it's gotta mean something, right?

Mia: Also, side note. Please don't give Matt Grissom my number. I *might* flambé his.

I bark out such a loud laugh, I'm certain the guys in the other room hear it.

Triple text.

I'm no expert, but that *definitely* means something.

Austin: Good to know my balls will remain intact, and don't worry, you're number is safe with me. I wanna be the only guy you're texting 😊

As I press send, I immediately regret it. I just sent her a winky face. What the hell am I doing? Flirting? Because sixteen-year-old's on TikTok have better game than this.

Shaking my head, I roll my shoulders and close my eyes. *Stop putting pressure on yourself.* Deep breaths. Deep breaths.

I just need to relax; pretend I'm talking to Griss or one of my roommates. Make it no big deal and be fun.

Mia: Wow, Austin. I gave you the benefit of the doubt when I met you. Thought you might be high on adrenaline, but you really do have the frat boy energy down pat, don't you?

Smiling, I read the message and start to feel myself calming. She's joking with me, so I couldn't have screwed it up too much.

Austin: My answer depends on if you like it or not.

Send.

Mia: Unsurprising FBE response again.
Austin: ??
Mia: Frat Boy Energy. Think that will be your nickname from now on.
Austin: One day in and you're already giving me nicknames. I'm flattered.
Mia: Don't be. I'm only speaking to you for tickets.
Austin: You sure about that? Because your BG energy tells me something different. You wouldn't take any shit from me just for free tickets, I'm sure.
Mia: BG Energy? Am I an electricity company now?
Austin: Boss Girl Energy. Guess that will be your nickname from now on, too.
Mia: Spoken like a true Frat Boy.
Austin: I can assure you that I'm not a frat boy.
Mia: You sure about that? You're cute with muscles galore, so you've got the look down. Admittedly, your charm could be improved, but I'm sure you're working on that.
Austin: You do know that I was too young in college to be allowed in a frat, right?
Mia: Seems to be a pattern for you.
Austin: What does that mean?
Mia: Nothing. You just have a youthful look, that's all.
Austin: I'm Twenty-one.
Mia: I know.
Austin: You been looking me up?
Mia: Don't have to. Jett knows everything about you.
Austin: So you asked him my age?
Mia: Yes, because I wanted to make sure I didn't just give my number to a minor.
Austin: Why would it matter if you're only talking to me for tickets?

Mia: Big Leagues next week. How do you feel about it?

I smile at the interesting change of subject. I wonder what else she asked Jett, but wants to avoid admitting.

Austin: Like I want to pee my pants and show them what I got all at the same time.

Mia: Aren't the Catfish uniforms gray? Might want to pee before the game, otherwise everyone is going to see.

Austin: Thanks for that little nugget, BG. I'll make sure to remember it on Monday.

Mia: No problem, FB. That's what I'm here for. Can't have Jett's favorite player embarrassing himself on his first outing.

Mia: Although, I wonder what a pair of wet Austin Adams pants would go for on the black market.

Austin: What makes you think I'd give them to you?

Mia: You wouldn't, but you might give them to Jett if I'm judging you on past behavior.

Mia: Thanks for signing his shirt, by the way. It's all he's talked about since we got home. In fact, it's the most he's talked in three years and that's all down to you.

Austin: Anything for my biggest fan.

Mia: 😑 His favorite player would be a twenty-one-year-old frat boy.

Austin: Like I said before, you've got me all wrong. I'm not a frat boy. Far from it. I was drafted when I was eighteen, so didn't even finish college.

Mia: I know. You seem to be forgetting that I have Jett at home.

Austin: What else did Jett tell you?

Mia: Everything. The kid is like your personal encyclopedia. Your dog's name growing up, your sister's birthday, the school you attended, the year your parents married, the first baseball team you played on. It feels like the only thing I don't know about you is what color socks you're wearing.

Austin: Not wearing any right now.

Mia: Well, there we go. The fountain of knowledge is full.

Austin: So you've really been trying to get to know all about me today?

Mia: Relax. No This is an accumulation of knowledge from the three years Jett has watched you and I'm only now putting together that it was you he was talking about. I didn't go fan girling back to him after I gave you my number.

Austin: It's okay to admit you're interested, you know?

Mia: I'm not interested, per se. I just happen to know everything about you.

Mia: Urgh. Can you please pretend you didn't get that last message? I can't delete it because you've already read it, but it sounds way worse than I intended. 🪦

Austin: It's okay. I get it. You know a lot about me. Now it's time I learn about you.

Mia: Not likely.

Austin: So prickly, but I like it.

Mia: And that's all you're going to find out about me tonight.

Austin: Well, there is one thing that Jett hasn't told you about me that you need to know.

Mia: Oh, yeah? What?

Austin: When I want something, I go after it relentlessly until I get it.

Mia: What's that supposed to mean, FB?

Austin: You'll find out soon enough.

Mia: Oh, FB, flirting with a MILF. What has your life become?

Austin: Everything I could ask for.

Still grinning like an idiot because she called me cute and admitted she asked her son about me; I place my phone on the bedside table. I don't want to come on too strong, and over text. Besides, Griss would tell me I need to keep her wanting more.

CHAPTER
FOUR
MIA

Austin: Is it just me, or does the Carolina Catfish mascot look more like a depressed shark than an actual catfish?

I nearly spit up my soda as I look at the picture Austin attached to the text. There he is with his beaming smile and a brow raised while he holds Catty the Catfish's head in what looks to be a first aid room. The setting, his messages, and how funny he is have a way of making my heart skip every time my phone buzzes. And honestly, it scares me.

It all feels like an illicit affair. I shouldn't be replying to texts from a twenty-one-year-old ballplayer, no less starting conversations with him. And I'm beyond guilty of that. Over the last two weeks, whenever I've had a free minute, or I haven't heard from him in a few hours, there I am desperately tapping away, sending him messages like some obsessed cleat chaser.

But he responds. Almost instantly, every single time, usually with a picture to make me laugh. It feels a whole lot more than just a wholesome interaction that I can share with Jett. So I keep it to myself for now because I have no idea what we're doing talking to each other, but there's something about him that keeps me coming back.

Austin: What do you think, BG? Catfish or Shark? Do I need to put it on to get the full effect?

"Why are you smiling like you've just been sent Henry Cavill nudes?" Charlie, my teaching assistant, asks as she walks into the classroom. My third-grade class is all outside for lunch, and I'm enjoying the only break for the day. "Not that I'm disapproving, but if you get caught with those on school grounds, you'll be fired. If you're gone, I'll be upgraded to teacher, and I'm not sure anyone is ready for that to happen. So, think about the kids before you scroll down and see that monster."

"I'm not looking at Henry Cavill nudes." I wave it off, but then I think for a second. "Wait. *Are* there Henry Cavill nudes?"

She touches her nose, only offering me a slanted smile. "Wouldn't you like to know?" She peers over my phone. "So, if it's not Cavill's Cavalry getting you all hot and bothered, who's making you smile like you've just sat in a bath full of chocolate and the only way to get out is to eat it?"

I roll my eyes, pushing my phone away, but making sure the screen is blank before I leave it. "What makes you think it's a who? I could be smiling at a funny meme, or a video I saw on social media."

"Because you're a grandma when it comes to the internet. I'm surprised you even know what the word meme means, let alone pronounced it correctly."

Pushing my lips out, I pout. "I'm not that bad."

She raises a questioning brow. "The fact that you just called it 'social media' and didn't reference a platform tells me everything I need to know about your internet habits."

I roll my eyes. "I'm sorry we aren't all spring chickens like you." My phone buzzes and I take no chances this time, grabbing it, I stuff it in my pocket, so she won't see any potential messages from Austin.

"You're thirty. That's only five years older than me, yet you act like you're sixty-five."

"I'm thirty with a thirteen-year-old at home," I add that very important point. What I don't add is that I'm flirting with a guy younger than her because that's a whole can of worms I don't want to open. Even now, I question my sanity. I should be looking for a mature man that will accept mine and Jett's screwed up life. A good guy that could help take care of us and ease the load. Instead, I'm flirting with a guy who sleeps in a single bed, in a house full of ballplayers, and has no intention of settling down anytime soon. He's the personification of a Frat boy.... But

47

with each passing text, I can't help but enjoy his boyish charm.

"Having a kid at home doesn't mean you're dead and devoid of desires. You do you, Mia. If those Cavill nudes, do it for you, enjoy them. Preferably with one of those new rose sucker things. I've read the reviews, they sound awesome," she pops out with an 'OK' sign.

"Just to be clear. I don't have pictures of Henry Cavill's dong."

"You should. I've spent one too many nights in my reader groups zooming in on photos I know I shouldn't. The only thing I will say is, don't look up 'Henry Cavill Sweatpants' ever. Not unless you want to be truly disappointed with your partners for the rest of your life." She smirks, looking to the side as though she's remembering something fondly. I'm not sure I want to know what.

"Charlie, we need to get you a date."

Flipping it back to me, she points at my face. "And we need to get you a *man*. You're surprisingly picky for a just turned thirty-year-old with Cavill nudes as your only way to get off."

"Charlie, we've been through this before. I'm not going to date the janitor. He's in his sixties."

She shrugs. "And you act like you're sixty. You'd be the perfect match."

"I don't act *that* old."

"When was the last time you went out? Like full on, dressed in a sparkly dress, had your hair and makeup done, and danced the night away like you didn't have a care in the world?"

"Senior prom."

"In college?"

"No. High school."

She shrieks so loudly that I'm concerned the window panes will shatter. "Now that is just sad." Her eyes are big as she takes me in with the same pity I was used to seeing three years ago, when everything went to shit, and my sister passed away.

"Is it? Because I'm perfectly content over here."

"Exactly. Content. Don't you want to live a life that makes you more than just content?"

"I guess."

"Perfect. So tell me who's put a smile on your face so I can make sure you don't mess it up. And don't tell me it's a meme because there's no way a cat playing a piano is going to make you smile like that."

"Fine. It's Austin Adams." I say his name like it's a lead balloon on my lungs that I've finally managed to force off.

"Austin Adams?"

"The baseball player?"

"Oh," she sighs out. "I knew it was too good to be true. Have you been watching the highlights of some baseball game with Jett or something? Or is it that you've found his nudes? What's this guy look like, anyway?"

"No. I'm not looking at his nudes." But now that she mentions it, I may want to. Especially if his arms are any indication of how thick he is elsewhere.

"I get it. With ball players, you can just look at their pants and see it. That's the great thing about men's sports and the only reason I watch football. Have you seen Devin Walker's bulge?" She waggles her eyebrows, poking her tongue out of the side of her mouth. "Let's just say his fiancée is one lucky lady."

"Will you stop talking about men's crotches? It's getting weird."

"No weirder than you watching the slowest sport on earth."

"It's not the slowest. Cricket is slower."

"I don't even know what that is."

My phone buzzes, and this time I check it because I'm concerned it might be Jett.

Austin: I thought the mascot head would be enough of a hint for you, but it looks like you decided to leave me on read instead.

Austin: Ouch. That hurts.

I flick my gaze back to Charlie.

"Just tell me who it is already?"

"I already did, but then you went off on some bulge tangent, and I can't control the places your ADHD brain goes. I'm talking to Austin."

She gasps, looking around the room in surprise, but there's no one there to join in. "Wait. You're sexting a ballplayer?"

"No. We're not sexting. We're just talking." I shrug it off, holding back my smile as I look at the little picture next to his name. Even though it's small, his wide smile fills the screen, and his light eyes draw me in. I want to look at all the other pictures he's sent me, but I can't risk doing that here. Not with the way Charlie is snooping.

"So that's it? You're just talking to a hot ball player? No big deal. We all do it, right?" She shakes her head with a sarcastic laugh. "How'd he

49

get your number in the first place?"

I groan, laughing at the memory now, still unsure of how we got here. "He wanted to give Jett tickets to his game."

"Oh, I like his moves. Goes through the kid to get to the parent." She winks and sits on my desk, trying to get more information.

"No, it wasn't like that. I don't think he knew I was with Jett until after he offered the tickets."

"What makes you think that?"

"Because he started stumbling over his words when I introduced myself and offered me a hotdog out of the blue."

"A hotdog?" She barks out a laugh. "Like he offered you *his* hotdog?"

"No. He offered me a hotdog to eat." That makes her laugh harder. "There was visible sweat trickling down his forehead, and his voice went really high at some point."

A slow smile grows on Charlie's face. "You know why, right?"

"Not sure about the hot dog, but I'm guessing the sweat was because I yelled at him."

She leans in close to emphasize her point. "No. That's not it. It's because he likes you."

Scrunching my face, I look at her with confusion. "He's twenty-one."

"Didn't stop *you* looking, did it?" She smiles smugly because she knows she got me there.

"That's different. He's a celebrity in our house, and we're always watching baseball, so I'm allowed to look, but it doesn't work the other way around. A guy like him wouldn't be looking at me." Disappointment dripped down to my toes as I admitted the harsh reality aloud for the first time.

"And why would you think that? You're a hot commodity."

She pinches my side, but I back away in fear that she'll get a fat roll. I could only wish I was twenty-five again and looked like her. Perfect skin and a tight body. Now that would be something for Austin to look at. Not my beat up, old body.

I hate feeling sorry for myself, but Jett's dad really did a number on me. I barely had time to shower, let alone work on my appearance or go on dates, which made me feel about as hot as week old bread left out to mould on the counter. There's no way a sexy, young baseball player would ever look at me twice. I'm delusional if I think otherwise.

I shake my head. "No. I think the only thing he's interested in is winning a bet with his buddies over getting my phone number, which he did."

She holds out her hand even though there's nothing in it. "Case in point. He likes you, and his friends were helping him out."

"No. It wasn't like that. One of his friends told me he thought I was a MILF, which makes me think he's a guy with a mommy kink or they're just messing around to see if they can get the old lady interested in him."

"Will you stop with this older woman bullshit? You're hardly old at thirty, and by talking like that, you're already aging yourself out of the market just because you don't think you're good enough."

"I'm not aging myself out of anything. He's nine years younger than me. That's a fact."

She stares at me blankly, as though she doesn't get it. "So what? Guys date younger all the time, and nine years isn't even that big an age gap. I've dated guys fifteen years older, and it's hot."

"He's closer in age to Jett than me…. Let that sink in for a second."

She screws her face and glares at me with disgust. "Why are you thinking about it like that? That's weird shit. He's twenty-one, and in his sexual prime. Have fun with it."

His sexual prime? That description sends a shiver up my spine, reminding me of all those inappropriate thoughts I had about Austin when I first laid eyes on him. Not that I can actually remember what it feels like to have sex that I enjoyed with another person. I've been too scarred to do anything with anyone after everything that happened with Hailey and Simon. Maybe that's why I'm happily flirting with Austin, because I know it won't go anywhere, and that makes it safe.

"Nothing's going to happen."

"Then why are you texting him?" She points at my phone with a raised brow.

"Because he promised me he'd get Jett tickets to his game."

"Come on, Mia. Even you don't believe that. I can hear it in your voice."

"It doesn't matter what I believe. Nothing's going to happen between me and a twenty-one-year-old ballplayer. Imagine the threats I'd get if Simon found out."

Charlie takes in a sharp breath because she knows she can't win when I pull out the Simon card. He's a manipulative asshole who's always finding a new way to blackmail me, and this would just be another way to play into that. He'd probably use it as some kind of threat to get the courts to side with him.

"When was the last time Simon texted?"

"Anything other than a threat over money? A year ago."

"Ever think that he's lost interest in you as anything more than a cash cow?"

"I wish, but no. He's done this before. Puts me on a metaphorical shelf for a while and then pops up every now and again to remind me who he is and what he can do if I stop sending him those monthly payments."

Charlie offers me a sympathetic smile. I didn't want to tell her about all of this, but it seemed impossible not to after she found me sobbing in the bathroom over a legal letter Simon sent me. He knows how to hurt me, and that's pointing out how easy it would be for him to take Jett from me if he really wanted to. Not that he does. He'd only do it to spite me.

"So that's it? You've just resigned yourself to never being happy? Because Simon won't like it?"

"No. I just -" I don't know what to say because when she puts it like that, it really does sound like a crappy excuse. "It's complicated. That's all."

Folding her arms, she narrows her eyes, running her tongue across her teeth while she assesses me. "Can I give you my take on the whole thing?"

"I'm sure you'll give it to me even if I say no," I mutter, but she doesn't hear.

"I think Simon is a good excuse to not be happy. It's the easy way out and means you can play victim for the rest of your life instead of taking accountability and going for things you want."

"Are we still talking about me dating a ballplayer?"

She nods. "Yes. If you want to ride that young stallion until the cows come home, you should be able to. Simon be damned. He doesn't own you, and you certainly shouldn't be sitting at home on your own because of him. You're hot, and it's only right that you get some action before you get cobwebs down there."

"Are you finished?"

She shakes her head. "I won't be finished until I've helped you get your itch scratched. When are you seeing Austin again?"

I sigh, holding back the urge to check my phone and see if he's sent me more messages. "I might see him this weekend at his game, if he invites me." I try to make myself sound cool and unbothered by the whole thing, but internally, I'm freaking out because I think I might actually want to see him. "Which is still a big if."

"Why are you waiting for the invite? Just ask him where the tickets are."

"That's not really my style."

"Again. This is why you're sitting at home on your own. You need to take life by the horns, or the balls if they have any. What have you got to lose? Just ask."

As if by some act of fate, my phone flashes again, causing us both to look down.

"That's him, isn't it?" Charlie asks with excitement.

I hum out an agreement and check it.

Austin: I've got two tickets behind the dugout for Saturday if you want them?

Smiling, I look up at Charlie. "Looks like I won't have to ask. He's just invited me and Jett to watch his game on Saturday." There's a tingle of excitement in my belly, which I try to tamper down because he's just keeping his promise to Jett. This has nothing to do with me.

Charlie squeals. The math sheets she's holding flutter to the ground as she hops over to me. "Please let me come. I did a class on body language in college. I can help figure out if Austin's really into you."

As I stare at her overeager face, I ask, "Why does it feel like this is just an excuse to get you to the game?"

She shrugs. "Because it *is* just an excuse to get me to the game. I want to be there and see this guy in action. On and off the field."

"There will be nothing to see."

"If there is, I can at least entertain Jett while you let Austin woo you." Her eyebrows wiggle, and she's got that facial expression that I know well. She's not going to give up until I've caved.

Groaning, I push back from my desk. "When you put it like that, this whole thing feels all kinds of wrong."

Charlie frowns, and her eyes bore into mine. There's a seriousness that I don't see in her often, which makes me feel a little uneasy. "It's not wrong to be interested in a guy. You've put your life on hold since Hailey passed away as if that's going to somehow make her come back. But that's not what she would have wanted for you. She would have wanted you to live the life that she can't. You're great with Jett, but when he leaves for college, what are you going to do? You need to live for yourself as much as for him."

I force through a smile, trying not to show that the mere mention of Hailey can still turn me into a hot mess. She was my best friend and the fact that she died thinking I betrayed her still haunts me even though it's been three years since she passed. I think about her every single day at least three or four times. Even more when I look at Jett. I know if I had someone to confide in, they'd be just as honest as Charlie and tell me I need to move on, but sometimes I'm so lost in grief that I feel defined by it.

"Mia," Charlie presses, coming to my side. Clearly, I'm not as good at hiding my emotions as I thought. I pull out a tissue from the box at the end of my desk and dab at my tears, careful not to mess up my makeup because the kids will notice, and no doubt ask questions. "I'm sorry for bringing Hailey up."

"It's fine. You're right. Hailey wouldn't want this life for me. Living life paycheck to paycheck and waiting for the next threat from Simon isn't what I want, but sometimes it's hard to see how I get out if it." I offer her another smile, but this time, it feels a little less forced.

"I didn't mean to upset you, but Simon surely can't have any objections to you going to a Catfish game with Jett? That's something he should do himself."

"You're right." I swipe my nose one last time, and take a deep breath. "Do you still want to come?"

"Yes!" She squeals. "I don't have a clue about baseball, but I'll be happy just looking at the tight pants."

Laughing, I quickly type a message to Austin, smiling at Charlie once I finish.

Mia: We'd love them. Any chance you'd be able to snag a third one?

Austin: Sure. Who's it for? So I can register their name at the front desk.

Mia: Charlie Davenport.

Austin: No problem.

Charlie squeals, and her little fists start shaking in the air. "I'm going to a baseball game for the first time in my life just to meet your toy boy. Two things I never dreamed of happening in my lifetime."

"Toy boy?" I raise an unimpressed brow.

She dips her chin, looking at me with a wicked grin. "Oh, stop denying it. If he hasn't sent you a dick pic yet, you'll be getting one soon. I guarantee it."

"You're delusional."

"But I'm right. Do you think Austin has any older teammates?"

"Older?"

Charlie draws a sly smile. "You might like to date young, but like I said before, I like a daddy."

Staging upright, I adjust my shirt. "Do I want to know why Daddy rolled off your tongue so smoothly that it sounded like a pet name?"

"Probably not. We've got the kids coming in ten minutes, so we should probably get back to being professional." She rolls her eyes.

Just as I plan to put my phone away, I notice a notification come through and quickly check it. That's when I crack a smile, because Austin sent me another picture. *Where did he find this?* It's a picture of the first day we met. Austin's signing Jett's shirt and I'm looking at him admirably, which is surprising because I was pretty ticked off with him at that point. For all intents and purposes, you'd think it was taken by a professional, but there's something different about it. Something's off. It's only when I read the message, I realize what.

Unknown: Good for you, Mia, but I gotta say, stalking a ball player isn't low key. Not that I'd expect anything different from a cougar like you.

That picture isn't from Austin.

Swallowing, I feel my body heating, and I instinctively look around the room, expecting to see someone watching me. To see *him* watching me, but there's no one there. There never is when I receive a message like this. I'm in a secure school that no one can get into. He's just messing with me to point out how much control he has over me.

"Ooh, did Austin send you another message?" Charlie drops the last paper on a desk, along with her hip, as she looks at me with a smile. "Is it a sexy text? You're looking all dark and broody."

Shaking my head, I quickly shove my phone into my desk and do my best not to think about that text from Simon, which is hard, considering that picture keeps flashing in my mind. Was he there with us? How else could he have found it?

"It's nothing. Just one of my neighbors complaining about the noise after school."

"Again? I thought they accepted your apology after Jett broke the window?"

"Yeah, well, what can I say? They hold a grudge." Thankfully, the bell rings, cutting short our conversation. Kids stand outside the classroom waiting to be called in, and I force out a smile, showing no emotion as they file in. It's not their problem, and only I can deal with him. So, I'll do what I always do and ignore it.

21.

CHAPTER

FIVE

AUSTIN

"Why is your leg shaking so much?" Tate Sorenson, our shortstop, elbows me in the rib as he looks down at my bobbling knee. "You need to calm down." Easy for him to say. He's just put us two runs ahead by scoring the first homer of the game against our biggest rivals. He had nothing to worry about because he's a Catfish legend. The guy could fart a nuclear bomb, and someone would want to bottle that shit up and sell it in the gift shop. Tate Sorenson can do no wrong in this place. "Is it because you're nervous about your at bat?"

My at bat? I hadn't even thought about it this inning since I'm five batters away. Unless we start a rally, it's unlikely that I'm going to be up since I'm at the bottom of the lineup. It's strange because these at bats are what I've been training my whole life for, yet I'm not nervous about them. I've done my time. I've worked years and years for this, and I've homered in my last three games. I'm confident that I can keep my hot streak going because of all that work.

I nod, agreeing with Tate because I'd rather he believed that instead of the real reason behind my twitching leg, which is too embarrassing to admit in a dugout full of my teammates. If opening up to Griss taught me anything, it's keep my sex life private. Or should I say *sexless* life.

"Don't be. You're on a hot streak. Ride that shit like the wind and keep winning. The crowd loves you; the team loves you. You're a Catfish through and through." He laughs to himself. "If you keep playing like this, Greg is going to have to compete with you to get his spot back. He knows it too. We talked about it the other night."

I raise my brows and hum out in acknowledgement because, as per usual, I don't want to jinx myself. They're only saying this now because I'm playing well. Let's see what happens the minute I go cold for longer than a game.

"You know what?" Tate leans in, and I follow suit. "When I get nervous, I always like to remind myself about the first time Grayson pitched for the Catfish. Did you see it?"

I cut my gaze down the dugout to our ace veteran pitcher. Looking on one of the pre-approved iPads, he's analyzing the opposing pitcher with Max. After seven years on the Catfish, the guy is almost part of the dugout furniture.

"No." I inwardly laugh, shaking my head because, after all this time, I can't imagine Grayson being anything other than a formidable force to be reckoned with. The idea of him ever being a rookie is hard to imagine. "Well, when he came out of college and entered the draft, there was so much hype about him. He did all these crazy things to make himself a better pitcher. Things like using those shake weights while doing yoga, but the thing is, he's never cared about what other people thought about him. I remember there was so much hysteria about his curveball, I genuinely expected him to hit a perfect game on his first outing."

"But that's not what happened?"

Tate shakes his head. "Nope. I'm sure you would have heard about it if that was the case. The guy doesn't shut up when he ties his laces correctly. Imagine the talk we'd get if he ever hit a perfect game?" He groans and rolls his eyes at he looks over at our teammate with a smirk. Then he leans in. "First time he was out on the mound, he let in three runs within his first five pitches."

"No way?"

"Yes." Tate can't hide the amusement on his face. It's like he's telling me the biggest secret of our time. "If that wasn't bad enough. He was so nervous after starting the game with a three-run deficit, he threw a pitch so wide, it made Fifty Cent's toss look like it was on target."

My lips curve into a smile as I watch Grayson casually talk to Max.

"Grayson Hawk? How is that not all over the internet? He's got an ego the size of Charlotte. There's no way he'd let something like that go."

"He didn't. That's why if you look it up. You'll find no information on his first start. He scrubbed the internet and used his entire signing bonus to hide it from the world." He raises his fingers and tilts his head. "Now some say that the story isn't true, and it's just lore. A whispered fable amongst the dugouts made up to make opposing batters feel better when they're going up against him."

"That would explain a lot. The story just doesn't sound legit. There's no way Grayson could hide something like that."

Tate shrugs. "Maybe not, but if there was anyone that could do it, you know it'd be Grayson. He does all kinds of shady shit. But you're right. It's probably just an urban legend. The guy's been in the league so long, I'm not even sure they had TVs on his first start."

I snort, trying to hold back my laughter, but it doesn't stop the Coaches grumbling at me. Sitting up a little straighter, I bring my fist to my mouth and pretend to clear my throat. Then I take a handful of seeds and shove them in my mouth, hoping that it will help control my laughter.

Tate knocks my knee, and whispers, "There we go. That's what I wanted to see. You forgot your problems for a second."

"Thanks," I mumble, but unfortunately, my problems are much bigger than my next at bat. At bats are nothing compared to the conundrum I face. Mia. The girl, or should I say woman, sitting out in the stands with her son, is the dilemma that has my leg shaking with uncontrollable nervousness. She's a conundrum, and I don't have nearly as much experience with solving that as I do at bats.

I don't know what we're even doing. She has a son, and yet we've been texting like teenagers without a care in the world over the last two weeks. Only, she *does* have things to care about.

Her son being one of them.

Charlie being the other.

At least I *think* Charlie is someone she cares about. She's bringing him to the game today, so he must have some relevance to her. Charlie and Mia. Charlie, Mia and Jett. I hate the sound of it. I hate that this might be the sign I've been looking for. Charlie Davenport could be Mia's partner.

But I still have no idea.

After spending the better part of two hours sleuthing the internet for pictures of him, I came up with absolutely nothing. It was like he didn't exist, but Mia was the same.

Which leaves me with only our texting to go by. And those have all been positive. When I thought the conversation had fizzled out one day, she initiated more texts, and they felt far from friendly. In fact, if I didn't know any better, I'd say she was flirting with me. I want to ask someone, but the only one who knows is Griss and it's not like I can ask him for advice without him getting overly involved. Therefore, I've concluded that I'm either getting stonewalled or catfished and she was only messaging me for free tickets. Which she got because apparently, I'm a chump for her, and I still want to see her.

Even if it's *with* Charlie.

Is he Jett's dad? Does he know that Mia's been texting me? Is he in on it? Will he punch my lights out when he sees the way I stare at his wife? His girlfriend? *Jett's* mom? I don't know at this point, but I've decided that finding out the truth will at least make it easier to focus on my game.

I should have just been up front and asked her, but there was a very real possibility that I would have scared her off if I did. I was hoping that when we started talking, she'd open up about it, but she didn't. Something I've learned about her is she's thoughtful, potentially strategic about what she shares, and she certainly doesn't say things she doesn't mean. Every answer with her is earned, and I plan on earning every single one that's been running through my head tonight.

Tate slaps my leg and dips his chin. "Looks like you're up." I glance to the field, and we're still several batters away, but the manager is beckoning me to get ready just in case. I push myself up, put my gloves on, and grab my bat from the side.

As I take a few steps out of the dugout, the crowd cheers close by. I turn around, offering them a smile as a thank you, but instead of leaving it at that and focusing on my at bat, I do something incredibly stupid. I look for Mia. I can't help myself, and it feels like a car crash. You know the ones where you know you shouldn't look, but you can't stop? Yeah. It's like that. Blood pumps through my veins, the adrenaline taking its toll as I look five rows back in the center behind the dugout, because I know exactly where the seats are.

"Austin!" Jett immediately sees me, and waves in excitement.

Way to be subtle.

There's no way I can casually look at Mia now. The whole section is watching and I try my hardest to keep my eyes from venturing to the two seats next to him until I realize I can't see them anyway. Catty the Catfish, our mascot, is doing an intricate yoga routine on top of the dugout, making it impossible to see around him.

I do catch what looks like a shoulder next to Jett that doesn't look like Mia's. It must be Charlie, and my stomach drops because there was a tiny part of me that hoped I'd gotten the wrong end of the stick but now, I can see he's right there. Next to Jett.

And I'm the chump in all of this. The little virgin boy who was too naïve to see he was being played.

"Austin," Coach warns, and I divert my attention back to the game, and what I've come here to do.

"I got this," I whisper to myself, gripping my bat a little tighter. Whatever is going on between Mia and me can be dealt with later. Right now, the only thing that matters is showing the crowd and my team exactly why I will be the National League Rookie of the Year without question.

***

"Good game," Tate pats me on the back as we walk into the locker room. "Again."

"Thanks." I keep it brief because even though two singles, a double and a homer are nothing to be sniffed at. I need to keep grounded.

"Seems like you're having no problems reading the Big League pitchers."

I nod, hardly focusing on Tate and his compliments because I've still got Mia on my mind. In the fifth inning, I could have sworn I saw her snuggle up to some man in a suit, but when I blinked, I couldn't find them in the crowd. I've officially lost my mind, but funnily enough, it might not be a bad thing. That whole scenario riled me up enough to score a homer on the first pitch without trying.

As I strip my shirt off, I decide to check my phone, and I'm disappointed that there's still nothing. I've received nothing from her since last night. Not even a good luck text, and from the way we were talking, I kind of expected one.

Damn.

Just like that, I've fallen back down from the high of playing my ass

61

off and feel completely deflated. I was right. This confirms it. Mia was only talking and flirting with me because she wanted those tickets. Now that she's got them, she doesn't need me.

I shake my head because she couldn't even send a thank you for the tickets? All I've got is an empty inbox. Well, that's a lie. I do have a text from Griss.

Griss: Awesome game, A! So proud of you.

And my mom.

Mom: Honey. What's gotten into you? That homer in the fifth was phenomenal.

More messages from Griss come through, my mood lowering with each buzz.

Griss: You're never coming back down to see me again, are you?

Griss: No sharing a bunk bed and talking about our favorite plays of the week ever again.

Griss: Just me and Travis still here, and that guy barely talks. Probably because he thinks he's going to get traded this month.

Griss: I think he's right.

Griss: A? I can see you've read these. Why aren't you responding?

Griss: Am I going to have to resort to some annoying gifs to get your attention? Because I haven't used that frustrating coin one that never stops spinning in a while.

Griss: Seriously? I feel like a desperate ex, trying to get the attention of a guy who's changed his number and found a new girl.

Griss: Real talk, though. Don't forget me when the Catfish offer you a ten-year extension and you're making more millions than you'll be able to count in a lifetime. Save this message because it's going to happen.

Austin: Wow, Griss. I know it's lonely down in Triple A, but give a guy some time to at least shower.

As I see him typing a response, a new notification hits my screen, and I raise my brow, smiling in surprise.

New Message: Mia

Sorry, Griss. Your whiny ass is just going to have to wait.

Mia: Thank you so much for the tickets, Austin. I thought nothing would be better than you signing Jett's jersey, but those tickets were phenomenal. Behind the home dug out with Catty dancing on top. I hope Jett's prepared for a lifetime of disappointment with his birthday gifts because I'm never going to live up to this.

Austin: You're welcome. I'm glad he had fun.

As I stare at my sent message, my thumbs stop because I don't know what to do. Here's another opportunity for me to end the conversation. I could wish her and her family well, even half-heartedly offer her tickets to another game, knowing she's too polite to say yes. Then that would be it. The endpoint to a relationship that was never really there.

But apparently, I'm a glutton for punishment, and seeing her snuggle up with a guy in the stands isn't enough to turn me away just yet. It seems I'm too selfish and obsessed to let her go without meeting the guy she's picked first. I need to see her with a good, age appropriate fit before I can move on.

Austin: Hope you enjoyed yourself too?

Mia: How could I not enjoy watching you hit a two-run homer on your first home game of the season? I hope they got the ball out of that fake waterfall in the back, so you can keep it.

Austin: They did. They're just drying it off. Where are you?

Mia: Heading to the car with Jett and Charlie.

My jaw clenches at the thought of Charlie. He's probably got Jett on his shoulders, taking advantage of the high Jett's riding from being at the game. *My game.* He didn't have to do anything for that smile. It was all me.

Why am I so jealous?

There are plenty of other women in this world. Most without a kid and a husband, but here I am still ready to fight over her because after spending ten minutes with her, I can't stop thinking about her smile.

Okay, what I need to do is see them together to see where I stand. That's the only way I'm going to get over this.

Austin: Heading out already? I was going to show you the locker room. Come back to gate 3 and ask for Lenny. He's waiting for you.

Mia: Wow. Now you're trying to ruin Christmas too?

Austin: Is that a yes, you're coming?

Mia: We shouldn't. It already feels like we're taking too much.

Austin: Too polite for your own good. I've got something for Jett, so you need to come down and get it.

Mia: Fine. We'llSee you in ten minutes.

My pulse spikes, and I'm more nervous now than I was at the start of the game. I sniff my armpit and nearly keel over at the stench. Cringing, I flick my gaze between the shower and my new white shirt. There's no

63

way I'm going to get a shower in before they get here. So I'm going to have to improvise. Grabbing my deodorant, I roll it all over my chest, my neck, and my armpits before putting on a clean shirt. That'll have to do.

With only a few players and their partners left in the room, it's private enough that I could have a conversation with Mia if I wanted to. But what would I say? *Damn it.* I knew I should have rehearsed. I'm probably going to do something stupid like blurt out 'Hotdogs,' again.

Shaking my head, I throw my deodorant in my bag before shoving it into my bag. That's when I hear the door to the locker room open.

"It's just through here." Lenny's deep voice fills the room, and that's got to be them. I tip on my toes, taking in a shaky breath and run a hand through my sweaty, wet hair.

Am I nervous?

I feel like I'm going to throw up again and I haven't even turned to look.

"Thank you." Jett's familiar voice comes out next.

"Now or never," I whisper to myself, turning on my heel to finally look at them.

Then I stop.

My whole body feels paralyzed, and my vision tunnels because all I see is her.

Green eyes—brighter than the first time—twinkle back at me as Mia flashes a coy smile. Does she know that when I look at her, it feels like my heart is trying to leap out of my chest? Still as gorgeous as the first day I met her, she's got her arm over Jett's shoulder, and I brace myself for Charlie. I can only imagine he's some hot Charlie Hunnam type of guy, ready to kick my ass for looking at his girl the wrong way, and once he's beaten me to a pulp, he'll ride into the sunset with Mia.

I wait for a little while, but no one else walks through the door. Where is this guy? Did he decide to wait in the car?

Jett looks around the locker room in awe, heading straight for my cubby. "This is amazing," he coos, completely unaware that I'm staring at his mom like she's a piece of cake, and it's my birthday.

"I'm glad you like it," I reply, still staring straight at Mia. I haven't taken my eyes off her because I've been trying to read her facial expression, but she's giving nothing away.

"Hey," Mia says timidly and as she steps toward me, I don't know if she's offering me a handshake or a wave. It's too formal, either way, and

I feel like we're beyond that now. So I do what feels right. I hug her. The same way she did with me when I promised not to screw her over because, after texting her these last couple of weeks, I want to prove that I kept my word.

"It's good to see you again," I say into her hair, lavishing in the fruity scent, which only serves as a reminder of how perfectly she fits in my arms. She's small enough that I can protect her, but tall enough that I wouldn't strain my neck kissing her.

God, I really am a fool, aren't I? I'm thinking about *kissing her* while I wait for her boyfriend to strut into the room. What am I? An idiot?

Pressing her hand tightly into my back, she says, "You too."

As we look at each other, I feel this undeniable connection. Electricity sparks through my veins. She smiles. I do too. She laughs. Me too. And when she opens her mouth, dropping her bottom lip to say something, I tip on my toes, eagerly awaiting whatever she's about to say.

Bang.

"Oops," Jett cries as several bats fall from the cage, completely ruining the mood. Reluctantly I pull away from Mia, the electric feeling dampening with every step as I head to a fumbling Jett who's now desperately trying to shut the bats back in the cage but can't reach the lock at the top. This is only going to end in disaster if I don't help.

"Don't worry about it. Those are our practice bats, anyway. No one is going to notice if there's a scuff or two on them." He smiles hesitantly as I save him by picking up a few of the bats and placing them back in the cage. Then I fiddle with the lock at the top of the gate and smile back. "See. No big deal, and no one has to know."

When I pat Jett's shoulder, Mia clears her throat from behind. "Uh, Austin?" Hesitation is laced throughout her voice.

"Yeah?"

I glance over my shoulder as I play with the lock to find her looking as timid as she sounds.

"I'd like to introduce you to Charlie."

Lock closed. Ah. That's why she's looking so distraught. The woman is about to break my heart and she knows it.

This is it. This is the guy that's going to dash all the hopes and dreams I had for Mia and I being something more. Cringing, I take my time to turn on my heel as I brace for impact. I'm fully expecting to see a six-foot behemoth man staring me down while clapping his hand against his fist. Dude's probably a hockey player for the Charlotte Thrashers and I'm about to get my ass whooped for even thinking something could happen between me and his wife. She's probably shown him the text messages, and there's no denying my intentions in those.

Fully turning, I slow in confusion.

Petite blonde. Smattering of freckles across her nose. Beaming, bright smile.

Not what I was expecting.

"Charlie?" This girl looks more wholesome than my old high school cheerleaders. She nods, making the blue Carolina Catfish ribbon holding her hair up bob. "It's nice to meet you," I say, doing my best to hide the surprise.

She takes my hand, shaking it with intention, and offers me a knowing grin. I have no idea what it's for. "I'm sure it is." Then she winks with a giggle and looks around the locker room in awe. It's pretty empty now, making it seem even more intimate between us.

"So…" Charlie drawls out, looking around. "Any single over thirty-five players that you want to introduce us to?"

"Charlie," Mia hisses. "Stop with the weird Daddy stuff." Her comment is low, and almost a whisper, but I hear it clearly. Daddy stuff? Mia can't be Charlie's mom too, can she? Is she looking for a boyfriend for Mia? A new daddy? No. There's no way that's possible. Mia's definitely not old enough to have a kid in her early twenties. But then again, maybe she is, and she just looks freakishly young for her age. I still haven't figured out how old she is.

This woman is a bigger mystery than how a team like the Seattle Starfish openly cheated an entire season without getting penalized by the league. At least that mystery didn't give me a boner every time I thought about it. Mia is a different story.

Why is her older woman vibe turning me on so much?

Maybe Griss is right. Maybe this is my thing. Maybe it's my sexual awakening and I need to lean into it.

"What?" Charlie raises her hands in exasperation. "Are you trying to tell me you're the only one that is allowed to sample some baseball bats?"

Relief washes over me because that's confirmation. They're just friends, and apparently Charlie's just as kinky as me.

"Umm, there might be some guys hanging out in the replay room." I point my thumb at the back of the lockers, focusing all of my attention on Mia because Charlie's comment has suddenly made me feel more confident in myself. That baseball bat sampling has got to be a reference to me, right?

"I always knew you were my favorite," Charlie giggles, making her way over to the room. The only reason I feel comfortable about offering my teammates up on a silver platter is because it gives me some time with just Mia, and the only ones still milling around don't have a family to rush back to. Who knows? Maybe I'm doing them a favor.

As I watch her skip past Jett, I stop myself from laughing because she's the same height as him. And here I was worried that I was about to be beaten up by her.

"Hey, Jett. Do you want to go outside and run the bases before the grounds men cover the field?"

"Yes!" Technically, we shouldn't go back out there, but I'm in a good mood after finding out that Charlie isn't a threat.

"Are you sure?" Mia interjects, making Jett stop by the door. "I don't want to get in anyone's way."

"Wouldn't have offered if it wasn't a possibility. Come on, let's go." There's a second where I contemplate taking her hand, but I don't. We need to talk before I get too cozy with the idea that Mia might be interested in me too. "It's just through the doors. You'll be in the dugout, and I'm sure you'll be able to find the entrance to the field."

Jett nods, already several paces ahead of us, but I stay back with Mia.

"Thank you," She whispers.

"You've got to stop with all this thank you stuff. I wouldn't be offering if I didn't want to do it."

"Well, then you've got to stop being so generous."

"Never."

We fall into a comfortable silence as we step through the dugout, which has been cleaned since the game, thankfully. Otherwise, she'd be walking on half-eaten seeds, which doesn't exactly scream romantic. Mia grabs the railing and takes a step up to look at the field. She looks tiny in this position, and I have an urge to saddle up behind her, wrap her body in mine and kiss her on her neck.

Woah. Where did that come from?

Talk about taking it slow and talking to her first. But the idea of fooling around with her in the dugout is way more thrilling than I'd like to admit.

"So that's Charlie," I say, stuffing my hands in my jeans and rolling onto my toes as I stand next to her instead of behind her. I can't hide the amusement on my face because I can't believe how much I built that whole situation up.

Mia smiles, watching Jett stand on the field, looking up at the stands in awe. "Yeah? She's my TA." I try to hold back my smile, but Mia's brows cross.

"You're a teacher too?"

"Mhmm."

"Griss is going to have a field day when I tell him this," I mutter. Older woman who's a teacher…. Just the type he thought I'd like.

"Why do you sound so surprised?"

It's now or never. There's no Charlie Hunnam husband, and if I want to get the girl, I can.

"Because I've been trying to guess everything about you over the last couple of weeks and have gotten nowhere." Scratching the back of my head, I look up at her, cringing. "I kind of thought Charlie was your husband."

"Husband?" She chokes out in surprise, raising her hands. "There is no way that I have a husband."

Yet. But that could change very easily.

"You sure?"

"Are you asking me if I'm sure I'm not married?" I nod. "Yeah, there are a lot of things I'm not sure about in life," She laughs. "My marital status is not one of them."

"So, you're single?" I ask with a raised brow.

"Why do you want to know?"

For the first time in my life, my brain and dick are working in tandem, and they both want me to fight for her. If I ever want to have a relationship with a woman, then I've got to take the same chances I did with baseball and go for it.

Taking a deep breath, I puff my chest out and I don't miss that she glances down, and her breath catches. She likes what she sees. "Haven't I made it obvious? I'm interested."

Then her smile falls, and she looks at me like I just stripped naked and covered myself in mustard.

Well, shit.

That wasn't the reaction I was expecting. I get it. I'm not Tate or

Grayson, but I hoped I'd get a little more enthusiasm than that. Mia's face is going a little green, and that's when it hits me. I've totally read this wrong, haven't I? She's so far from interested in me; it's laughable, but I came out so cocky and confident with my response that there's no way to back out of it now. Keeping my 'Frat Boy Energy' vibes would at least make it easier to shrug this all off and pretend that my ego hasn't just been crushed into a thousand tiny pieces.

What do I say next? That it was a joke and I'm surprised she fell for it? Yeah, I doubt that would go down well. *Fuck.* She's still staring at me. I've totally screwed this up and now all I can do is stand here and smile at her like an idiot. This must be what Griss feels like on a daily basis.

"Hey, Austin. Can I go to the outfield?" Jett asks, unknowingly breaking the awkward silence. Thank God.

Still frozen in place, Mia hasn't flinched since I opened up about my intentions. It's like I've hit the pause button on the remote and she's waiting for me to press play. I've broken her and my own confidence in the process.

"Sure," I drawl out, watching Mia as I slowly step backward, expecting some kind of response. Still nothing from her, so I turn to Jett and direct him to the back. The ground men are about to tell Jett that he needs to get off the grass, but when they see me step on the mound, they back off.

"Woah. This is huge." He takes a few steps past second base, looking around the stadium in awe. It reminds me of the first time I walked out on this field when I was in the minors and made a promise to myself that one day I'd be MVP of the Catfish.

"Yeah, forty-one-thousand-and-eighty-one people can watch a game here when it's full."

"Have you ever played in full capacity?"

"Surprised my biggest fan doesn't already know that," I joke. "Last year I only played thirty days in the big leagues, half of which were away games. The other half were against teams with smaller fan bases, so no. I'd love to get to the postseason because then I'd be guaranteed full capacity, but I have no idea when that will be."

"You'll get to the postseason this year," Jett says confidently, punching the glove he's been wearing the whole time. It looks a little small, and I make a note to fix that because who gives a shit that his mom doesn't want me? Jett's interested in baseball, and he deserves someone to show interest in him. "And I bet you'll be Rookie of the Year."

I look at him wearily. "I hope you haven't just jinxed it."

"I haven't. Just watch." Without warning, he runs to first base.

"And there goes Jett James, celebrating his first four-hundred-and-fifteen-foot homer with the Carolina Catfish." He sounds like a broadcaster as he hypes himself up, trotting the bases like a true pro. "Do you hear that crowd?" He makes a crowd cheering noise as he rounds third base, doing a hopscotch around it like Tate Sorenson does.

As he inches to home plate, I catch him off guard. "Hey Jett. Catch." Like a true catcher, he stops in place, gets in his box and catches my ball. The kid's got speed and accuracy. There's no denying that.

I can't help myself; my gaze drags over to the dugout for more than a few seconds. Mia's sitting on the benches in the dugout, not even registering us because she's too busy staring at her phone. Probably texting her friends about me. The creepy ball player that only invited her and her kid to a game because he's been trying to get into her pants the last two weeks.

Stupid. Stupid. Stupid.

I should have never taken Griss's advice. Even if he wasn't here to technically give it. I still took it and failed.

Jett throws the ball back to me, and I move to the pitcher's mound, watching him take his position as catcher seriously. As I throw pitches to Jett, I give him pointers, and he soaks it in like a sponge, immediately applying the critiques. He's a hard-worker, and I've no doubt that I'll see him in the Majors if he keeps it up.

We spend another ten minutes playing ball without a care in the world. All the while. Mia's eyes are glued to her phone as she gnaws at her bottom lip. I'm surprised it's not bleeding with how hard she's chewing on it.

Stop looking at her!

I'm going to make it worse. She's going to catch me staring soon, and then I'll really look like a creep. But I find it hard to look away. Not just because she's so beautiful, but because I want to know what she's thinking. She pushes a strand of her dark hair behind her ear, and I clench my fists. That look. Sultry, but innocent at the same time. She reminds me of a damsel in distress and I want to do everything in my power to save her. But what if who she's running from is me? What if I'm the creeper in this story?

"Jett," She calls. "We should get home. It's late and we don't want to take up too much of Mr. Adams's time."

So, it's Mr. Adams now? I get it. She's trying to maintain a professional distance since she's got what she wanted. She doesn't need a naïve virgin fawning all over her now. I'm just the idiot that fell for her charms, hook, line and sinker.

"Okay," Jet sighs, trudging to the dugout. By the time we make it to her, she's put her phone away and zipped up her jacket. There I was excited that she was wearing my jersey, but I've just been put in my place, yet again.

"Thanks for everything, Austin," she says with unspoken finality.

And there we have it. I have officially made a fool of myself.

"No problem." I turn to Jett, beckoning him to follow me back into the locker room. "Before you go, there's something else that I'd like you to have."

Mia puts a protective arm around him as they step into the dugout and follow me.

When I get to my cubby, I rifle through my bag until I find my muddied jersey and push it in his direction. "Here. I want you to have this."

Jett stares at the fabric in shock. "Is that the jersey you wore today?"

"Yup. It will look good on you." Just as Jett's about to take it, Mia steps in front of him.

"Austin," She sighs, looking exhausted, and there's still something in me that wants to take her in my arms and hug it all away. "That's really generous of you, but we can't accept this."

"Good thing *we* aren't accepting it," Jett sasses back. "I am."

"Jett," She warns. "You can't accept that. This is the jersey from Austin's first home game. Thank you for thinking of us, but really, it's too much, especially after everything you did for us today."

"Don't worry. I've played in the fishbowl plenty of times. I don't need this jersey as a reminder. Besides, they salvaged my home run ball, so I'll have that to commemorate the day."

Jett finally takes the jersey, and threads his arms through the holes, buttoning it up. It swamps his small frame, but he wears it with confidence. "I've also signed the back for you, so you have a matching set. From the Macon Minnows to the Carolina Catfish."

Jett tries to look at the signature over his shoulder, and beams when he finds it. "Thank you so much," he says, running into me so hard that

I nearly fall back.

"Anything for my biggest fan, and I can get you tickets anytime you want them." I put the offer back out there, just in case.

Still hugging Jett, I look up at Mia. Her lips are turned in, and she's staring at me as though she wants to say something but doesn't know what it is. After a few seconds, she finally mouths a 'thank you.'

As Jett backs away, Mia takes his place, and I'm fully expecting one of those quick half-hearted hugs you give to your opponents when you're forced to show that there are no hard feelings. What I don't expect is for Mia to come hurtling toward me, hugging me as though I'm her only life force. That's a different take. I accept the hug because I'm thinking that this might be her thing. Hugging someone to the point of suffocation. I'm not complaining, though. Just nervous that she might feel my half-mast boner because of her damn fruity shampoo.

"Thank you so much, Austin. For everything," she says, muffled against my shirt. Even though I can't see her face, I know she means every single word, and judging by her tight hold on me, she doesn't want this to end as much as I do. But it's not for the same reasons. She's just thankful I've given her son a role model to look up to. That's it.

"Austin," Jonah the team photographer calls. I pull out of Mia's hold to look up at him because I didn't realize anyone was still here. "Any chance I could get a picture of you guys? For the website?"

I look down at Mia, and I can't read her facial expression, but she's not as green as she was after I told her I was interested, so that's a plus. "Uhhh. Would you guys mind?"

"Sure. That sounds great." There's a reluctance in Mia's voice, but I put it down to the fact that my hand is still resting on her hip, and she's already told me she's not interested. *Way to make yourself look like a persistent fucker.* I pull my hand away so it's hovering behind her back as Jonah takes the picture.

"Perfect. Thanks." Jonah smiles then walks away without a second glance, completely unaware of the awkwardness he left behind.

As Mia pulls away from me, she wets her bottom lip, and makes the tiniest of noises, as though she's about to say something. She's cut short again when the locker room door violently slams open.

Charlie skips into the room, a smirk brandished across her face and her hair bopping to a beat that's playing in her head.

"Hey guys," she croons, but slows down when she looks between us and notices the awkward tension. "What did I miss?" Mia doesn't immediately answer, which makes Charlie narrow her eyes, examining me suspiciously. "You guys look like someone farted, and no one wants to fess up."

"You didn't miss a thing," Mia finally mumbles. "We just need to head out. Austin's got another game tomorrow, and it's a school night."

Jett groans. "Tomorrow's Friday. Can't I skip? It's not like we learn anything important on Fridays anyway."

She raises her brow and dips her chin. "You're out with two teachers and you think you're going to convince them to let you skip school? Sorry bud, not going to happen." Mia turns to me, her face still marred with intensity. "Thanks again for everything, Austin." If only she could say that while making eye contact, then it would be much more believable.

"Yeah, thank you." Jett's beaming, and I feel a sense of pride for at least making his night, even if I shattered my own ego in the process. "This is probably not something you'll be able to do since you're so busy, but maybe when you're on your off season, or have a break in your schedule, you could come watch me play sometime? I'll try putting your pointers into action," he says with an eager smile.

"Jett," Mia warns. As much as I want to brush him off politely because I think that's what Mia is insinuating, I don't want to end this night on a sour note.

"No. That sounds fun. You should also look into the Catfish youth program. They run a few yearly events that could use a player like you. You're a fantastic catcher with a lot of talent, and they need to see it."

"I will." He nods eagerly. "Thank you so much."

After another round of goodbyes and the promise of more tickets to games, I wave goodbye to Mia, Jett, and Charlie. All of whom seem reluctant to leave. Or maybe that's just my wishful thinking.

I offer to walk them to their car, but Mia refuses to let me take them any further. So, I guess this is it. They've come to my game, and she'll refuse an offer of more tickets because I've made this whole thing awkward. I might see Jett again if he looks into any of the Catfish programs, but that's it.

We're finished.

There's no reason for me to text or see Mia again.

Lenny, the guard, winks as he shuts the door for them, leaving me alone in the locker room and feeling more like a chump than I ever have before.

I'm interested.

I shake my head, feeling my cheeks heat. What a stupid thing to say. I'm more embarrassed about that than I was walking out of Caterina's dungeon, which is saying something. This is just another reminder that I am completely clueless when it comes to women, and it's going to take a heck of a lot of work for me to get anywhere near a date, let alone lose my virginity at this rate.

Laughing to myself, I start to pack away the rest of my gear, ready to head to the Charlotte hotel I'm staying in.

Austin: Griss, I'm never taking your advice again. I can't decide if it's useless or terrible.

Griss: Woah, where did that come from? I'm just sitting at home trying to relax and watch a game with Rhode, but then you send me this aggressive text. I feel attacked.

Austin: Attacked? Imagine taking your best friend's advice and being shot down while her kid watches.

Griss: 🐵 Call me tomorrow morning. We need to discuss.

I guess getting shot down is a normal part of dating and putting myself out there. Maybe this whole experience is just a lesson about coming in a little too hot.

That's the end of that.

Damn, though, because I really, *really* liked her.

CHAPTER SIX

MIA

Jett practically skips to the car, the wind billowing through Austin's jersey with the movement. Austin was a perfect gentleman tonight. But I shouldn't be surprised. He always has been every time I've met him. I still can't believe it was just us in the dugout. I'd assumed he'd invited a bunch of people, but it was only us. He's treated Jett with so much kindness; it's overwhelming. So overwhelming that I had no idea how to say goodbye.

"Hey." Charlie elbows me. "What happened back there?" She whispers so only I can hear.

"What are you talking about?"

"You and Austin. That had to be the most awkward interaction I've ever witnessed. Although, walking into the showers and seeing one of the player's dongs earlier was pretty awkward, so maybe it was the second most awkward interaction of the night."

I stop, turning her to me. "Hold up. You can't just say something like that and keep walking."

She rolls her eyes with a faint smile adoring her face. "Okay, do you remember when Austin directed me to the press office, or whatever?" I nod. "Well, there was no one in there, so I may have walked around the

75

clubhouse to just have a brief look." She raises a hand, trying to make it sound innocent, but I've known her long enough to know that she was snooping. "As I was moseying around the place, I heard someone singing that song. You know, from Top Gun. 'Highway to the danger zone,'" she sings, and I'm surprised at how in tune she is. "Well, it's a great song, and they were pretty good, so I thought I'd tell them."

"Okay, but where does the dong come into it?"

"Well, I was in the room with all the showers."

"How the hell did you end up there?"

She shrugs. "One door led to another, and then there was just steam everywhere."

"So you thought you'd venture further in?"

"Well, my contacts were fogging up, so I couldn't find my way out." Raising her hands to the width of her chest, she says, "That's when I saw it. His dong, that is." She makes the width of the space between her hands bigger, clearly referencing the unbelievable size of his appendage.

I shake my head, feeling the second-hand embarrassment that apparently Charlie lacks. "Did he see you in there?"

"Oh yeah. Screamed louder than a banshee while he tried to cover his third leg. Unfortunately for him, there was too much to cover if you catch my drift." She waggles her eyebrows and I check Jett is far enough away that he didn't hear that.

"Yeah, you've made that pretty clear. So then straight after that, you somehow miraculously found the door?"

"Yup."

"Funny that."

"No funnier than him asking me what my name was while I ran out like Cinderella."

"You left it at that? I would have thought you'd want to give him your name after that?"

"And have him call the police? No, thank you."

With her chin tipped high, she walks with intention. "Why are you smiling? If he finds out who you are, you could be arrested."

She flips her hand, walking ahead of me. "You worry too much. He's never going to see me again, let alone find out my name. We're good. Besides, if something happens, I think I'd do okay in prison. I went to Alcatraz once and thought it looked like a good time. Crafting during the day, beach side sunbathing, and the food looked delicious."

I roll my eyes. "Yeah, it sounds like a real good time." I pause, watching her with ease. "I'm glad he was worth the risk of prison, then."

She lets out a puff of air. "Oh, he was. Let's just say I found my daddy." She waves her hands across her body, flashing me a smile of appreciation. "He had hair everywhere. Face, chest, balls. I could barely see the muscles underneath." With wide eyes and pursed lips, I glare at her with intention, but she doesn't take the hint. She just keeps talking. "I know what you're thinking. Was he playing hide the pickle? And I can tell you, that is not one of his issues. He manscaped that baseball bat with immense detail."

"Charlie, Jett is right over there," I whisper sharply.

She looks at him, and then back at me. "What? He's talking on the phone to his friend. I doubt he's eavesdropping on us."

"Still, be careful. The kid's been through enough. I don't want to scar him for life because he has to hear about some guy's hairy balls."

She waves her hand flippantly. "Please, me interrupting a shower spank session is nothing compared to finding out that you did something to Austin."

I decide to ignore the 'spank' comment, because it's better that I don't ask. "I didn't do a thing to Austin."

"Then why was he looking at you like you kicked his dog when we left?"

"Was he? I didn't notice."

"Of course you didn't," She groans. "Because that's your toxic character trait. You're oblivious to every man's advances."

Groaning, I knock her with my elbow. "If you mention the janitor one more time, I'm going to scream."

"No problem. I wasn't going to mention him since your love life has finally raised from sweet with heat to three chili pepper spicy in the last couple of weeks." I raise my brow, not sure what she's talking about. "What happened with him after I left?"

"Nothing happened."

"Nothing except you broke his heart." My brows furrow in confusion. "Let me guess. You've been texting the last couple of weeks, and when you accepted the invite back to the locker room, he thought it confirmed that you were also interested in him." She looks to the ceiling of the parking lot and laughs. "Which is kind of funny when you think about it. When an athlete invites you to the locker room, they are essentially showing you them at their worst. Unshowered and dirty. It's like seeing them naked without seeing them naked, if you catch my drift."

"Is that why you snuck into the showers? So you could see *daddy* naked?"

"Changing the subject again," she tuts, and slows, so Jett is still far enough away from us that he can't hear our conversation. "The cynic in me believes you're trying to avoid this long enough that you won't have to answer because Jett's in the vicinity."

"How'd you guess?" I smirk, noting that Jett's already relaxed against our car, texting away.

"Come on, I told you about my shower incident. The least you could do is tell me what happened, even if it's highly edited. I didn't come all the way out here for nothing."

I roll my eyes. "Fine, but only because I know you'll be pestering me about it all day tomorrow if I don't tell you." Taking a deep breath, I relive the memory and cringe. "Right before he offered to take Jett out onto the field, he asked me if I was single. When I asked why he wanted to know, he said it was because he was interested. In me."

Even when I replay that conversation, it makes no sense. Austin *can't* be interested in me. He's got everything going for him. No strings to hold him down, and he's just at the start of his career. I'm a liability. I'm nearly a decade older and have a kid to look after.

"What?" She yells, the noise echoing throughout the parking lot. It's so loud, even Jett looks up for a split second before he's distracted by something else on his phone. Grabbing me with both hands, Charlie forces me to look at her. "Are you serious?" I nod, feeling a little sheepish about the whole thing. She breathes in before taking a long, slow breath out. "You let me stand here and talk about invading *Daddy's* privacy when you were over here contemplating whether you're going to go on a date with Austin?"

"I'm not contemplating. It's not going to happen."

"Why not?"

"Because I didn't know what to say when he told me that."

"How about I'm interested too?"

I give her a sardonic look. "It's not as easy as that."

"Sure, it is. You could even nod your head if words are too much for you."

"Charlie," I warn. "There's more to it than that, and you know it."

"If you weren't interested in him, then why were you texting him all week?" She throws her finger at me. "And don't you dare say it's because you wanted to get Jett tickets to the game because we both know that would have happened either way."

She got me. "Look, I didn't know what to do. I was lost for words. I've never had a guy be so forthright with me, and he's not just a guy. He's more successful at twenty-one than anyone I've met in their thirties. I just couldn't, and still can't, believe that he'd be interested in someone like me."

Charlie lifts her lips to one side, looking at me sympathetically. "You're a catch, babe. It's time you finally started realizing that. What did he say after you brushed him off?"

"That's the thing. I didn't brush him off. I didn't say anything because after I didn't respond, Jett asked him if he could go onto the field. By the time we could talk again, the moment had passed, and I didn't want to get into it."

"So, how did you leave it with him?"

"I hugged him goodbye and thanked him for tonight."

"That was it?" She raises her brows in surprise.

When I nod, Charlie rolls her eyes, and makes some ungodly noise. "This is why you're still single. My god. How much more obvious can he make it? He likes you and you just brush him off like it's nothing."

I raise my hands, checking Jett's still not listening. "I didn't know what to do or say. Honestly, I was just confused that he was interested in me, even with all my *baggage*."

The baggage sounds unbelievable when I think about it. Unknown numbers and threatening messages flash through my mind. All things I've been dealing with in secret over the last three years. Anxiety churns in my stomach because I can't imagine what he'd think of me if he found out about the Unknown texts. Of Hailey? Of my life here as a whole? And therein lies the main reason I don't date. Because explaining my situation is too complicated, and I'd rather not put someone else in danger.

Charlie points her finger at me. "Jett is not baggage, and if you ever refer to him like that again, I will pull your lady bits apart."

I grimace. "I wasn't referring to Jett. Jett's the best thing that ever happened to me. I was referring to Simon, and all the *emotional* baggage left behind after Hailey…"

I still can't finish the sentence. No matter how hard I try, it's nearly impossible for me to speak the truth, and I hate it. But acknowledging it could have dire consequences, so instead, I stay stuck in this endless battle with keeping Simon as far away from Jett as possible.

Charlie squeezes my shoulder. "Is he still not paying any support?"

"I don't want his money." That statement is laughable when you think about the actual situation, but I'd rather live paycheck to paycheck than get a cent from him.

"Is everything okay?" Jett's voice breaks through my thoughts, and I blink away the tears before he sees anything. If he knows I'm crying about Hailey, it will get him worked up too. It's a sad reality that we've both come to. Misery loves company, and that misery has only strengthened our bond. I guess that's what happens when you're living with grief, and it confronts you every single day.

"Everything's fine, J." I look down at his jersey, and my heart warms for Austin and his kind gesture. "You're not going to wear that to school tomorrow, are you? That shirt's a collector's item."

His concern washes away as quickly as I'm able to keep up with my happy façade because I will be damned if Jett has to go through any more pain in his life.

"We'll see." He smiles, and once I unlock the door, he drops into the back seat.

Just before I walk around the hood, Charlie holds me back. "Mia, I know things are tough, but remember, I'm always here for you."

Placing my hand above hers, I mumble. "Thanks."

"But also, I think you should let yourself live a little. You've focused entirely on Jett's happiness for the last three years. Maybe it's time you considered focusing on yours. Have some fun with a ballplayer. It doesn't have to be anything serious. Who knows? You might be entering your cougar era, and that sounds like it would be a lot of fun. After all, it's always good to get the cobwebs cleaned out, if you know what I mean?" She winks, and I push her shoulder slightly.

"Yeah, I'm going to pretend you didn't say that and get in the car now."

"Just think about it."

"I will."

Getting in the car, I put my conversation with Austin to the back of my mind and focus on Charlie and Jett. It's only when Jett is in bed, and I'm in my room, that I start to feel a distinct sense of loneliness. The ceiling needs a good paint as it's started to yellow, and the trinkets left around are all Hailey's from when she used it as a guest room. I haven't bothered to change things because I never felt comfortable making myself at home in her house. Even in death, it's her house. Everything was chosen by *her*, not me. If she could see me now, I'm sure she'd tell me to make this place my home. She'd want me and Jett to be happy; I know that. I just haven't had the guts to change our lives since that day.

But maybe it's about time I did.

Maybe it's time I tried to move forward because sitting in my grief will not bring her back or help Jett with his baseball aspirations. The grief does nothing but steal time away from things she'd want us to be doing until we're too old to enjoy them.

Ultimately, grief's been a good excuse to stay put.

Austin's over-eager face comes to mind, and I chuckle. There's something about him that I'm really attracted to. Okay, that's a lie. There are *plenty* of things about him that I'm attracted to. His eyes, his smile, his thighs, his kind nature, that BDE he gives off. There are so many things about him that make him seem wiser than his years, but then he does something so awkward that makes me see his boyish charm. And I kind of like it. I like him more than I've liked any guy before.

What would happen if I gave it a shot?

He's already told me he's interested. Even if it's just for fun, hanging out with a ballplayer would certainly get my mind off any of my other issues.

That's when I grab my phone and decide to message him because I know if I don't tonight, I'll chicken out tomorrow.

Mia: Hey Austin. I just wanted to say thank you again for everything today. Jett hasn't stopped talking about how much he loved it and honestly, I don't think I've ever seen him happier.

Austin: No problem. I meant it when I said you're welcome anytime. Just let me know.

I frown. *That's it?* No flirty message back? Okay, maybe I did more damage than I thought when I stared at him blankly, so I'll have to try a different route.

Mia: Thanks. You're an amazing guy.

Surely complimenting him will help bring the magic spark back.

Austin: Appreciate it.

Nope. Nothing. He's not going to initiate anything because he's already tried opening that door and I didn't just slam it in his face. I shut it on his fingers, pushing until the bones cracked. If I was rational tonight, I might think that maybe this should be it. That maybe the flirtation has run its course, and I should let it go, but I'm too pig headed for that.

After leaving it for a few minutes, I decide to take a chance.

Mia: Austin, there's something else.

Austin: Oh yeah?

Mia: I'm sorry that Jett interrupted us earlier, and I didn't answer you.

Austin: It's fine. I think we can all agree it wasn't my finest hour.

Biting my lip, I consider flirting, but decide I need to make it clear what's going on between us first.

Mia: Remember when you told me you were interested?

Austin: How could I forget?

Mia: Well, I just want to clarify that I'm interested too.

I squeal in my bed, my heartbeat thrumming in my ears because I've never been this bold with a guy. My lack of dating life is only becoming painfully obvious in this interaction and how excited I am by it.

As the bubbles appear to tell me he's typing, I feel the anticipation beating through my veins. If anyone could see me now, they'd be questioning why I'm acting like a teenager, waiting for a guy to reply when I'm in my thirties and have a kid sleeping in the room upstairs.

Austin: Really?

Mia: Yeah.

Austin: You sure? Because I don't want to get excited about this, only for you to tell me it's a prank.

Mia: Dramatic much?

Austin: Coming from the woman that waited six hours to tell me she's also interested in me? You could have at least started your text with that, so I wasn't wallowing in misery the whole night.

Mia: Please. You weren't wallowing. I'm sure you were already looking up your next target.

Austin: Mia, let's make one thing clear. I'm a busy guy. I don't have 'targets.' Never have. The only woman I've seen that I'm interested in is you. I don't have time for cleat chasers, and I'm not interested in women like that, anyway.

I'm taken aback by his words because I don't know if I believe them considering the number of women that probably throw themselves at him. But I'll take it as a compliment for now.

Mia: Ditto.

Austin: Can I take you out on a date? As you know, I'm only here in Charlotte for another two days. Both days I'm playing ball, so won't be able to see you. Then I'm on the road for two weeks, but once I'm back, I'd like to take you out then if you're interested?

Mia: I'm interested.

CHAPTER SEVEN

Five Days Later

Mia: Jett told me to tell you that you had a good game, and that stolen base attempt was elite.

Mia: His words, not mine.

Austin: Oh, I didn't know he knew we talked.

Mia: He doesn't. He thinks this is my first attempt at speaking to you after you offered us tickets. He was very insistent that we maintain contact.

Austin: Why?

Mia: He probably wants more tickets.

Austin: You sure? Because I gave him our Marketing exec's number for that. He has tickets whenever he wants them.

Mia: Wait, you did what?

Austin: It's the fastest way to get tickets.

Mia: Let me get this straight. You gave my thirteen-year-old some random marketing exec's number without telling me?

Austin: She's not just some random exec. She's Tate's girlfriend, and she's cool.

Mia: Okay. So maybe he wants me to text because he wants to keep the connection with you.

Austin: Or maybe he wants *you* to keep the connection with me.

Austin: Is your son trying to set us up? 😳 I knew I liked him.

Mia: You're delusional.

Austin: Then why are you smiling like that?

Mia: Like what?

Austin: Made you look.

Mia: You're an idiot, and really starting to show your age.

Austin: Yet you're the woman talking to this idiot every night.

Mia: Has it been every night? I'd say that's wishful thinking on your part.

Austin: Scroll up. I think you'll be enlightened.

Mia: Wow. How did this happen?

Austin: It started with those two words 'I'm interested,' and now you can't get rid of me.

Mia: Shouldn't you be focusing on your game?

Austin: It might surprise you to know that I can multi-task. I play the game on the field and then I try out my game off the field. How am I doing?

Mia: I'm still texting, aren't I?

Austin: I can stop if I'm bothering you.

Mia: Don't stop. I like it.

Austin: Me too.

Two Days Later

Austin: So… I finished playing three hours ago and there's still no text from you. Were you just not going to text me tonight?

Mia: I wasn't sure you'd want to talk.

Austin: Why? Because we lost?

Mia: Yeah. I didn't want to rub salt in the wounds.

Austin: You can rub salt in my wounds whenever you like. Maybe lick them clean, too.

Mia: Austin!

Austin: Sorry, was that a dream I had or were you talking about licking and rubbing me? Because shit. I completely forgot about my bad game.

Mia: Please, please, please don't sext me right now. I've got Jett in the room, and I would die if he reads my messages over my shoulder.

Austin: No offense, but I doubt he's that interested in his mom texting.

Mia: Not even if it's a ballplayer sending me porn.

Austin: Porn? I think you've got the wrong guy.

Mia: You sure? Because that picture you sent me yesterday of you smirking at the camera with no shirt on in bed was pretty obscene.

Austin: Was it?

Mia: You were dripping wet.

Austin: Mhmm, that's another thing we should add to the repertoire along with licking and rubbing.

Mia: Austin!

Austin: Sorry, BG. Can't help myself when talking to you, but it's your fault. You shouldn't have sent me that picture of you with the green face mask. That was 😨

Austin: Can't wait to see it in person.

Mia: Does this cute little flirting act usually work for you?

Austin: You tell me?

Mia: I'm rolling my eyes so hard right now that I'm giving myself a headache.

Austin: Don't. You're giving me ideas.

Mia: What kind of ideas?

Austin: Ideas on how I can help relieve that tension.

Mia: Austin...careful.

Austin: You asked for it.

Mia: You're right, I did, but I bet you aren't thinking about your loss now?

Austin: Nope, and I only have you to thank for it.

Five Days Later

Austin: So, I know you're a third-grade teacher, but I don't know how long you've been teaching?

Mia: Since I graduated.

Austin: Smart response. I bet you tell those seven-year-olds where to stuff it.

Mia: They're 8 or 9.

Austin: My bad.

Austin: Who was your favorite cartoon character growing up?

Mia: Kim Possible. Why?

Austin: Ah, I remember her. Long red hair, tight leather pants. She was hot. Not as hot as this brunette I've met recently, especially when she wears a Catfish Jersey with 'Adams' on the back.

Mia: Why are you asking me such odd questions?

Austin: Just bored on my off day.

Austin: So, when did you graduate?

Mia: I can't remember the year.

Austin: Have you had your ten-year reunion?

Mia: Yes.

Austin: What about your fifteen year one?

Mia: If you think I'm thirty-three, I'm using the wrong night cream.

Austin: I knew that. I was just testing you.

Austin: What songs do you remember from your high school prom?

Mia: I don't like to think about that night, but why are you asking?

Austin: It's been a week and a half of texting, and I'm still trying to get to know you.

Mia: Really? Because these questions seem a little random.

Austin: I'll make sure I stop taking notes from '100 things to ask the girl you're interested in.'

Austin: Who was President when you graduated High School?

Mia: What?

Mia: You're trying to figure something out, aren't you?

Mia: Wait a minute. You're trying to figure out how old I am, aren't you?

Austin: 🙈

Austin: Maybe.

Austin: Not all of us can go on google and find out your place of birth, parent's names and work history all in one place.

Mia: Oh, the woes of being a famous ballplayer.

Austin: Not famous yet. The only person looking me up is you.

Mia: Oh, but you will be famous, according to Jett. He loved your three-run homer against Washington yesterday btw.

Austin: Tell him thanks. Is he still trying to set us up?

Mia: You know, the more the days go by, the more I think your whacky theory might not be so whacky at all. He's asking me to message you a lot and so far, he seemingly believes that I'm leaving comments on your social media and you're only responding because I'm a 'top fan.'

Austin: Did you just call it Social Media? Are you sure your face cream isn't fantastic and you're actually seventy?

Mia: I'm thirty.

Austin: So, I'm dating an older woman.

Mia: Dating is a bit strong; don't you think? We've met twice and texted for a couple of weeks. And I still have no idea what I'm doing talking to a guy with a nine-year age gap except maybe living out fantasies from The Graduate.

Austin: I stopped reading after fantasies. What kind of fantasies are you having?

Austin: Oh, just finished reading your message. What's The Graduate?

Mia: Dear Lord. You are definitely too young if you don't know that movie reference.

Austin: I don't know that movie reference because I've been too busy playing ball. Who knows, I could have missed the release.

Mia: You weren't even born when that movie was released.

Austin: And you were?

Mia: Well, no, but that's not the point. The point is, I'm nearly a decade older than you.

Austin: Not really. My birthday is in a couple months, which means you'll be eight years older than me soon.

Mia: Good to know…

Mia: How do you feel about that?

Austin: What's there to feel about you being a few years older? I think you're the hottest woman I've ever seen. You're the only person I'm looking at. Besides, older women are great. They come with snacks in their handbags. 😆

Austin: Mia?

Austin: Are you really going to stop talking to me after you tell me your age? Because if you want to go down that route, I've got some pretty big secrets that I need to tell you.

Mia: Secrets?

Austin: I knew that would get you.

Mia: 🫥

Austin: I'm back in Charlotte on Monday. When can I see you again?

Mia: I don't know.

Austin: Come on. You promised you'd let me take you to dinner. Let me live out my biggest Mrs. Robinson fantasies.

Mia: YOU SAID YOU DIDN'T KNOW IT!

Austin: I lied, but I didn't want you thinking that was why I was talking to you. I like you. Your age means nothing to me, and I want you to come to my game so I can prove that.

Mia: You want me at another game?

Austin: I want you at every game, but we can start with one.

Mia: You know I can't make a habit of it.

Austin: Why not? I get family tickets every game, and my family moved out to Michigan a few years back, so you aren't taking them from anyone.

Mia: But the more we hang out, the more Jett is going to suspect there's something going on between us.

Austin: Isn't he trying to set you up with me, anyway?

Mia: We've got to think realistically. If this doesn't work out, then how am I going to explain to Jett that we can never go to a Carolina Catfish game again?

Austin: That won't happen.

Mia: Optimistic much?

Austin: I didn't get to where I am today by not believing in myself.

Austin: I've got the day off next Wednesday. Got a thing to do in the morning, but I'm free after.

Mia: Working until six at school, but I could see if Jett could have a sleepover at his friend's that night.

Austin: Does that mean *we* could have a sleepover?

Mia: Stop with the FBE.

Austin: Sorry, BG.

The Next Day

Austin: So, I can't stop thinking about this sleepover. Do you want me to wear my Batman PJs or my Spiderman ones?

Mia: Funny. I don't remember inviting you to one.

Austin: I know I'm dating an older woman, but I didn't realize we were at the point of you losing your memory.

Mia: And you seem to have that youthful exuberance about you. Too much optimism.

Austin: What can I say? I'm back tomorrow and I can't wait to see you.

Mia: Gotta get through that double header first.

Austin: Double header to get double….

Mia: Take me out first, then we can talk about some double headers and sleepovers.

Austin: I'm biting my fist, just waiting.

CHAPTER EIGHT
MIA

Strolling down the hallway, I balance a stack of papers for my class's English assignment, and nearly drop them when I hear a door squeak open.

"Mia," Charlie whispers sharply. Her head is poking out of our classroom, and she looks somewhat shell shocked. "Everything okay?" I ask as she clutches the door as though her life depends on it. The concern on her face quickly grows into a smirk as I get closer.

"Did you arrange this?" she sings, smiling as though she's waiting for me to drop all my papers.

"Arrange what?"

She tilts her head to the classroom, and bits her bottom lip. There's a slight flush to her cheeks as she pushes herself forward in a vain attempt at privacy.

"You brought my Daddy back to me."

"Daddy?" My brows cross in confusion, and I shift the papers under my arm so I can move swiftly to the classroom. "I have no idea what you're talking about. I haven't spoken to your father before, and can I just say it's super weird that you call him daddy and drawl it out all low and husky like that?"

Thinning her lips, Charlie tries to hide her grimace. "Not my father. My *daddy.*"

Then it clicks. The guy she walked in on in the shower. "I still have no idea what you're talking about. I don't even know who your *daddy* is."

Before I can push past Charlie to see, she rests her hand on my chest, stopping me in surprise. "So, you aren't the reason there are three very hot and very familiar baseball players standing in our classroom right now?"

"Baseball players?" I stumble out before my breath stills. The adrenaline pumps through my body so fast it's the only thing I hear. That and a high-pitched beeping sound, which I think is my blood pressure.

She huffs out a little laugh. "Oh, I get it." She proudly wags her finger at me. "You need to pretend you had nothing to do with your little toy boy coming in today in case the principal finds out. Don't blame you for arranging it. Baseball schedules are brutal, especially on new relationships. Gotta find the time where you can."

When she finally takes a breath, I gently brush her hand off. "Charlie, I genuinely have no idea what you're talking about." I push past her and immediately stop.

Whiskey eyes.

Wide smile.

Austin looks just as surprised to see me. "Mia?" He spurts out, then closes his eyes and swallows. "I mean Mrs. James."

"It's *Miss.* James," Stuart, the smartest kid in the class, pipes up.

"That's, uh, good to know." I melt at his deep voice because I didn't realize how much I missed hearing it until right now. Smooth with the hint of a sharp edge. It's everything I could remember from our first encounter, but nothing like I imagined when reading his texts. "Miss. James."

I catch my breath, and I don't know what comes over me, but the papers slip out of my hands and fall to the ground haphazardly. "Sorry," I mumble, but no one can hear me over the ruffling papers and laughter of eight-year-olds.

"What is going on?" Charlie whispers as she leans down to help. I make a mental note to curse her out for not warning me earlier about these guys being here because it's not just Austin Adams randomly in my classroom; it's Tate Sorenson and Dalton Reed.

"What the hell are they doing here?" I reply, scrambling to put the papers on my desk. This isn't exactly the way I wanted Austin to see me after a long away trip. I'm exhausted. My make up is minimal, my hair is in a messy bun and I'm certain I've got a hole in the armpit of my shirt from reaching for a textbook earlier.

Still, he's staring at me with a goofy grin, and I just glare back, hoping my eyes convey the '*What the hell are you doing here?*' that I want to say but can't.

He shrugs before turning back to the class, shuffling on his feet so he's closer to Tate.

"Miss. James," Evie, another one of my students calls, and I turn to her with a smile. My knees are knocking wildly and I'm barely holding it together, but somehow, I'm not being questioned. When the principal mentioned I'd have some special guests drop by the classroom this afternoon, I was expecting the lunch lady with her baby chicks, not this.

And by this, I mean three hulking men that barely fit into the room and their PR team standing in the back taking pictures. The guys are staring at me like I've got three heads, but that could be because I'm staring at them like *they've* got three heads.

Either way, this whole thing is a mess.

"Yes, Evie?" I say, trying to come to my senses as Charlie pushes herself further into the room, inadvertently pushing me into Dalton. I'm so close to him, I can smell his cologne, and I'm sure he feels as equally awkward about our proximity.

"Is that man Miss. Davenport's daddy?"

"Excuse me?" I spurt out, feeling the heat of both Dalton's and Charlie's eyes on me.

Forgive me, father, for I have sinned. MILF's, Daddies... Just a couple of the things I've accidentally introduced children to through meeting ball players over the last month.

When I open my eyes, Evie is pointing to Dalton, who has turned redder than a tomato. Austin and Tate can't help themselves. They burst out laughing. All the while, Charlie lets out a roll of awkward giggles, scurrying to the sanctity of the desk and shuffles papers as though ignoring the question will make us all forget it was asked.

Dalton clears his throat, and immediately the room falls silent. Letting out an embarrassed groan, he scratches the thick stubble on his chin before saying, "I, uh, don't have any children."

"Then why did Miss. Davenport call you daddy when you walked in?" Another inquisitive student asks.

"That's enough," Charlie squeaks from my desk, refusing to look up. Unfortunately for her, her face is so red, it now looks like she may pass out any minute.

I look between the two of them for a split second, stopping to really look at Dalton. Rugged, bearded and manly. It all makes sense. He really *is* her daddy. The guy she walked in on in the shower and she liked it. Little, preppy Charlie likes him, which is unexpected, but not something I can dwell on when I have a classroom full of over-eager students, ready to ask more questions if I don't shut this down.

Charlie continues talking, but her voice is much higher than usual. "Some members of the Carolina Catfish have dropped by today to discuss a new youth program that's launching at the stadium this Saturday. Mr. Sorenson, I'll let you explain." That's an interesting segue coming from the woman who can't look up from the papers on her desk.

Like the pro he is, Tate steps forward, capturing the children's attention with ease as he explains the new program. It's the same one Jett mentioned to me the other day after Austin suggested he look into it. I've already secretly paid the fifty-dollar fee and signed him up because I know he wants to try out. I might go into my overdraft if Simon doesn't let me skip this month, but it's worth it. Jett's always been an incredible athlete and they need to see how good he is.

When I look up at Austin for the tiniest of seconds, I lose my breath. I've finally registered what he's wearing, and it's like I forgot how good he looks in jeans. There's a rip at the largest part of his thigh, leaving me to wonder if that happened when he put them on or he knows what he's doing, and that was there to draw attention to his thick leg. I swallow because he looks... good. In fact, he looks *better* than he does in his uniform, which is something I didn't think was possible.

When our eyes connect, Austin's lips curve into a smile because he caught me checking him out. That smirk. I swear it's so hot it could melt my panties off.

But then I look away because those unknown texts come to mind. Am I risking everything Jett and I have made for some potential hook up that might only last a few nights?

"We're holding open try outs at the stadium as part of this Saturday's launch, and we'd love to see you all there." He lifts some flyers while

Austin hands them out, and I curse myself because I shamelessly watch his ass and thighs in those jeans. With every step, I see a new muscle that I didn't know existed move. He's thick and chunky. Just the way I like them.

"We'd love to see you all there on Saturday." Tate smiles and right before he can finish, a tall, pregnant blonde ushers him back to the front of the room.

"Would it be possible to get a picture of the entire class?" She asks me and I nod, but purposely make sure I'm far, far away from Austin, almost out of the shot, just in case I look over-eager in his presence.

After the guys have signed a few autographs and are set to move to the next room, I pull Charlie aside. "I'm just going to walk them out."

That makes her smile. "Of course you are."

"Just cover for me for ten minutes."

"No problem. Just don't kiss him in the hallway. That will definitely get you in more trouble than those Cavill nudes." She winks, then smiles at the class, preparing them for the next lesson.

As I slink out, I follow the entourage of marketing and PR people down the hall. As they all turn left to go to the next class, I pull on Austin's shirt, getting his attention. He whips his head back, his jaw tense. That is, until he sees it's me. Then his lips lift into a smirk and he follows me down the hall.

There's nowhere to hide, but I bring him far enough down the lockers that no one can hear our conversation.

"What are you doing here?" We say simultaneously. "I asked you first." Again, we're pointing at each other, and I curse. I don't have time for this.

Austin's lips pull into a wry smile. "You know, we gotta stop meeting like this."

He takes a step forward. I take one back until I feel the lockers hit me from behind.

"Maybe we just gotta stop meeting," I mumble loud enough to turn that smirk into a frown.

"Aw. I don't think you really want that, do you, BG?" He's playful back, but is being careful not to touch me. "After all, weren't you the one to say that you were interested, too?" Tilting his head, he frowns.

I let out a breathless laugh because there he is with his frat boy energy again. Shaking my head, I look at the other players going into the third-grade classroom. "Why are you all here today?"

"Why are *you* here?" He asks with a smug look on his face.

"The fact that you have to ask makes me think you might need a few lessons yourself."

"Sign me up if it means you'll be my teacher. Then we can live out those Graduate fantasies you were talking about the other day." He goads me, but I just silently glare back. There's nothing I can say here without potentially getting into trouble.

Austin frowns, but it's quickly masked with another playful smile. "Marketing put these school visits in our schedules a couple of weeks ago. The entire team has been split up and we're all at different schools around Charlotte today. I may have seen your school and asked if I could come here."

"And you thought you'd come and surprise me while I look like this?" I dust off my pleated black skirt, noticing a whole lot of lint on my tights. I know I look like an absolute wreck today because I had to drop Jett off for practice early and got up late after texting Austin all night.

"You look beautiful." It's a simple statement, said with so much confidence, I believe it. "But I'm surprised this whole thing wasn't on your agenda. Kind of thought you'd know I'd be here."

I shrug. "I got an email last night about something, but after marking papers and texting a certain someone all night, I didn't go back and re-read."

"And that's what's wrong with education today. Even the teachers don't know what they're teaching."

I roll my eyes, leaning into him, but then I stop myself because we aren't alone. It doesn't matter how at ease I feel with Austin, I shouldn't be drawing attention to us. "But that's beside the point. Tell me more about this ballplayer."

"There's nothing more to say that hasn't already been said." I sigh dramatically and look off to the side. "Really, I should probably stop talking to him because he's started stalking me at my work."

Austin's mouth drops in surprise, but there's a little tilt of amusement in the corners. "But what about the sleepover?"

Snorting, I roll my eyes and shunt my shoulder in protest. "What sleepover? I don't remember agreeing to anything."

Tipping his chin, he holds his hand to his heart. "Wow, BG. Way to break it to the guy you're dating."

"Austin," I whisper sharply, looking both ways. "We aren't dating."

He drops his hands and rolls his eyes. "Semantics. We're getting to know each other."

"Maybe, but the delicacy of the terminology isn't something we can talk about here."

"Good thing I'm taking you out tonight then. I can talk about your delicacies all I want." His gaze connects with mine. "And there are a few things that we need to talk about."

I smile, pushing him lightly. "You're insufferable."

"And you're hot, especially when you use big words like terminology." He wiggles his eyebrows. "What time and where should I pick you up?"

I bite my lip, watching Tate speak to the blonde woman from earlier. There's a tenderness in his eyes, and when he squeezes her shoulder, and drops his hand onto her stomach, I realize that they must be dating, and they aren't afraid to show it. "I'm not sure I can do tonight. I've got a few things that I need to finish up here..." I trail off, playing a little hard to get.

"I can do as late as you want." His over-eager face takes the bait. "Come on, BG. What's stopping you?" His hand gently grazes across mine. The movement was so fast, that there's no way anyone noticed it. I noticed it, though. My whole body lit with electricity in that mere passing touch, which was just a small indication of what this man can do to me without trying.

"Austin," Tate calls, and Austin raises his finger, focusing solely on me. The way he does that makes it hard not to feel like I'm the only person in the room.

"Come on, BG. One date. I promise you won't regret it." He's tipping on his toes and everything in me wants to say yes.

So I do.

"Pick me up at seven. I'll text you my address."

Austin's smile grows wide. "Can't wait," he says smoothly.

"I better get back to class." As I slide past him, he brushes his little finger against mine, gently hooking them together for the smallest of seconds before letting me walk back to the classroom.

My entire body is brimming with excitement, and even though I try to tamper it down, the smile on my face won't fade.

Humming to myself, I skip to the door as I think about how I'm going on a date with Austin Adams. So many things could go wrong, but I'm excited. He makes me feel so carefree and happy. The same way I felt when I was in my twenties, before Simon ruined everything. Maybe that's why I'm drawn to him, because he reminds me of all the things I feel like I missed out on. Time will tell if this is more than a fling, but I'm going to make sure I enjoy myself while it lasts.

CHAPTER NINE

AUSTIN

"I did something stupid," I say, holding my phone under my chin. Griss's grinning face flashes at me as I sit in the dark in my truck parked opposite Mia's driveway.

"You talking about that tagging error you made the other night? Because yeah. That was really stupid. The guy had nowhere to go, but you still threw to second and he essentially stole a base. It was embarrassing."

"How did you find time to watch my game?" I run a shaky hand through my hair, feeling the nerves shoot through my veins. What the hell is wrong with me? I wasn't even this nervous about my first Catfish start. I've sweated through three shirts already tonight and I have another two in the back, just in case my deodorant falls through.

"I didn't. It was on *Chally Sports* highlights, and I've been meaning to talk to you about it. I thought a text was too impersonal though, so in a way, I'm glad you called me on the only night I get to hang out with Rhode this week, because at least it means I can point out your issues."

"Hey, Uncle A," Rhode calls, and my eyes widen because this is certainly not a conversation I want her to hear. "Loved those three runs you batted in against Boston."

That's when she grabs the phone and waves. "Thanks, sweetheart. Are you going to the tryouts for the Junior Catfish on Saturday?" She nods proudly. "Good. The team needs to see your pitching skills."

"As long as they don't put me on the softball team, I'll be happy."

"They won't. You've got a faster pitch than most boys your age. You'll do just fine."

"We'll see. What are you doing in the dark?" I blow out a breath and look at the house opposite me. It's beautiful, with a large porch and an old bench under the window.

"Crap," I whisper, dropping my phone and crouching as far down in the seat as I can get. It's just my luck that Mia looked out the window while I was staring at her house. I don't think she can see me from here since the closest streetlight is ten feet away, and my windows have a slight tint, but I can't be too sure.

"Uncle A, what's going on?" Rhode asks, and I look between my legs to the phone sitting on the truck floor by my foot. Her face fills the screen, and I grab it, ready to come up with some elaborate lie.

"I think Austin might be going on a date tonight." As I bring the phone back to me, Griss pushes his daughter to the side so both of their faces are visible in the frame. With wide, cheesy grins, they're waiting for me to respond, as though I'm going to give them some kind of logical answer.

I roll my head to the back of the chair, glancing up at the sky through my sunroof. Calling Griss for advice was a stupid idea, but I seem to be drawn to them these days.

Sensing my nervousness, Griss gestures off the phone. "Watch this inning for me, Rhode. There are rumors that the starfish might be cheating again, and I need you to listen out for any suspicious noises."

"Okay," She drawls out, not questioning her dad.

Griss waits until she's out of earshot and then shuts the door to his bedroom. "So, what's the stupid thing you did? Because if it has anything to do with using the vacuum as a masturbation tool, I have no sympathy for you. I *told* you it was a bad idea."

"It's not that. I may be a virgin, but I'm not stupid enough to suck my junk up a hose before it's been tested."

He pauses, mulling over that. "Does that mean that you'll do it *after?*"

I stop that line of thought immediately. "I've been flirting with Mia." Silence. He stares at me, and there's a moment that I think I've lost connection, so I shake the phone. "You still there?"

"Oh, I'm here." He nods. "Is that it?"

"Yeah."

"And that's bad because?" His voice lilts at the end of his question, and his brow raises.

"Because," my voice is equally as high, "I'm almost certain she thinks I'm an experienced dater."

He scrunches his face and scratches his ear. "You've been *flirting* with her for the better part of a month, and you haven't told her you're a virgin?"

"I haven't even kissed her yet."

"I gotta be honest. I'm gonna need to know what your kind of flirting is because I think you might be getting a little ahead of yourself." I drop my shoulders, feeling more deflated than when we lost to the Armadillos 21-5. "Is this your first date?"

"Yeah. I saw her at her school today, but apart from that, we've just been texting."

"Dirty texts?" He drawls out with a grin.

"No. Maybe it's light flirting."

"Coming from you, I'm guessing that means you asked her favorite ice cream flavor?"

"I'm not that bad."

"Look, you just need to relax." He rolls his shoulders back. "Go in there with your head held high and your thighs on display. She's going to love you. I guarantee it."

"But what if I fumble?"

"You're not going to fumb-. Wait a minute. Do you remember that conversation that we had about bases?"

"Mhhm."

"You didn't answer the question. What base have you been to?"

"Making out," I spit out, my leg shaking under the wheel. "I've made out with a few girls, but that's it."

Griss takes a minute to respond. "It's fine. She likes you, so she'll like it." That sounded believable.

"What adult woman likes a virgin?"

"Plenty, I'm sure. Experience is overrated. This way, Mia can mold

101

you into whatever lover she wants." A chill runs up my spine with his emphasis on the word 'lover.' What does that even mean for a guy like me? "But seriously, calm down. It's not *that* big a deal. Just relax, give yourself some time and don't think about it too much."

I blow out a breath. "Okay, don't think about it too much." I repeat, already knowing I'm thinking about it too much.

"Just treat it the same way you treat your first at bat going up against a new pitcher. Keep your expectations low, but your senses high. Learn what moves she likes and figure out how you can work with it."

I nod with pursed lips before replying, "That's a good idea. Just think of it like a game."

"You got this, Boo. I believe in you. But I've got to go. The pizza's here and Rhode is waiting for me. She'll ask questions if I'm gone too long."

"Okay. Thanks for the mini pep talk."

"Let me know how it goes."

I turn my phone off and lean against the headrest. "You can do this, Austin," I whisper, in a vain attempt to hype myself up. Something I've never needed help with before. I turn the phone off, blow out a breath, and look at Mia's house one more time. "Oh, crap." She's on her porch, making her way over to me.

How long has she been out there? Has she been watching me this whole time?

Adjusting my shirt, I scramble out of the truck, stride across the street, and meet her in the middle of her driveway.

Fuck. She looks hot tonight. The breeze makes her short, ruffled skirt skim across her thighs, and I'm certain my dick's getting a little hard just looking at her. Thankfully, it's dark out, so she can't see the ever-increasing bulge in my pants.

"Austin," she purrs out with intention. Her heels click against the concrete as she zips up her leather jacket and flicks her hair over her shoulder. "I thought I'd come out to make sure you weren't getting cold feet." She smiles, and I swear it lights up the street as well as my heart.

"You saw me?"

"Hard not to notice the lights of a mammoth truck like that pull up." She tips her chin toward my g-wagon. "It's almost as big as your thighs." Then her gaze flicks to my jeans, and I instinctively stuff my hands in my pockets. Not much protection, but it should at least cover the half-mast boner I've got going on.

Breathe. I remind myself to calm down, and treat this whole thing like I'm dealing with a new pitcher. Don't let her see your nerves. I lift my lips into a smile and when she's close enough; I pull her into a hug. My hands hesitate before I rest them on the small of her back.

"Sorry, I was early, and I didn't want to interrupt you. I also wasn't sure if you told Jett I was coming, so I didn't want to surprise him."

With her hands locked behind my neck, she draws back to look at me with a flirty smile. "I may have arranged a babysitter and told him I have parent / teacher consultations tonight." She bites her plump bottom lip, and I have the urge to bite it for myself before licking that gloss coating off.

Her minty breath fans my lips as she looks down at mine. We're close enough that I could kiss her right now. Is it too early on the date for that? We may have flirted via text, but I haven't spent any quality alone time with her. Has the date even technically started?

Okay. Stop. I'm overthinking again.

Breaking away from her, I cut a look at her outfit, taking in her toned legs for just a little longer, and speak my mind. "And he thought you were going to speak to parents in *that*?"

"What's wrong with this?" Opening her arms, she looks down at her dress before spinning in a circle. The fabric flits up, and dances across her thighs so high that I nearly see her ass. I swear she wants me to lose my mind.

"All I'm saying is, you're the hottest teacher I've ever met, and if I was a dad at the school, I wouldn't be able to concentrate with you in that." I look up at the sky, noticing the flicker of stars above us. It's a nice change to see them since I'm too close to the city in my hotel. "Although, come to think of it, that tight black skirt you were wearing this morning in class was pretty hot, too. Pretty much anything you wear makes me lose my concentration."

She snorts, pushing me back as she shakes her head. "I can't believe you saw me in that. It had butter stains from my bagel on it."

"All the better to lick off, my dear."

I frown. She pauses.

What. The. Fuck. Did. I. Just. Say?

She's looking at me.

I'm looking at her.

Nothing.

Have I already fucked this up?

Mia tucks an errant hair behind her ear, looking down coyly before looking at me straight in the eyes. "Maybe a little later."

Am I dead? Or just dreaming? Because there's no way in hell, she actually said that all shy and shit, did she?

Mia scrunches her nose, and I'm feeling so hyped from that little comment alone, I want to bite the end. I give her hips a squeeze instead. "Sorry. That was a little lame, wasn't it?" She says, shaking her head, giving me no time to respond. Then she laughs hesitantly. "I've got a confession to make. I might be a little rusty when it comes to dating."

"Me too," I blurt out without thinking.

"How is that even possible? Didn't you just start dating a few years ago?" Cringing, she slaps her forehead. "And there I go again, making it awkward because I still find it hard to believe that a guy like you would be interested in a woman like me."

I chuckle, bringing her hips so they're against mine again. "Firstly, there's no reason for me not to be interested in you. You're sweet, but could kick my ass if I ever crossed the line." I wink, and she slaps me on the pec, dropping her forehead onto my chest. I smooth down her hair, kissing the crown of her head before smelling her fruity shampoo again. "Secondly, you're right, I'm a little new to the dating scene, so maybe we can just go with it?"

"I like the sound of that."

"Great." I break away from our hold and shift my elbow out, offering it to her. She slips her hand through, kissing me lightly on the cheek. "Are you ready to go on this date?"

"Mhm," she hums out with a smile.

"Alright. Then let's do this." I lead her to my car, unsure of how the night's going to go, but hoping desperately that I don't do something stupid like admit to her that this is my first real date and I have no idea what I'm doing.

CHAPTER TEN

MIA

Slipping my hand in Austin's, he helps me step out of his truck, and I land safely in his hulking arms. Nose to nose, our mouths are a whisper apart, and the moment feels magical. I shiver. He smiles, and I smile back, tracing his full lips with my gaze. My fingers tickle the edges of his jacket as he pulls me into him tighter.

His woody cologne warms me, and all I want to do is feel his lips pressed against mine as I melt into his touch.

Only, I don't think that's ever going to happen.

We've been out for a couple of hours now. Sparks have been flying the whole night, and I've never felt so instantly comfortable with a guy before. There hasn't been a lull in the conversation, and he hasn't let me go all night. But there's just one glaring problem with this whole thing. He hasn't tried to kiss me.

At first, I thought it might be because he was trying to be a gentleman, but after so many opportunities, it's starting to feel like he's actively avoiding it. Tipping my chin up, I go for broke and try one more time. I plump my lips out, giving him a look, telling him to kiss me without outright asking for it.

Austin's gaze drops to my mouth, and he bites down on his lip, letting out a low groan. But still nothing. Have the rules of dating changed since I last went on one? Maybe his generation is a lot more conservative than I thought.

He's had at least five opportunities to kiss me, but he hasn't taken a single shot.

Austin lets out a shaky breath, but that's it.

I frown, holding back my frustration. Maybe he's just not that into me, and he's suffering through this date because he doesn't want to be rude.

If that's the case, I think I'll die on the spot.

"Thanks for tonight." Still in his hold, I close the car door with my foot, and as I try to step away, he holds me a little tighter. That's a good sign, right?

Smiling, he says, "No. Thank you for taking a chance on me." My stomach flips, and I try to tame down my excitement that maybe there is hope. One thing's for sure, he's keeping me on my toes with his whole 'will he, won't he?' act.

His eyes are still on my lips, and he drops his chin, bringing his mouth closer to mine. Shivers run up my arm, and I tip my toes in anticipation. Has all the waiting finally paid off? Swallowing, I anticipate his kiss as he slowly drops his lips closer to mine. We're mere centimeters apart, and just as I think it's about to happen, his lips brush across my cheek instead.

Disappointment slithers through me, but I try to mask it with a forced smile.

"I've had a great time," he husks out, his hands firmly on my hips as he gives them a little squeeze.

A squeeze.

On my hips.

That's it.

Why won't he kiss me?

I brushed my teeth twice and chewed a hell of a lot of double mint gum before coming on this date. I even made sure I had the blandest salad I could on the menu at dinner, so I wouldn't have bad breath. I don't think I've said anything to totally screw up my chances, but I just don't know. He's so back and forth with me, I can't figure him out.

He backs away, and even though it's dark, I can see that his face is a little flustered. There's a sheen across his forehead, and he pushes out a shaky breath.

Then it hits me.

Maybe he wasn't trying to make me feel better when he said he was newer to the dating scene. Maybe he was telling the truth, and he hadn't been on many dates. That would make more sense. Why date a girl when he just has to flash his jersey to get them to drop their panties? I guess I should be flattered that he's taking his time with me instead of trying to get me straight into bed, but I can't help but feel a little weird about it.

Pushing his shoulder, I try to make light of the situation, to ease his nerves. "I still can't believe how terrible you are at basketball. That giant bear would have been mine if you could have made a shot."

He cracks a smile, letting out a grunt. "Basketball was never my thing. Between playing football, baseball and graduating early so I could get collegiate level at bats, I didn't have time to perfect my shot."

"Football *and* baseball?"

"Yeah." He gestures down his body, looking at me with the utmost seriousness. "And what about me screams 'good shot'?" That move alone is just an invitation to flick my gaze to his chest and soak him in.

Dressed down in jeans and a plain white shirt, he's yet again managed to surprise me with how good he looks in whatever he wears. His shirt effortlessly hugs his arms and anytime he's accidentally flexed, I've had urges to rip it off so I could feel his muscles underneath. Not that he's noticed. I could lift my skirt and reveal my thong, and he'd still think it was because I needed to feel the breeze, not because I want him to touch me.

I take a step closer, swaying my hips to not so subtly tell him I wouldn't reject him if he tried to kiss me. Reaching out for his hand, he waffles his fingers with mine and pulls me back into his body. His woody cologne makes me feel dizzy and I so badly want to feel his stubble scratch across my skin as he kisses my neck. "Yeah, but you're a professional baseball player. I just assumed athleticism is universal."

"Have you ever watched a basketball game? Guys who play are tall and lean. I'm anything but that." He sounds almost awkward about it, but his big bulking frame is one of the things I like most about him.

"I'm not that either," I joke, and again, he teases me with what I hope is a potential kiss until he swerves away from my mouth, down to my neck. When I feel his lips connect with the skin there, I close my eyes and sigh in relief. This is exactly what I wanted. Him feeling like it's okay to touch me and actually doing it. I thread my hands through his hair, letting my nails lightly scratch his scalp. He moans out an approval, and I'm getting a little excited.

"You're perfect. That's what matters," he mumbles into my skin, and I feel light-headed all over again. This guy is like an aphrodisiac, making my entire body melt into his touch. If I'm like this after a little kiss to my neck, what the hell would I be like with his lips somewhere else?

Don't think about that right now, Mia.

"Is it okay if I walk you to your door?" He whispers as he draws his eyes back to me.

I crack a smile, tugging at the short strands of hair at the back of his neck. "Dinner at a diner, carnival date, walking me to my door. Why does this all feel like we're teenagers again?"

In an instant, Austin's face drops, and mine does too, because I've clearly said something to sour the mood, and that's far from what I wanted. "Yeah, sorry. I'm not good at this whole dating thing. I guess I thought taking you out to dinner at a fancy restaurant was a little too stuffy, and something an old guy with no imagination would do." He pulls a hesitant smile, gauging my reaction.

"And you'd be right. I had a great time." I squeeze his hand in another attempt at reassurance, and he gives me a small smile back. "Would you like to come in for coffee?" I tilt my head to the house behind.

Austin looks down at it, but says nothing. Did he miss my innuendo? Or do guys his age not drink coffee? "I can't believe this is your house," he says in awe. With yellowed planks and rusty hardware, it's had better days, but we don't have the time or money to fix anything right now, so it will just stay as it is until I figure out how to fix my Simon problem.

"Mhmm," I drawl out, linking my arm with his.

He lets out a low chuckle as I drag him down the path to the front porch. "It's beautiful. Reminds me of my grandmother's home when I used to come and visit her in Charlotte." When we get to the steps, he halts, watching me as I go up. He wraps his large hand around the beams of the porch, checking it out as though he's confirming it will hold a guy like him.

I roll my eyes, dragging him up the steps before he can think about it too much. "Come on." Leading him to the rickety white bench, I take a seat and pat the spot next to me, inviting him to sit too. He offers me another hesitant glare, probably worried about his weight again, but I ignore it and force him down.

The wood creaks, and there's an obvious dip, but I'm confident that it can hold him. Leaning into his side, I say, "This is actually my sister's place." Cringing, I run my hand across my face. "Sorry. I meant to say that it *was* my sister, Hailey's, place." I pause for a moment, worried that this conversation might be a little too deep for a first date, but he seems mature enough to handle it, and it's important he knows the truth before this goes any further. After all, he deserves to know what he's potentially getting into. "She passed away three years ago."

I feel those words with the whole of my body, and my toes anxiously tap as I watch his reaction. "I'm sorry to hear that." His hand squeezes mine, and when he looks at me, I can see sadness there. "Were you close?"

"Extremely." I give him a small smile, holding back the lump forming in my chest. Sometimes when I think about her, I get a feeling that if I say or do anything, I might just cry, and unfortunately, this is one of those times. "She's the reason I'm in Charlotte. I moved from Rome, Georgia, to attend Charlotte U just so I could be near her. When she passed away, I had the opportunity to move closer to our parents, but there was no way I was uprooting Jett."

"Well, I, for one, am glad you stayed."

Laughing coldly, I nuzzle into Austin just a little more to steal his warmth, and he takes that as his cue to lift my legs and rests them on his lap. With the low light of the streetlamps and the crickets as the only sound, it all feels magical, even though the conversation is heavy. He hasn't run away so far. In fact, he's inviting more. His hands stroke my thighs, sending little jolts of electricity through my body. "There's also something really important that I've been meaning to tell you." His hands stop moving, and he looks up at me with concern. Wetting my bottom lip, I admit, "Jett's not my son."

He takes a few seconds to digest that. "What?"

I pinch my lips into my mouth before shaking my head. "He's my nephew, and I've been helping Hailey raise him since he was born. Now it's just me and him, so sometimes it feels like he's my son."

"But you don't correct people?"

Shrugging, I adjust my knees, and scoot closer to him. "Not when I first meet them. We live in a town where everyone knows what happened, so it's not something we talk about. I only tell people after it feels right."

He looks down at my thigh, frowning. "But you're only telling me now? Even though we've been talking for nearly a month?" His finger draws a circle around a freckle on my thigh, and I suddenly feel like shit.

"Honestly. I wanted to tell you, but I just didn't know how to bring it up. It wasn't appropriate when I first met you because I thought you were a frat boy trying to get your kicks off and I didn't think you were actually interested in me."

He lets out a low, disbelieving breath. "And why on earth would you think that?"

I push out a laugh, watching his hand on my thigh, letting it calm me. "Because I'm an old hag and have a kid to take care of. Not exactly things that would entice a guy in his early twenties."

Without another word, he pulls me fully onto his lap, skimming his nose against my collarbone as he does it. Instinctively, I wrap my arms around his neck, bringing him closer. "If you call yourself an old hag one more time, I'm going to have to…" He trails off, and I so badly want to know what he's going to have to do.

I raise my brow with a smirk. "To what?" I challenge.

He shakes his head. "Doesn't matter. What matters is that you know I'm interested in you. You're the one making the age thing a big deal."

"Because I'm over here just waiting for you to loose interest and find yourself a girl your age."

"See, that's the thing about girls my age. They don't make me feel half the things I feel when I'm with you. They don't see the sacrifices it took to get to the big leagues. All they see is a quick root to money and notoriety. You wanted nothing to do with me.

"I'm sure not all of them are like that."

"No. you're probably right, but the only ones showing up at my games are."

"You mean like me?"

His smile grows. "You weren't there out of choice. You're different. You've been ready to flambe my balls at any opportunity, and I like your feistiness. Besides, you were wearing my name on the back of your shirt, so you were already mine."

Narrowing my eyes, I study him. "Surely, a stunt like that should make you more concerned about my intentions?"

"No. it only confirmed mine," he replied confidently.

"Which are?"

"That I don't want to see any other man's name on your back ever again."

I try to spurt out a laugh, but Austin catches my breath when he rests his hand on my cheek. Placing my hand on top of his, I hold back my excitement as he draws me to him.

This is it.

Finally, it's the moment I've been waiting for.

As his eyes skate across mine, I feel the hesitation flow through his hand as he says, "What happened to your sister, if you don't mind me asking?"

And the mood has just been killed. Hacked to death by Austin's clunky questions. I should like the fact that he's asking about me, and he's interested in the answers, but I'd like it a whole lot more if he was getting to know me in other ways.

"I don't mind." I lean back, giving him a little space. "I'm just surprised you'd want to hear it."

"Mia, I think we've established that I want to know everything about you." Taking a deep breath, I feel Austin's thumb gently rub across my palm, offering me a little comfort.

"She and Jett were in a car accident. The car flipped off the highway, but it was a quiet part in the middle of the day, so no one knows how they ended up like that."

"Not even Jett?"

I shake my head, feeling slightly sick that I'm revisiting this. "Jett left that accident with a concussion and a broken arm. He clammed up when the police tried to question him and didn't speak for nearly a year." I flick my gaze to his, giving him a small smile. "The only thing that got him talking was the Minnows game I took him to after I had run out of ideas on how I could make him talk. It got him out of his rut, but now he won't talk about anything other than baseball." I inwardly laugh, a proud feeling emanating through my chest because of all the things Jett's managed to overcome.

"What about Jett's father? Is he around?"

Simon's wicked grin comes into my mind, and I involuntarily shiver as guilt drips through my veins. He played us all, and now he's got us all on the hook. "Jett's father is worthless. When Hailey found out she was pregnant, he skipped town and wanted nothing to do with her. When he found out she was moving on with her life and seeing other people, he did something heinous that I'm too embarrassed to talk about now." I close my eyes and take a breath. "The important thing to know is that he's not in the picture."

There's a silence between us, but oddly, even after that confession, it's comfortable. It feels like he's willing to accept me, warts and all. Pulling me into a tighter hug, I let the warmth of his embrace fill me with comfort. "I'm sorry that you and Jett had to go through that." He kisses the top of my head, and it makes me smile.

"It's okay." I breathe into his chest. "We've started to figure things out, and ultimately, I'm happy I was here for him. He would have had to move out of the state to live with my parents otherwise. This way, he has the least amount of disruption." I can feel my eyes tearing up, but I push through the pain of talking about this. "Hailey always loved being a boy mom, so I'm doing everything I can to live up to it. Didn't know a thing about baseball until that first game. I peppered Jett with so many questions that I essentially forced him to talk."

Austin gazes at me tenderly, like I might break, but he stays quiet for a few seconds. Then he says, "You're a really good person, Mia. Your sister would be proud of you."

Not comfortable taking a compliment, I tuck a strand of hair behind my ear and look down at our connected hands. "I'm only doing what my sister would have done for me had the roles been reversed. He's my nephew, and he needs to be with his family."

Austin brings his hand to my face again, cupping my cheek in his palm until I look at him. His thumb rubs across my skin, wiping away a tear that I had no idea was trickling down my face. Then he leans in and places the simplest of kisses against my lips. It wasn't as sexually charged as ones I've had before, but it felt just as intense. It was a kiss of admiration, and as much as I appreciated it, I'm not in the mood to be admired for something any decent human would do. As his fingers gently caress my cheeks, I adjust in my seat because I need a different fix. One I didn't realize I needed until Austin's lips touched mine.

I shift closer. He does the same. His tongue swipes tentatively across my bottom lip, and I take it. I open my mouth, inviting him in, and make my head feel dizzy in the process. As our kiss deepens, the tenderness of his touch starts to fade, replaced with a little tighter grip as he pulls at my hair, directing me where he wants me.

His large paws control every aspect of this kiss, and then Austin does something wholly unexpected. He gives my neck a little commanding squeeze, and a shot of arousal runs straight to my core.

A purr emanates from my chest because I liked that. A lot.

But did Austin?

With his hand still on my neck, he pulls away, staring at me with wide eyes. His mouth parts as though he doesn't know what to say because he wasn't expecting that either. I don't want him to think he did something wrong, so I lean in, kissing him one more time, just as passionately. It takes him a second to get back in the groove, but when he does, he gives my neck another testing squeeze, growling into it when I push myself against him.

My thigh rubs against his, and I gently tickle my fingers across Austin's knee, traveling them ever closer to his crotch. Granted, I didn't think I'd be attempting to cop a feel after one date, but I can't deny how much I want to feel him now.

His tongue licks at my bottom lip before he sinks his teeth into it, keeping a tight hold on me as I try to back away. His light eyes darken with lust. The same lust that's burning inside me.

My hands are high enough that they're at the button of his jeans, and even through the thick denim fabric, I can feel his impressive bulge growing against my palm. His thumb gently grazes across my thighs, sending burning heat to my core.

I'm hot, tingling and want more. Feeling Austin like this isn't enough. I want to feel every part of him on me.

Would he be tender as he towers over me, suffocating me in his presence? Or would he throw me over his shoulder, toss me on the bed and then spank my ass?

I'd sure like to find out.

I give his bulge the smallest of squeezes before asking, "Do you want to come inside?" My hoarse voice sounds nothing like me, which only seems to draw Austin's attention to the question more. Even in the darkness, I can see my red lipstick smeared across his chiseled jaw. He looks good. Smoking hot, and I have an urge to trace the red lines with my tongue.

His gaze shifts to the door, and it looks like he's about to say yes, but then a pained expression draws on his face. "Is Jett home?"

"Yeah," I mumble as I feel my cheeks burn because it's the first time I've forgotten about him. I was so lost in my drunken Austin haze that I invited my nephew's favorite ball player into the house. To what? Sleep with him? While Jett sleeps in the room upstairs. That's all kinds of messed up.

Austin squeezes my neck again, forcing me out of my thoughts. "As much as I want to go inside with you, and I *really* want to go inside, I shouldn't. I've got a lunchtime game and Coach will kill me if I'm in anything but perfect condition in the morning. That, and I don't want Jett to hear anything."

"What would he hear?" I push, wanting something to think about tonight when I'm all alone in my bed.

"Let's save that for another time." His heated gaze burns me with its intensity and does little to help soothe my pent-up sexual frustration. It's been nearly four years since I last had sex, and I know this little make-out session will not cut it. I'm probably going to have to help myself when I get inside.

"I guess you're right," I sigh out, moving my hand from his crotch and placing it on my lap. Austin takes my hand again, waffling it with his. "We should probably stop because I like Jett's babysitter and I'd rather not scare her away with my over-eager crotch grabs."

"Your over eager crotch grabs won't scare me away." He lifts our hands and brings them to his mouth so he can kiss each of my knuckles individually.

"When can I see you again?" I ask.

He takes in a sharp inhale and rests his head against the chair. "I'm not sure. I've got a game here tomorrow night, but then I'm away for two weeks."

Disappointment rips through me, but I'm not sure what I expected. He's a ballplayer, so he's always on the road. That's something I knew before we started talking. But that was when I didn't think Austin's advances were serious. Now, it feels a little more difficult to manage.

"What cities are you visiting?" I ask, because focusing on that is better than my slightly damp panties and my over-eager hands.

He raises his brow with an amused expression on his face. "I'm surprised you haven't got my schedule memorized yet."

I roll my eyes, giving him a gentle swat on his chest. "Please. I'm not a cleat chaser."

His elbow lightly knocks against my side. "No, you're not. You're just a ball buster." He winks, throwing me his usual flirty grin.

"Let's make one thing clear. If I have a pair of balls at my disposal, I'm certainly not going to bust them."

I inwardly cringe, because that sounded so much sexier in my head. Austin's still smiling, though.

"Oh yeah? What would you do?" His voice is low. Sexier than usual, and he drops his hand onto my thigh, digging his nails lightly in.

Is he trying to be sexy with me?

"Let's save that for another time."

Austin throws his head back onto the seat, closes his eyes, and blows out a long breath. "You're going to be the death of me, Mia James. Everything about you is intoxicating, and I feel like a drug addict because I can't get enough. I can't even remember where I'm going on this road trip because you're the only thing filling my mind."

Giving him a small smile, I point to the door. "Do you want me to go check with Jett where you're going? I'm sure he knows." I make a small attempt to stand, but Austin pushes me back down onto the bench. If only this joking around could ease away the sexual tension.

"And lose out on the last few minutes I have with you for two weeks?" He crinkles his nose, kissing me on the cheek. Then he pulls out his phone. "I'm good." He flicks his thumb over the screen before stopping and reading. "We're going to Kansas City, Miami, and San Diego."

"So nowhere near each other. Why don't they plan that better?"

He shrugs. "Gotta play all the teams at some point. Besides, I'm not paid to worry about the logistics. I'm paid to keep my focus on that little white ball."

I deepen my voice, mocking Austin. "I'm paid to focus on the ball." Laughing, I revert to my real voice and slap him on the chest. "You're making yourself sound like you're just a piece of man meat who can't think for himself."

"Am I? Because if you want to see how well my man meat can think for himself, I'm happy for a little Show and Tell, Miss. James?"

I gasp, whacking him a little harder. "Shh. What if Jett hears?" I look at the door just in case he opens it.

"From the woman who was literally grabbing my balls and inviting me to her bedroom two minutes ago."

"At least I whispered that request." Biting my bottom lip, I ask, "So what are we going to do now?"

"What do you mean?"

"You're gone for a couple of weeks, so we won't see each other."

"We'll do what we always do. We'll text."

I raise my brows in surprise. "Are you sure you have time?"

He narrows his eyes, looking up at the sky. "Guess it depends."

"On?"

"What would the content of these texts be?" My mouth drops in amusement. "Am I going to get some explicit ball busting material, or are you just going to send me texts about my games?"

Rolling my eyes, I poke him in his side. "Is that how it's going to be now? I'm going to have to pay to play? No nudes, no fun?"

He gives my knuckles another kiss. "No. I'm not too busy to text you. I might not respond immediately, but know I'll text you back. Then when I get home to Charlotte, we can meet."

"I can't wait."

"Me, either, BG. Me, either."

He kisses the top of my forehead, and we stay snuggled together for a few more minutes, not wanting the night to end, but knowing we have no choice soon.

21.

CHAPTER ELEVEN
AUSTIN

Running into home with my arms wide, I yell at the crowd, but no one can hear me. The stadium chants are just too loud.

"MVP. MVP. MVP."

My teammates are rushing out of the dugout before my foot has even touched the plate, and as I tip my toe on the white base, Tate pulls me into a hug. Arms are flying everywhere. I'm getting hugged and patted on the back by every teammate as they scream along with me.

"YOU DID IT!" Tate yells above the voices, straight into my ear.

I did. I really did.

"Elite!" "Goat." "Rookie of the Year."

I'm hearing every possible compliment thrown my way, but I have no idea who they're coming from because everyone is shouting in my face. Adrenaline runs fast and furious through my veins, to a point where I can't hear the chants because of the loud beat of my heart.

Without warning, Grayson lifts me onto his shoulders, shaking as he rises to a stand. The guy may be over six foot, but he's lean, and I'm not sure how long he can take my weight. "Hold on tight, Rookie." Grayson clamps his hands on my thighs and jogs around the field with the team behind. It's a bumpy ride, to say the least, but with everyone celebrating behind me, I don't care.

It's just game Fifty-four, but we're celebrating like it's a world series win because we're now twelve games ahead in our division, and we just keep adding W's in the column.

Dalton pushes Grayson's shoulder, and I can feel him losing balance, which forces him to drop me in the middle of the field. Once I'm on the ground, he stretches his back out, wincing in pain. "Oh, yeah." He rubs the base of his spine with his eyes still closed. "Coach is going to kill me if I can't throw my slider tomorrow."

"Just blame it on the Rookie," Tate jokes, sticking his tongue out before rushing me and carrying me in a tackle to the dugout.

My feet barely have time to hit the ground when Sienna, our dugout broadcaster, shoves a microphone in my face. "Austin!" She coos as the cameraman and sound guy stride beside her. I quickly glance over to Coach, and he tips his chin, mouthing a 'congratulations' to confirm he's happy for me to do the game ending interview.

By the time she's talking, the team has somewhat calmed down as they all hurry into the dugout. This isn't my first game. They aren't done. I know they're up to something.

"Austin Adams." Sienna's voice echoes through the stadium and as I look at the seats, I suddenly feel so small. They're pretty much empty now, save for a few of our fans trying to talk to players by the dugout, but I'm so pumped, I'm ready to play another nine innings.

"Congratulations on your win. This is your fifteenth home run of the season. Over half of your home runs have come from runners in scoring positions. Tell me, what allows you to come through clutch in those moments?" Sienna holds the microphone so close to my face I swear she wants me to lick it. With the high I'm on right now, I might just playfully do it.

"It's really about settling down and having more focus in those moments. Just trying to actually do my job and I guess in that moment I did it. I'm a big believer in focusing in on the fastball, and when I saw it coming my way, I just put a barrel on it."

Before she can ask another question, she glances at something over my shoulder and takes a step back. That's when I brace myself for what's coming.

Ice cold.

Freezing water splashes down my jersey as ice cubes ricochet off my back and bounce onto the field. Chills run through my veins, but in the Florida heat, it feels good. Shaking my head, I open my eyes to see Brett holding an orange cooler and laughing hysterically. Giving Sienna a little wink, I run over to Brett, attempting to shake out my wet hair on him, but he's too quick, and he jumps away before I can get to him.

"Austin." Right. Sienna's voice brings me to reality, and I have to get my head back in this. With the cold-water trickling down my back, and my adrenaline high, finishing this interview is the last thing I want to do. But I've got to do this for the team, and the fans.

"Just over two months ago, you were down in the Macon Minnows. Now, you're one of the most vital players on the team. What's it feel like to have crowds chanting MVP at you this early in the season?" Teammates slap my ass, making an audible *thwap* because my clothes are soaked. Pain radiates through my butt as I try to focus on the microphone.

"Ah." I scratch the back of my head, holding back my smile because some of the crowd chant MVP in response to her question. I chuckle, giving them a wave because I'm still in shock that I just walked off against one of our biggest division rivals. "It's pretty awesome, even if it's far from the truth. At the end of the day, I'm just trying to help the ball club win, and anyway I can do that whether it's defensive or offensively, I will."

As I wave at fans in the crowd and look at Sienna, ready to answer her next question, I can't help but feel like there's something missing, and I know what it is without too much thought.

Mia.

She's already become someone I want to share my successes with, and there's a pang in my chest because I wish I could just kiss the crap out of her right now. Maybe even wear off some of the adrenaline pounding through my body with her. Feeling her supple, warm curves would be more fun than the cold ice bath I just went through. There's also the fact that if she was here, I might not be using my hand as much as I am at night, and my wrist could use a rest.

Gah. Just thinking about Mia makes me harder than the Catfish Tower in central Charlotte, which is why I'm low-key thankful that Brett poured that cold water over me. At least he dampened down one thing. Lord knows, I don't want the cameramen catching a glimpse of my boner, and I become a meme, forever living in internet history.

"Have your teammates told you yet that you're supposed to make this game look a little harder?" Sienna asks with her usual curt smile.

I chuckle, shaking my head, and look down at my teammates because everything about this them and how we're playing feels right. "Nah. They do it themselves. They make it look easy, so I guess it helps me out, too."

"Riding on a five-game winning streak has gotta feel good, right?"

"Oh yeah, especially against our division rivals, but no matter how good it feels, we've got to go out and keep winning some more if we want to make it to the playoffs."

"Well, we are looking forward to you guys winning more games. Have fun and we appreciate the time as always. Thanks, Austin."

"Thank you."

Sienna signs off, talking to the broadcasters in the booth as the camera pans away from me. As I step down into the dugout, almost everyone else has packed their stuff away, ready to get the bus for the hotel.

Before I go, there's just one other person I want to speak to. When I open my bag, I immediately pull my phone out, ready to text Mia, but I can't because it's blowing up with messages. Numbers I've never saved send me congratulatory messages, and it makes me wonder how many people have the time to watch me. It's an afternoon baseball game on a Wednesday, after all.

Thumbing through the responses, I look for the only name I'm interested in. The name that I believe has helped me play the best baseball of my life. Funny, I've never worked harder to keep a woman's interest, but I like it. Impressing her almost feels like a sport to me, and I'm competitive as hell.

Mia: Walk-off homer, huh? Jett's always talked about how good you are, but I had no idea you were that elite.

Austin: Are you doubting my abilities?

Mia: Never. I'm congratulating you on an amazing game.

Austin: Did you watch it? Don't you have class this afternoon?

Mia: My last class finished at two, so I put the last hour on while I marked some papers. Don't tell Jett though. He'll be bummed if he finds out I watched it before we do tonight.

Austin: You're going to watch me again?

Mia: Yup, and I'll pretend I have absolutely no idea about your abilities. 👀

Austin: Wait. Which abilities are we talking about here? Because I'd like to show you more of them the next time I see you.

Mia: Careful, A. Letting off some of that FBE again.

Austin: Think I'm allowed. Bet not many guys you talk to can say they just finished a game of professional baseball with a two-run walk off homer?

Mia: Only the other five I'm talking to.

Austin: Give me names.

Mia: Calm down, FB. Your abilities are the only ones I want to sample.

Groaning, I bite down on my tongue, ignoring the splitting pain because I'm conflicted. Flirting with her is fun. She's hot and easy to talk to. I can say what I want, and I know she won't judge me. Kissing her the other night was perfection, and I got excited as hell.

There was just one problem. When she grabbed my balls, all my bravado went out the window and the realization of what was going to happen between us dawned on me.

What's going to happen when she finds out my secret?

I hate to admit it, but Griss was right. With a girl like Mia, being a virgin feels more like a problem than a perk. I thought it wouldn't be that bad, but now that I know it's Mia I want to be with, all kinds of thoughts run through my mind.

How would I compare to other guys? Would she even want to have sex with me? What if I suck?

Don't get me wrong. I'm a confident guy, usually, but I don't have any experience on how to get a girl off, and she's probably used to guys that could make her come with one finger.

Urgh, and now I'm thinking about Mia with other guys, and the jealousy rages through me, because she's mine.

Mine. Mine. *Mine.*

And I've got so many plans for her. Things like fingering her in the dugout at the end of a winning game and hauling her up to the nosebleeds seats where I proceed to eat her out until she crumbles on my tongue. You know, normal things.

All of these thoughts are great, it's just carrying them out is where I'm worried I'll stumble because suddenly, scoring on the field feels a whole lot more manageable than scoring off it.

Mia: When you get back in town, we'll have to celebrate.

Mia: Maybe spend a little time showing each other our abilities. 😜

Her line is corny as hell, but I'm nervous. I can't tell if I'm breaking a sweat because I'm imagining the next time I see Mia, or I'm still soaked from the impromptu ice bath. I look around the room, cursing myself because I could really use someone to talk to like Tate, but he's not here. No one is.

"Hey, Rookie. Game ended thirty minutes ago. What are you doing still in your uniform? You'll miss the bus to the hotel if you're not careful." Grayson struts out, adjusting the gray suit they require us to wear when leaving the building for the photographers. He's the only person who keeps it on the entire way back. Most players switch into something more comfortable on the bus, but not Grayson because he likes to make an entrance wherever he goes.

"Yeah, just busy."

"Well, answering messages about your performance can wait. The bus can't."

I snort out a laugh, re-reading Mia's message. Yeah, messages about my performance *can* wait because I have no idea what to say without getting a huge boner that I'd have to deal with. Tossing my phone in my bag, I take the towel from the peg and head to the showers. As I walk past him, Grayson picks at the collar of my jersey, forcing me to stop and look at him.

"Dude, why do you look like someone slapped your butt and called you Colonel Clucker? You should be running around this locker room naked with happiness, not shivering like a newborn puppy."

"Do you want to know why?" He nods and I raise my brows, holding back a smile. Picking my phone back up, I pretend to look at something because I want to mess with Grayson. "It's because I just saw a video of you playing peekaboo with a toddler while you were in the dugout last week. I've got to be honest, it shocked me to my core because I didn't know you had a soul."

His smile immediately falls. "Where did you see it?"

I turn my phone screen off before he can actually see what I'm looking at. "Literally every sports outlet is sharing it because no one believes you're human."

He adjusts his shoulders and rolls his eyes with an audible groan. "If I had known someone was recording, I would have just ignored the kid. Not like he was old enough to remember the interaction, anyway."

"Grayson, everyone has a smartphone these days. Privacy is dead, and you're famously one of the angriest pitchers in the league. Just take it as a given that your picture is going to be taken in some form or another."

He scratches his chin in contemplation. "You know, I'm really not all that angry these days. Cocky?" He raises his brow, asking himself a question with a smile. "Yeah, I'm cocky, but that's because I can be."

"You're right. You haven't tried to start a fight in a while."

"Blame my lawyer girlfriend. She told me I wasn't allowed to."

"Surprised you listened. You don't listen to anyone."

"And that's where you've got a few things to learn, Rookie. Always listen to the woman who can suck your cock better than those insidious barnacles that suck the life out of crabs."

Cringing, I sigh. "Not an image I wanted before going into the shower."

"You should consider yourself lucky. Ivy and I are hot together."

"Okay." As I attempt to walk past him again, Grayson uses his body to stop me this time. "What?" I ask, slightly annoyed because I'm definitely going to miss the bus now.

"Same question as before. Why are you looking so nervous? This should be one of the happiest days of your life, but you look like you've just been yelled at by the principal."

Grayson isn't known for the warm and fuzzies, so I'm not sure why he cares. "Nothing, just some stuff back home that I need to figure out."

"I know that face," he says, narrowing his eyes as he points at me. "This is to do with a woman." He smirks when I don't immediately answer. "It is. I knew it. What's wrong? Maybe I could help?"

"Unlikely," I mumble, trying to walk away, but apparently, Grayson is just as persistent as Grissom when he wants to know something. Even though water runs up the fabric of his pant legs, Grayson stays stuck to my side.

When all I give him is a furrowed brow, his shoulders go lax, and he drops his head. "Okay, I have a confession. It was something I was never going to bring up, but I overheard you."

"Overheard me?" I ask, confused.

He nods with his eyes still closed, as if he can't bear to look at me. "Spring training, out in the bar. When that joker Matt Grissom convinced you to have one too many shots."

Too many shots?

My mind races, trying to figure out what he's talking about.

Too many shots? Too many shots?
Then I still.

I'm suddenly feeling so hot that any remnants of the water from the ice bucket have evaporated because I know exactly what night he's referring to. It's the only night I've ever had shots, and I still regret it to this day.

"Did anyone else hear?" I can't look at him, so I focus on my cleats.

"No. Tate was too busy fawning over the first scan of his twins, and Max was… well I don't know what he was doing, but I'm pretty sure he was too busy to care about the fact that you've still got your big V because he hasn't mentioned it to me, and it feels like something we'd talk about."

My eyes widen in annoyance, but I don't know what to do. What are you supposed to say when the best pitcher in the league knows the secret you've been trying to hide?

"Relax. I don't care, and I don't plan on telling anyone."

"No. you just plan on torturing me with this information."

"Wrong again." He wraps his arm around my shoulder, unbothered that I'm getting his suit wet, and he walks me to the showers. "I get it. You've had a tough time. Girls aren't your strong point. Beating balls seems to be your MO, but I will offer you one piece of advice."

"Oh, yeah?"

"Yeah. Don't hold back. You need to grab the proverbial bull by the horns, otherwise you're going to sink deeper and deeper into a hole and it will never happen for you." Tapping the side of his head, he smiles. "It's all in the mindset."

Is this really happening? Is Grayson Hawk really trying to give me sex advice? Am I really considering accepting it too?

"Thanks, Grayson," I quip, not wanting to take this conversation any further, but, as per usual, Grayson refuses to let it drop.

He clutches my shoulder and winks. "I don't do this often because I don't want people to think I can stand their presence, but if you need any more advice, I'm here." He squeezes my shoulder, and now we've just gone to a whole new level of awkward.

"Will do." After giving him a gentle nod of acknowledgement, there's a moment where we're just looking at each other. Will he leave? When my phone buzzes in my bag, he gives me a knowing wink.

I don't know what's more embarrassing. The not so 'Playboy Pitcher' offering me sex advice, or Caterina the Cat Dom trying to unintentionally take my virginity.

Grayson turns, checking himself out in the mirror at the end of the room. He adjusts his collar, giving himself a satisfied smirk before looking down at his watch. Taking in a sharp breath, he tips his chin and stares at me through the reflection in the mirror. "Bus is leaving in three minutes. I guess you're getting a taxi to the hotel."

I look down at the towel in my hand and consider skipping the shower, but maybe a little alone time is what I need. After all, if I go with the team, they're going to want to talk about my homer when all I want to do is text Mia. "I guess I am."

"Do you want me to stay?"

"I'm good. You go. I'll see you at breakfast."

Hauling his bag over his shoulder, he stalks out of the room, leaving me in the empty locker room, alone with my thoughts and my phone. Before I can get caught up in overthinking things, I check my messages.

Mia: Did I come on too strong?

Mia: I hope I didn't offend you.

What's this? She can't be concerned about that, can she?

Austin: You couldn't offend me, Boss Girl. I was just about to take a shower. Didn't mean to leave you hanging.

Mia: A shower? Show me.

Show me?

I blink a few times, re-reading the message, because I wonder if my brain has malfunctioned, or if I'm actually talking to Mia. Maybe some super-savvy AI took over? Mia's never initiated the flirty talk, and now she's asking for a dick pic. Okay, maybe she doesn't want me to start with my hard cock. That would probably be me coming on a little too strong, but now that I'm thinking about it, she's got my blood boiling. I keep my erection to myself but pull off my shirt and pants so I can wrap my towel around my waist. Then I lift the phone over my head, taking a shot of my sweaty chest and send it to her.

As it sits on my phone screen, Mia's bubbles appear, then disappear, then appear and disappear. She does this dance for a few more minutes until I can't stand the wait.

Austin: You still there?

Mia: Did you keep your smudged eye black on just to tease me?

Austin: Haven't taken the shower yet, remember. Why? Don't you like it?

Mia: No. I like it. I like it a lot. Maybe you should wear it next time you see me.

Groaning, I put the phone in my bag, giving myself time and space to think of a response so I don't say the wrong thing, and head to the shower.

By the time I get back, I notice there are a few messages on my phone.

When I open it up, I'm met with a picture of Mia.

Dead.

Am I dead? Because I definitely stopped breathing for a few seconds, but it must take longer than that to die. Welp, that cold shower was worthless. Blood rushes straight to my groin as I stare at the quid pro quo picture she sent me.

Lying in her bed, she's biting her bottom lip and the neckline of her pink top dips down just enough that I can see the outline of her large breasts. Big, perky tits that would look great with my dick between them, or my tongue, and I debate over what I want to try first.

Did I just think that?

Breathing in and out, I try to center myself because there's a very serious possibility that I'm going to come in my pants without touching my dick if I don't calm down.

Shit. If I'm like this from just seeing a photo, what the hell am I going to be like if she looks like that in person?

As another notification comes through, I scroll down to see what else Mia has to say.

Mia: I definitely came on too strong with that picture, didn't I?

She's joking now, and I know she's got some kind of idea about how she's making me feel. So, I decide to toy with her too. After all, Grayson said, I need to take this by the balls and play. I send her another picture. This time it's of my face, now clean of the eye black, but still dripping wet.

Austin: Nope. That picture just made me come on strong. I was in the shower.

Mia: 😊 Is that your way of telling me that you just jerked off to me?

Shit.

Austin: No. No. Just that I liked the photo.

Mia: Too bad. I wanted to know more...

Umm... Where do I go from here? My cock's hard, I can barely think straight and she wants to dirty talk with me. I've flirted but we've always skated the line of funny one liners. So I go back to what I know.

Austin: Believe me, if you saw these showers, you wouldn't want me spanking one out in there. I'd probably get athletes foot on my dick.

Mia: Spanking? Who said anything about spanking? But good to know that's what you're into.

What the hell has gotten into Mia? She's feisty tonight. Maybe turning her down when I was at her place got her riled up. I don't know. All I know is that I don't hate it. My thumbs hover over the words because I'm sure she wants me to dirty talk back, but I don't know what to say.

Mia: What else do you like?

I scratch my face, grunting because I've really got to get it together. Okay, let's think about this. What would I *like*? Bondage? Spanking? Anal? Mhmm, maybe these are a little out there to be suggesting since I'm a beginner, and if I say I'm interested now, that could come to bite me in the ass in the future. Literally.

Oral? I nod to myself because, yeah; I think I'd like oral. Getting it definitely, but would I be good at giving it? Girls have told me I'm a good kisser before, but I don't know if that technique translates. Maybe I can avoid answering the question again.

Austin: Please don't make me send videos of myself shirtless while I lick fruit suggestively. I'm just not into it.

Mia: Voyeurism isn't your jam. Good to know. It's not mine either.

Austin: What do you like then?

I figure if I ask her, at least I can prepare myself for it. Maybe read a few things

before we do anything. After drying myself off, I take my time putting on a pair of sweatpants and a shirt since I've missed the team bus already.

Mia: I really liked something you did the other night.

Something *I* did? I barely remember what happened because all the blood in my body had gone straight down to my dick. I swear, the number of times I've gotten hard over her is unreal. Even when I watched porn as a teenager, I could never get it up as often as this. What magic does this girl possess?

Austin: What did I do?

Mia: I'm too embarrassed to say. 🙈

Austin: Can't do it again if I don't know what it is.

Mia: How about this? You're away for another seven days, right?

Austin: Yes.

Mia: Good. So, how about each night, we tell each other one thing we like in bed, and then maybe when we see each other next week, we can pick our favorite to act out?

Shit. Reality hits me hard. We're going to have sex next time we see each other. If not sex, then some foreplay will be on the cards. Am I ready for that? Yes, because my hand is getting tired from all the wrist action, but I can't let her go in blindly. I need to be honest with her and tell her the truth. She needs to know what she's getting into—or what I'm getting into.

Austin: Good idea, but I'm a giver. I want to hear all the things you like.

Because was I really going to say no to that offer?

Mia: Sure, but you do realize that just told me something very hot about you?

Austin: And that's all you're getting. Now, tell me, what did you like?

Mia: Don't judge me.

Austin: How could I if I did it?

Mia: Fine. The other night, when we were on the porch, I nearly lost my mind, and it wasn't because you're an amazing kisser.

Austin: Ouch.

Mia: Believe me, you're an amazing kisser, but right after you kissed me, when you squeezed my neck, I swear I nearly came on the spot.

New kink unlocked.

I remember that moment vividly because even when I had my hand wrapped around her neck; I felt an arousal deep in my core that I hadn't thought possible. When I gave her the lightest squeeze and she looked at me with those doe eyes, I was ready to do everything and anything with her.

Mia: I was so hot, I could feel tingles in my core, and I had to stop myself from moaning and making a complete fool of myself.

Memories from that night flash through my mind. She tasted as good as she looked, and her body was so warm and soft against mine. I didn't know what to do with my hands, so I let them roam. Somehow, they landed on her neck, and well, that happened. Never in my life did I think I would find a new kink doing that.

I scrape my hand over my face, wondering how the hell I'm supposed to last the next week if she's sending me messages like this. I'm going to have to knock a few out just to feel normal.

Mia: There was something else that made me really hot. Do you want to know what it was?

Austin: I think you already know the answer to that.

Mia: Good.

Mia: While you were squeezing my neck with one hand, you were squeezing my thigh with the other. When you squeezed both at the same time, I felt like goo, molding to your every little touch.

Austin: I liked it too.

Again, another pathetic virgin response. Closing my eyes, I sit back, trying to relax and think about what I could say that would make her feel as equally as hot as me.

Austin: Your eyes went wide, and your mouth dropped open ever so slightly. All I could think about was how good you'd look on your knees while you begged for me to feed you my dick.

I have no idea where that came from, but I'm going with it.

Mia: Not sure you'd fit. From what I felt, you were huge.

Austin: Only one way to find out.

Mia: Austin, how am I supposed to make Jett dinner when all I can think about is you?

Austin: How am I supposed to hit those baseballs without thinking about you?

Mia: Doesn't seem to be a problem for you.

Austin: Then you should be able to work around it too. Now, where were we?

Mia: Did you just get out of the shower?

Austin: Yup. Already dressed and about to head to the hotel.

Mia: Hotel? Too bad. I was going to ask you for another picture.

Austin: Don't you have enough?

Mia: Do you have enough?

Austin: I'll never have enough, so why don't you be a good girl and send me more?

Mia: Good girl?

Austin: You're right. Sorry, you're Boss Girl.

Mia: No… I like the sound of Good Girl too.

Have I just accidentally revealed another kink?

Austin: Okay then. GG it is. I've got to catch a taxi to the hotel, but if you're around, I'll talk to you later.

Mia: Can't wait.

As I put my phone in My pants pocket, and haul my bag over my shoulder, I can't hold back my smile because making Mia my little good girl has a nice ring to it. Now if only I could become her bad boy, and do bad things, we'd be in good shape.

CHAPTER TWELVE
MIA

Austin swipes away the sweat on his forehead, smearing the dirt along with it. It's hot today, but Austin's making me ten times hotter as I sit in the stands watching him below. He's in his uniform, talking to some other players in the dugout, completely unaware that I'm staring at him like a hawk. Of course, I shouldn't be watching him because he's not even playing today. He's just mentoring the kids while they try out for the Catfish Youth program. My eyes should be solely focused on Jett, who hasn't moved from the catcher's spot since they asked him to try out in the fourth inning, but I can't help myself. It's like my body knows when Austin is in the vicinity, and I can't help but home in on him.

It's been another week of talking, and when I say talking, I mean we've been low key flirting, and I've been getting off on it. He's such a player, acting nonchalant when he knows he's getting me hot, but he just shrugs it off, like he's used to it. Maybe he is. Who knows? All I know is that I have accepted the fact that I want a piece of him for myself.

"Strike two!" The umpire yells, and half the crowd cheers. The other half mutter things under their breath, annoyed that their children aren't playing on the winning side. I roll my eyes because it's typical baseball parent behavior, but they need to calm down. It's just a game.

However, maybe I'm not shouting at the ump because Jett's doing so well. As I look around the stadium, I laugh at how seriously the rest of the parents are taking this. It feels more intense than an actual game, yet here I am, completely oblivious to it all because I'm too busy getting hot and bothered over the third base coach for the day. But who wouldn't? The man is solid. Built like a brick house, and I can't stop thinking about how it would feel to have him throw me against the stadium wall and kiss me the way he did the other night.

Yeah, I've been thinking about it a lot.

Hot and demanding. Controlled and dominant. My body tingles just thinking about his hands wrapped around my throat, and it's ridiculous. We've only kissed, yet I can't stop thinking about what it would feel like to have his hands all over me.

When Austin turns to the stands, he finds me and winks. It's a hot day in Charlotte, but that's not what's making me melt in my seat. It's his attention. I've had boyfriends in the past, ones I'd rather forget, and they were nice, but none of them looked at me the way Austin does. None of them made me *feel* the things that Austin does.

"Which one is yours?" A woman with dark hair leans in to ask. When I look over, I'm immediately stunned by her beauty. With her perfect bow lips and dark eyes, she looks like a doll. She's wearing a Macon Minnows jacket over a white crop top, emphasizing her perfect proportions. To say she looks effortlessly cool would be an understatement.

She raises her brow, waiting for me to respond, and that's when I realize I'm staring.

Umm okay, which one is mine? She's most definitely not talking about Austin.

I point to the catcher's box. "The current catcher. Mike 'Jett' James," I say proudly, as he squats in place, effortlessly catching another strike. I've watched Jett play in plenty of games over the years, but seeing him wearing a Catfish jersey, in a professional team's catcher's box, hits different.

His dreams are coming true, and I'm so glad that I'm here to see it... I just wish Hailey was here to enjoy it, too.

"I'm Mia, by the way."

"Selena." She smiles brightly as she shifts her hair to one shoulder and looks at the field. Lifting a perfectly manicured eyebrow toward the pitcher's mound, she says, "*She's* mine. Rhode," just as proud.

"No way? That girl out there pitching better than any of the boys today, is your daughter?"

"Yup. Dare I say, she's even better than her father."

"Oh?"

"Her dad is a stud when it comes to baseball. He just gets… distracted. Can't focus on one thing at a time, and baseball needs a lot of patience. But Rhode got his athleticism and my determination, which means she's hard to push back on when she's on the mound."

"I can see that," I muse, watching Rhode and Jett have what looks to be a heated conversation through their mitts. She's about a foot taller than him, but he's holding his own. "You must be so proud of her. How old is she?"

"Thirteen."

"Same as Jett. They look like they could make a good partnership."

"Yeah," She drawls out. "He hasn't tried to throw a ball at her head like the last catcher." She throws her head back on a laugh, making her black hair shine in the sun. "That's always a good sign for us. We've had to leave a few teams because Rhode can be a little hot head."

"Oh, really?" I notice Jett tip on his toes, which usually means he's angry, but maybe it's just nerves.

But suddenly, Rhode steps in front of Jett, towering over him, and glares like she wants to punch his lights out. Jett lifts his chin, unbothered by her and stares back with confidence.

Rhode drops her mitt, pushing past Jett and steps off the mound.

Now I'm no baseball aficionado, but I do know that coming off the mound during play isn't a good thing.

"What's going on?" I ask Selena, and she leans back, sighing.

"Not again."

"Maybe they're switching someone out," I offer, but as the argument gets more heated, I realize I'm being naïve.

Jett throws his mask up and grabs her arm. When she glances behind, he shouts at her as other players join the heated discussion.

"What the-" I don't finish my sentence because Rhode pushes Jett, and I find myself standing, rushing to the front so I can hear what they're arguing about.

"I told you to stop calling pitches that make me look bad," Rhode grits out. Nose to nose, she's staring at Jett like a lion about to eat its prey. When she pushes him again, he's not ready for it and staggers back, but quickly regains his composure.

Jett adjusts his chest protector, and for a second, I'm proud that in the heat of the moment, he's not letting the stress get to him. He's calm and composed.

For that second.

But then he sees Rhode's face, which makes him whip his helmet off and throw it to the side. "It's not my fault your fastball is as slow as Billy McGill trying to run bases." He pushes Rhode back, just as hard. "Maybe you should stick to softball."

The crowd sucks in a breath, and I cringe. "Jett!" I yell, to no avail. He can't hear me, and he doesn't back off when other players hold him back.

Neither does she.

Rhode is ready to tackle him down.

"Rhode! Baby girl, what are you doing?" Grissom's voice cuts through the fervor, and Jett instantly backs off. He's at Rhode's side in a heartbeat, checking for bruises even though she was the one doing the pushing, not Jett.

Austin stands beside Jett, squeezing his shoulder for moral support.

"What am *I* doing?" She laughs out, as she points at Jett. "It's not my fault they've paired me up with the worst catcher here."

"Hey!" Jett steps up to her, but is held back by other teammates, and then Austin steps in front of him. Grabbing Jett by the shoulder to pull him away.

"Jett," Austin warns. "This is not a fight you want to get into."

As I watch both Jett and Rhode get dragged through the field, I look at Selena, who won't take her eyes off her daughter. The stadium is still silent because there's an awkward energy ruminating through it. "Kids will be kids," I say with a shrug, trying to relieve some of the tension.

Austin has pulled Jett far enough away from the others so that he can whisper something in his ear, slowly calming Jett down.

Selena smiles. "Don't be. This isn't the first time Rhode's had a bust up on the field. Won't be the last."

"Oh."

She shrugs, unbothered. "Comes with the territory. Being the only girl on the team can be a pretty lonely place."

I suck in my lips, giving her a knowing smile, but I really don't have a clue how tough it must be to be pushing against all odds to get people to take you seriously in a game that's not made for you.

After some discussions between the coaches, Rhode and Jett are escorted to the dugout, and I feel sick to my stomach with the implications. Have they both just lost out on their dreams because they couldn't stand each other?

Pointing my finger to the dugout, I say, "I should probably check if Jett's okay."

"No problem. It was nice meeting you. I'm sure I'll see you around."

"You too," I reply brightly as I turn on my heel, rushing down to the stadium exit. I'm not usually concerned when Jett gets into an argument on the field. That's part of being in a competitive environment, but today feels a little different.

After several arguments with security because they won't allow me in the locker room, I'm asked to leave, which I do without a fuss. Jett's already made enough of a scene for the both of us.

As I sit on a bench outside waiting for someone to come out, I check my phone constantly, hoping someone will tell me what's going on.

When a couple of the stadium doors open, I whip my head to see Austin walking out with his head hung low. All kinds of emotions come rushing through me because it's the first time I've been close enough to hug him since he came back from all of those away games. Offering me a weary smile, he looks exhausted, but I don't let that stop me from running into his arms.

He takes a step back, but catches me with ease, clasping his hand at the back of my neck.

"Hey, Mia," Austin husks into my ear, seemingly unfazed by my clinginess.

As I pull back, I want to kiss him, but I stop myself because I'm technically at his place of employment, and if any other parents see me, they might think I'm doing it so Jett has an unfair advantage.

I slide my legs down his body, so I'm standing in front of him instead of mauling him like a koala, and back away. "Austin." I do my best to sound neutral, but it's hard when you know what a guy looks like without a jersey on. "I'm so sorry about Jett." Embarrassment suddenly rolls through me because this wasn't how I was expecting our first meeting to go.

He sighs out with a little smile. "Don't be. You should have seen me at my Little League games. Once, when I was eight, the ump got so tired of my taunting, he threw me out of the game."

I cross my arms, taking him in. "Wow. I didn't think they took the game so seriously at that age."

His smile widens. "Yeah, well, the ump may have been one of the parents who didn't like that I kept pointing out that he was calling the strike zone wrong."

"I'm glad you can see the funny side of Jett losing his place on the team." I wince, not knowing how I'm supposed to talk to Jett about this when he gets back. He's a good kid and I've never really had to chastise him over anything, so this feels out of my comfort zone.

Austin tilts his head, pursing his lips. "I'm not so sure he's lost all his chances. He's a good player, and they both showed passion for the game, which is very important. It's also not the first time Rhode has had a run in with someone."

"I bet it's hard being one of the only girls on the field."

"Oh, yeah. Griss is her dad, and he's had to use his name within the organization to get them to even look at her. When they do, they're shocked at what she can do. I guess that's why he's so mellow about his own career. He knows he's not the best, but his daughter might be."

Just then, another door slams open, and Jett comes trudging out, holding his helmet in one hand and dragging his bag with the other. "I don't want to talk about it," he grumbles as he walks past me and Austin looking at the ground. I follow his form as he walks past, giving Austin a silent glare.

I brush my hand against his, sad that this is the closest we're going to get to touching today after so long apart. "I guess we better go. Can I call you tonight?"

Austin has other plans. He clasps his hand in mine, not caring who sees. "You can't leave yet."

I tilt my head to the back. "I can't exactly stay with a sulky teenager who's been kicked out of the game."

He looks over my shoulder to Jett standing by the car, who's still not looking at or acknowledging us. "I get it. I was just kind of hoping we could talk." He brushes his thumb across the back of my hand, looking more serious than I've ever seen him.

Talk? Is that all he wants to do? Because I want to do a hell of a lot more than that. Not that I can mention it in front of my teen.

"I'm leaving town again in two days."

Two days?

And therein lies the issue between us. The elephant in the room that neither one of us wants to admit. Although we have this crazy connection, how are we supposed to see if we can be something if he's never actually here?

"Austin!" Jett yells, finally acknowledging us. He looks over, surprised. "Are you coming?" Austin dips his chin, looking at me questioningly.

Out of all the things I expected to happen tonight, I didn't expect Jett to invite Austin over. Maybe this is the universe's way of telling me something, or maybe it's a nephew trying to set up his aunt so he can get more access to the Catfish. Either way, I can't let go of the opportunity. "Do you want to come over for dinner? I've got pizzas in the fridge." I try to hide my smile as best as I can, but it's hard when Austin gives me one straight back.

"Sure." His hand crosses mine, but I'm careful not to show much affection. Something he lacked earlier. "I've just got a few things to tie up and then I'll be right behind you."

***

After a long, silent drive home, I look over to Jett. He hasn't made a sound since I got in the car. No look, no explanation, and he doesn't seem to realize the opportunity he lost out on. In fact, he's acting like *I'm* the problem, and all I've done is sit here.

"We're home," I say but it feels like I'm talking to myself since there's no acknowledgement from Jett.

Still no words as he opens the car, slamming the door behind him like it personally offended him.

That's it.

I don't need to take this. I open my own door, and step onto the car ledge so I can see Jett from over the hood. "What the hell was that for?! I understand you're ticked off with how today went, but you do not take it out on the car, especially because we can't afford a new one."

When he looks back at me, his shoulders slump and he frowns. "I'm sorry, Aunt Mia, but I don't want to talk about it."

The words make the surrounding air fall silent because we're not on the same page. Jett and I are always on the same page. This can't be happening.

"Jett," I drawl out, already feeling exasperated, knowing that we're entering Jett's teen years, and this will be the first of many tantrums.

"I already said I don't want to talk about it," he says definitely. By the look on his face, he's as shocked as me that he's being so upfront.

Hopping off the car and slamming the door, I make my way around him. "Michael James. You do not take that tone with me."

As if he has to go with it, he says, "Fine. I won't take one at all." He spins on his heel, stalks up the path, and makes his way to the house.

What on earth has gotten into him?

"Jett," I warn, traipsing after him, and stop when I get to the porch.

When he turns, he looks as if he's just about to say something but stops himself when he sees what's over my shoulder. Then tips his chin. "I want to talk to Austin."

Austin? I'm so taken aback that I nearly fall off the step of our porch. Luckily, I land in a familiar set of arms. Austin is already behind me, and I must have been arguing with Jett so loudly that I didn't notice him coming.

"Hey, Austin." Resting in his arms, I look over my shoulder to my equally stunned boyfriend–wait, scratch that–man friend. We may have dry humped and sent each other a few racy texts, but I'm not sure we can consider ourselves anything other than friends just yet.

"Hey," he says hesitantly, looking between Jett and me. "Did I miss something?"

"You didn't miss anything," Jett speaks for us. "But I need to speak to Austin about everything that happened today."

I'm trying really hard not to be offended here, but he wants to talk to Austin? Not me? Breathe. Don't take it personally. Austin's a guy and a professional baseball player. Of course he'd want to talk to him. He's got more experience getting over setbacks like this, and I should let him have this.

Resigned, I look over to Austin with a questioning brow, and he smiles back, albeit somewhat hesitantly. "Are you okay with that, Austin?"

"Sure," he drawls out, his confidence a little shaky, but Jett hardly notices because he's too caught up in his own problems.

"I guess I'll just make those pizzas," I pipe up, not knowing what else to say as I climb out of Austin's arms and walk up the porch. I move around Jett, but he follows close behind and as I step into the kitchen, he turns to go up the stairs.

Austin takes my hand, squeezing it one time before letting out a hesitant breath. "See you in a minute," he rolls out, following dutifully behind Jett.

Well, this should be interesting.

CHAPTER THIRTEEN
AUSTIN

"So, what is it you want to talk about?" I ask, stuffing my hands in my jeans as Jett enters his room, falling onto the bed dramatically. I imagine our mascot; Catty the Catfish, living in a place like this. The walls are covered with so many posters of Catfish and Minnows players that I can't tell the color of the room, and the only three shelves are filled with more bobbleheads than I can count. The only person I've seen with more bobbleheads than this is Tate's baby mama, Cali, and designing those is part of her job. I make a mental note to snag a couple of the exclusive ones for him next time I'm in the marketing department.

Most noticeably though, there's only one picture in his room, and I'm not usually an emotional guy, but seeing it chokes me up. Sitting on his bedside table is a picture of Jett with Mia and I assume his mom at a baseball game together. Hailey's arm is wrapped around his shoulder, proudly looking at the camera. He looks young in that photo and I wonder if it was close to when she passed away.

Jett sits up, pulls his socks off and throws them dramatically into the laundry basket. I don't point out that he misses.

"I hate her," he mutters without looking at me.

"Who? Mia?" And in that moment, I realize I'm ready to do

something I thought I was too young for. I'm ready to give Jett a lecture about how good he's got it with an aunt that loves him and is trying her best. "Because she-"

Jett winces, flippantly waving his hand. "No. Not Mia. That woman is a saint, and I will apologize to her once I've gotten myself out of this funk."

"Well, I'm glad we're in agreement about that. But if it's not her, then who are we talking about?"

"Rhode."

It takes me a second. "Oh, Rhode Grissom. Why?"

He looks at me, dumbfounded. "You're kidding right? Because don't you remember you had a front-row seat to her ruining my chances of getting onto the Junior Catfish team?"

I wince. I hadn't forgotten; I was just thinking about other things. But now it's my time to step up, and I need to think back to all the lectures my dad used to give me. "I'm not sure we can blame Rhode entirely for what happened out there, J. I'd say it was more of a joint effort."

He mumbles something half-heartedly, and I sit next to him on the bed, noting the dent I leave. Jett refuses to talk, still riled in anger as he cracks his knuckles.

"What got her so riled up, anyway?"

He raises his hands and shakes his head, feigning innocence. "I have no idea. I was calling pitches I thought would get the players out. That's all I was focused on."

"And you didn't do anything to make her look bad? Like suggest she throw something that you knew she couldn't throw?"

He blows out a breath, smiling to himself. "Nothing could make her look bad, and she can throw anything."

Uh oh. Those googly eyes. The goofy smile. I know that look. It's the same look I have when I think about Mia. Jett *likes* her. And I've known Rhode since she was six years old. The only thing she's interested in is baseball and impressing her dad. Jett doesn't have a chance.

"Austin, can I ask you something?"

"Sure." It's reluctant because I've got a feeling I know what's coming, and I have no idea how I'm going to handle this.

"Have you ever felt like you want to hurl when a girl looks at you?"

"Plenty of times?" I laugh bitterly because that happens pretty much every single time I'm in Mia's presence. "But what has that got to do with anything?"

He opens his palms, and shakes his head. "Maybe I accidentally called a bad pitch or two," he admits. "But I wasn't doing it on purpose. She was staring down at me, her eyes pinning me in the catcher's box, and I felt frozen on the spot. I just started feeling queasy and didn't know what to do. It wasn't that I was trying to give her bad calls, it's that I couldn't think straight."

I shake my head, chuckling. "Jett. I'm sorry that I have to say this, but I think you have a crush on her."

He cringes, pushing back. "And what am I supposed to do about that? I've got a game to focus on."

I shrug. "Do you *want* to do something about it?" I throw the question back to him because I have absolutely no idea what I'm talking about, or doing, for that matter. I've never had a girlfriend, and I wouldn't say I'm killing it with Mia. I have no idea what I'm doing half the time, and the other half, I'm questioning my decisions. Like the one where I agreed to come upstairs and give Jett dating advice.

"I don't know." He growls, and falls back onto the bed, staring at some glow in the dark stars stuck to the ceiling. "I've just never met someone like her."

"Yeah, I get it."

"She's awesome, and she's amazing at baseball."

"Yup."

"She could kick any guy's ass."

"That's true."

"And she hates me," he sighs.

"Hate's a strong word."

"She told me to eat rocks."

"You told her to play softball."

"Because then she'd be less distracting, and I'd be on the team."

"Distractions are a part of life, and they're definitely part of baseball."

"How do you stop yourself getting...." He waves a hand over his face. "Distracted?"

"Luckily for me, the person I'm interested in isn't staring me down while I'm trying to do my job."

"And the person you're interested in is Aunt Mia, right?"

"Yes," I say without hesitation, and I feel ridiculous looking for validation from a teenager, but here we are.

Jett smiles smugly. Probably because he thinks he had something to do with the outcome. "I never thought I'd be saying a famous baseball player is my uncle."

Uncle? Is Jett already talking about marriage? Rings? What the hell? I'm a twenty-one-year-old virgin. Mia doesn't even know that yet, but I'm in no way ready for that kind of commitment. This conversation is not going the way I'd planned.

"Woah, woah, slow down there. We aren't that advanced yet."

"But you're dating?"

"I guess."

"How'd you do it?"

"Do what?"

"Convince her to stop hating you?"

"Did she hate me?"

"She didn't like that Griss called her a MILF in front of me, that much is for sure, and the entire way home she was silently cursing you."

"I thought you said you didn't know what MILF meant?"

Jett's face falls. "Look. I love my aunt, but I'm thirteen with access to the internet. I feigned ignorance for both our sakes. But she definitely hated you then. So, how did you convince her to give you a chance?"

I shrug, thinking about all the things Griss and Grayson suggested, surprised that their words of wisdom are coming in handy now. "I didn't need to convince her to do anything. I just started talking to her and let it go from there."

"So, you became friends first?"

"Yeah, I guess you could say that."

Jett blows out a sarcastic breath. "There's no way that Rhode will ever want to be friends with me."

"Do you want to ask Rhode on a date?"

"Maybe." Jett runs a hand across his face, groaning in embarrassment. "Yeah. I do." I knew I shouldn't have asked. I knew this was coming, but I still did it because apparently, I'm a glutton for punishment. "It's just she's everything. She's strong. She's determined. She's got these beautiful hazel eyes and I can't stop thinking about the way she looked at me."

"Okay." I stand, knowing I need to nip this in the bud, otherwise things are going to get out of hand. I don't want to tick Mia off by giving advice she doesn't want me to. "It's not my business, but you're only thirteen and I think that's too young to be dating. You should focus on

143

baseball and have fun with your friends. Dating can come after."

"Is that how you got so good at baseball? You didn't date."

"Yep," I pop out the 'P', rolling back on my heels a little. "But that wasn't entirely out of choice. However, that's not the point. When I was thirteen, all I was thinking about was the best way to break in a glove." I point at him before I get to the door. "Focus on the game. Everything else will fall into place."

Jett nods. "Okay. Focus on the game." He blows out a breath and I already know that this little crush spells trouble for him, but I'm not going to be the one to burst his bubble.

As my hand grapples with the doorknob, Jett says my name, and I look over my shoulder at him. "Thanks for the talk. It's nice to speak to someone that isn't Aunt Mia about this."

I offer him a smile. "No problem. You've got my number, and I'm always here. Whether you want to talk about baseball or Rhode. I'll answer."

"I hope so."

I hope so, too.

"I'm going to check on Mia, but I'd suggest you coming down in ten minutes, apologizing and then eating every slice of pizza she offers you."

"Sounds like a good plan."

"See you in a minute."

As I shut the door to Jett's room, I blow out a long, exasperated breath and run a hand through my hair. *What the hell was that?* I'm the last person who should give advice on women. I have only slightly more experience than the thirteen-year-old asking for advice.

The smell of pizza, and dishes clattering draw me to the beautiful woman downstairs. I miss talking to her, so I follow the noise. By the time I'm on the bottom step, I can see Mia is standing in the kitchen loading the dishwasher as she hums to herself. She shakes her hips to an imaginary beat, dancing because she doesn't know anyone is watching. She's beautiful.

So happy. So carefree. So mine.

Mine. Mine. Mine.

Something warms my chest. Feelings that I have no right feeling bloom. Feelings like this is exactly where I belong, and maybe I don't need to find an apartment because I could just move in here. Mia, and even Jett are everything I didn't know I wanted, and now that I have a small semblance of something real, I want to have it all the time.

She doesn't notice me behind her until I wrap my arms around her waist and nip at her exposed neck. Tilting her head down, she gives me better access, but swats me in the arm to feign protest.

"How did that go?"

I swipe my tongue across her skin, loving that she lets out a little giggle. "He'll survive," I say loud enough for her to hear. "But I'm not sure his heart will," I mumble under my breath because I already know Rhode and Jett are a lost cause.

"What was that?"

"Nothing." I'm sure Jett doesn't want me telling his aunt about his crush.

"So, I was thinking," she hums out, drawing her finger around the button on my shirt. Her voice is low and melodic with invitation. Her eyes are hooded, and she's got this sexy little smirk on her face. "Maybe after pizza you should spend the night. You know, as it's getting late." Spend the night? Fuck. Maybe she just wants to sleep. Although it's unlikely since she's gently rocking her hips into my crotch, and I'm hard just thinking about touching her. She has no idea what she's doing to me. "My room is just down that hall, so you don't have to walk up those pesky stairs again." She tips her chin to a room downstairs, and I long to go down and open the door just to see where she sleeps. I've imagined it plenty of times. Have even seen the sheets when she's sent me a picture or two, but I doubt it's anything like I envisage. "It's also far, far away from Jett's room," she adds to entice me, but the more I think about the implications lacing her words, the more I start to freak the fuck out.

Her bedroom.

She wants *me* in there with her, and I'll probably come in my pants before I've reached the doorknob.

Damn it.

Why didn't I try fooling around with Caterina when I had the chance? Sure, she may have been two kinks away from anal, but at least she would have been able to show me a thing or two.

Mia's hand tickles up my chest, which is unusually heaving. If she notices my shaky breath, she says nothing, but her eyes are zoned in, focused solely on me.

"Remember how we talked about all those things I liked?" Gently squeezing her throat comes to mind, and my dick goes hard without my

145

permission. "Thought maybe I could be your good girl tonight."

She bites her bottom lip, and for some reason, I find myself backing away.

Am I scared?

I think I might be.

Mia's hot. She's all woman, and I have no idea how she'd take the idea that I'm a virgin. I should just blurt it out and tell her. I can feel my dick softening, but now I'm worried this admission will make it impossible to get it back up.

With my crisis of confidence firmly obstructing anything, I respond the only way I think I can. I look to the hallway, then back to Mia, who's staring at me with expectation. "Mhhm. As much as I'd love to join you. I don't think I can."

I want to. I really, *really* want to, but I'm nervous. I don't want to fail. I need to psych myself up and prepare myself to tell her the truth. I can't do it too because I'm exhausted after a long day at the stadium. Also, I've waited this long. What's another day to figure out how I'm going to broach the subject with her?

"Okay," she says with pressed lips, obviously unhappy about my brush off.

Holding her hands against my chest, I wait until she's looking at me. "How about we go for dinner tomorrow night?" I say, looking at her with more expectation than I thought possible. Tomorrow night, I'll tell her, and she'll be fine with it. I hope.

Mia's eyes trace our laced fingers as she looks down at my chest longingly. Kind of like she's remembering what I look like with nothing on. I can't do this tonight. Not after all that talking with Jett. I just need some time to decompress and think about my situation first.

"Tomorrow sounds good. Today sounded better, though."

Fuck me.

She's batting her eyelashes now, and what does she expect? For me *not* to get hard over her?

"Tomorrow. Definitely tomorrow." My voice is so high, I sound like I'm auditioning to be orphan Annie.

"Pizza smells good." Jett's voice breaks the ice like a sledgehammer, and Mia immediately backs away, tending to the dishes as though she wasn't just trying to jump my bones. "Everything okay?" He slows, stopping at the bottom step and looks between us with a raised brow.

Red-faced and flustered, I comb a hand through my hair and laugh awkwardly. "Everything's good. Let's have that pizza. I'm starving."

And that's how I manage to dodge having sex with my girlfriend for the night.

Chapter Fourteen

Mia

When the doorbell rings, I tip on my toes in excitement. He's early, and I'm so ready to see him again. My heels click against the hardwood as I make my way to the door, and when I open it, I can't help but smile. Tight jeans, white shirt and a Catfish ball cap greet me, along with Austin's trademark sexy smirk. Grappling at the door, I'm more than ready to skip dinner entirely and devour this man instead. Talk about holding out. I've given him every opportunity to take me to my room and screw me senseless, but he just keeps brushing it off like it's nothing.

But I know it wasn't nothing. I could feel it in his pants. He wanted me just as much as I wanted him, but Jett being home held him back again.

"Austin," I say in a breathless whisper. "I'm so glad you're here." As my smile widens, his turns to a frown and I stop my advances, studying his reaction earnestly.

"Mia." It's short and curt, and there's a moment that I think this is it. He's going to break up with me. What other explanation is there for his flustered, red face, and the sweat dripping down his forehead? Oh my god. Was Jett just an excuse last night? "It's nice to see you again."

It's nice to see you again.

That's super formal, and super confusing, so I decide to take things into my own hands. I take a confident step forward, planting a welcoming kiss on his lips before taking a step back.

It does nothing to calm his nerves, and he chokes out a hesitant laugh, then looks at me with an intensity I'm not used to. It's as if he's trying to search my face for an answer to a question he never asked. "Let's go out." It comes out of his mouth rushed as he runs a hand through his hair. Is his hand shaking?

"Um, if you want to. I kind of thought we could order Chinese... maybe watch a movie..." I point behind me to the sofa with the pillows already laid out. It by no means looks like a sex dungeon, but I have tried to make it look somewhat enticing and cozy.

Austin lets out a low groan, his eyes widening at the sight. He's caught my drift.

"Are you sure you want to stay in?" His voice sounds more tentative, and I don't know what's gotten into him. He's usually a burly, cocky man. Not a bumbling mess. "There's this little Italian restaurant by the stadium that I've been meaning to check out."

"The stadium?" He nods. That's like thirty minutes away. "I thought you said you didn't mind staying in with me tonight?" And by in, I meant inside me, but that's pretty obvious at this point.

"I don't," he answers, but I don't believe it. Something's wrong. I can feel it. "I'd love to stay in tonight." Also, not believable. "Just thought you might want to go out?"

I shake my head. "No, I want to stay in."

"Okay," He answers reluctantly. "Have you got a movie picked out?" Taking his hand, I lead him to the sofa, and he sits next to me. A foot away, but I'll take it.

"Not just yet." Biting my bottom lip, I figure that maybe Austin's the kind of guy I need to be bold with. He's too much of a gentleman to take something without it being given, so I'm going to offer myself up to him. Scooting a little closer, I pull on the opening of his jacket, tipping my head up to make it clear what I want.

I feel him hesitate again for a second, but then he drops his lips on mine in a sweet, respectful kiss.

Then he backs away with a small, placid smile.

Is that it? Where's the fire from the first night we kissed? Where's the energy that I see coming from him when he's out on the field? I want more than that, and I know he does too.

So I take it.

Snaking my hand around his neck, I draw him back for another kiss, which he eagerly accepts. His tongue slips into my mouth, testing the waters. He's still tentative, but I can feel him slowly relaxing.

As the kiss intensifies, I melt into his hard chest. His touch is like fire in the freezing cold. Scorching hot, but I need it to survive. Kissing endlessly, his hands slip into my hair, gently scratching at the nape of my neck. I haven't felt this alive in years. My core is tingling, and my bones are aching to feel him on top of me.

This is what I wanted.

When I try to pull him down so he's lying on top of me, he holds me still in the position.

Okay. Maybe he's worried he'll crush me or something.

So I try a different move. With my lips locked on his, I shuffle toward him, my hands landing on his thighs. His hands rest on my hips, not moving anywhere, and I like it. It makes me feel in control.

Taking the plunge, I throw one leg over and sit on his thighs, right against his jean-covered crotch where I can feel his hardness. He wants this, and I so badly want to feel him.

As we kiss, I unbutton his shirt, revealing his hard, muscular chest underneath. His hands move down my spine, and he gently scratches my back, but makes no effort to rip my shirt off.

Am I missing something?

"Austin. I love how this feels," I say, trying one more time to pull him down, but he stays still.

He cuts his steely blue eyes over my face and then looks to the stairs. "But what about Jett?"

I laugh. "Did you really think I'd create this little pleasure palace in the living room with him upstairs?" I toil with some of the fluff from a pink pillow as I watch his facial expression. "He's at a friend's tonight. It's just us."

"Just us," he repeats, and as I go to kiss him again, his body tenses.

"Is everything okay?" I cup his jaw, and he scoots as far back as he can with me sitting on him. I feel his hands shaking against my hips. Why on earth is he so nervous?

With my legs still wrapped around him, he sits himself up, looking at me before cracking his knuckles. "There's, uh, something I need to tell you before anything can happen between us." He cringes, cursing under his breath. "Not that I'm implying anything *will* happen between us tonight, but if it does, there's something that you need to know." He lets out a hesitant chuckle. "I really do like you."

Showing his age, I give him a quick kiss to stop him from rambling. How is it that this big, hulking man turns to jelly when I'm around him?

I rub my thumb against his jaw as I gently coax him to look at me. "It's okay. You can tell me anything." The irony of that statement. He can tell me anything, yet I still haven't told him the whole truth about Jett's father. Not like there's really been a good time to tell him.

"Yeah, but this is just awkward, and hard to explain." He leans into my touch with his eyes closed, taking all the comfort he can from my hand.

"Is this your way of telling me you're into something kinky? Are you a furry?" I scratch the back of his ears, poking my tongue out playfully. "Because I could be a good girl and give it a go," I purr out.

His eyes widen. "No. No. It's not that. I'm most definitely *not* into that." Okay, so he's tried it. That's fine. "I mean, I don't think so. I don't know, maybe with the right person, but that's not what I've got to tell you."

"Okay."

"I've never done this before." My brows cross as I study him, unsure of what he's referring to. Then he clarifies. "I've never had sex."

He's never had sex?

I sit there, letting the words sink in, and when they do, I drop my hands and stare at him in shock. But then it all comes together, and I smile. "Is this a bit?"

"A bit?"

"So you're into role play. Was it the good girl talk that got you into it?" I gasp, slapping him on the chest. It all makes sense. He's been acting out this character since the start of the night, I just didn't realize until now. "Or wait, is this another graduate reference? Are you pretending to be my inexperienced student, and I have to *teach* you?"

I lean into him, ready to take this fantasy to the next level.

"Well, Mr. Adams, I guess the first thing we'd need to check is if everything works." I drop my hand and grab his crotch through his jeans.

He jolts up, wincing. "This isn't a bit," he squeaks out. As I loosen my grip on his jeans, he opens one eye, and then the other. "It's the truth. I'm a virgin. You are the closest I've been to dirty talk in my life."

"Wait, are you being serious?" He nods. "So you're actually a virgin?"

He cringes. "Don't say it like that."

"Like what?"

"Like I'm about to give you a contagious STD or something." Finally, he squirms enough that I slide onto the sofa next to him. Talk about mood killer. Not the virgin part, but the fact that he's so unconfident about it. Why was he hiding it from me? Did he think I'd have a bad reaction?

"I'm sorry. I didn't mean to make you feel bad. I just didn't expect to hear that from a guy like you." I raise my hand, flailing it in his direction.

"What's that supposed to mean?" When I look at the concern on his face, everything clicks together. The over-confident, somewhat clunky texts, the nervousness whenever I'm close. The need for me to confirm that I'm okay with it. Everything about his actions screams inexperienced. I was just too preoccupied with other things to really notice.

"You don't act it. You're hot, know how to flirt, and you play baseball. I kind of thought you were a playboy, not a choir boy."

"Yeah, that's what I hear from most people," he relents, focusing his attention on his hands that are resting on my thighs.

I scoot back a little, giving him some space. "Is it because you're waiting for marriage, or you don't want to?"

He laughs sarcastically. "I'm not waiting. Believe me, I've wanted to. For a long time. But it was just never my top priority. Baseball was, and with each passing year, it started becoming more of an issue. Especially when I ended up in college at sixteen with all these older women."

"No one would look at you," I state as a fact.

"Nope," He pops out.

"Is that why you like me? Because I'm older?"

He shrugs, his cheeks going ruddy. "I didn't know you were older when I first met you, remember? I thought you were Jett's sister, not his aunt." I purse my lips, holding back on saying anything. "When I found out you were older, it kind of helped my confidence. I just spoke to you in the same way I spoke to my friend's girlfriends, and that seemed to work."

"I hope you weren't sending your friend's girlfriend's shirtless photos like the ones you sent me."

He chuckles, the first sign that he's relaxing after that revelation. "Nah, but I'd joke with them and maybe flirt a little. I was four years younger and a minor. They knew I was harmless."

"Well, I appreciate you letting me know."

He looks up at me, confused. "So does that mean you aren't put off by it?"

I shake my head. "No, of course not. You weren't put off by me when you found out I looked after Jett. Even when you thought I was a single mom, you just went with it. Why would I be put off by something as trivial as you being a virgin?"

He sits up straight and squeezes my thigh with a little grin. "There's *nothing* trivial about me, I'll have you know."

I let out a small laugh. "You're right about that." I glance down at his package. Untouched, all mine. "You know," I start, glancing up at him. "It's actually kind of sexy." He narrows his eyes, looking unconvinced. "I mean it." I drop down, kissing him on the lips. "Exploring you is going to be fun, knowing no one else has had the opportunity to do it."

He stays still as I kiss his jaw, so I move down, kissing his neck. When he takes a sharp inhale, I smile because I bet no one else has made him feel like this before. But then he grasps my wrists, shackling them to the side of me.

"Let's be clear. I might be new to this, but that doesn't mean I want you to treat me like it." His voice is gruff with a heady edge, and I roll my chest against his, feeling myself melt into his words.

Finally, he pushes me onto the couch, so I'm lying down and he's straddling above me. With my wrists still clamped by his hands, his gaze sweeps over me. I'd hate to know what I look like right now, considering Austin's mouth has the faint smearing of red across his lips, and my hair is everywhere.

He drops down, leaving a trail of kisses on my neck and I tilt my chin up to give him easier access, moaning in approval. Darting his tongue out, he runs it back up my neck until I can feel his breath against my ear. "Every time I do something you like, I want to hear it, okay?"

With my eyes closed, I'm too lost in the feeling of having Austin on top of me to fully take in his words, but when he growls and thrusts his hips against me, he's got my attention. "Mia," He warns. "Are you going to be a good girl and let me know when I'm doing something right?"

"Yeah," I drawl out. It's hardly coherent, but he accepts it. His big paw of a hand drags up my body until it rests against my neck. I swear I'm wet just from the feeling of his warm hand because I can sense what's coming. Kissing me again, it's much more passionate this time. His mouth clashes against mine, and just as I get into the kiss, he squeezes my neck, and I moan again.

Austin growls in response, his body moving against mine, creating a delicious hot friction between us. Clutching onto his shirt, I jerk my hips against his, pulling him closer, wanting more. Like putty in his hands, I let him pull my shirt over my head, revealing my neon pink bra. He lifts himself onto his haunches and stares down at me in what I hope is awe. Unfortunately, because he's so silent, my thoughts turn sour. Were my stomach rolls turning him off? Were the stretch marks on my breasts a little too obvious? Was my age finally showing for him?

I wrap my arms around my stomach, and he flicks his gaze to mine; his eyes laced with confusion. "I just wasn't sure you liked what you saw," I answer the question he didn't ask.

He grunts, moving my arms out of the way. "You can let me decide for myself."

He pushes down on top of me, kissing at the nape of my neck, and I roll my head back, crashing into the pillows. My back arches, begging for Austin's touch, and just when I think I'm going to get it, he backs away, looking over at me again. This time, he licks his lips, his hands running across my arms as he pushes them up and holds them above my head.

"Then why are you looking at me like that?"

His gaze flicks up to my eyes for the smallest of seconds before he's straight back to looking at my body. "Because I'm trying to decide what to do first. Finger fuck you to oblivion or play with your nipples until I have you begging for me to make you come."

My nipples immediately harden at the thought, a zing of electricity bursting in my center. "Austin," I whisper, surprised.

"What? Did you think because I'm a virgin I wouldn't know what I want? Mia, I've waited twenty-one years for this moment. I'm starving and you're the feast laid out for me."

I bite my lip, holding back a smile as he cups my full breasts. Full enough to fit his large hands perfectly. He drops his head down and rubs his face in between them, lavishing them both in attention. Kissing, nipping and licking, He does everything I want, listening out for when I moan, and repeats the motion that gets the best reaction.

"Good girl," he husks out, as if I needed more encouragement than this. The build up has never felt as intense and it's like a slow burn that has me begging for more. With the weight of his body on top of mine, and his mouth tasting me as though I'm a delicacy, I'm already feeling as though I'm on the precipice. But that can't be possible. He's barely touched me.

"Austin." I pull at his hair, not sure what I want, but knowing he can't stop. His hand skitters down to my jeans and I instinctively lift my hips, letting him unzip them with ease.

The pop of my pink thong flashes as he eases the jeans off. There's a chill in the air that is quickly replaced when his body is back, towering over mine. Austin kisses me again, mumbling something under his breath, and before I know it, his hands dip into my thong. Without warning, two of his thick fingers rub against my clit in a slow massage.

"You're so wet," he says in surprise, and I have to taper down the little self-conscious voice inside my head because, of course he'd be surprised. He's never done this before. He's never felt a woman get aroused like this. "Am I making you feel good, Boss Girl?" I answer with my hips, motioning in a way that lets him know I like what he's doing. As he moves faster, he circles my clit in such a way that I start to lose sense. Pleasure jolts through my body in a way it never has before.

I'm going to come. It's not a maybe now, but a foregone conclusion. It's going to happen, but this can't be it. I want more. I *need* more. So I tilt my hips just a little, letting my wetness guide him. Still nipping at the nape of my neck, I pull on his jeans when his fingers dip lower, and finally sit at my entrance.

That's when I suddenly feel his hesitance again. "Austin," I beg, lifting my hips one last time, and finally one of his thick fingers pushes inside me. There's a pinch of pain because it's been a while, but when it's fully inside me and his thumb is circling my clit, the pain is the last thing on my mind.

Pure pleasure, and I can feel how much he likes it, too. With one of his strong thighs between mine, the pressure keeps building, and I can almost imagine what it would feel like to have him inside me.

"You feel so good," I moan, with my head resting on the back of the coach. I can't open my eyes because I'm too embarrassed to know what I look like. "Add another finger."

Did I just say that?

155

His hand stops moving as he adds another digit, and I relax into his touch, feeling so full from the pressure of both of them. He takes his time, watching me as he curls his fingers, stroking me from the inside. I gasp audibly, and my hips buck against his hand, chasing the pleasure. He responds to every moan with ease.

Then, I lose all sense.

"I'm going to come." I barely get out before he's furiously working his thumb around my clit.

"Be a good girl, Mia and come all over my fingers."

Then it happens. With no warning, black stars fill my vision as my body explodes in pleasure. Austin keeps his fingers in place even though my hips flail wildly, letting me milk the orgasm through its entirety.

I fall back onto the sofa, trying to catch my breath, but I'm exhausted from the most intense orgasm I have ever felt. My body feels like a wet noodle, spent from being overstimulated and overworked by Austin's hands. With my eyes closed, I breathe slowly, taking in the moment. Austin's fingers are still inside me, but I don't bother asking him to remove them because I like how full they make me feel. As long as he's not moving them too much, then it still feels nice.

His lips are back on my neck, traveling down my body as he kisses away my orgasm, but leaves more heat behind than he knows. Slowly, as I bathe in the afterglow of my climax and Austin's faint touches, I feel my body warming up for another round.

With every kiss, every lick, every slight twitch of his fingers inside me, my body wants to go again. It seems Austin wants to keep going too. I groan in displeasure when he pulls his fingers out. "Don't worry, I'm not finished with you yet," he mumbles into the skin of my torso. With both hands, he pulls my soaked thong off, throwing it across the room, and I think they end up behind the TV. I make a mental note to find those in the morning before Jett comes home because I don't want to scar the kid for life.

Sitting up, Austin opens my legs wider, positioning me so my left leg falls to the floor and my right rests against the back of the sofa. Wet and flustered, my entire body is bared to him, and as he looks down at me, all I see is a feral hunger.

His hooded glare alone is making me wet, and I can't help but squirm as he studies me. Dropping one of his hands to my pussy, he ever so gently skates his thumb across my slit. His gaze jerks to me when I gasp.

"Sorry. I'm still a little sensitive."

He doesn't move his thumb, though. He just moves across me slower, making my body tingle in anticipation. He dances his thumb across my clit, and I moan when he pulls my lips apart.

"You look delicious," he says, cutting me a mischievous look before dropping down and giving me one long lick with his tongue.

I can't speak. I can barely move with Austin's head between my legs, but if I thought his fingers were the best thing to ever happen to me. I was wrong. His tongue is just as thick as the rest of him. As he gets to the top of my slit, he gently laps at my clit, playing with it a few times as he looks up, and watches my reaction.

I can't think straight. I've never been worked up again so quickly after an orgasm, but Austin doesn't let up, and his cool tongue laps against my heated flesh so quickly that I might just come again. When he pushes a finger inside me, I know I'm done for. I thread my hands through his hair, pushing his face into my center as his tongue swirls around and around. "I, I, I," I cry out. I have no idea what I'm trying to say, but the burst of pleasure is obvious as I spill out another orgasm.

I keep my eyes closed as he laps at my center, slowly and carefully, taking all my essence. I don't want to open my eyes because, for some reason; I feel embarrassed about what we just did. What *he* just did. I'm the first woman he's ever sampled, and he went at me like a man possessed. That second orgasm was so intense, there's a very real possibility that I peed, but I couldn't feel it. And it's not something I can ask him, especially knowing that it's the first time he's done it.

After a couple of minutes, I open my eyes to find him sitting back on his haunches, breathing heavily and looking at my center.

"Everything okay?" I ask with hesitancy. Then he casually licks his lips, and closes his eyes, and something like a low growl emanates from his chest.

"I don't think I've ever tasted something as delicious as you." Well, there goes my concern. "I can't wait to do it again."

He lifts my legs in a move that I'm nervous might be him going for round three, but I push back on his shoulders. "No, not yet. I need some recovery time after that. How about you let me show you what I can do instead?" I keep pushing him until he's lying back on the sofa. My breasts hang down, only emphasizing what little clothing I'm wearing compared to him. "You know, you really are wearing too much."

157

Austin places his hands over mine, stopping me in my wake. "As much as it kills me to say this." He closes his eyes, takes a moment to compose himself, and then starts again. "And it *kills* me to say this, but I think we should wait on that."

I drop my hands, immediately feeling embarrassed. I've never felt that before, but here I am, naked and soaking wet for this guy and he's just turned down a blow job.

"That doesn't seem entirely fair."

"What isn't fair is that your scream nearly made me come with no other stimulation. I know the minute you get your mouth on me that I won't last, and I refuse for my first blow job to be two seconds. I've waited this long. I want to lavish in the fact that you're sucking my cock."

"Hold on. You've never had a blow job either?"

"Mia, who's going to give me one?"

I smile, embarrassed. "I don't know. I just thought that a lot of guys don't count those."

"Like I said, I've never dated, and I don't have the flexibility to give myself one... not that I would try if I did." He cringes, and my heart blooms at his off-kilter charm.

I squeeze his thigh, smirking. "I guess we'll just have to take care of that another time. Maybe in the morning?"

That's when he backs away and takes a sharp inhale. "Wish I could stay, but I've got to be at The Fishbowl for nine."

"And yet you're still here."

"Yeah, because I was bad and had my dessert early." As he looks down at my naked form, I grab a pillow and cover my crotch. He lets out a little chuckle and shakes his head. "Your lasagna smells delicious, though."

I sit up a little straighter and look over the back of the couch to see that the timer still says twenty minutes. Happy that I haven't burned anything, I look at Austin with a lazy smile.

"Where are you staying tonight? The stadium is only thirty minutes away. It can't be *that* much closer. Can it?"

"Yeah, it's actually at the stadium. There's a hotel on site that I'm using because I haven't found a place to buy yet."

"Oh. You're living in a hotel?"

He waves it off. "It's nicer than it sounds. Lots of players are there because you don't know how long you're going to be in the Bigs for. I need one of those long-term contracts before I can set down roots anywhere." I shake my head, holding off the laughter. "What's so funny?"

"Oh, Frat Boy. You just inadvertently admitted that you'd rather be alone in a hotel room than here."

"You know that's not true. It's just that if I don't work my ass off, there's a very real possibility that I'll be sent down to the Minnows again. And if I'm there, I'll be in Macon, which is even further away."

"Has anyone ever told you that your dedication to the game is admirable?"

"Not really something you hear from other players who are putting in the same amount of work in as you."

"I doubt many of the guys would turn down blow jobs and sex to make sure they get to the stadium on time."

He looks to the side and nods. "Good point."

I smile, rolling into him. "Well, the invite is always there if you want to stay and endure that thirty-minute journey to the Stadium in the morning. I'm going to be all alone here, and you'll be all alone in your hotel room. Just makes sense to keep each other warm."

"In Charlotte in July?"

"Mhmm. Sometimes I like to sleep naked in the heat."

He purses his lips, contemplating. "My uniform is at the clubhouse, so I could always go straight there."

"I like your thinking." I pull him in for a kiss, his body covering me in warmth, and my hand skates under his shirt. Then he slaps it away.

"Uh uh," he says, pulling at my bottom lip with his teeth. "I may have jumped the gun a little when it came to tasting you, but I couldn't help myself. You're downright delectable, and I want to savor every moment I have."

I look at him with wide eyes. "Is that your way of saying that you're going to make me wait?"

"Not long. Just not tonight. Tonight, I'd like to lie next to you, and see what it feels like to have a nice-smelling, beautiful, naked woman next to me, instead of a sweaty Grissom."

"A sweaty *naked* Grissom?" I ask with a raised brow.

His lips crumple together, hiding his smile. "You're filthy."

"And that's not an answer."

Grabbing me by the thighs, he lifts me from the sofa with ease. "If he ends up in my bed, it's because he's too drunk to walk the rest of the way down the hallway to his, and I can confirm that does sometimes entail

Griss in a certain state of undress."

"Why does that sound so hot?" I bite his shoulder, licking the pain away as he carries me down the hallway.

"Believe me, seeing Griss drunk and crying over a woman that doesn't care he exists is not hot."

And he leaves it at that, stopping at the only door down the hallway. "Can I safely assume this is your room?"

"Mhhmm," I sing, kissing his neck.

"Great. We aren't going to come out of it until morning."

"What about the Lasagna?" That stops him in his wake. "We've probably got ten minutes until I need to take it out of the oven."

His lip curls in amusement. "Oh, Boss Girl. Is that your way of timing me?"

"No."

He shuts me up with a kiss. "I want to see how many orgasms I can give you before the timer goes."

I bark out a laugh. "Okay, Frat Boy. Let's get some practice in."

After kicking the door open, he strides in so quickly that I let out a little squeal and laugh because I can only hope that's not the only squeal I let out tonight.

21. Chapter Fifteen

Austin

"Austin?" Mia groans, her back arching into my chest.

"Morning," I whisper in her ear, leaving a small kiss as I push her oversized shirt up and play with her nipples. A fun fact I learned about Mia last night. She loves her nipples being played with. Almost as much as I enjoy playing with them. And play with them, I did. Once she realized I wasn't joking when I said I was off limits for the night, she let me ravish her in ways I didn't think possible.

There wasn't a mole on her body that I didn't touch or lick last night, and I lost count over the number of orgasms I gave her. Not bad for a Rookie.

Mia groans sleepily, "What are you -." She stops, her body jerking a little, and I smile. "Oh, that feels so good." She drops her hand on top of my other one, forcing it further down her center. Did I forget to mention that my hand was already caressing her panty-covered clit when she woke up? It was just a few innocent strokes at first, but then my mind started racing over the possibilities, and well, now we're here.

"Keep going," She cries, her hips bucking against my hand as she directs it into her underwear. My cock thickens because I'm met with her now familiar warm, wet heat. I'm so hard, I have a genuine concern that

161

I might burst, but I kind of like it. Mia seems to think it's because I'm into edging and she has all these things she wants to try out with me. I'll let her think that because it's better than admitting the truth that I was just too chickenshit to let her touch me.

Another cry leaves her lips, and she scrunches her eyes shut as she tries to hold on to the feeling. Little breathy mewls escape her mouth as she grinds her ass cheeks into my dick. I should move back, but I've been too good for too long, so I stay in place, letting her rub herself against me.

When I dip my finger inside her, she drops her head to my shoulder and turns to the side so she can nuzzle her nose against the column of my neck.

"Do you like that, Boss Girl?"

"Mhm." She moves against my hand, and I add another finger, rubbing my palm against her clit a little. She likes it, careening at my movements, so I keep going, guided by her every hip flex and moan. When her fingers clutch my palms, I know I'm going in the right direction. Then her nails dig into my skin, and I repeat the action over and over again, enjoying the feel of her skin against mine.

With every stroke of my fingers, she gets louder, until she doesn't. With her hips frozen in place, and her eyes scrunched shut, it's like she's trying to hold onto the pleasure for as long as possible. But just as I think she's about to come. Her head drops to my shoulder, and her hand skates between us. I'm too busy dropping a kiss on her neck to realize she's skated her hand to my crotch, and she grabs my cock through my boxer shorts. "What are you doing, BG?" I warn, giving her neck the tiniest of bites for the indiscretion.

Her head stays on my shoulder as she presses her teeth into her bottom lip, looking at me with a grin. The smirk is perfectly in time with her little fist moving up and down while she uses the fabric of my shorts to create the perfect friction between us. "I can't let you have all the fun, can I?"

Curling my fingers inside her, I look for her g-spot again, thinking I did a good job finding it last night. This position is a little harder, though, since my hand is a little more restricted. Mia returns the favor and slips her hands into my boxers.

I freeze, focusing on the tiny hole in the wall instead of what's happening because I have no doubt that if I really think about what Mia's doing, I'm going to blow all over her hand, and I can't be done after one stroke.

No. No. No.

I try to think of something. Anything. But nothing can distract me away from this moment because my fingers are in her wonderful, wet pussy.

That's it. Focus on her.

Dipping down, I bite her ear, digging my palm into her center as I go. Just focus everything on making her as wet as possible. Then I won't have time to register that her hand is too small to wrap around my dick and that even though her movements are uncoordinated, I love the feeling.

Her nails occasionally scratch against my shaft, sending a new sensation straight to my balls. It's the first time anyone else has tried to get me off, and I now fully understand why it's so much better to get someone else to do it for you.

I can't predict what her smooth, feminine hands are going to do next, and it's driving me wild. My eyes roll to the back of my head when she swipes her thumb across the top of my dick, dragging the pre-cum down my cock.

"You're so thick," She moans, not caring that my current fingering technique is haphazard at best, but what does she expect? I'm doing everything I can not to explode in her hand like a teenager. There's no way I'm going to be coordinated with my moves.

Make her come first.

That's the most important thing. Make her come first. Then she won't notice the bucket load of cum I'm no doubt going to spill all over her back. As I finger her, I stroke against her walls, feeling for that spot that I think I found last night. I'm still unsure of whether I found it, but Mia goes speechless before she thrashes against me, her pussy clenching around my hand.

Have I hit her G-Spot?

I have no idea, but I keep going just in case.

"I'm-, I'm-"

I know this routine by now; I spent most of my night exploring Mia, learning all about her wants and needs. She's about to climax, and I can't wait to feel her fall apart in my hands again. Her body jerks with another moan, and then it happens. I feel her clenching against my fingers as they slide in and out of her with ease.

I can't wait to know how it would feel to have my dick inside her instead.

Kissing her shoulder, I keep my fingers in place, waiting for her body to calm down so I can work her up all over again. But I lose my train of thought when Mia's hand works me harder. Up and down. Stroke after stroke, she's bringing me closer and closer.

"Faster," I command, moving with her because now that I'm close, I want this so badly. Her hand, her smell, her pussy. Everything has my adrenaline pumping, and my body is ready for more.

Buzz. Buzz. Buzz.

"An alarm on a Saturday?" She groans, her hand ceasing all movement.

"Don't stop," I grind out, moving my hips against her hand to get some friction back. But then she takes her hand away completely, and meets my hand in between her thighs, pulling it out of her pussy.

Oh Shit.

I've fucked up, haven't I? I can't get her off, so she's going to get herself off. She probably wants me to watch and learn, but I'm so close to coming, I'm not sure I'll be able to look her in the eye after blowing my load all over her back without stimulation.

From what I can see, she covers her pussy with her hand, pushing a few of her fingers inside herself and she sighs with pleasure. This whole thing would be hot if it wasn't a direct reflection on my inabilities. And just like that, my dick softens. Well, at least I don't have to worry about coming on her back.

"What's wrong?" She asks, taking her hand away.

"I'm, uh, I don't know. I'm sorry?" What the hell does she want me to say? I thought I'd been doing a pretty good job of getting her off over the last few hours, but apparently, I'm wrong.

"Don't be. I'm so close, but it won't happen without your fingers inside me."

Um, okay? Now I'm confused.

She seemingly doesn't notice but then raises her hand to show me the wetness between her fingers. Fuck. That's hot. Then she dips under the cover, wrapping her hand around my cock.

Fuck. That's even hotter.

My dick is fully hard again, with the new slickness from her hand making the friction feel so much better. As I draw my hand over Mia's hip and down to her center, she looks at me from over her shoulder. "Taste me on your fingers first."

"You're not such a good girl, after all, are you?" I smirk, and she watches me closely as I shove my two fingers into my mouth, tasting her and licking away every ounce of her essence. Then I draw my fingers out of my mouth, dragging them against her collarbone, across her breasts, down to her navel. When I'm at her center, she parts her legs for me, and I do as she asks. Sinking my fingers in her to the hilt.

My alarm is still blazing through the room, but we're both lost in a haze of arousal, that it's not stopping us. "Austin, it's never felt like this," She whines out, and I can only assume it's a good thing as she's withering in my hands, so I pump in time with her hand, getting as close to the feeling of being inside her as possible.

Smooth and fast. I'm nearly at the point of blacking out when she finally cries out, and her greedy pussy clenches around me. Even through her climax, she keeps her hand on my shaft, working me just as fast.

"Mia, baby. I'm going to come if you don't stop."

"That's the point," she mumbles out with a hint of amusement. "I want to feel you all over my hand."

Well, if that's what she wants, who am I to deny her? With my hand still inside her, I close my eyes and let the pleasure take over. Black hazy dots blind my vision as I feel my release all over her hand, and then I cringe because it's still coming. Thick and fast, I've never felt myself come so hard and I think the sheets show it.

There's silence in the room and when I'm brave enough to open my eyes, I wince because it's everywhere. The sheets, her hand, my boxers, her back, my stomach. No surface went unpunished because that's what happens when you leave it as long as I have apparently.

"Sorry."

God, this is awkward. I knew it would be. I should have listened to Grissom and jerked off in the bathroom beforehand. Mia lifts her shoulder and looks at the damage before her gaze lifts to mine. A small smile plays on her lips, and she giggles, seemingly unfazed by the mess.

She leans over, grabbing a bunch of tissues from her bedside table and throws a few at me before wiping her hand off. Scrunching the tissues in my hand, I clean her back first, but frankly, she's going to need a shower if she wants to get rid of all of it.

Mia rolls onto her other shoulder, faces me, and starts to clean my cock. "To be honest, I think that's the last place you need to worry about cleaning." I smile hesitantly, still feeling a little embarrassed. "I pretty much got it everywhere *but* my cock."

"I know," She sings. "Sheets can be washed, though. I have no idea when you're going to let me touch your cock again, so I need to take advantage."

When she tilts her chin up, I can't help myself. I kiss her, and she snuggles up to me, unbothered that we're sticky as hell. Mia pulls away from me with a lazy smile.

"That was not the wake up call I was expecting." Her hand cups my face, drawing me in for a kiss, which I eagerly take.

"Same. How do you expect me to play today after that?"

"Always thinking about the game." She pouts playfully, pulling the sheets over her like she's going to sleep again. "You play like two-thousand games during the season. I'm sure you could get away with playing badly one time?"

I chuckle, pulling her and the bundle of sheets she's surrounded herself in into my chest. "Playing poorly is the quickest way back down to Triple A."

"Says the Catfish's Rookie of the Year candidate."

"And if I want to keep that potential title, then I've got to work at it."

"All work, no play. Why am I not surprised?"

"I think you'll find I played with you pretty well last night." I tickle her sides, nipping at her neck before she can slither away.

"Austin, I'm ticklish."

"I know." She giggles into my chest, squirming, and when I stop, she turns to me, breathing heavily. Her chest is heaving, her eyes cutting a gaze down my body, and I know if I don't leave now, I never will.

"I'm sorry to cut this short, BG, but I've got to go shower," I say reluctantly. Getting out of this bed with Mia is the hardest thing to do, but I know it won't be the last time.

"Can I join? Been thinking about a few of those texts you sent me. You know the ones where you tell me to drop to my knees?" Oh, I remember those. Is my dick hard already? I thought I'd be worn out by all of Mia's antics, but it turns out my dick is insatiable. That, or the prospect of watching Mia suck my dick, is enough to get me off on its own.

"I'd love you to join, but I'm already late, and I've got a feeling that if you join me, I'll never leave this room. Something we both need to do."

She glances at the door, sighing. It may only be six am on Saturday, but Jett will be back anytime now, and I'd rather not do the walk of shame in front of a teenager.

As I get out of her bed, I pull up my boxers just enough to make me decent, and when I look down at Mia, I immediately regret my decision. "Maybe I should call in sick."

"Don't. We'll have plenty of time to share a shower." She wiggles her eyebrows, which makes me laugh.

"What are you doing tonight?" I ask eagerly.

Her smile fades with confusion. "Uh, I don't know." She sits up, taking the blankets with her so they keep her body covered, and cringes when she tries to run a hand through her hair, but it gets stuck.

"Why don't you come to my game tonight? Surprise Jett with a couple of tickets behind the dugout."

"I don't know." She's still working at getting her hand out of her hair instead of focusing on my request, so I kneel beside her to help.

"Come on," I say gently, as I manage to untangle her fingers. "You're going to let me stick my tongue inside that delicious pussy of yours, but you aren't willing to come to my game?"

"It's not that." She blows out a breath. "It's just." Another pause. "Complicated."

"Uh oh." Suddenly, all those insecurities come back. "Complicated, meaning I was terrible at eating you out?" Fuck. I couldn't have been that bad, surely? I know there were times I was getting a little tongue-tied, but considering her legs didn't stop shaking, I thought I was doing a pretty good job.

Unless she was faking it to satisfy my ego.

Smirking, she kisses my knuckles, bringing me out of my thoughts. "You weren't terrible. Believe me, I wasn't expecting that." Her eyes widen. "I lost count of the number of times I came on your face. I'm almost embarrassed about it."

"Five."

"Five?"

"You came on my tongue five times. My fingers, two." Just like that, the memory of tasting her makes me want to do it all over again, but I hold back, solely because I have to go play a game. "I'll shoot for nine next time. But until then, you should come to my game. I want to see you out there in the crowd, watching me."

Her eyes are closed, and she's got this dreamy look on her face that makes my stomach drop.

"Okay," she wisps out. "If Jett's up for it, I'll try to be there."

"Good. Then after we can come back here and finish what we started." Smacking another kiss on her lips, I hop to the bathroom and ignore her protesting mewls as I head to the shower with all the things I'm planning on doing to her, running through my mind.

CHAPTER SIXTEEN
MIA

"Hey, Jett," Austin calls from the side of the field. His voice is just deep enough that it breaks through the chattering in the stands. Jett smiles, racing down the metal stairs to get closer then wiggles his way in between a couple of kids to hang over the railing to see Austin. There's a six-foot drop separating them, but this is the closest they'll get until the end of the game.

Waving, Jett yells, "Hey, Austin!" Jett's practically bent his entire torso over to see him, and in all his eagerness, he hasn't noticed that I'm right behind him, holding onto his jersey in case he loses balance. As I look over his shoulder, I'm stunned by the intense gaze Austin is throwing my way. Dark and heady, I know he's thinking about this morning, and I almost feel like it's indecent in this setting.

He not-so-subtly licks his lips, and my body tingles at the thoughts of him touching me again. *Tasting* me again. He doesn't say anything, just leaves me with a sly, subtle smile as he takes in everyone else around me.

Did I just wet my panties? Because that intense stare, the eye black covering his face, those tighter than tight baseball pants; everything about him is making me want to hop this railing and jump his bones.

169

There's no doubt that I want him, but right here, in front of everyone in the stadium, is not the time to divulge those thoughts.

"Get ready," Austin says to Jett as he steps back to third base. Raising his arm, he flashes a baseball before throwing it straight toward Jett, who catches it with ease.

"Is that a new mitt?" I ask, and Jett gives me a sneaky smile over his shoulder before throwing the ball back down to Austin. They do this for another couple of minutes as kids around us watch. Did they plan this?

Catty the Catfish slinks over with a film crew following him and he stands directly behind Austin. Catty taps him on the shoulder before pushing him away and attempts to catch the ball Jett threw down. Unfortunately, his fins get in the way and it whacks him on the head instead. Catty falls to the ground dramatically, his arms and legs flailing everywhere until Austin revives him.

More kids rush to the railing to watch the little show, and I can't help but smile. Austin's so goofy, but I love him. Frowning, I take a step back because did I just say I *love* him? I know it's been a long time since I've dated, and he's amazing at giving head, but damn, I need to cool it if I don't want to freak him out.

Buzz. Buzz. Buzz.

I quickly pull my phone out of my purse and when I see the **UNKNOWN** number, my heart sinks. I haven't received a message from him in so long, I almost forgot about him. But I guess I should have remembered that's his usual MO. He lets me forget, then comes back with a vengeance with a thinly veiled threat.

Unknown: At the Catfish game? Wearing an Austin Adams shirt? Not the first time I've seen you with him. Better be careful, Mia. People might think there's something going on between you. Doubt he'd want to date a fat ass like you after he finds out what you did to your sister.

I close my eyes, feeling the raggedy breath in my chest. Simon is the dark cloud from our past, and a constant reminder of why I'm protecting Jett at all costs. Looking over my shoulder, I brace myself and fully expect to see Simon standing right there, ready to threaten me, but when I turn, there's nothing. Just some parents happily watching Austin throw baseballs to their kids.

The organ plays idyllically in the background, and the atmosphere is electric. Unfortunately, there's no way I can feel comfortable in it after receiving that. Turning back around, I take a deep, calming breath as I try to shake off the uneasy feeling that someone's watching me.

But then it dawns on me. There's a camera batting between Jett and Austin, which is probably airing on the TV broadcast. That's the only way he could know I'm here, right?

My thighs tremble as I try to shake off the guilt I feel for bringing Jett somewhere so public. I should have known better. Simon's always been a huge Catfish fan. He never misses a game, and here I am offering up our whereabouts on a silver platter.

What a stupid mistake. I've been too caught up in Austin to really think through the consequences of my actions.

"Did you see that, Aunt Mia?" Jett says over his shoulder, all smiles because he's blissfully unaware that I think I might hurl. I force out a matching smile, pulling at Jett's jersey to bring him close to me.

"I did. Where'd you get the mitt?" I ask, looking at the leather suspiciously because I haven't been able to afford a new mitt.

Jett pulls back, his lips lifting to one side. "Austin may have gotten it for me after the Junior Catfish try outs. Showed me how he breaks his in and everything," he answers, punching the leather as he talks.

"Did he?" I raise my brows in surprise, and as I look to the field to chastise him, he's gone. The camera crew has finished, and Catty is further up the field, dancing for another part of the crowd.

Jett slowly punches his glove to a stop. "Please don't tell me you're going to make me give it back because I've already broken it in, and it's helped me play better. My coaches have told me."

My shoulders slump. "No. I won't make you give it back. Austin got it for you. I just wish you'd have told me."

He looks at me sheepishly. "Yeah, sorry. It was after I had that meltdown last week. Thought you might take it away as a punishment."

Draping my arm over his shoulder, I say, "You know what? That's a good idea. I'll keep that in mind next time you yell at me." I push my hip into his side, smiling. Jett smiles back, clutching onto that mitt like it's his lifeline. "Should we get some snacks before the game starts?" I offer. Now that the camera is off us, I doubt Simon will try to contact me again. He won't know where we are.

Jett nods, and we walk to the food stalls. Even though I know it's near impossible that Simon's here, it would be stupid of me not to check as we pass the other fans in the crowd. I check every single face as we make our way through the line at the food stand.

Something still doesn't feel right.

I shake my head, trying to rid my brain of these thoughts, and when I turn to Jett, he's reading the menu. "What did you say?"

I do my best to smile for him, and remain present in the moment, all the while thinking about the exits in case we need to use them. As long as we stay in this big crowd of people, then we're safe. Simon won't try anything with this many witnesses. He's too much of a coward.

"Sure thing." My voice is high-pitched and peppy. A little too peppy to be normal, and his brows furrow when he looks down to his arm at my clutching hand.

"Everything okay, Aunt M?" His eyes narrow, and I turn my attention to the menu, looking anywhere but my suspicious nephew. He has no idea about all the things that went down with his father, and I don't intend to tell him on The Fishbowl Concord.

"I'm good, thanks." Turning to the cashier, I raise my hand and point to the menu board. "Can I get two Catfish dogs, and a large popcorn please?"

My fingers thrum against the counter as I stare the cashier down. Really stare him down. "Sure thing, lady," he says hesitantly, looking up at me a couple of times with a furrowed brow. Good. He probably thinks I've lost my mind, but I don't care. At least that will make this interaction memorable. It will make *us* memorable.

Soak in my eye and hair color, and the crazed look on my face. Notice that I have a teenager with me who has dark hair and blue eyes, just like his mother.

I glance at the ceiling and see a camera in the corner, making direct eye contact with it, hoping it's not too fuzzy to take in my features.

Jett's hand rests on the top of mine. "Aunt Mia?" He goads me, and I finally look at him, only seeing concern laced across his features. "What's wrong?"

I tip my toes, and an involuntary high-pitched squeal falls out of my mouth. "Nothing's wrong. I'm just starving."

We move to the side, and I lean my elbow against the counter as we wait for the food. "Is this about what happened back there with Austin?"

"Is what about who?"

He shrugs his shoulder. "Austin. The last time you acted all high-pitched and giggly like this was when you watched that movie and saw Thor's butt."

Eyes wide, I screech, "What does that have to do with anything?"

Jett stifles a laugh. "Please. My mom told me you had a huge crush on Chris Hemsworth and that's why you were giggling the whole movie. Because you knew it was coming."

"She told you that?"

He nods proudly. "Yeah, you were ruining the movie for the rest of us. We had to watch it again a week later while you were out so we could hear the dialogue."

"Well, I'm sorry I was such a pest."

"You weren't." He points at my face, wagging his finger up and down. "But you have that same nervous energy. And I think it's because you like Austin, but you don't know if he likes you back." I don't know what's worse. My teenager questioning me about my love life or admitting to him that me and Austin are more than fine. So fine that I jerked him off this morning. Not that I'd mention that detail. "Because you have nothing to worry about. I know he likes you, too."

"You do?" Whose voice was that? It came out like a constipated hyena... Not that I know what one of those sounds like, but it's what I imagine.

"Ma'am. Your order." The cashier pushes the tray of food in my direction and gestures behind me to the long queue.

"Sorry about that." Grasping the food, I quickly stuff some popcorn into my mouth before handing the hot dogs to Jett. I figure if my mouth is full, he won't be able to question me, and we can all forget this conversation ever happened.

"You don't have to be embarrassed. I get it. Not everyone is as cynical about dating as my mom was." I keep my mouth closed. If he knew what was going on before he passed away, he might think her view was warranted. "But my mom always talked about how she believed you'd get married and have a few cousins for me to play with."

I nearly choke on my popcorn. "Cousins?"

"Yeah, I always talked to her about how much I wanted a sibling to play ball with, and she promised me cousins instead. Didn't get either in the end..." He says, frowning.

"Woah. Your mom promised you cousins? Without consulting me?"

He shrugs, a wry smile across his face. "She said you were too much of a dreamer *not* to have kids. Guess she was wrong."

"Hey. Wait a minute. I never said cousins were off the table

173

completely."

"So, does that mean things are serious with you and Austin?" Oh, I see what he did there. I seriously underestimated my nephew and his ability to fish for information.

"It means nothing. Absolutely nothing. Oh, do you hear that? Is that organ playing? I guess the game is starting. We better get to our seats." I drag him back to the stands, carefully taking in the surrounding people again to make sure Simon isn't amongst them.

When I'm certain it's just us and the crowd, I lean back in my seat and focus on the game. There's a stop in play for a second while Max talks to the pitching staff and I catch Austin's eyes. He raises a curious brow in my direction. A subtle question that I can't answer without looking like a lunatic and freaking out.

But I shouldn't be freaking out. Simon isn't here, and this is all in my head. I just need to calm down.

The loud crack of a bat echoes through the stadium, and the crowd breaks into a crescendo of cheers and boos, as Holden Fox hits a bomb against us. The ball flies into the top deck of the stands, opposite home-plate. "Woah. That's at least four-hundred and fifty feet," Jett says in awe.

"Yeah, they don't call him The Legend for nothing," I surmise, blowing out a breath. A homer from the other team usually isn't a big deal, but this is Atlanta we're playing, and they have a habit of winning games they score first in. "This is going to be a long game."

"Oh, no."

"What's wrong?" Jett eyes me, waiting for an explanation.

"Nothing. Just forgot something at school." I lie, mainly because I don't want him to worry about the Unknown text message flashing on my phone again. Two in one day seems a little excessive for Simon, but I guess he wasn't happy that I ignored him.

Unknown: Diamond Reserved, Stand 138. Right behind third base. Interesting seat choice. Are you stalking Austin Adams or is he using you to get his rocks off? Don't bother responding. I'll see you later.

See you later. See you later?!

What the hell is that supposed to mean, and how the hell am I supposed to concentrate on the game if I'm worried that he's going to show up at any point? He effectively knows our seat numbers. Dread fills my body because I can see my future and I know this will never end. He's always going to have a hold over me, and I'm never going to get away from him, or the guilt that rings heavy on my heart. He'll always be there in the background, haunting me with his presence and reminding me it's my fault Hailey died.

Sweat prickles my brow. My body goes into fight-or-flight mode. "Jett," I say, hearing the hesitancy in my voice. "I think I left the oven on."

He rolls his neck to look at me with a questioning brow. "And?"

"And that means we have to go home and check. We can't leave it on because it could blow up the house."

His shoulders slump and he drops his head so all I can see is the Carolina Catfish logo on his baseball cap. "Seriously? But it's only the bottom of the fourth."

I nod my head, not really paying attention because I'm trying to subtly look around the stadium without drawing too much attention. Jett knows Simon comes around from time to time, but he has no idea that I'm paying Simon to keep Jett. I've never told him because I'm worried he might do something stupid, like confront Simon, and his safety is my top priority.

"I know, I'm sorry, but remember, Austin's given us season tickets, and there are at least thirty more home games this year. We'll be back. I promise." The smile I pull is forced at best because my mind is racing with too many potential scenarios over what might happen if we stay.

In a crowd like this, it would be easy to go undetected. My mind immediately goes to the worst scenario. What if he had something that could threaten the lives of people here? I'd have no choice but to go with him to save everyone else. Grabbing Jett's hand, I squeeze it, and look him straight in the eyes. "Come on. We need to go."

"Okay." He packs his things quickly, and we're out of the stands in a matter of minutes, walking through the stadium hall. Crowds of people fill the edges, and my head flicks from side to side, checking out every single person I can. I haven't seen him. He was surely bluffing. There's no way that he was at the Catfish game tonight. It would have been too much of a coincidence.

"Can't you check with the neighbors?" Jett asks as I weave him through the people.

"I could, but-"

No.

I'm wrong. I'm all wrong.

I lose my breath.

Cold, dead eyes and a sinister grin stare me down, and my blood runs cold because there's nowhere to go.

I'm so scared, my heart feels like it's going to break through my chest at any minute. He found us.

"Aunt Mia?"

I blink and am brought back to reality when Jett shakes my shoulder. Then I look back to the spot I saw him, and he's not there. Glancing around, I don't see anyone that looks like him either. The place is too full for him to get away that quickly. Was he there at all?

"Aunt Mia. Are you okay?" Jett's squeezing my shoulder, watching me with concern.

It's then I realize that I've suddenly stopped walking, frozen on the spot by a figment of my imagination. He's not here. He never was. I'm just paranoid, crippled in fear that he might follow us to the car. Come to think of it, if we leave now, no one will be in the parking lot, and we need witnesses.

"Yeah," I say with a slow shoulder roll, trying to act normal. "You know what? You're right. I should just text Miss Robins. She has a spare key and can check for me." As I cut my gaze to Jett, he's looking more confused than ever, but doesn't question my erratic behavior. "Shall we finish watching the game?"

"Okay," he drawls out with pointed annoyance. "That's cost us a whole inning, but let's get back to our seats before we miss the top of the sixth."

Reluctantly we head back to the seats, and although it's a thrilling game, I can't concentrate on any of it because with every move in my periphery, I swear I see him. Watching me with those cold, blue eyes that once held such warmth. He's here, just waiting for me to make the wrong move, and I haven't figured out what I'm going to do when I see him.

"Go Catfish!" Jett jumps out of his seat, cheering. I look down at the game in surprise. I've been so lost in my own thoughts that I've only just realized he's cheering the last out. How did I miss four innings? Catty the Catfish runs out onto the field with a long catfish flag, and the entire crowd stands, roaring because we won.

"Can I go down and congratulate Austin?"

My gaze flicks to the bottom of the stands, and then the concourse exits. People are leaving, and we need to be in the crowd if we want to be safe. "How about we call him when we get home? We've got to go."

"Still worried about the oven?" He asks with a sarcastic edge, but when I nod, he nods diligently. Following behind me, we head up to the stairs, but then Jett taps me on the back. "Wait, we can't go yet. Austin is trying to get our attention."

I don't dare to look because as much as I'd love to be with Austin right now, that will only waste valuable time. "Ah, I'm sure he's just waving to the crowd. He's not looking for us. Besides, if he wants to talk to us, he can just text me." I look Jett up and down with a raised brow. "Or you, apparently."

Jett doesn't fight back, probably because I've shut him down so many times tonight. "Let's go." With my arm around his shoulder, I make sure we're sandwiched between a group of college guys who are burly enough to take on Simon if he tries anything.

As we get to the parking lot, I can hardly hear myself think with the echoing chant of the college guys bouncing around the walls. Having walked by them for the last ten minutes, I've learned that they're all here celebrating their friend getting drafted onto the Charlotte Crossbills, which only made me cuddle up to them closer since I know Simon can't take on a line backer.

Thankfully, we parked close to the door so that when we're both in the car and the doors are locked; I feel safe.

"So," Jett drawls out, buckling his seatbelt. "Was there a reason we had to rush out like that? I'm pretty sure Austin wanted to talk to us, and judging by the amount of missed calls you've got, I'm guessing he's pissed that we left without so much as a wave."

"What are you talking about?" He tilts his chin toward my phone, which is obnoxiously flashing Austin's name in my security approved clear bag. "I'm sure it's nothing." Unzipping the purse, I grab the phone and decline the call, ignoring the other ten missed calls and turn it off, and slip it into the cup holder. "He probably just wanted to talk about the win with his biggest fan."

I start the car, and reverse out into the queue to exit the stadium.

"Then why decline his call?"

"Because I'm driving." I tap the steering wheel pointedly, but I can tell he's not buying it.

"You weren't when he called? But also, that hasn't stopped you answering calls before because it goes through the speakers.

Damn Jett and his logic.

Waving my hand to the windscreen, I raise my brow. "Have you seen how bad the traffic is? I can't get distracted."

"You mean the traffic that isn't moving?"

"Right now. You know how these things work. It goes slow, but then will suddenly pick up."

"Fine." Jett sinks into his seat, and I think I've finally got him on my side, but then he says, "Austin wants to know why we didn't go to the clubhouse after the game."

"How do you know that?" Jett raises his phone, flashing a long text chain, and I shake my head. "I still can't believe you and Austin text."

He shrugs, looking unbothered by my surprise. "He might be my uncle soon. I should probably get used to him being around."

"You did NOT just say that!" I shriek, swerving a little because Jett keeps bringing this up. Here I am wondering if I'm dating Austin to relive my youth while Jett's planned my wedding. "Have you planned my bridesmaid dresses, too?"

"Chill out, Aunt Mia. It was just a joke. You're so jittery tonight."

"You would be too if you left the oven on."

"Just saying. I could use an uncle, and he's got the right intentions."

"Oh, does he now?" I whip my head in his direction, narrowing my eyes at him.

"Yup. I've already had the talk with him."

"The talk? What talk?" If I find out he's had the birds and the bees talk with Austin, I'll kill him.

"Just wanted to check he had the right intentions. I needed to make sure that Austin treats you better than Simon treated my mom." He spits his father's name out, his hand clutching his phone hard.

Looking at him now, I realize that I'm no longer staring at the cute kid that loved ice cream and Paw Patrol. Jett's growing up, and he's becoming a man right in front of my eyes.

"Simon's a bit of a low bar."

"Agreed. That's why I'm here to make sure I don't lose another woman in my life, because a guy takes her for granted." That statement feels like a punch in the gut. His father is awful, but he doesn't know the full extent of Simon's involvement in Hailey's demise. Or, at least, what I suspect is Simon's involvement.

The car suddenly feels heavy. Jett stopped talking, and I can tell there's something more bubbling underneath, so I quickly swerve into another parking space, ticking off a few cars behind me. That move gets me a couple of honks, but who gives a crap? We're moving at a snail's pace and my nephew is more important than any of them.

Jett's looking down at his hands now, and I don't say anything when I see him wipe away a tear from his cheek. I know how he feels.

"Jett." I place my hand on his knee. "Your mom would be so proud of the man you're becoming. I'm proud, too." I pause for a second, holding back my emotions. "You're the most important thing in the world to me. I love you, and I will fight for you the way your mom would if she were here."

He tries to disguise his sniffles, sucking his lips into his mouth, stopping him from choking up.

"That's why I need to look out for you, too. No one is going to hurt you."

Smiling, I give his knee a squeeze. "I appreciate you looking out for me."

He glances up for the slightest of seconds before dropping his gaze to my hand. "It's the least I could do since I couldn't look out for her."

What does he mean?

The silence is deafening. The pain in his words sitting heavy in the car. "Jett, you were ten. You weren't expected to protect her then."

"But I could have," he mumbles, shuffling his shoulders.

"What do you mean?" He doesn't respond. "Do you think you could have stopped the accident?" More silence, and I can see the guilt dripping across his face. "You were in the backseat, and I'm just so damn lucky you survived because I would have been broken if I lost both of you."

Jett takes a deep breath, so I keep going. "You know, when you were born, you looked nothing like Hailey. You had this bright blonde hair and the most mischievous smile I'd ever seen. But as each year passed, I saw more and more of Hailey." He continues to concentrate on his hands, not looking at me. "Now, all I see when I look at you is her, and it makes me feel a little less lost in this world. You give me a reason to push for better, because that's what she would have wanted for us."

"It's my fault," He whispers it so quietly, I barely hear it. I squeeze his knee a little tighter, desperately trying to show him how much I care.

"No, it's not."

"How can you even sit there and say that?" He finally lifts his chin.

179

Watery, bloodshot eyes meet mine. "If I'd never been born, then she'd still be alive."

I sit up straighter in my seat. "Jett. If you weren't born, then Hailey's life would have been meaningless, anyway. She had no regrets about having you. She always wanted to be a mother and loved you with all her heart."

"No," he grits out, frustrated more than upset at this point, but I don't know why. "You don't get it. If she didn't have me, she'd be alive." He speaks slower this time, as though a change of pace will change the meaning of the words.

"How do you know that?"

"Because *he* told me."

"Wh- wh- what are you talking about?" The words come out harder than before because I'm almost afraid to hear what he has to say.

"The accident. He was there."

"Who's he?"

"Simon. He was at the accident, just after it happened."

I press my lips together, trying to remain calm and composed, so I don't freak Jett out. "Are you sure? Because I thought you were passed out until the emergency services cut you out of your seat?"

The pain only mars his face further. "Aunt Mia, there's something I need to tell you."

"You can tell me anything."

He takes a deep breath, pushing his tongue against his teeth before admitting, "I think he was the one who hit us."

Trying to breathe myself, the confession hits me like a wrecking ball. There isn't a bone in my body that thinks he might be lying. "What makes you think that?"

"Because I remember."

"What exactly do you remember? The police think you know nothing."

"A black car hit us." That's not new information. The paint against their car confirmed it, and they searched for a black car with that damage for months. "Mom freaked out when it rammed into the side of us because it caused us to lose our balance. That's when we rolled. The last thing she said to me was 'hold on.'" He swallows, watching my reaction as I try to stay as neutral as possible because I need him to finish this. "The car rolled so many times and only stopped when we hit the tree.

Mom bashed her head against the steering wheel, and I called out for her, but I knew she wouldn't answer. I knew she was gone, but I hoped with every part of me I was wrong."

"Oh, Jett."

"When I heard footsteps, I lost my voice. I was so afraid of who was coming for us, I froze. Then a man put his face against the window, and as much as I wanted help for mom, he scared me. It didn't feel like he was there to help, so I took the coward's way out and pretended to be passed out."

My heart's beating so wildly that my brain's barely able to process what Jett's telling me.

"He opened my mom's door. I thought if he pulled her out to help her, I'd tell him I was awake, but instead, he laughed, and slammed the door shut."

My eyes burn, tears threatening to spill because it sounds so callous, and it's not something Jett had to see. He's just a kid who lost his mom in one of the most tragic ways possible.

"Jett, did he do anything to you?"

"No. He didn't bother to check on me." Thank God. "But he did smack the car window, and I heard him call me a bastard. It was Simon, Aunt Mia. I just know it."

If I hadn't already had a million reasons to hate Simon, this would have pushed me over the edge.

"I'm going to kill that man." I wasn't thinking straight, but how could I be after hearing that? Every fiber in my being wanted Simon to pay for what he did to our family.

"Please do."

"Are you sure it was him?"

"Yes. I remember before Mom passed away, I was snooping through her things, and I found a picture of them together. I recognized him immediately."

"But why are you only telling me this now?"

"Because there hasn't been a day, I haven't thought about it. I was scared that if I told the police I was awake and saw him that Simon might find out and come and finish the job."

My blood runs cold. Fury emanates through my body.

"Tomorrow morning, we're going to the police to tell them what happened," I say calmly, gripping the steering wheel. "They need to know the truth."

"What's the point? The case was closed, and who's going to believe a kid whose story has changed over several years?"

"You were a kid afraid of his father."

"Don't call him my father. He's done nothing to earn that title. He acts like I don't even exist. Not that I want anything to do with him.

"Oh, he knows you exist, alright." I close my eyes, knowing that the statement alone is going to bring out some hard truths.

"What are you talking about?"

Turning to face him, I lean my head against the car seat. "Since you've been honest with me I've got to be honest with you." I wince, and when I look at him, I'm surprised that he's not upset. He just raises a brow, waiting for me to explain. "Simon's been blackmailing me ever since the accident."

That makes him sit up. "Blackmailing you with what?"

"You." I keep it short at first to gauge his reaction. The sad, scared kid is long gone, replaced by an angry and tense teen. "He's been threatening to take me to court over your custody if I don't send through monthly payments."

"He has?" His face falls, and he becomes expressionless.

"Yeah. I didn't tell you because you'd already been through enough stuff with the accident, and since you didn't know him, I assumed you wouldn't want to live with him."

"There is no way I'd ever live with that man." Jett's lip quivers in disbelief as he processes the words I've been reluctant to admit to anyone for three years. "Why didn't you tell me? I could have quit baseball and got a job to help."

"That's exactly why. You're thirteen, J. You don't have to be the hero in this story."

"But you don't have to face Simon alone." He wraps his hand in mine, his eyes welling. I'm right there with him, but I try to stay strong for the both of us.

"Neither do you. We'll figure something out." I give him a weak smile and then look outside, only to realize that through all my best efforts, I failed miserably at getting out of here in the rush. It's quiet, and we're like sitting ducks in this now empty car park. "Look, let's get home. I don't like being alone here."

"Yeah," He drawls out, going straight back into his shell.

Tapping his knee pointedly, I say, "This conversation isn't over. Let's talk about it when we get home."

"Sure." He sounds unconvinced, but I'm more determined than ever to listen to everything he wants to tell me. We are going to fight to get a better understanding from the police over what happened with Hailey.

As I turn the ignition back on, and back out of the space, Jett rests his forehead on the window, looking out in thought. I don't try to disrupt it because I want to get us home as safely as possible.

By the time we got home, Jett had fallen asleep against the glass, and I didn't have the heart to finish the conversation. So, I sent him straight to his room to sleep.

As I sit on the sofa in the living room, I take another sip of my peppermint tea in an attempt to relax. After lying in my bed for what felt like hours, I couldn't sleep. Jett's confession made that near impossible now because I always knew Simon had something to do with Hailey's accident. I just had no proof. Guilt slithers through my veins, because I feel like we could have somehow stopped all of this before it got to the accident.

But I just don't know.

Grabbing my phone for the first time tonight, I swipe past all of Austin's missed calls. I should have texted him earlier, but I'm pretty sure he's on a flight now, so I'll call him in the morning. I sweep my thumb up the screen, until I find the number for the detective that worked on Hailey's case, already planning what I'm going to say.

Knock. Knock. Knock.

My thumb stops, and I freeze, fear settling in over just who's behind our front door. Would Simon be so bold to waltz over here in the middle of the night? Surely not. There's a security camera right at the entrance. I close out the contacts on my phone and pull up the security app.

"Mia. It's Austin." I drop my phone because his voice immediately soothes me, and my whole body relaxes. "Will you let me in? I'm worried about you guys."

Tip toeing to the door to not wake Jett, I check the peephole. Sure enough, it's him.

"Austin," I say with a weary smile as I open the door. "What are you doing here? It's one a.m., and I thought you were traveling to Seattle tonight?"

He gives me a lopsided smile, trying to cover the concern and stress marring his face, but I know him well enough to see it now. "We're leaving tomorrow morning, but I couldn't sleep. You didn't stay after the game or answer any of my calls or messages. Jett suddenly stopped replying too."

As if I didn't feel guilty enough tonight, Austin's worried face only adds to it. Jett and I have been alone for so long that I didn't think of the impact us not responding would have on someone else who might care for us. "I'm sorry. Everything's fine. Jett fell asleep on the way home."

He raises a brow in disbelief. "Are you sure about that? Because you kind of look like a bee stung you in the ass." He lifts his lips, and I laugh at his stupid joke, whacking him in the chest lightly.

"No. I don't."

He sighs out. "Yeah, you do. The entire game you were distracted. You wouldn't even look at me."

"How on earth did you have time to notice where I was looking? You were playing a game."

"Oh, believe me, I had time to notice." He chuckles sarcastically. "I just didn't have time to make a big scene over it." He steps closer, and I shut the door, offering him a seat on the couch, which he gladly takes. "I seriously considered climbing over the railing so I could catch up with you guys."

"I'm glad you didn't. What if you got hurt?" He takes my hand, pulls me to his side, and kisses me on the cheek.

"Being on the IL doesn't sound so bad if I have you there to nurse my injury," he whispers in my ear. His breath tickles my neck, sending shivers down my spine, straight to my core, but my phone on the table tampers down any dirty thoughts because it reminds me of everything that happened tonight.

"Sorry, Austin. I didn't mean to ghost you. I've just got a lot on my mind." And a lot of things I should probably tell him before he gets any deeper involved with me, but just maybe not tonight.

"That's it? Just thinking too much?"

"Yup." His fingers dance across my shoulder, and he watches them with a flirty smirk on his face.

"Because if overthinking's got you down, I can come up with a few things to distract you." He grins, leaning a little closer, and kisses me longingly on the lips. I indulge it, pretending that I'm twenty-years-old for a second and that none of this real-life shit matters. It's just me and

Austin, young and in love.

The kiss only intensifies, and I trace my fingers across the bottom of his shirt, dipping them under to feel his warm skin. He pulls away, looking down at my hand, and then lets out a low chuckle. "Before we get into any of that, I have a question for you." He scrubs his hands together, letting out a long breath. Oh, no. He's not going to ask *that*, is he? His cheeks are going red, and his breathing is labored.

Don't do it. Please, don't do it. I shout in my head because this is like watching a car crash. I can't look away, and I can't do anything to stop it.

He's going to ask permission to have sex with me, and I don't know where to look.

"A question?" I feign ignorance, trying to sound nonchalant, but after everything that happened today, I feel drained and exhausted, and the only thing I want to do is get lost in my bedsheets with Austin.

"Yeah," He looks up to the ceiling. "So, you know it's my first season as a Catfish." Okay, not where I thought this was going, but it sounds a lot better than asking for sex.

"Yes?"

"Well, I've just had my one-hundred-and-thirtieth at bat."

"Congratulations." Cupping his cheeks, I give him a quick peck.

"You do know what that means, right?" I shake my head, and he smiles. "It means I'm officially a rookie."

"Oh," I say, sounding surprised, but shake that thought and give him a hug. "Congratulations." I pull back out of his hold. "That's fantastic news. I'm just surprised because everyone has already been talking about how you're in line to be-"

"Don't say it." He raises his shaky hand to my mouth. "Why is everyone so hell bent on jinxing me?"

"Sorry," I mumble against his hand, giving it a teasing lick.

"But since I'm officially a rookie, I've been invited to the Rookie ball."

"That's awesome news."

"It is." He nods, and I still feel like there's something he's skirting around. "I've also been given a plus one."

There it is.

"Okay," I say with a wry smile.

He mimics me. "And I'm sure you can see where this is going, but I was hoping you'd be my date."

"Your date?" He nods, and as much as I want to say yes, after

185

everything that happened tonight, I'm not sure if I can. Should I really being going further with Austin when I have so much other stuff to deal with?

"Damn, Boss Girl. You're really going to leave me hanging like I'm some loser at school, hoping you'll accept my promposal?" He looks down and shakes his head.

"Austin," I say, and he takes a second to look back at me.

I smile nervously because I so badly want to say yes. It feels right. Just sitting next to him, I can feel the connection between us. It's like this buzzing static energy drawing me closer, but there's just one nagging thing that's stopping me from leaping into his arms and saying yes.

Simon.

Because if what Jett admitted to me today was true, then I have a much bigger problem than I initially thought, and Simon's payments are just the tip of the iceberg. If he did have something to do with Hailey's death, then there might be a long trial in my future, and I know for sure that's not something a Rookie Ballplayer would want to get involved in.

"Where is it?" Not technically a yes, but it seems to have worked.

He takes my hand and rubs his thumb over my skin. "Tampa. Is that what you're hesitant? Because I've looked into it, and there's nothing to worry about. It's on a Saturday, and the team pays for hotels and flights."

"But what about Jett?"

He smiles. "Did you really think I'd forget about my biggest fan? In an awesome stroke of luck, he won't be here that weekend, anyway."

I narrow my eyes. "Is he coming with us?"

"No. No. I probably shouldn't tell you this." He pushes his lips from side to side in contemplation, but now I need to know. "But I guess he'll find out in a couple of days. Jett got selected."

"Selected?" It takes a minute for it all to click. "For the Catfish Youth Team?" Austin nods, looking almost as proud as I feel. I want to shriek in happiness, but I'm still so shocked.

"I should stress it's for the reserve team, though."

"What?! Are you serious? And you haven't told him?" I spring up from the couch, ready to wake him up. "We have to tell him."

"Woah. Woah, woah." Austin grasps my arm, stopping me. "You can't tell him now because that will ruin the surprise. Catty the Catfish is going to come knocking on the door in the next couple of days with a camera crew to get his unfiltered reaction. I'm sure the team will call you about it tomorrow."

"How on earth did he get on the team after that whole incident with Rhode?" I ask, "Did you help him get this place?"

He raises his hands in defense. "Nope. I had absolutely nothing to do with it. Jett's a talented catcher. He and Rhode had a good connection, whether they liked to admit it or not. Before their argument, they were striking out batters left, right and center."

"So they just told you he got a place?"

"Nah. I'm friends with Tate's girlfriend, Cali." He gives me a lazy, wistful smile, and for the slightest of seconds, I feel jealousy rage through my body because he better not be smiling over her. "She works in marketing, and she may know that I've got the hots for you."

"You've got to be kidding me?"

"I don't kid about things like that, but," he drawls out. "That leads me back to the ball. There's a team building event for the Youth Team on the same weekend as the Rookie Ball, which means Jett won't be home."

"Jett won't be home." I repeat, letting it sink in.

"So," He says, waiting for me to fill in the blanks. When I don't, he starts again. "Mia James. Would you do me the honor of being my date for the Rookie ball?" He asks with a lot more confidence than he started with.

If Jett's safely away from here, and I'm not in Charlotte, Simon won't be able to get to either of us. "Yes."

"Yes?" He laughs.

"Yes." I jump into his arms, my hands cupping his face as I kiss him senselessly. He responds by lifting my thighs and wrapping my legs around his waist, laying my back flat against the sofa cushion.

With every swipe of his tongue against my lips, our movements become more erratic, and we're both chasing a high that we know can't come to fruition. Not on the sofa with Jett upstairs, at least.

As I pull away from him, he bites down playfully on my bottom lip.

"I can't believe you said yes."

"Why are you so surprised?"

"Because this is the first time I've ever asked someone to a dance."

Stroking my hand across his cheek, I look at him with admiration. "You're just too pure sometimes." Austin frowns, and I immediately regret my words. "I didn't mean pure *pure*. I just meant you're so wholesome. You know, like apple pie." Then I cringe because the only

187

thing that comes to mind is Jason Biggs and *that* scene in *American Pie*, but he's probably too young to get the reference.

He kisses my nose. "Relax. I know what you meant."

"Do you want to stay over?" I ask against his lips, toying with the buttons of his shirt.

His hands rest against my shoulders, and although he gives me one lingering kiss, he groans as he pulls away. "I wish I could, but…"

"I know. Baseball comes first."

"I didn't say that. Let's be clear, you always *come* first. Whether it's through a door, on a date, or in the bedroom. You are my top priority. Or should I say, you and Jett are my top priority. But, as I would very much like to take you to the Rookie Ball, I need to keep playing, and I don't know how good I'd play after eating you out all night long." He smirks, and I like how proud he is of himself.

"Well, next time, I hope I can do more than give you a hand job."

He squeezes my shoulders. "Boss Girl. As long as we've had dinner at the Rookie Ball, we can do whatever we want the rest of the night." He wiggles his eyebrows with amusement.

"This sounds more and more like prom by the minute."

"I wouldn't know. I never went. What happened at yours?"

I cringe. "Do you really want to know?" When he nods, I have no retort, because I walked right into this one. Closing one eye and squinting at him with the other, I admit, "I lost my virginity, and it was a terrible experience."

"Why?" He shuffles forward, his jaw clenched, his fists tight like he's ready to pounce. "He didn't hurt you, did he?"

I gently rest my hands on his shoulders, looking into his eyes with a smile. "No. Johnny MacMan was a nice guy from what I remember. I'm pretty sure he's an accountant now and has settled down with his college sweetheart."

His jaw ticks, but I can tell he's trying to hide that from me. "What made it terrible, then?"

I wince, thinking about it. "Let's just say he couldn't find the right hole and he was a little too eager. Come to think of it, I'm not sure if I technically *did* lose my virginity that night. I just thought I did because I didn't know any better."

He laughs, folding his fingers with mine. "Well, I'm pretty sure I don't have that problem. I believe I've already found the right spot plenty of times."

I blush just thinking about the sheer number of orgasms he's given me with just his hands and mouth. Six? Seven, maybe? I lost count after the first three, since we've only spent one night together. One amazing night that I can't stop thinking about because everything felt so good. I was calm, tangled up in my bed sheets with Austin, even if he hadn't let me fully return the favor yet.

He kisses me quickly on the lips. "So, is that you sold? You and me at the ball with a shared hotel room?"

"Yes. I can't wait."

I kiss him again, sealing the deal, and as I sit on his lap ready to take this further tonight, he groans, gently pushing me away. "As much as I want to continue this. I've got a flight to catch in." He looks down at his watch. "Forty minutes, and the guys will kill me if they have to hold the plane."

I shouldn't be disappointed because I knew this was coming, but I can't help but feel cheated out of more time with him.

"Hey, hey," He whispers, cupping my cheeks. "Next time you see me will be at the ball, and until then… we can always talk."

"Talk?" I repeat.

"Yeah, all night long if we want." His lips lift in amusement.

"I guess that doesn't sound too bad."

With that, he kisses my forehead and leaves me in a mess of couch cushions, with mixed emotions. The excitement I feel about going to the ball with Austin is tempered by the whole situation with Simon. Something I *need* to talk to Austin about. I just haven't figured out the best way to approach it yet, but I'll need to do it out soon, otherwise I risk losing him, and that's not something I'm ready for.

21.

CHAPTER SEVENTEEN

AUSTIN

Mia: Good game tonight, A.

When the text drops over the top of my screen, I immediately stop scrolling the sports pages because she's up. Smiling, I sit up in my bed, replying to her immediately.

Austin: Thanks, but what are you doing up at two am on a school night?

Mia: Rebelling.

Austin: Funny. You don't strike me as a rebel.

Mia: And you don't strike me as a naughty boy, but here we are.

And there goes my dick, springing to attention because of one little phrase. This is the longest stint I've had away from Charlotte since joining the Catfish, and the first time in my life that I think I might be suffering from blue balls. Fourteen days so far, and four more to go before I'm back on a flight to see Mia, but it feels like years. Now that I've had a taste of her, it's like she's got a direct line to my dick, and all she needs to do is send me an emoji and my dick is ready to go, which is why I only check her messages in the safety of my room.

Austin: Can you guess what I was thinking about when I hit that homer in the fourth?

Mia: Philly Cheesesteaks?

Austin: As delicious as they are, no. I was thinking about something just as tasty, though.

Mia: Oh yeah? What?

Austin: You.

Mia: That sounds like it could be distracting. I'm surprised you could hit anything.

Austin: On the contrary. It keeps me focused.

Mia: What you were thinking about when you hit that double in the sixth then?

Austin: You. Naked and withering underneath me while I rail you into the kitchen countertop.

Mia: Okay, naked on a kitchen countertop? How cliché, and unless there's a towel underneath me, it's not going to happen. It's cold and unhygienic.

Austin: Way to ruin a guy's fantasy. What am I going to think about now?

Mia: Not that. Besides, doesn't that make it extremely difficult to play? Don't you have a boner at the most inconvenient times?

Austin: I'm half-mast at best. It's going to take a lot more than imagining you to get it up fully with all that distraction. I'd need to see and feel you.

Mia: Don't get naked at your games. Got it.

Austin: Good. I don't want anyone else seeing your perfect tits but me.

Mia: Possessive.

Austin: I know when I've got something good. But that doesn't mean I haven't thought about railing you in the dugout when the Stadium's closed.

Mia: Where are you?!

Austin: In my room? Why?

Mia: So not out celebrating your win?

Austin: It's midnight. I don't think we'd have many more wins if I was out celebrating after each one this late. Got 75 more games to go, don't you know? So much could happen.

Mia: Good point.

Mia: So, does that mean you're alone?

Austin: Yup, I'm on my own. This isn't AAA anymore. They give me my own room. Where are you?

Mia: Obviously I'm alone in my room too…

Then I sit up a little straighter because those dot dot dots suggest something that I've been waiting for.

Calling Mia.

She answers on the second ring; her face lighting up my screen as well as my heart. "Hey," I say, feeling like a goofy teenager as I look at her pixelated smile and big, doe eyes beaming back at me.

Why didn't I try this sooner? Facetiming Mia means I can see her in real time, and the mere sight of her is already making me hot and bothered.

"Hey," She whispers on a sexy giggle as she sits in the darkness of her room. A shot of sadness runs through my body because I miss her, and I don't know if it's appropriate to say that. We're at the point in our relationship that I'm starting to feel like she and Jett are family, but I don't want to freak her out.

Mia rolls down her bed, throwing her blanket over her head.

"What are you doing?"

"I don't want Jett to hear us," she whispers, moving down her bed, and flashing just the tiniest hint of bare shoulder. It's enough to pique my interest.

"His room is on a different floor on the other side of the house."

"Your point?"

"What are you planning on doing that he might hear?"

She smiles shyly at the camera, trouble sprawled across her face. "Isn't that why you called?"

I raise my brows, smiling. "Partly, but mostly because I wanted to see your face. I miss you." And there I go, blurting it out because holding it back was like edging with no end point.

"Aww. I miss you too." She giggles, thankfully, not in a sentimental mood. She shuffles around and I move my phone, falsely assuming it will show me what I want to see of Mia.

"Are you naked?" I ask, scrutinizing the screen harder than Sherlock Holmes.

Rolling her eyes, she looks down, patting what must be clothes, otherwise she's just patting her bare breasts and if she dips the phone down, my heart might give out. "No. I've got this cute little satin PJ set on." Then she does it. She drops the camera down, and all I see is a little pink, a little flesh and a whole lot of darkness, but it's more than enough to have my mind reeling over what I couldn't see.

"Mia," I say really slowly, with command. "Take a picture of what you're wearing with the flash on and send it to me."

Her smile morphs into a mischievous smirk as she does what I ask. I can already tell she's getting hot over this. Something I've learned about her is that she likes it when I'm in control. Give her a command, and she's like putty in my hands. But then again, something I've learned about myself in all of this is that I like telling her what to do.

The picture comes through, and I reduce her FaceTime for the slightest of seconds to look.

Yup. I'm hard.

Satin, light pink silk hardly covers her vivacious curves, and if I were there, all I'd need to do is push those tiny little straps to the side, and I'd be able to bite her nipples. I grind my teeth in annoyance, the 'four more days' mantra doing nothing to satiate my appetite for her.

"Are you as horny as I am?"

"Mhmm," she moans out like that's an acceptable answer.

"Show me." Her eyes pop open, and she glares at the screen, fully expecting me to laugh off the command. Well, I'm not joking, so I make it very clear. "Drop your hand down your little silk shorts, touch yourself, and then show me how wet you are for me."

I admit, this wasn't how I envisaged my night going when I left the team at dinner, but here I am. Waiting for Mia to finger herself and show me. She takes a sharp breath before her shoulders shuffle. "Open your eyes, Mia." She hardly opens them, but I let her off as it seems like she's following my orders.

"Tell me exactly what you're doing."

She bites her bottom lip, and the video gets a little shaky. "Umm. Well, my fingers are at my stomach right now, just circling my naval."

"Keep going."

"Okay," She sings. Her eyes are fully closed now, and I know when she's touching herself because her mouth falls open, and a tiny, tight smile forms at the edges of her lips.

"Tell me what you're doing Mia," I grit out. My cock is straining against my boxers, but I'm too concerned about Mia to think about it.

Her teeth release her lips as she says, "I'm sliding my fingers across my clit, circling it the same way you did when you touched me." I groan, and before I know it, my hand is on my cock. "I'm soaked." Her voice is all hot and breathy as she smiles.

"Push two of your fingers inside yourself."

Another sharp inhale, and I know she's doing as I asked.

"Good girl. Does it feel good?"

"Would feel better if it was you."

"That's not an answer to my question. Does it feel good?"

She tips her chin forward, her eyes still closed, and I can see her shoulder moving. She hasn't just dipped her fingers in, she's finger fucking herself, and I want her so badly, I feel like a might explode, and not just in my pants.

"Mia. You need to show me."

Taking her fingers away, she brings them up to the camera as she lets out a reluctant mewl. She holds them so close that it's blurry and I can't see. "Hold them back a little so they're in focus, BG."

She does as I say, and that's it. I have to stroke myself because all I see is a soft sheen across her fingers. Her taste comes back to me, and I lick my lips, wishing her essence was there again.

"Is that good? Can you see it?"

"It's perfect, but I want you to get yourself off, Mia." Too turned on; she doesn't protest, but just drops her hand back down. "Are you missing me?" She nods, her eyes are closed, and a serene smile adorns her face. I'm imagining it now. She's naked from the waist down, with two fingers inside her because one would be far too slender. "Tell me what you're thinking about?"

She opens her half-lidded eyes, and looks so tempting. My dick is rock hard, just looking at her face, and what I wouldn't give to have a peek under her covers, but I'm thousands of miles away in a hotel room I don't want to be in.

Biting her lip, she takes a sharp inhale before she builds up the courage to answer. "Just thinking about the last time I saw you without your shirt on."

I look down at my chest, surprised she can see much with the angle I'm holding my phone, but happy because the last time she saw me like this, my head was between her thighs, and I was eating her out like she was my last meal.

I lick my lips, still expecting them to taste like Mia. When they don't, I frown. "I miss your taste, baby."

She groans, wiggling in protest. "Don't say things like that. I'm already close."

"Good. Show me."

With her eyes closed, she furrows her brow. "But I already did."

"I'm greedy. I want more. I want to see your delectable pussy, so turn your flashlight on, flip the camera and show me what you're doing."

She pauses for a moment in contemplation, but I know she'll do it because I've asked her. Offering me a lazy smile, she says, "I will if you will."

I growl involuntarily like a caged animal because the idea of watching her finger herself is so hot. Doing as she says, I turn my torch on and flip the phone, and Mia follows suit. When I see her body, I nearly come all over my bedsheets at the sight. Her hand is covering her mound, so all I can see are her knuckles moving at a ferocious pace. That's enough, and better than I imagined. She's working herself up so well, all I can hear is the sloppy wetness of her fingers moving. It's like the most deliciously sexy ASMR I've ever heard.

And it's so. Fucking. Hot.

"What are you thinking about?" I ask as my hand moves against my shaft. She groans but doesn't answer. "Tell me what's making you so wet, Boss Girl."

"Your tongue," she blurts out. "I'm thinking about your tongue circling my clit."

"Oh, yeah?" my hand moves quicker as I think about the last time Mia had her hands on me.

"Yeah. You did this thing that just made me feel good."

"What was it?"

"You flicked your tongue so fast; I couldn't catch a breath." Her confession comes out on a sigh. "What are you thinking about?" She asks, barely able to get the question out.

"I'm thinking about how good it would feel to have your mouth all over my cock, and your hand playing with my balls."

"I want to do that so bad," She groans out, her fingers moving faster.

"Next time, baby. Just think about my tongue on you, lapping you up right now. Tasting every part of you."

"Austin," she calls, her hips bucking against her hand. I follow the movement, only able to imagine how tight she'd feel.

"Mhm. I love the way you call my name like that. It's even better when you're pulling my hair, letting me know exactly what you like."

My balls tighten, and I know that I'm close, so I watch her intently. Her fingers work faster, her hips move a little and then pause. I know what that means. I watched her fall apart enough times to know.

"Come for me, BG."

That's all it takes. Her hips raise from the bed, jerking in movement as she comes, holding back because she can't make much noise.

Watching and hearing her fingers move, I'm on the precipice too. "Mia," I cry, coming too, and letting the liquid spurt all over my hand like a teenager, but I don't give a fuck. That was the best hand job I've ever given myself, and the first time I've had phone sex.

Her hips drop to the bed, and she moves her fingers from her center as she flicks the screen back to her face. I do the same.

With red cheeks, her face is flushed, and she gives me a lazy, serene smile. "Did we just do that?"

I chuckle, biting my lip. "Yeah, we did."

"Wow, I must really miss you. Can't that kind of thing be recorded and sent around the internet?"

"I think that could only happen if I record it." She looks at me in disbelief. "What? Do you think there's some hacker watching us get off? Because I'll tell you what? That's one lucky hacker."

She barks out a laugh, looking like a satiated kitten, and I wish I was there so she could fall asleep in my arms.

"Only four more days until I see you."

"Yeah. Four more," she replies sleepily.

"I should probably go shower, Boss Girl, and I've got a feeling you're going to fall asleep any minute."

She nods, giggling. "Oh, after that, I most certainly am."

"Goodnight, Mia. I can't wait to see you."

"I can't wait to see you either."

CHAPTER EIGTHEEN
MIA

Unknown: Noticed a new truck's been coming in and out of that shit hole of a neighborhood of yours. That's the fanciest F150 I've ever seen.

Unknown: Tell me, Mia. Is there a new man in your life? Is it the same ballplayer that you're trying to convince to be Jett's new daddy? Guess you haven't told him about what happened with Hailey, otherwise he would've skipped town by now.

That's it.

I'm tired of this shit.

If this man thinks he can scare me with these stupid threatening texts, he's got another thing coming. My blood is boiling and there's a new fire in my belly because I know for certain he was involved in Hailey's death, and I've no doubts that he hoped Jett went along with her. He wanted to take everything away from me as punishment, and when that didn't work; he found a new way to control me through blackmail.

Mia: Leave me alone, you sorry piece of shit, or you're going to regret it.

Clutching my phone so tightly, I'm certain I'm going to crack the glass. I curse under my breath because I let my anger get the better of me. Why the hell did I respond? Name calling is only going to goad him, and he'll contact me more.

If I ever want the messages to stop, I've got to stop paying him and be unresponsive. At least, that's what Detective Hamby suggested I do if I wanted to prove that *he's* harassing me and not the other way around.

My mind still reels from the meeting I had with the detective last week. So much has happened in those three years since the accident, yet the minute I saw Detective Hamby, I felt like I was right back where I started. When I mentioned Simon's possible involvement, he wasn't surprised. It was a theory I had back then, but he urged me not to pursue it because Simon was claiming I was harassing him. Even after I told him about Jett's confession, he didn't seem that convinced. He said they wouldn't be able to use that to get a warrant, so there'd be no way to get any evidence for re-opening the case.

The only thing he did warn me about is that I'm on record 'harassing' Simon, and the best thing I can do for myself right now is leave him alone.

Urgh. What a stupid move. I need to delete that last message before he sees it.

Raising my phone, I'm bitterly disappointed because I'm too late. He's already responded.

Unknown: Baby, was that supposed to be a threat because I'm laughing? I can't leave you alone. You should know that by now.

I swallow the bitter taste in my mouth, frustrated that just a few words can bring me right back to the worst day of my life without fail. He's always had this ability to make me feel like the smallest person on earth with just a few words.

"Crap," I whisper, re-reading his text before tossing my phone into the cup holder in the car, and regretting every key stroke.

"What's wrong, Aunt Mia?" Jett asks, concerned from the back seat.

Shit. I forgot he was back there for a second. I make eye contact with him in the review mirror and smile. It's false, but he won't be able to tell in the reflection.

"Nothing, J. Just forgot something at home." I lie again because he doesn't need to be burdened by the truth. After thinking about his confession and the detective's response, I decided not to tell him about Simon's harassment because I don't want him riled up any more over something we might not be able to change. I'm his defender, not the other way around, and I'll take all the blackmail and stalking if it means he'll leave Jett alone.

"Come on, let's get inside. I've got some lasagna ready to go." My voice cracks a little, which I mask by opening the door and pulling my handbag out. I scan the neighborhood and relax when I don't see his car. But that's the thing with Simon. He isn't going to make himself known. That's not his style. He prefers letting me live in constant fear instead. Never knowing when he's going to show up, or what he's going to do.

"What's that?" Jett points to the top of the porch and right in the middle of the entryway, a perfectly packed brown box sits on the top step. My blood runs cold because I didn't order anything, and I've seen enough horror movies to know that this isn't a good sign.

Tucking Jett behind me, I say, "Stay here for a second. I'm just going to check out what it is."

"Why do you sound scared about an Amazon package?"

"I'm not. I just want to see what it is first in case it's a surprise for you."

He raises a brow, looking at me unconvinced, but he doesn't bother pushing back. He just dips down to pick up his catcher's gear.

"What? Can't an aunt spoil her nephew without him getting suspicious?"

I can feel my heart beating as I tentatively make my way to my porch, wondering if it's overdramatic at all to think that this could be my last moment on earth. After what Simon did to Hailey, I wouldn't put it past him.

With each creak of the step, my anxiety rises, and I wince, preparing myself for the worst. When I reach the top of the steps, and nothing happens, I feel somewhat relieved. That's short-lived when I see the cursive writing on top of the box. 'Mia James' is scrawled across it, but the writing is too neat to be Simon's, so I should take some heed in that.

I glance over my shoulder and see Jett is right where I told him to be. He's lost interest in me, already too busy with reading something on his phone, so I turn back and delicately lift the package, surprised that it's lighter than I expected. A severed head is like, what, eleven pounds? It's definitely too light to be that.

"What is it?" Jett calls from the end of the driveway. If it's not a head, I could handle a sawn-off finger or an ear, right?

"Not sure." I shake it, and I hear something scratch across the cardboard, which most certainly doesn't sound like a body part. I place the box on the table next to the bench and rip the tape off. As I push the flaps down, my brows furrow when I see the pink envelope sitting inside, gently placed on top of some perfectly uncreased tissue paper. The handwriting is familiar, but it's not Simons.

It's Austin's.

My shoulders drop and I feel a little more relaxed, knowing that a bloodied body part isn't going to greet me when I push the papers aside. Taking the note out of the envelope, my heart beats wildly, but this time it's for a completely different reason than when I was in the car.

Can't wait to see you in this dress, Boss Girl.

I flip it over and nearly snort at the message on the other side.

I also can't wait to see you out of it.

Frat Boy

When I hear Jett's clunky footsteps make their way up the path, I stuff the card back into the envelope and tuck it into the side beside the tissue paper. "What is it?"

"Austin sent me something."

He cringes. "I don't want to know why I had to stay away while you opened it, then. Why can't my future uncle get you jerseys and mitts like he does me?"

I roll my eyes, pushing back the tissue paper to reveal the red fabric shimmering at me. "He's not your future uncle, and relax, it's just a dress."

"And you wanted me to stay back for that?"

"I thought it might be a bomb," I say, with a hint of humor. I drop the box, pulling out a long off the shoulder dress with a slit up the thigh.

Swallowing, I hate that the first thing that comes to mind is that I'll look fat in this dress. It's beautiful and if I was ten years younger, I'd feel great rocking an outfit like this. It's daring but sophisticated, and when I see the Balmain label, I freeze. He must have spent a fortune.

"Overdramatic much?" Jett laughs, tilting his chin as he looks at me pointedly as he drags his bag into the house. I've never felt more judged. "I like the dress," he calls over his shoulder, and I smile because it's only two more days until I see Austin again.

Gently placing the dress back in the tissue paper, I pick up the box and follow Jett inside. "I'm going to take a shower," he says over his shoulder as he heads up the stairs.

"Wasn't going to say anything, but you stink," I joke, heading to my room. After locking the door, I lay the dress across my bed, admiring it for a few minutes before the urge to try it on gets the better of me. Never in my life did I dream that I'd be able to wear a pair of Jimmy Choos, let alone a Balmain dress. That's like a completely different level of luxury. I put it on, telling myself that I need to know if it works for me, so Austin can return it if it looks terrible. As the fabric falls across my hips and I zip the dress up, I tip toe to the mirror, pretending I'm wearing those Jimmy's that I've always wanted.

Now, I'm not usually one for self-love, but I don't think I've ever liked looking at myself more than right now. Even with my weathered make up and haphazard hair, the dress hugs my curves in ways that I never imagined possible. I feel like it's molded to my skin, emphasizing my every curve instead of highlighting my fat rolls. I don't think I've ever felt more beautiful, and I can't believe Austin picked this.

I don't waste another minute; I grab my phone and quickly text him.

Mia: A new dress? Balmain, no less. What did I ever do to be so lucky?

Austin: Existed.

Mia: Well, who knew breathing came with such perks.

Austin: And your perks make me come… Does that mean we've gone full circle?

I smile coyly even though it's just me in the room, because it always feels a little naughty receiving texts like this.

Mia: You know that makes no sense, right?

Austin: I don't care. All I care about is whether you like the dress or not.

Mia: It's gorgeous. Funny, I was looking at a much cheaper dress like this on a rental site. It's like you read my mind.

Austin: I wish I had that ability. But alas, I may have had the help from your shower stalker co-worker.

I laugh, realizing that must have been why Charlie was so invested in picking an outfit with me the other day.

Mia: Can't believe she helped you.

Austin: It didn't come without a price. She only agreed to help me if I gave her information about 'Daddy Dalton.' Poor guy has no idea what's coming his way.

Mia: What kind of information did you give her?

Austin: Normal stuff, you know. His age, if he has siblings… the size of his dick. You know, things regular people talk about.

Mia: You didn't tell her the latter, did you?

Austin: I made it up. She seemed content.

Mia: Well, thank you for going through all the effort and dealing with my TA.

Austin: Are you sure you like it? Because if not, I have the receipt and you can go downtown to the Balmain showroom and pick something else.

Mia: I absolutely love it, but it's too much. I'm not sure I can accept it.

Austin: Why not? I've already had dreams about the things I'm going to do to you in it. Are you going to deprive me of that?

Mia: Because it's too expensive.

Austin: We're going to an MLB Ball, and you're dating the potential Rookie of the Year. Let me indulge you.

Austin: Have you tried it on?

Mia: I'm wearing it now.

Incoming FaceTime Austin.

I decline.

Incoming FaceTime Austin.

Another decline.

Austin: Answer me, woman!

Mia: But you'll see me in the dress.

Austin: Exactly.

Mia: It will ruin the surprise.

Austin: Thought you weren't keeping it?

Mia: You insisted.

Austin: Good. I've also got Charlie on standby to go shoe shopping with you on the weekend. She mentioned you have a little obsession with Jimmy Choos? Pick whichever ones you want to wear for that night.

Mia: Austin. That's too much.

Austin: Don't make me come over there and spank you.

Mia: What if that's exactly what I want?

Austin: Don't start. I'm going on the field for my warmup in a minute. Don't need my dick standing to attention for that.

Austin: Did Jett get the rest of the gear I sent over, by the way?

Mia: Of course he did, but again, you didn't have to do that. You spent way too much.

Austin: No, I hardly spent a thing. I get huge discounts from sponsors on gear. If he's taking baseball as seriously as I think, then he needs it, and I want to give it to him.

Mia: Thank you. That saved a whole lot of money I didn't have.

Austin: If it makes you feel any better, I got it for each kid attending the Carolina Youth program. They had a similar program in Michigan growing up, and a ballplayer did the same for me. Thought it was time that I paid it forward.

Who is this guy? Sometimes when I talk to him, it feels like I'm talking to a middle-aged baseball vet, not a rookie that's still trying to make an impact on the game himself.

Mia: Thank you, Austin.

Austin: Gotta head out to the field. Watch me tonight, I'll hit a homer for you.

Mia: Sure thing, Frat Boy. Can't wait to see you.

Austin: Ditto, Boss Girl.

21.

CHAPTER NINETEEN
AUSTIN

Did I just win Rookie of the Year? The World Series?

No, but I still feel like the luckiest man alive.

As Mia takes a few steps down the stairs, it's like my entire world stops spinning. Was she always this gorgeous or has being away from her made me want her more? When I catch her eyes, she beams with happiness. Wearing the red dress I bought her, she looks breathtaking, which would explain why I can't breathe. Holding the train so she can walk down the steps, her strong thighs are on show, and jealously courses through my veins. Jealousy that all these men get to see her like this when all I want to do is take her back upstairs and rip that slit until her dress is in pieces on the floor.

My feet move at their own fruition, taking two steps at a time to meet her in the middle of the stairs. Standing on the landing, we drink each other in for a few seconds before I wrap her in my arms because I can't take it anymore. Her fresh, floral scent triggers memories from the last time I was with her, and my heart beats faster than I've ever felt before.

My stomach pits out, my chest feels light. There's something going on when I'm around her, but I can't describe it. I've never been that romantic of a guy because I've always been more focused on my career than anything else, but being with her makes me want to work harder and be better. For her. Because seeing her smile once isn't enough. I want it all the time.

"Mia," I breathe out, and there's that smile again. The one that makes me feel like I've already won in life. I kiss the nape of her neck, running my nose across the skin there. It's my place and I've been away too long.

Resting her hand on my cheek, she guides me to her deep red lips and kisses me. When her lips touch mine, it's like I'm a bull that's been unleashed, ready to take on the world for her. Tongues clashing, hands gripping at the fabric of her dress, all I can think about is hauling her over my shoulder and dragging her back to the hotel room because who gives a fuck about a Rookie Ball when you've got the hottest woman alive, dressed in a beautiful gown just for you?

Pulling away from her, I rest my forehead against hers, breathing heavily as my fingers swirl across the small of her back. I knew the dress was backless, but I'd never imagined how low it would go. It's low enough to have me wondering if she's wearing anything underneath it.

Despite kissing me fiercely, her lipstick is still perfectly in place thanks to the make-up artist I arranged for her. As good as she looks, I'm devastated. Devastated that her lipstick isn't smeared all over my cock. Gah, why have I waited so long to let her get me off? Seeing her like this is torture.

"You look beautiful."

"Thanks. Gotta say, I couldn't imagine you in a tux." She grabs my bowtie, dragging her fingers across the fabric. "But now that I have, I can't decide what you look better in. Your uniform, this tux, or just those gray sweatpants from that picture you sent me the other day."

"I'll wear whatever you want me to as long as you keep looking at me like that." I drop another kiss on her lips, and she giggles. It's so light and carefree, I'm not used to it.

"Good to know."

I drop my palms to the curve of her ass, giving her a gentle squeeze. "I've missed you. Two weeks feels too long." I sound like a desperate teenager fawning over his first love, but I don't care what anyone else thinks anymore. As long as she's smiling.

Her lips curve, and she drops her head coyly before pushing a strand of hair behind her ear. "I've missed you too."

I tickle my fingers against her skin, watching as she takes in a sharp breath, and clutches at my perfectly pressed white shirt. Groaning, I whisper into her ear. "The last time you made that noise, my tongue was flicking against your clit."

"Can we do it again?"

"After dinner, I promise."

"You know," She drawls out, wrapping her arms around my neck. She kisses my ear before whispering, "I think it's about time I returned the favor. Don't you?"

Growling, I rest my forehead against hers, gripping her arms to hold back from grabbing her ass. "Don't tempt me. I might just suggest that we skip the dinner altogether."

"Would you lose your Rookie of the Year eligibility if you didn't show up at the ball?"

I shrug, unsure. "It would be worth it if it meant I could taste you again."

Slapping her hand across my chest, she looks around, but there's no one here. Everyone's already in the ballroom. "You've got to stop talking like that, Frat Boy. It's making me a little hot."

"Good, because that dress is making *me* a little hot, and if I'm going to have to suffer through this dinner horny and uncomfortable, then it's only right that you do too." I drag my hands so they rest on her hips, and my thumb is so close to her thigh, I'm tempted to follow the slit and see how close I can get to her center. But I stop myself because she's right. We're here for dinner, and she looks beautiful. She should at least show it off before I wreck her dress.

"Austin. Don't," She warns as though she can hear me talk, and that's going to stop me.

"Dinner starts in thirty minutes. How long do you think we need to be there before I can bring you back to the hotel room?"

She purses her lips, pushing them to one side in thought. "I think we have to at least stay until coffees."

"Coffees?" I say, surprised. "Can't we sneak out between main and dessert at least? They always have these long, drawn-out speeches. No one would notice."

As I dip down to kiss her on the lips again, she drapes her hand over mine and says, "They may not notice we're gone, but they'd sure as hell notice my hair after coming back."

"Oh baby, if you think that's all that will be messed up after I get my hands on you, then you're sorely mistaken."

"Stop." She slaps me on the chest, moving her face away so I can't ruin her make-up.

"Never. Now let's get this dinner over with."

Lacing her hand through my arm, I help her walk down the steps in her new red heels, and I stand proud as we walk into the ballroom, knowing that I have the best prize of all on my arms.

***

Three hours. It's been *three hours* of speeches, dinners and talking with other rookies across the league, and as much as I like these guys, I'm ready to get out of here. More specifically, I'm ready to get out of here and *in* toMia.

Now if only I could find her. She excused herself twenty minutes ago, and I haven't seen her since, but I find it hard to believe that the line to the bathroom is that long. I scan the crowd, looking for the beautiful woman in the red, shimmery dress with curves to die for.

When I spot her amongst a set of baseball wives and girlfriends, smiling and laughing, looking like she belongs, I know I'm in trouble. My heart is beating so fast, it feels like I'm having palpitations, but I know it's not that. The Catfish have a team cardiologist which I have to see weekly, and he's told me I have one of the healthiest hearts on the team. No. It's because I want to spend every second I can with her, and I've never felt that about another person before.

Thrumming my fingers on the back of her chair as I wait for her to occupy it, I whistle to myself, going over all the things I want to do to her when we're alone. That red lipstick is still immaculately in place, and as I watch her talking to someone, I imagine all the ways I'm going to try to rub it off.

'Could everyone please take their seats for the Commissioner's speech?'

The announcer's voice breaks through my thoughts, and I can't hide my disappointment. *Another* speech, when we have a free hotel room waiting for us upstairs. As the crowd disperses, and everyone heads back to their seats, I notice Mia stays in place. So I decide to get her. As she looks at something on her phone, she hasn't noticed me, so I use it to my advantage, and sneak up on her. Wrapping my arms around her midriff from behind, I kiss her neck in my now usual spot. "Should we sneak out now or do you want to listen to the boring Commissioner talk? I know what I'd rather do."

When I place my chin on her shoulder, I feel the muscles still.

"Austin," she says uneasily, and when I glance down, I realize why. She's reading a text from someone else.

Unknown: Hard to deny you're dating Austin Adams now, Mia. I'd say he's an upgrade, but the only reason a guy like him would be interested in a fat ass like you is because you give good head.

My body tenses so much, I wonder if she can feel it. "Mia, is everything okay?" I grit out because I'm holding back my fury. Who the fuck is sending her messages like that? An ex?

Breathing out, she drops her phone into her handbag without a word. Then when she turns around to face me, she gives me with the most awkward smile I've ever seen. "I'm fine," She quips, sounding like one of those Stepford Wives. Mechanical and unbelievable. With a short, quick kiss, she toys with my bowtie, and says, "Shall we go upstairs? I've had enough of other people. I just want you for myself."

Yeah, she's trying to make me forget the message, but it won't be that easy.

What the fuck isn't she telling me, and who doesn't she want me to know about?

"Let's go." I take her hand, leading her out of the ballroom, but instead of going to the elevator to our room, I pull her into a quiet corner.

As she lays her back against the wall, I rest my hands on either side of her face, studying it. Her lips are pressed with tension, her eyes darting from either side. She's hiding something. I just know it, and that fact annoys the shit out of me because I thought we were beyond keeping things from each other.

"Mia," I breathe out. "Is someone harassing you?"

She pulls her lips into her mouth and shakes her head. "No. It's nothing. Just some idiot trolls that are jealous I've kept you interested."

"People are messaging you vile things like that because of *me*?"

Her eyes widen, and she waves it off, her gaze drifting to the side. "No. No." She refuses to give me eye contact. "Just some idiot found my number and they're playing with me, that's all."

"Do you know who it is?"

When she finally looks up at me, tears coat her eyes, and she blinks a few times as though that's the only thing stopping her from crying.

What the hell is going on?

We were having a great time tonight, and now suddenly she's on the verge of breaking down because she's hiding something from me. "They're always unknown numbers."

That wasn't an answer to my question. It was a statement of fact, but laying into her about it won't get me anywhere. "*They?* Are you getting messages from different people?" She doesn't answer me. There's just a slight tremble in her bottom lip. Fuck. If she's getting harassed, I need to fix it. "Tomorrow morning, I'll get you a new phone. One with the best security features they have and then we'll contact the police. Get them to trace those numbers and find out who it is."

"No." She throws her hands to my chest, looking at me as though she's let something slip. "I don't need the police involved. I've tried to get their help before and nothing's changed."

Before?

What the hell is that supposed to mean?

"Look, I don't want some idiot troll running our night. It's been two weeks, and I don't know when I'm getting you alone again." She quickly changes her demeanor, her finger dipping into my shirt as she drags her nails across my chest to get my attention. "I want to spend the night *with* you." She lifts a brow, a slow, sexy smirk pulling across her face. "I want to see everything you have planned."

Everything I have planned?

I gulp.

Was there something else I was supposed to plan other than a room and condoms? Griss did tell me to jerk off before, but I've heard that end in disaster. What else could she be talking about?

Mia's freshly manicured nails swirl across my skin, and her sexy, sultry eyes take me in. Just like that, I can barely remember my name, let alone what we were talking about. The only thing I can think about is what it would feel like to finally have her naked body against mine as I slide inside her.

Her finger stops, and she frowns. "You aren't having second thoughts, are you?"

"Second thoughts?" I laugh. I'm nervous, a little sweaty, with a roll of condoms in my jacket pocket. Apparently, I'm living out what would have been my prom night three years late. "No. You're everything I want."

She smiles before tucking her hand inside my shirt, pulling me in to kiss her. Long, slow and passionate, she takes her time melding our bodies together in a way that's almost indecent when anyone could walk by. I'm already high on Mia, and we've only just started.

As she pulls away from me, her cheeks are flustered, her eyes a little hooded. Her lipstick is a little faint, and it's smeared around the edges. A thought runs through my head that I don't dare voice out loud.

Is this what she'd look like after giving head? What would my dick look like?

"Take me upstairs, Frat Boy," she whispers with a giggle.

Without another word, I grab her hand, weaving through the rest of the guests and refusing to make eye contact because I only have one goal, and that's spending the rest of the night with Mia naked.

CHAPTER TWENTY
MIA

Austin slams me against the wall of our hotel room, kissing me so fiercely, I can feel his growl rumble down to my stomach. He grabs my hands, pushing them up above my head, holding me in place as his hard body presses against mine, and I feel like putty, melding into him.

I didn't realize teasing him in an elevator full of guests would work him up so much, but I like it, and it had the added benefit of getting his mind off that unknown text.

"Grabbing my dick in the elevator," Austin says firmly between kisses. I close my eyes, lost in the sensation of being sandwiched between him and the wall. "Did you really think that was going to end with anything other than a spanking from me?"

"Spanking? You've been thinking about that a lot lately."

"Can't help it when my girlfriend needs to be taught some manners." I smile, thinking he's joking, but when I meet his heated glare, I realize he's being serious.

"Oh yeah? How are you going to teach me?"

"You'll see." I don't have time to ask him what that means because, with his hands holding my hips in place, he's already dropped to his knees. His hot gaze watches my chest heave as he pushes the slit of my dress apart to reveal the tiny G-string I wore tonight.

He takes me in for a minute with a low grumble. "I've been waiting to do this all night." Then he tips his chin forward, leaving a kiss on the small piece of fabric covering my mound, watching my reaction the entire time. "As hot as you look in these, I think they need to come off now."

Twirling the strings in his hands, he pulls my panties down my leg, almost tearing them. Before I can chastise him for potentially ruining my favorite G-String, his mouth is immediately on my pussy, and he's eating me out like a man possessed. His tongue flicks across my clit, his mouth covering every inch of my center. My body trembles at the sensation, and my legs wobble as they try to keep me standing up. In a desperate attempt to stop this from ending, I look for anything in the vicinity that I can grasp onto just to keep me standing.

I settle for the frame of the door to the bathroom, but my wrist is twisted, making it hard to hold. Lick after lick. Caress after caress. I'm lost in the pleasure, and as if Austin can tell I'm in trouble, he grabs one of my thighs and throws it over his shoulder. When I yelp in surprise, he does the same thing to the other, so I'm essentially straddling his face.

"What are you doing?" I pant out, already too close to coming for comfort. He can't answer because his mouth hasn't left my clit since he removed my panties. Swirling round, he sucks the little bud into his mouth, flicking it with his tongue, and I swear I've never felt a sensation like it before. He's relentless, and every time I think I'm about to come, he slows down, edging me until I'm dizzy. With Austin's shoulders as my only point of balance, there's a very real possibility that when I come, I'll fall over before it's finished. I thread my hands through his hair, hoping that's enough to spare a trip to the ER.

As if he knows why I'm clutching, he looks up at me with a grin, and he dips his tongue down to my center, using his nose to graze across my clit.

It feels phenomenal.

Breathing out, I greedily ride his face, letting his tongue dip in and out of me. Austin slams his palms against either side of the wall, and I gasp in shock, pulling his hair tighter because he starts to stand. "Austin," I shriek, but again, he doesn't answer because he's a man possessed, only interested in watching me fall apart because of his mouth.

As he moves, my body follows the line of his shoulders, so I'm effectively doing a reverse piggyback while he eats me out. Austin's hands grasp the fleshy part of my thighs, keeping his tongue firmly inside me, and I feel so alive.

Did Austin have this position planned, or was it spontaneous? I've never done more than the standard missionary, and this, well, this is something else. My head is spinning. My hips are riding his face, and this has never felt so good.

Pleasure tingles up my spine, and I crush my eyes shut because I'm so close.

"Ouch!"

When Austin pushes to his full height, my head whacks the ceiling and I have to crouch forward to make space. Austin is unfazed, though. It's like it didn't happen as he continues to lap me up, determined to keep going and giving me no time to catch my breath.

My head whacks the ceiling, and I nearly lose my balance as I crouch forward, making sure I don't hit my head again. Austin is unfazed. Giving me no time to breathe, he's lapping me up, determined to keep going, and I'm just along for the ride.

Where the hell did he learn this move from?

Unless something drastic happened while he was on the road, he's still a virgin, and I'd never expect him to have moves like this. So he's either watched a lot of porn, or he's just naturally good at getting me off–which is also a strong possibility.

"Oh, my." Is all I get out as his tongue swipes down, pushing into me with as much force as his fingers. Hyper-focused on making me come, his nose rubs against my clit, his hands dig into my thighs, and I'm right back to where I was before I whacked my head.

Panting and desperate.

"Yes," I call out, pulling at the strands of his hair, still crouching, but it's made his tongue feel that much better. "Keep going." As Austin notices my legs tremble, his fingers bite into my thighs, keeping me stable. Then he squeezes harder like he did the other night - firm and demanding - and that's it. I'm completely done. I fall apart with his tongue inside me, screaming so loudly that I'm sure we're going to get some noise complaints from the neighbors.

He holds me tighter, letting my hips rock against his face as I ride the wave of pure pleasure.

As I come down from my high, he languidly licks me, and kisses my center one last time before gently guiding me back to the floor.

"Where the hell did you learn to do that?" I ask, still somewhat breathless, and feeling a little ungraceful as he drops my thighs down and expects me to stand. With no panties on, and my dress scrunched to my hips, I feel utterly destroyed.

He shrugs, loosening his bowtie as he leads me further into the room. "My neck was hurting from the angle when you were standing on the floor. Didn't want to get a crick in my shoulder when I've got practice tomorrow, so it was easier to have you up there." Well, that confirms it. I'm a dripping wet mess because my boyfriend doesn't want neck strain. If this is him when he's not trying, then I don't know if I'll survive when he is.

I wobble behind him; my legs seemingly lost the ability to walk after that orgasm, with my heels not helping the situation.

"You okay?" He asks as he glances over his shoulder, his lips glistening with my wetness. He licks it away with a sexy smirk smacked across his face, and I nearly melt into a puddle. When did Austin become such a sexy, confident man in the bedroom? You'd think with the way I'm trembling that I'm the one planning to lose my virginity tonight, not him. Guiding me to the bottom of the bed, he stands behind me and pushes the dress straps off my shoulders to reveal my naked breasts. He traces an invisible line down my back until he gets to the top of my ass, right where the start of the zipper is. He strokes his fingers across the small of my back for a few strokes before grabbing the fastener and pulling the zipper down.

It's not long until the fabric falls to the floor in a heavy lump.

Austin's hand appears at my side, and I take it as I carefully step out of my dress because I'm already unsteady on my heels. There'd be nothing worse than getting caught fumbling out of my dress and falling on my naked ass in front of this man.

"Turn around," he commands, and I do as he says, fighting the urge to cover my heavy breasts. With my shoulders pushed back, I stand there, watching Austin take me in like he's trying to memorize every curve of my chest. "Have I told you about my biggest fantasy since meeting you?" I shake my head, licking my lips as I wait patiently for him to tell me. "Watching you kneel in front of me in nothing but heels while you suck my cock so hard, you leave lipstick stains."

His hands cup my breasts as his thumbs skate across my nipples, and I fight the urge to throw my head back. Before he can let me get lost in my own pleasure again, I push his hands off, stepping into his space. "I think we can make that happen, Frat Boy."

Pushing Austin's jacket off, he unbuttons his shirt for me, shunting it over his shoulders while I work on his belt. Unbuckling it, I pull his pants and boxers down in one fell swoop. His hard, thick dick stands to attention, and I kneel on the plush carpet to get a better view.

I rest my hands against his hips, and I nearly laugh because how the hell does he play baseball so well when he's got this behemoth of a bat in between his legs? It's a question I plan on asking him later. Right now, my sole focus is memorizing every inch of his cock. Wrapping my hand around him, I give him a squeeze and watch as he grows in my hand.

As I glance up at Austin, he lets out a shaky breath, and I swear he's shivering in anticipation. "Is this okay?" I ask, gently rubbing my thumb on the underside of his shaft before slowly moving my hand up and down.

"It's absolutely fine." He huffs out a nervous laugh. "You can keep doing that all night."

"I'd like to do a little more than that," I say as I bring my other hand to gently play with his balls. I take a swipe with my tongue at the tip of his cock, licking away the pre-cum that had already settled there. "Oh my God." He winces, throwing his head back but whipping it up again so he can keep watching me.

"Austin. Will you let me know what you like, and what you don't?" I swirl my tongue around the tip, padding it against the slit just to watch his reaction.

I'm not disappointed. He cries out in pleasure and starts panting as though he's just run a marathon. "I like that. I like it a lot," he huffs out and his grimace makes me stop for a second. I'm the first person to put my mouth on him, which must be a big deal. "Please don't stop so we can talk about this." His hand covers mine as he attempts to get me to keep moving. "I've held onto my virginity for long enough. All I want right now is your hot mouth wrapped around my cock."

Well, alright. He doesn't have to ask me twice. I kiss the top of his tip again before slowly sinking my mouth around him, gently sucking as I go. He chuckles sarcastically. "Why the hell did I wait so long to do this?"

I smile as much as I can with his dick in my mouth, and take hold of his hands for a minute, guiding them to my hair so he can direct me.

He scratches his fingertips across my scalp, sending bursts of pleasure straight to my core, and guides me to a pace that he likes. Slow and erotic. He seemingly wants to commit this moment to memory, and I'm going to do everything in my power to make sure it delivers.

I twist my tongue around his length as I force him deeper into my throat until there's nowhere else to go. "Mia." Austin can barely get out my name. His body is tense as his fingers clutch my hair. I'm sure he's worried about underperforming, but what he doesn't realize is that this is only the first time I'll have my mouth around him tonight. I'm going to have a lot more fun with him later.

I scratch my nails against his balls, tickling him, and his butt clenches. "What are you doing to me?" He shakes his head with a smile, but it doesn't stop me. I ever so gently scratch my nails across his skin, tickling the base of his cock as I'm there. I know he likes it. His legs are trembling, and his body is shaking right along with it.

Pulling my hair back, he does everything he can to try to stop me from deep throating him. "Mia, please stop. I'm going to come."

Not responding, I swirl my tongue around his shaft, taking him deeper and he throws his head in the air. "Why didn't I listen to Griss?" he cries. Massaging his balls, I suck a little harder, because I refuse to let him think about Griss while I'm sucking him off. "Oh shit. I'm sorry."

That's all he gets out before I feel hot, salty liquid shoot down my throat. His hips jerk into my face, and I keep my balance by holding onto his side as I swallow as much as I can. Well spent, his body limps forwards, and his eyes are closed with a pained expression on his face. As I pull him out of my mouth, I lick away every ounce of him and he lets out a low, drawn-out grumble while he watches.

His eyes close on a grimace, and he's still grumbling. He stays like that for so long, I'm worried that I've broken him. Gently dropping his length, I back away to give him some space.

Another few seconds later, he's finally garnered enough energy to haul his body up, and then he scrunches his hand over his face. Still groaning, he refuses to look at me as he runs a hand through his hair. "You shouldn't have let me come."

"Why not?" I say with mock innocence. Still on my knees in front of him. With furrowed brows, I look up at him with feigned confusion, and he rolls his eyes. "Why wouldn't you want to come on your first blow job?"

He cups my face, rubbing his thumb against my cheek lovingly, and then guides me to stand with him. Still a little wobbly in my heels on the thick carpet, I do my best to seem confident as I stand in front of him naked like this.

"Believe me, I wanted to come." As if on instinct, his face drops to the crook of my neck, and he leaves a kiss there. "It's just I didn't exactly plan on giving you a smoothie of my cum for the pleasure. I mean, hell, I had no idea that my body could produce that much."

I giggle when he nips at my skin and holds me in place. "Glad to know my mouth is better than your hand," I joke, but he still looks stressed. Snuggling into him, I thread my hands through his arms until I can scratch his back. "What's up? Why is coming after your first blow job as soul crushing as you're making out?"

Giving me a small peck on the lips, he offers me a lazy smile. "Because I'm pretty sure you just sucked out twenty-one years of sexual frustration, and I'm not sure there's anything left in the tank. Like ever again."

I raise my brow and crinkle my nose. "Come on, Austin. You're the best candidate for Rookie of the Year, and you're worried you won't be able to perform? You're young and in your prime. I'm sure you can get it up again if you try. If *we* try." Backing away from him, I turn, and make my way to the bed.

Sitting on the end of the mattress, I uncross my legs and then switch sides as Austin watches me with intensity. "Do you like what you see?" I ask him as my hand skims across my thighs, making my body tingle.

"Mhmm."

"Then tell me what to do."

Austin's eyes flare, and as he takes a step forward, I can already see his dick thickening again. See, he had nothing to worry about. Lifting my heel to his chest, I stop him from coming any further and shake my head. "Nope. You can't touch me just yet. You need to fill up your tank first." I grin when he frowns. "I want you to watch me for a little bit."

"You do?"

"And I want you to tell me what to do."

He smiles like he's a kid in a candy store and looks at me one last time to confirm this is what I want. When I drop my leg and keep my legs open lazily, he takes that as confirmation.

"Spread your legs further." His voice is commanding, his eyes burning into my center. I lean my hands behind me to the bed and slowly open my legs, feeling the cold air against my slick pussy.

Biting his lips as his hand falls to his crotch, he says, "Touch yourself."

"Where?"

"You know where, Boss Girl." I take my time, dragging my hand to my center, tickling the top of my mound to tease myself. I don't plan on working myself up to the point of climaxing because the next time I come, I want it to be when he's inside me. "Mia," Austin warns, but I continue to take my time in hopes that he'll deliver that spanking he's been promising.

My fingers tickle at the top of my clit, but I'm still a little too stimulated from when Austin ate me out, so I gently stroke myself. Not quite a feather touch, but close enough. Closing my eyes, I imagine it's his hands instead of mine and circle my clit, taking a sharp inhale as I moan out his name.

"Yeah," Austin groans, holding his now erect shaft. "You're not going to need to do that. I'm ready." He lets out an awkward chuckle as though he should be embarrassed that it took him all of three minutes and looking at his naked girlfriend to be ready for another round.

"Good." I smile, moving my hand away to make space for Austin's body. I've been thinking about this moment for too long. Not as long as Austin, but long enough. "Have you got a condom?"

Austin nods. "Yeah, it's in my jacket. Wait." He looks over his shoulder and grunts. "Where did my jacket go?" Moving off me, he looks around the bed haphazardly.

"Austin," I sing, but he's too busy cursing under his breath to pay attention.

"Shit. Shit. Shit."

"Austin." I try one more time.

"I can't believe this." He curses again, throwing everything he finds out of the way.

"Austin."

"What?" He finally looks at me and I have to hold back my laughter. Here he is completely naked with a hard on that reaches his belly button and he can't stop swearing over a lost condom.

I tilt my chin toward the lounge area. "Did you check the TV?"

He follows my gaze and sighs. His jacket somehow ended up there in the haphazard undressing. "Dammit. I'm sorry." He saunters over to his jacket, pulling it off the screen, and digs into his pocket until he finds a gold foil packet. I snort when the roll of condoms drops. He has at least twelve with him tonight, and even with his impressive stamina, I don't think we'll get through that many.

"Lucky you didn't lose that," I joke, trying to lighten the mood. He rips a condom off, dropping the rest on the floor, and watches me as I lie back on the bed. With my elbows as the only thing propping me up, I open my legs for him.

After taking a deep breath, Austin makes his way to me. Grabbing both of my legs, he pulls me down the bed until my ass is leaning against the edge and he's standing in between my thighs. He rips the condom wrapper with his teeth and pulls out the rubber, rolling it down on himself meticulously to make sure it has a good fit.

"Looks like you were paying attention in health class." I say, and he's still not smiling.

Once the bright blue condom is in place, he huffs out a long breath and gives me a hesitant smile. "Are you sure you're okay with this?"

I laugh, sitting up a little higher. "I'm literally lying here, legs wide open, dripping wet for you, and you want to check that I'm okay with it?" I wrap my feet around his shins in an attempt to feel him against me. It works. The subtle brush of his condom covered cock is enough to make me let out a little moan in surprise. "Please make love to me, Austin. I want to feel you inside me."

He looks down at my hips, and I know if I don't take action, then this isn't going to work. Clasping my hands around his neck, I kiss him passionately while dragging him onto the bed, hoping the move helps him relax.

With the pressure of his body on top of me, I sigh in relief, feeling his hardness against my thigh. He kisses me, long and slow, before adjusting himself, so his cock is sitting at my entrance. Taking one more breath, he uses his hand to ease himself in, kissing my nose as he does. "That feels good." I arch my back, thinking it might help, but I'm so wet for him, I doubt it matters.

"Shit," He groans, his hands slapping the bed on either side of my head. Stretching me in all the right ways, I've never felt fuller, and he sits inside me, letting me get used to his girth. Delicious pain pricks at my center because when I think he's done, he adds another inch, letting me get used to that before adding more.

"Oh, Austin." I run my fingers up his arms, scratching them across his naked back to encourage him to keep going. But he stops, and when I look at him, he silently assesses me. Drawing my hand to the back of his neck, I bring his face down until his ear is next to my lips. "You feel so good, Austin," I whisper. "Keep going." Then I bite at his earlobe before licking away the pain.

Panting hard, he says, "I want to, but you're so tight and warm that I'm worried I'm going to come after two pulses again."

I smile, scratching his back a little as I move my hips to get going. "You won't. That's why I gave you a blow job. You'll last longer, I promise."

With his hands resting on either side of my shoulders, he moves, and it's absolutely everything. Never has anyone filled me so completely. Not just sexually, but the connection I feel between us right now is unlike anything I've experienced before.

Austin's deep breaths skate across my skin, igniting my body as he adjusts himself. Grasping onto his biceps, I kiss him on the lips, offering him some encouragement. "I like that. Keep going."

His thrusts are languid at first, as if he's worried he'll break me. His slow and steady pace hits me in just the right spot. I'm becoming a withering mess underneath him, yet he's barely moved.

Biting my lip hard, I close my eyes, taking in the feeling of being so complete.

"Oh, God." He groans, and I open my eyes, surprised, but my lips curve into a smile no less.

"Is everything okay?"

His whiskey eyes drop to look at me, and he offers me a lazy smile. "Everything is perfect." Still seated inside me, he kisses me. Long and languid. "You're perfect," he says, kissing my nose. "This moment is better than I could have ever imagined." Then he burrows his face into my neck again, pulsing his hips in and out of me.

As Austin picks up the pace, tingles of pleasure run through my body. In and out. Hard and fast. His eyes darken as he watches me squirm underneath him, focusing on when I moan, and repeating that motion over and over again until I cry even louder.

My mind is dizzy, my body feels like it's on fire. With every thrust of his hips, I'm closer to the edge, and I have to grip the sheets for stability.

"Austin," it's all I get out before my body takes over. I can't hold back any longer. My center numbs, and back arches. I crush my eyes shut because it all feels too intense, and when Austin kisses me, I'm done for. White-hot pleasure sears through my body and my hips shift as I come.

"Shit, Mia. That's..." Without another word, Austin comes right along with me. He drops his head to my shoulder, his hips barely rock as he takes his own pleasure.

Exhausted, he falls on top of me, his weight stealing my breath as we both come down from our respective highs. Sweaty and wasted, I slap his back, uncurling my legs from him. As he rolls off me, I take in some much needed air and push back my damp hair.

Grinning, I say, "That was..."

"Everything," he finishes.

"That's a little dramatic, don't you think?"

He shakes his head, his hand capturing mine before he brings my knuckles up to kiss them one at a time. "Nope. I'm certain that there's a very real possibility you've ruined me for all other women because there's no way it can feel that good with anyone else."

I slap him on the chest, trying to roll away, but he holds my hand firmly in place and throws my thigh over his waist. We're sweaty, lying in our own mess, but it's blissful. "I'm pretty awestruck by the experience, too."

"Is it normal for my legs to feel so shaky after that?"

"Oh, Frat Boy. If your legs are shaking after that, you're going to be wrecked by the time I'm through with you tonight."

He bites his bottom lip, holding back a smile. "Oh yeah? What else have you got planned."

I sit up and straddle his hips, just above his dick, ready to have some more fun with him. "Lie back and find out."

***

Buzz. Buzz. Buzz.

Disappointment drips through my veins when the sound of a phone going off wakes me up instead of Austin. Last time we were in bed together, he lavished me with attention before I'd even opened my eyes, and part of me just assumed that was how it was always going to be between us. My body was Austin's playground, and I'd happily have him play with me all the time. Although, come to think of it, as much as I like the idea of being woken up by Austin's hands, I don't think my pussy could handle any more sex. The whole night feels like a blur. Countless orgasms in so many positions have brought me to the point of exhaustion that even getting out of bed feels unachievable. I ache in places I didn't know were possible, and when I turn over, expecting to feel Austin's warm body next to me, I'm greeted with cold sheets.

As I hear the water, I realize he must be in the bathroom, and as nice as it would be to join him, the bed is to comfy against my sore muscles to move.

Buzz. Buzz. Buzz.

What is that noise? I roll my head to the side, looking for Austin's phone, only to realize that it's *my* phone. I quickly grab it from the bedside table and check that it's not Jett.

Unknown: Wow. The Rookie Ball and a night in his fancy hotel room? I always knew you were a cheap whore, but I didn't realize you were that desperate for a quick buck. Am I really draining you dry, or are you spending all your money trying to snag a ball player?

Unknown: What does a Rookie make these days, anyway? Half a million dollars a year? Better hope Jett's new daddy is generous because I'm about to up my monthly child support bill.

I sit up, re-reading the words, feeling a chill run down my spine. He's going to try to get *more* money out of me? I can barely afford the money he takes already. What have I done? Why did I let this go so far? Could he get Jett?

"Mia, what's wrong?" Austin's in a towel by my side instantly. Had I made it that obvious that I was upset? A single tear drops onto my phone and there I have my answer. Unbeknownst to me, I've been crying the whole time. "Did you get another message?"

Initially, I find it hard to speak because how do you tell the man you're falling in love with about a past you'd rather forget. A past that, no matter how much you want to ignore it, will not go away. "Mia. Talk to me. Please."

Austin's kneeling between my legs, looking up at me, pleading for me to talk, but I can't do it. Not just yet. I fall into his arms, crying because I need to feel his arms around me one more time before he finds out the truth. How will he look at me after?

"There's something I need to tell you." I finally get out and pull away from him so I can see his face. He tries to hide it, but he's disappointed. He probably thinks I'm going to talk about online trolls, but he has no idea what I've been hiding and I'm not sure how he's going to take it.

"Okay. You know you can tell me anything, right?" He gives me a slanted smile, his hands holding me just a little tighter. "Even if it's that you have a secret husband you hate. You don't have to worry; I'll take him down and marry you in a heartbeat. Age be damned. It's you and me now. You get that right?"

His words are perfect and hit a little too close to the truth to be comfortable, but I try to give him a smile. It's the least he deserves since he's probably going to drop me like a hot frying pan when he finds out the truth. I just know it.

"So, Jett's dad's been messaging you," he starts because it's obvious that I can't build up the courage to tell him the truth.

"You read all that?" He nods and I scoot closer.

"Are you paying him child support?" Something about the way he says it makes me panic.

"It's a long story, but I hope you don't think I'm dating you because I'm trying to swindle you out of money."

A small smile passes his lips before it turns into a frown. "Didn't think that at all," he sighs. "I'm a Rookie. If you were dating for money, you would have gone for Brett or Max, or any other player on the team. Does he always send you threats like that?"

"From time to time, but they've gotten a little more frequent recently."

"And do you respond?"

"I tend to ignore them. Unless he gets particularly threatening."

"Seems to be working for you," he replies sarcastically. "How did he find out about us?"

"He has a particular knack for finding things out about me, but I guess it doesn't help that he's a Catfish fan."

Still so stoic, I can't tell what Austin is thinking, and it's unnerving. "How long has this been going on?"

"Too long."

"Since before we met?"

"Yeah," I sigh. "Seeing us together is just a bonus for him. This whole thing started before Hailey passed away."

"What happened?" He looks at me with genuine concern and care, which makes me balk for a second. Will he look at me the same way when he finds out the truth about Hailey? We've just had the perfect night, and I'm going to potentially ruin it. "Mia. Talk to me. Please. I want to understand."

Taking in a deep breath, he slowly caresses the top of my hand. He's still here. He hasn't walked away yet, so maybe I should give him the benefit of the doubt.

"Do you remember I told you I moved to Charlotte to go to college?" He nods. "Yeah, well, that wasn't the only reason. Hailey had been living there for a few years at that point, and she'd gotten pregnant after a messy one-night stand. I was leaving Georgia to go to college, and Charlotte Tech was one of my top choices anyway, so I thought it would be nice to come and help my sister out."

"Okay, and Simon wasn't in the picture?"

I shake my head. "I had no clue who Jett's father was. Whenever I asked her about it, she would give me the same answer. That she was irresponsible, and didn't get his number, and the name he gave her was fake. I believed her. I had no reason not to. For the first seven years of Jett's life, it all seemed fine. We were happy. When I wasn't completing my teaching degree, and then my masters at Charlotte Tech, I'd look after Jett while Hailey worked as a Personal Assistant in a local doctor's office. It was a great life." Tears prickle my eyes, threatening to fall at the mere memory of her.

"After graduating, I moved out and started a Teaching Assistant job, which was stupid really because I was at Hailey's house all the time. I guess one of my biggest issues was building a life outside of my family. I didn't really have any other friends or relationships, and at the time, I was okay with that."

Swallowing, I prepare myself for Austin's reaction to the rest of this story. "But then I met someone."

His face stills, and I don't know why it feels like I just cut Austin's heart out with a blunt knife, but it does. I'm sure there were people he was interested in before me, but it just seems so wrong to think that there were people in my past when he's the only one I see in my future.

Beside the tiny bit of tension in his jaw, he has no other reaction. "What happened then?"

Feeling a little flustered, I laugh humorlessly. "His name was Joey, and he told me he'd just moved to the area. I thought he was great. He swept me off my feet at the start. Took me on a bunch of dates and seemed genuinely interested. But after a couple of months, the initial excitement of having a guy interested in me had worn off. He had so many red flags. The main one being that he wanted to keep things casual. I wasn't into that, so I backed off, and he got the message."

"So, you stopped seeing him?"

"For the most part. I didn't have a reason to block him, so we'd talk every now and again. He said I was the first person he met in the area, so why not be friends? After a while, I would get fewer texts. We could go several months without speaking and I'd hardly notice. But then he'd come back in some loved up haze over me, and I'd go with it. I was in my twenties with no commitments, after all. Why not have some fun?"

Embarrassment scorches through my body at the admittance that I had fun in my twenties, but it's not something I can change.

"How long did that go on for?" His voice is stone cold, and he looks emotionless, like he's about to go up for an at bat against the best pitcher in the league and he doesn't want them to know how he feels.

"Nearly three years. On and off, but I knew it wasn't serious. He was too aloof and couldn't keep my interest for longer than a day. But every time I thought we were going our separate ways, or I'd meet someone else, I'd get a text from him asking to see me. It got to a point where it all started feeling a little too coincidental, you know? I couldn't speak to a guy without receiving a text from him. When I confronted him about it, he got a little possessive."

"Possessive in what way?"

I bite my bottom lip, wanting to hold back the truth, but knowing I can't. Not if I want this to work with Austin. "He started threatening me." I try to stop myself from wincing because I need to see Austin's reaction, and surprisingly, he took it better than I expected. He's clearly annoyed. I can tell from how hard he's squeezing my hand, but he seems to want to hear the rest of the story first.

"Did he hit you?" The calmness in his voice is threatening in itself.

"No. Just verbal threats. I didn't let him close enough to me for more."

"So that was the end with him?"

I raise a brow, thinking back bitterly to the day I had that argument with him. The day that would change everything. "I tried to, but he wouldn't accept it. He'd text and call me at all hours of the day. When I blocked his number, he'd get a new one. If I did answer, he'd say weird things like, 'I'm going to show you how much you're going to regret this,' and 'you can't leave me. I'm the one who decides when it's over.' All the usual things a threatening ex would say, so I didn't take him seriously. I kind of thought if I ignored it, he'd get bored and move onto someone else. Looking back now, I know that was the wrong move, and I should have gone to the police with the threats."

"What happened?"

Closing my eyes, I suck my lips into my mouth, hiding what I really want to say, and skipping to the most important part. "The day after I told him to leave me alone, Hailey and Jett were in a car accident. I was told she slipped on black ice, and to be honest, I was too devastated to really think straight. Within an instant, I had a ten-year-old that needed my help, and a funeral to plan. It wasn't in my mental capacity to question anything else."

I swallow the lump in my throat from the memories of that awful phone call with the police and picking Jett up from the station. He looked as lost as I felt. Austin ups my cheek with his hand, wiping away a tear from my cheek before grabbing a box of tissues from the side and offering me one.

I can get through this. I repeat to myself the same way I did when I was trying to heal after her death as pull a few tissues from the box.

"It was only after a few weeks that I started getting suspicious. The police were slow to release Hailey's body for her funeral, and then they started asking strange questions about where she was going. Apparently, she had three bags packed, and they assumed she was going on vacation. Jett wasn't talking, and I had no idea what they were talking about until I found a note on her fridge for me. All it said was she would call me when they got to where they were going. No stipulation on how long they'd be gone, or why they were leaving. She'd just left."

"Why would she do that?"

"To this day, I still don't fully know. I can only assume it had something to do with Simon."

His eyebrows cross in confusion. "But you didn't know him."

Laughing bitterly, I say, "Yeah, apparently, I did." I shake my head, only able to look at my twiddling thumbs because what I'm about to say is ridiculous. "When I started looking into getting legal guardianship of Jett because I didn't want him going into the system. I found his birth certificate, and that's when I first found out about Simon. His name was right there, added the same day Jett was born. Hailey knew the whole time about him, but she was keeping it from me. I contacted him because I thought he'd be able to help me." I push out an angry breath, and Austin pulls me onto his lap, and strokes my arms to comfort me. Not even his warm chest will make me feel better about this situation, and how naïve I was.

"And Simon agreed to meet you?"

I nod. "Yup. Even told me over the phone he'd be happy to give me full custody of him. I had all the papers ready and thought Jett was safe. But when I met him, that's when I found out that Simon and Joey were the same person."

"And Simon knew you were Hailey's sister?"

"It was the only reason he started talking to me in the first place. Pretty sure he was blackmailing Hailey to fund his drug habit since Jett was born. It kind of explains why his contact with me was so sporadic. I'm guessing he'd only call me when she'd stop paying and use it as a threat against her. It's all guesswork because they couldn't find Hailey's phone after the accident. All I know is that something led her to thinking she needed to leave to keep Jett safe."

"Do you think he hurt Hailey?"

"I believe he wrecked Hailey's car with every fiber of my being." It's a short statement, but Austin hears the power behind it.

"If you felt like that, then why didn't you go to the cops?"

"I did, but imagine how crazy I sounded telling them that story? No one believed me, and I didn't have an ounce of evidence."

"What do you mean? You said you dated him for like a year?"

"On and off. He said he didn't like his picture taken, so there were none of us together. Not to mention that they couldn't find any evidence that Joey and Simon were the same person. They had different numbers, different apartments, and were completely different people on paper. But I didn't drop it. I was so adamant that they needed to look into it that Simon threatened me with a restraining order. I was looking obsessed with him, and the detective working on my sister's case said he'd likely get it if I didn't drop it."

"Did he sign the papers?" I shake my head. "Then how do you have custody of Jett?"

"I was signed off as his temporary legal guardian after the accident. It seems no one will bother looking into it unless someone contests it."

He puts it all together. "And that someone is Simon?"

"Mhm."

"And that's why you're paying him? He's blackmailing you?"

"Yup." I laugh bitterly. "He's never wanted Jett, yet somehow, he had the power to take away my nephew. He told me he knew how easy it was to get Jett, and if I wanted to keep him, I'd have to pay."

"What an asshole."

"Paying him was the biggest mistake of my life, but I refuse to put Jett in a position that might mean he gets stuck in his 'father's' care. I've been afraid to go back to the police because a harassment charge on my record would bring Jett's custody back into question, and they could take him away."

"That won't happen."

"You don't know that, Austin." Breathing slowly, I choke out the last words. "I can't lose him. I just can't."

Austin crushes me in a hug, suffocating my tears. "Mia. I'm so sorry that you had to go through this." He kisses my cheek. "But you're not fighting this alone anymore. I'm here for you."

"But -"

"No. This guy is harassing the woman I love, and I refuse to let that happen. He's not going to get a cent more of your money."

"You can't stop him. Not without getting involved and giving him a reason to come after you."

"He's already using me to get more money out of you, so you might as well let him come after me."

"But he might," I pause.

Austin cups my face, leaning his forehead against mine. "Did you forget I can swing a bat pretty hard?"

"But he hurt Hailey." It comes out as barely a whisper because it's still so hard to say.

"If he hurt Hailey, she will get justice, but before we can deal with that, we've got to legally get Jett in your custody and take away his power."

"But what if we can't?"

He kisses my lips, making a silent promise with the peck. "But, Boss Girl, what if we can?" There's a determination in his expression that almost makes me believe him.

CHAPTER TWENTY-ONE
MIA

"Aunt Mia," Jett sings, spinning on the kitchen barstool as he watches the Catfish game.

"Yes?" I drawl out, barely paying attention to him because I'm too busy counting the brownies and sandwiches I've made to grovel to the organizers of the Carolina Youth program.

"Weren't you listening?" Jett pushes, because it's obvious I haven't.

"Nope," I pop out. When I finally look up, I see red. "Jett!" I grumble, swatting the pimento cheese sandwich out of his hand, and tuck it amongst the rest of the platter.

"Hey! I was eating that."

"How many did you eat?" I say, haphazardly counting the sandwiches again. When he doesn't answer, I look up quizzically.

Jett's lips are pinched as he tries to hide his laughter. "Only about four."

"Four?! I've just spent my whole Saturday morning making one-hundred-fifty of these to suck up to your team, and you're just sitting there, smugly eating my inventory."

He raises his hands in defeat. "It's not my fault you make the best pimento cheese sandwiches known to man." I roll my eyes, pulling out a brownie from the container and giving it to Jett before packing away the rest of the food in the cooler. "Besides, I don't think anyone is going to be counting the sandwiches. They'll be too busy wondering if that *Rhode* block of a pitcher got on the team."

Rolling my eyes, I look up at him, annoyed. "Considering you like that girl, that's the worst pun I've ever heard."

"Woah, who said anything about liking? Did Austin say something?"

My lip curls into a smile. "Didn't have to. You just admitted it all right there," I tease, and he blushes.

"Says the woman who's too busy staring at her boyfriend's butt to notice I ate ten brownies already." He smiles, popping the final brownie in his mouth, wiping any of the remnants on his shirt.

Staring at him slack jawed and surprised, I don't know what to say. Have we really gotten to the point in our relationship where he can say things like that? I feel seen, but for all the wrong reasons. "Jett," I drawl out because I still haven't figured out if I should chastise him or applaud him.

"Oh, wait." He turns to look straight at the screen, playing the Carolina Catfish game. "Did Austin just score another run?" I eagerly look up, expecting to see Austin running the bases, doing his little trot at third, but when all I see is a beer commercial, I frown. "Made you look."

"I thought you were thirteen going on fourteen, not ten."

"And I thought you were good at comebacks. Guess that's another thing you lose when you're old."

With pursed lips, I point my finger, desperately trying to be serious because Jett needs a mom figure, but watching him hold back his amusement makes me laugh. "I'm not *that* old."

"You sure about that? Because doesn't your birth year start with nineteen?"

"You know what? I'll remember this conversation when you're thirty, and we'll see how old you feel then."

He shakes his head, laughing. "And it will be the shortest conversation in history because I'll be in the middle of my baseball career with the Catfish, and you'll be living in a beautiful mansion up in the Charlotte Hills that I bought you."

"What?"

"That's always been my plan. I'm going to take care of you the same way you've taken care of me." My heart melts because I'm so happy I'm able to provide for him now. "Although." Jett narrows his eyes, looking at the tv. "Maybe I won't have to if you and Austin keep going strong. I bet he'll be a coach on the team by that point, and you'll be married with a couple of kids."

I glare at him with a furrowed brow. "Have you just mapped my life out for me?"

He shrugs. "I want to see you happy. Gotta have plans to make things like that happen, don't you know?"

So many questions, but so little time to get the answers.

Ding Dong.

"I'll get it." Jett jumps off the barstool before I've had time to respond. I just shake my head and take advantage of the quiet, packing away the sandwiches and watching the Catfish. They're losing at the bottom of the eight because their pitcher struggled in the first few innings, but it hasn't stopped Austin being productive. With a walk and two hits, he's had a pretty good morning if it's just his stats he's worried about.

"Umm, Aunt Mia?" Jett shuffles back into the room, confusion sprawled across his face. Wiping my hands on my apron, I take it off and rest on the counter before I make my way to him.

"What's wrong?"

"Nothing. It's just, um." He points his thumb over his shoulder. "There's some official looking guy at the door asking for you."

Some Guy?

It couldn't be Simon, could it? No. He wouldn't show up here because he needs to paint himself as the victim. Besides, it's way too early on a Saturday for him to be anywhere but at the wrong end of a toilet. "Wait here." I pat Jett on the shoulder, making my way to the door. My steps slow when I see a man in a suit that I don't recognize. He's running his hand across the beam of the porch, and I wonder why. There's no mortgage on this place, and I've paid all my bills this month, so why is he here?

Opening the screen door, I offer the man a tight smile. "Hi there. Can I help you?"

"Are you Mia James?" I nod, and that's it. He doesn't say anything else. Just shoves a brown envelope in my direction, and the minute it's in my hand, he takes a picture of me without my consent. "Thank you."

As he walks down the porch, I call out, "Wait. What is this?" I know he heard me, but he acts like he doesn't as he heads straight to his blacked-out car and leaves.

Staring at the envelope, my stomach fills with dread because as much as I hope it might be another surprise from Austin, I know it isn't. He wouldn't need to deliver anything to me like this. No. Deep in my heart, I know who it's from, and I should have known it was coming. Sighing, I look over my shoulder, making sure Jett isn't around, and then tear open the envelope.

Dear Miss. James,

It has come to our attention that you have unlawfully taken guardianship of Mr. Michael 'Jett' James.

With every word I read, my world crumbles just a little bit more because this can't be happening, can it? He can't be trying to get custody? Not after everything that's happened.

"Aunt Mia, what's wrong?" Jett asks, walking behind me.

I stuff the papers back in the envelope before tucking it under my arm so he can't see. I'll be damned if he finds out about Simon's manipulations. "Nothing." I swallow down the lie, not even feeling guilty because I know this move will protect him. "It's just a letter from one of the neighbors."

Jett surveys the area before eyeing me suspiciously. "Didn't look like any neighbor we have."

"Yeah." I wave him off. "It's one of their sons." I check my watch and look back up at Jett with a smile. "You know what? We don't have time to talk about this. We've got to get to your game, otherwise we'll be late, and we don't want to give them another chance to bench you, do we?"

Jett wiggles his eyebrows. "Not like they have many options since their first Catcher got hit in the shin yesterday. They have to play me, otherwise they have no one."

I raise my brow. "I wouldn't get so smug about it. You never know who they've got lined up on the sidelines. There are plenty of kids that would kill for the opportunity you have, remember?"

"Sidelines? That's football. We've got Dugouts. Have you learned nothing in the last three years?"

Groaning, I push him back into the house. "Get your stuff. I'm going in five minutes, with or without you."

When he heads up the stairs, I stuff the papers into my purse and immediately text Austin.

Mia: I know you're still out on the field, but I wanted to let you know that some guy in a suit dropped off a legal letter from Simon.

Austin: I'm off the field and we lost. I'm in the locker room, licking my wounds and preparing myself for tomorrow. What did it say?

Mia: I only skimmed it because Jett came over, but it looks like he's going to fight to get custody of Jett back.

Austin: Empty threat. That's never going to happen.

Mia: How can you be so sure?

Austin: The guy's a drug addict who has no relationship with his son. Think that pretty much rules him out immediately.

Mia: I hope so. Are you still coming to Jett's game today?

Austin: Of course. I'm already here. I will just take a shower and then I have a few things to go over with our manager, but I should be out in the stands with you by the fifth inning.

Mia: Good.

Austin: Bring the letter and we'll talk about it then.

Mia: Okay.

***

"Mia," Selena drawls out, throwing her arms around me in a hug as though we're best friends. I hug her back, because who knows, if Rhode and Jett stay on the same path, maybe we will be. "Can you believe our babies made it?" Her big, bright smile is contagious as she looks proudly at the Carolina Catfish field. The teams are just prepping for the fourth inning to a crowd full of scouts and proud parents. "I knew they'd regret making Rhode a reserve." She tips her head towards the bullpen, and sure enough, Rhode is warming up. Not surprised they took the starting pitcher out since he let five runs in over the first two innings. "First girl to play an official youth baseball game here," She says proudly. "They're both getting their chance."

"And I'm sure she's going to be awesome."

As the current pitcher stalks off the mound, cursing himself, Rhode jogs onto the field with a steely determination etched across her face. Selena cheers loudly before elbowing me in the side. "For a couple of kids that weren't supposed to be here, they're doing pretty good."

"Let's hope they can put their differences aside for this." Jett meets Rhode in the middle of the field, and he lifts his mitt, ready to talk strategy.

"Mia? What a pleasant surprise," Griss drawls out, saddling up next to Selena and draping his arm over her shoulder. She cringes when he kisses her cheek, but doesn't push him away. "Do you know Selena?" When I nod, he grabs his chest, looking between us, aghast. "You mean to tell me that you met my wife, and I didn't know about it? Why didn't Austin tell me? We could have gone on at least three double dates by now."

He leans closer to Selena, but she shoves her hand in his face, pushing his neck back. "How many times do I have to tell you? I'm not your wife."

He narrows his eyes. "Mhhm. So you have my baby, take my money, come watch my games, sleep on my couch when you've had a tough day, but you ain't my wife?"

Selena looks at me as though she's exhausted to be having this conversation again. "I have a boyfriend, and it's not him."

"You mean Trevor?" Griss spits out, looking around. "Because I don't see him. Haven't seen him around for a while now. Kind of think you're just using him as an excuse."

"Because he's tired of dealing with you."

"Good."

I raise my hands, looking between the two of them. "I think I might have walked in on something I shouldn't have."

"No, you're good," Griss smiles. "She likes roasting my balls. I've asked her to consider kissing them better, but she keeps saying no because she has a 'boyfriend.'" He mocks the word, looking at her with disbelief. "This Trevor guy is a real piece of work. Always cock blocking me."

"Stop it." Selena slaps him, wiggling out of his hold.

"Fine, fine. I'll leave you for now, but the conversation isn't over." He looks back at me with a sardonic smile. "So Mia, Selena, how did you guys meet?"

Selena points her thumb at the field. "I met her at the game last month before Rhode and Jett got kicked off the field, remember."

"How could I forget," he mumbles, shaking and then slapping his head with his palm. "That girl. How many bust ups is she going to have before she turns sixteen?"

"As many as it takes for her to get taken seriously," Selena retorts. "She's the only female out there, throwing harder than any of those boys, and she's only going up now because a pitcher worse than her is having a hard time under the pressure. It's ridiculous."

"I know, but believe me, they're taking her seriously. The number of prestigious high schools in the area offering her scholarships should be enough of an indication of that." He smiles proudly, but it fades a little when he looks at me. "I'm sure Jett's had the same. They might end up on the same team."

"He's had a few. Our luck, they'll probably end up rivals," I joke.

Griss lets out a low whistle. "Austin's not going to like that. Having to pick between his future nephew and his niece in everything but blood."

"Future nephew?" I spit out, my eyes widen in shock. We may be officially dating, but we're nowhere near the point of marriage. What is with all these people trying to marry us off?

"Uh oh, did I hit a nerve?" Griss smiles, watching my reaction.

"Not a nerve. Just it's only been a few months."

"Sure," Griss drawls out, unconvinced. He looks over his shoulder. "Where is the big guy, anyway? I thought he was coming out to watch in the stands for a little bit."

"He is." I look down onto the field, expecting him to be standing close to third base, but he's not. "He said he was coming up here for the top of the fifth and that he'd bring food."

Griss nods, laughing. "Ah food. I bet he's going to come out here with two hot dogs and bypass the fact that he ate four before seeing you."

"Why would he do that?"

"You've seen him. The guy's a beast. He has to eat a lot of meat to feed those quads in order to sustain them." Selena slaps Griss in the chest, chastising him. He holds his pec, rubbing himself, pretending it hurts. "What? It's the truth."

"Says beanpole over here." Selena elbows him in the stomach and Griss grimaces. For all intents and purposes, they seem like a cute couple, or ex-couple, I guess.

"You know what? I might just go and check where he is. We don't want him missing Jett and Rhode's joint start." They both nod as I flitter past them, heading to the central concourse as I look for the broad shoulders amongst the crowd. I nearly laugh, because never in a million years did I think I'd be standing in the Fishbowl, looking for my twenty-one-year-old boyfriend while my nephew plays on the field. It's like I'm living some crazy fever dream, and I never want to wake up.

I check my phone, and there's a message from Austin saying he's coming out, so I keep looking out for him. As I walk through the concourse, my feet slow because as I pass less people, an uneasy feeling bubbles in my stomach.

Austin's coming. He'll find me. I'll just make my way to the clubhouse entrance, and he'll find me. I drop my gaze to my feet in hopes that it will calm my churning stomach, but as the concrete floor meets the concrete floor, I realize I'm at a dead end.

"Stupid Mia," I whisper under my breath before turning around, but I nearly fall on my ass when I hit a hard chest.

A very familiar hard chest.

"Mia," he drawls out, venom spitting from his voice. I don't dare look up because this can't be happening. Not today. This has to be a nightmare. Nothing more. Memories of him have just come to the forefront because I talked about him to Austin this week. I'll wake up from this dream and be in Austin's arms any minute now. "Long time, no see."

So cold. So callous. That voice is like poison slithering up my spine, taking hold of the back of my neck, and paralyzing me.

What do I do?

I can't run. No one is going to hear me from here. It would only be a distant scream that would more than likely be mistaken for a random fan rooting for her favorite player. It's just him and me here, and nothing will change that.

"How have you been, Sweetheart?"

I take a shaky breath, trying to think about the positives. If Simon's here with me, then he's nowhere near Jett, so he can't ruin his big moment. Jett will be cheered on by the crowd without me in it, but at least he's safe.

Although every fiber of my being is urging me to push past him and run, my feet stay firmly planted on the ground. I can't move, much less fight off a one-hundred-and-eighty-pound dude.

"What are you doing here, Simon?" I do my best to sound strong, but something about this man makes me feel as shaky as a leaf.

He lets out a low chuckle, taking a step forward. He's practically in my face now, even though I refuse to give him any eye contact. His thick, fat finger touches my chin, tipping it up so that I'm forced to look at him. Black angry eyes and a sinister smile greet me. He looks tired, and a little more unhinged than I remember.

"My son is playing for the scouts at The Fishbowl Stadium. Did you really think I'd miss out on an opportunity like this? I even got him a gift. Bought by you, of course." He holds up a Catfish Jersey with Inwood sprawled on the back of it. "Figured he could wear his actual last name instead of yours."

I bite down so hard on my tongue, the metallic taste of blood rushes into my mouth. I snatch the jersey out of his hand instinctively and ball it up. "Why are you here now? You've missed every other opportunity that led to this point, so why is this one different?"

I don't care about the answer, but I know that the best way out of this situation is to keep him talking because that way I have more chance of someone walking by and seeing us.

Simon's smirk curls into a wicked grin. "Well, things change when you've produced a potential major league baseball player." He rubs his thumb and forefinger together, and I should have known he'd be after Jett for the potential money.

"You need to leave."

I try to sidestep around him, but he stops, standing in my way. "Aw, I can't leave now. That would be a waste of a good trip." He pouts his bottom lip out, mocking me. "If only you had responded to my messages with more than a 'fuck off,' then you could have told me not to come."

"Last time I did that, you got me monitored by the police and threatened me with a restraining order."

He laughs, looking up at the sky. It's full and hearty, as it echoes around the room. He really finds himself funny. "Oh yeah, I did, didn't I?"

I try to step around him, but he grabs me by the arm, pulling me back into his chest. The touch makes my entire body recoil in disgust, but I lift my chin up, refusing to let him see how scared I am.

"Where are you going? It's been so long; I hoped we could get reacquainted." His hands grab at my waist, but I swerve out of his hold.

"Reacquainted? Sorry, Si, but I've got to get back to my boyfriend." I emphasize, hoping that will make him back off because he knows there's someone waiting for me. Unfortunately, it seems to have had the opposite effect, and he steps forward, brazenly grabbing me again, and throwing me against the wall. I hit my head hard, and even though the pain throbs, I don't let it show.

Simon raises his brows in surprise, letting out a sarcastic breath. "So, you admit it. Austin Adams is your new boyfriend?" He asks with unrestrained glee. "Can't wait to share child support with him when I gain custody of Jett."

Closing my eyes because the room is a little hazy, I take a deep breath, trying to get my bearings, but that hit is proving harder to shake off than I'd like.

"You're never getting Jett, and I'm not paying you child support."

"Oh, but Mia, my darling, you already do." I crush my eyes shut, the pain getting unbearable. "What do you call the monthly payments you give me now?"

"Blackmail."

"Yeah, I can see how you might think it sounds like that." He tilts his head, contemplating something, and I look over his shoulder, hoping to see someone, *anyone* is coming our way so I can get out of this mess before I fall on the floor with a concussion. "But remember, you're the one who's paying me to keep my child illegally. That's frowned upon in most states, you know."

"That's why you're bluffing. You aren't going to tell anyone anything because it will get you in trouble, too."

He lets out a low laugh, his eyebrow arching in question. "Is that what you really think? That I'm too afraid to go to the cops about you kidnapping my son?" I tip my chin up because it's the only response I can muster. "You know what? The best thing that ever happened to me was you going to that ball with your lover boy. Got to see the pictures that confirmed you were together, which meant I could hire myself a fancy lawyer. It'll be on your dime, of course, because he's certain it's an open and shut case that I'll win."

"What are you talking about?"

"Haven't you read my court papers?" He tuts out. "Guess you didn't have time yet. How about I give you a sneak peek? I'm getting Jett back, and you'll be paying me a hell of a lot more now for the pleasure. Might even get a few charges thrown in for fun."

My head is spinning, and the words get caught in my throat. Dread trickles down my stomach, along with warm liquid by my ear. He's bluffing. There's no way anyone would see him as more than an addict.

"I don't believe you."

"You don't have to. All I have to do is convince a jury that I wasn't in my right mind after the love of my life was killed and I only agreed to an arrangement with you because I didn't want my only son going into the system."

"But I'm paying you to keep him."

"Exactly. You're trafficking my child." That word. Trafficking? He can't get me on that kind of charge, can he? "You were always so jealous of Hailey, weren't you? Makes sense. She was the funny, pretty one who had a good head on her shoulders. There was only one night where she lost control and that was probably more to do with the Rohypnol that I slipped in her drink than anything else."

Piecing those words together, I want to vomit, because that can't be true. He didn't drug her, did he? He's just trying to get under my skin. She would have told me.

"Must have been hard being nothing more than a sidekick, and a byline in her story. Hell, the only date you got for three years was me, and I was only interested because I wanted to tick Hailey off."

Simon's leaning over me now, his hands on either side of my face as I cower below him. What a stupid move on my part to leave Griss and Selena and getting stuck out here, alone with a head injury.

"I wasn't jealous of Hailey." It's a pathetic response, and my words are drawn out because I'm losing my ability to think straight.

"You're right. You probably weren't, but it sounded convincing, right? Won't be hard to convince a jury either. I mean, look at you. Living in her house, raising her kid, and you even dated me because your sister couldn't have anything of her own, could she?"

He lets out an arrogant laugh, his eyes roaming my body. "I don't think it would be hard to convince anyone that you were the one to ensnare me. Look at you now, acting like an immature cougar, dating a boy nearly a decade younger than you. What kind of impression is that leaving on my teenage son?"

I never fully understood what people meant when they said it felt like their world was crashing down on them until right now. Every fiber of my being feels like it's going to explode, to crash and burn because the one thing I've been dreading the most is happening. He's got it all figured out. He's going to take Jett, and there's nothing I can do about it. I always knew that my guardianship could be ended at any moment because I wasn't his parent and didn't have any legal holding, but I never thought Simon would come back and do this, especially since I'm still paying him.

"Simon. Please." I raise my hand, stepping aside, and surprisingly, he lets me.

"Please? Please, what?"

"Please leave Jett and me alone. We have nothing to offer you. I've never bothered you about Jett. You've shown no interest in him, and you have nothing to offer us because you're a deadbeat."

Simon grips my arm, making it impossible for me to move as his fingers dig deep into the skin. "Careful, Mia. You don't want to end up like Hailey, do you?"

My blood runs cold, and I search his dead, dark eyes for the confirmation of the fact I always knew to be true. Jett was right. He was there, and as I look at Simon longer, he confirms it with the nod of his head.

"What happened to Hailey?"

"I wouldn't know," he drawls out, still holding onto my arm so tightly that he's restricting the blood flow. "But I can't imagine smashing into the side of her car would have been easy. The person was probably pursuing her for a while before he forced her into a ditch. I'm sure whoever did it got a little thrill at watching the car roll three times, though."

He did it.

He killed her.

I have all the information and evidence I need, but no proof once we walk away, and he knows that. That's why he told me, because he knows I can't prove a thing and the more I try to push it, the more desperate I look.

"Was she leaving town because of you?"

"Did you really think she'd leave you voluntarily?" he asks, his stare so intense that I have to look down. I can only hope that the crazed glare wasn't the last thing Hailey saw.

"What do you mean?"

"I may have threatened your life a little." He holds up his thumb and forefinger, smiling. "Did you really think the woman that put you down as the legal guardian of her son, if anything happened to her, would just up and leave you without so much as a goodbye?" He shakes his head, tutting out in disapproval. "Wow, Mia. You're more naïve than I thought. I always knew that's why I liked you better. You were the damaged one. Easy to manipulate because you thought you were only ever destined to be your sister's helper. The one so desperate for approval from anyone that you'll date a child just to feel special."

With blood now matting my hair, I know I don't have long until I pass out. I need to get away from him before that happens, so I try to break my arm out of his hold, but he's not budging.

"Let go of me," I yell, but with no one there to hear, it's useless. His fingers dig into my arm, and I fall to my knees in pain like a broken rag doll. There's no way I'm getting out of this. He's so much stronger than me, and as he towers over me, I suddenly feel woozy.

I blink a few times and when I open them; I smile faintly because a familiar set of sneakers come into view.

"What the FUCK is going on here?" Austin's thick voice cuts through the air like a knife, making Simon jump.

He found me. I should have known he would.

CHAPTER TWENTY-TWO

AUSTIN

Stay calm. Stay calm. Stay FUCKING calm.

It's the same mantra I've been repeating in my head since I couldn't find Mia in her seats, and Griss had no idea where she'd gone. I searched the whole freaking concourse for her, before remembering that Jett had that stupid 'find my friend' app installed on his phone. It was only after delaying the start of the fifth inning so Jett could ping me her exact location that the mantra started to work.

However, the minute I walked down this quiet hallway, it took every ounce of resolve in me not to murder this idiot for touching Mia.

She's on the floor, her head bleeding, and this guy is doing nothing to help her.

"Mia. Are you okay?" She looks at me with a hooded glare, barely conscious, but just enough to give me a smile. Too bad that jack hole still has his hands on her, because I'm about ready to snap his neck.

"And here he is himself. The great Austin Adams, ready to save the day like any perfect Prince Charming would be."

Don't kill him. Don't kill him. Don't FUCKING kill him.

You will be worthless to Mia and Jett if you're sitting in jail beside this idiot. Just get him the hell away from Mia, and then you can deal with him legally.

"Glad to see you finally graced us with your presence. I was beginning to think this whole relationship was one-sided, and Mia was stalking yet another man."

I clench my fists, finally taking those breathing exercises that yoga instructor taught me seriously. I can't touch him. Mia will kill me, and I'll kill him.

He drops Mia's arm, and she slacks against the wall. At least I can take stock of the fact that he's not touching her now. As he takes a step toward me, I push him out of the way, crouching in front of Mia to check on her. "Austin," she wisps out, and even though there's blood tickling down her cheek, she's giving me a weary smile.

"Are you okay?"

"I'm fine now that you're here."

"Let me deal with this, Boss Girl. Call security for me," I whisper before turning back to the idiot that thought it would be a good idea to touch my girl. As I reach my full height, the confidence he had before I arrived slowly drains from his body.

He steps back, fully aware that I could easily beat the crap out of him if I did so wish.

Oh, and did I wish to kill him right now.

He leers at Mia one final time before holding his hand out to me. Strange, he wasn't who I pictured when Mia described the guy blackmailing her. I thought he'd at least have a couple of skull tattoos, and maybe a rat tail, but he's got nothing. He's just an average, nondescript guy – perfect for hiding in plain sight.

"I'm Simon." Of course he is. I knew that the minute I saw Mia's face when he touched her. "It's nice to finally meet the man who's not only taken it upon himself to become my son's adoptive father, but is going to help support my lifestyle from now on."

"Leave Jett out of this." Mia mutters from the floor, but I step in front of her, not wanting Simon to engage with her again. He needs to know that she and Jett are protected by me now. "Is there something I can help you with? As you heard, the fifth inning has just started, and I'd rather not miss any more of the game."

Simon shuts his mouth, a little taken aback by my directness, but instead of stepping back, he doubles down. "He's coming home with me tonight."

"Who? Jett?" The guy nods, and I clench my fists, holding back from punching him in the face at his sheer audacity. I'm not stupid. The guy probably has a taser hidden under that polo shirt.

"Yeah, he is my son, after all. Mia and I have agreed that Jett should be with his father and not raised by his hapless Aunt that's too busy fucking a teenager to look after her nephew properly."

My fist curls. The only thing stopping me from punching Simon is the fact that Mia's foot is touching mine, centering me. It's a reminder that we've already got a plan, and any deviation from it could affect us all.

"So at the end of the game, it would be great if you could fetch his bags and bring them to my car for me. Use those muscles you got for something useful since your brain has a few more years before it's fully developed."

"Simon," Mia warns from behind me.

"What?" He laughs, looking at Mia over my shoulder. "You can't say I'm wrong. He's barely legal, yet you're making a show and dance about fucking him. Don't worry, it's all good. It only helps my case for custody and that restraining order I'll put on you, too."

Ignoring him, I take Mia by the hand. "Come on. Let's get back to our seats." It's a ridiculous statement considering her face is covered in blood, and she's in serious need of medical attention, but I have to walk away from this guy before I do something stupid.

"Jett isn't coming home with you. Not tonight. Not ever. We will see you in court if you're brave enough to show up."

With Mia firmly protected under my arm, I shove past Simon, ready to take Mia to the first aid room.

"Austin, before you go. Can you tell me how it feels to be fucking a used, old pussy? Guess women give better head when they can take their dentures out." Simon throws his head back, cackling.

That's it.

Any ounce of decorum is out the window. I'm done listening to him threaten and berate Mia, and I don't care about the consequences. This idiot deserves a taste of his own medicine. Turning, my fist connects with his jaw before he's had time to register what I'm doing. His head bounces back as blood splatters to the floor and the sound of his jaw cracking reverberates against the concrete walls.

"Austin, no." Mia's yelling, and I can feel her clawing at my back, but she can't stop the inevitable. He's set me off, and there's no stopping me when I'm in this mood. He deserves this. Blow after blow, he connects a few punches himself, but he's about as useless as a wet dishrag in a pool, so I take it easy on him by just batting away his punches and pushing him out of the way.

With each attempt, the blood trickling from his nose becomes more obvious, dripping down off his chin and onto the floor.

He takes a step back, licking away the blood between his teeth. He looks crazed, and slightly feral, but happy. Not the reaction I'd expect from someone who just had their ass handed to them.

He cackles before resting his back against the wall, staring at me as though he's got a secret I don't know.

"What are you so happy about?"

He smiles, His gaze cuts to the ceiling, and I see the little white device in the corner. "Surprised a guy like you would forget that there are cameras everywhere in this place." He drags his body to the floor, lying in a way that makes it look like I threw him there. "I bet someone in security is calling the police right about now."

Color drains from my face, because, fuck, he's right.

What the fuck was I thinking?

I played right into his hands. He was purposely goading me, and I took it hook, line, sinker.

Fuck! Getting arrested will screw over my entire career.

Mia's hand wraps around my arm as she tries to pull me away. "Come on, Austin." People are walking towards us, and I know it's too late to get out of here without getting in more trouble for leaving the scene. Simon set this whole thing up to make me look like the bad guy. Planned it to not only fuck with me, but to fuck with Mia.

Mother fucker.

"Everything's going to be alright," Mia says, but as I come down from the adrenaline rush, I know that's not true. The leagues have rules on violence, and I just broke every single one. If that recording gets out, my entire career is over.

I hear footsteps, but everything happens so fast, all I feel is the cool metal of the handcuffs hitting my wrist like an ice-cold reminder that I'm screwed. As the officer reads my rights, I check out Mia, thankful that she's at least being treated for her injury.

How the hell am I going to explain this to my club? I've seen ballplayers lose their career over less than this, and there's video footage which I have no doubt will get leaked to news outlets.

As security drags me away, Mia watches me with interest and something inside my chest spikes. A strange sense of calmness radiates through my body when she smiles, albeit wearily, because I may have completely fucked my career, but at least it's for the person I

21.

CHAPTER TWENTY-THREE

AUSTIN

Clasping my hands together, I rest my head against the cold concrete and watch the slow dripping of water from the ceiling, across the yellow paint to the concrete floor. There's a pool of puddle building up around a hole in the floor. To what? I have no idea, but I'm hoping I won't be in here long enough to find out.

I close my eyes, thinking about everything that happened tonight and how ridiculous it all sounds. Simon tried to take Jett, and he seems to think he can just waltz into Mia's life and scare me away? So he can what? Torture her some more? Take her money? Fat chance of that happening. I'm going to end this whole thing if it's the last thing I do.

"How does it feel to be losing your career?" It's a short, succinct statement and I take a minute to open one eye to see a man in front of me. With swept back, perfect black hair, and sharp blue eyes, the guy looks like he should be behind a desk doing my accounts, instead of sitting here in an orange jumpsuit. "You're that ball player, aren't you?" He points at me with a wry smile. "Austin Adams."

Great. A guy that knows who I am. I've been here for the better part of four hours, and no one has bothered me, but I guess anonymity was too much to ask during my most embarrassing moment.

How does it feel to be losing my career?

It's a question I've been asking myself over and over as I watch the water drip. I can kiss Rookie of the Year goodbye once this gets out, that's for sure. Am I going to be a pariah on the team now? The one they treat differently because they know I tried to beat up a man who looked at Mia the wrong way.

Mia. Mia. Mia. Is she okay? Everything happened so fast. I don't know what happened to her after I was escorted out in handcuffs and she was getting medical attention. I tried to ask the police when I was transferred to them, but they wouldn't say a thing, no matter how many free Catfish tickets I tried to bribe them with.

"Yeah, how'd you know it was me?"

"They let us watch tv in prison, you know?" He sits beside me without invitation, looking at the large room in front of us. There are maybe ten or eleven other men in this room for 'recreational' time, which consists of us sitting around a large room that resembles a school hall while we ignore each other. I've been here less than a day, but time moves slowly, and I'm getting twitchy. Not to mention I look terrible in orange, and I'm having to wear XXXL pants because nothing else would fit my quads.

"Baseball is the easiest thing to have on in the background. It's on every day and takes forever to finish."

"Surprised you get coverage with all the blackout restrictions."

He laughs. "You know, I used to have that problem when I was outside the joint, but apparently, in jail, there are no territory issues to worry about."

"Glad to hear it," I say with a little sarcasm, but if he hears it, he ignores me. I should try to be nicer. I'm not ticked off at him, after all. I'm ticked off with the fact that I've been here so long and still haven't had my one phone call. The last time I saw Mia, she was barely stable on her feet and had dried blood smeared across her face and in her hair. I need to make sure she's okay, and the longer I sit here, the more annoyed I get. Especially when I think about the security guards that arrested me but didn't touch Simon.

Were any of those guys in on it?

He clearly had someone helping him if he knew where the cameras were, and I just want to make sure that Mia didn't get dragged into anything further when I wasn't there to protect her.

"You know what's funny? I've never really seen a baseball player in here before." The guy chuckles to himself, shucking his chin. "See a lot of hockey players, but never a ballplayer."

"Oh, yeah? How long have you been in here?" I ask with curiosity since I thought this was only a holding area for people until they were officially or unofficially charged with something. I assumed convicted prisoners were sent on to a different facility.

"Six months, and I've seen as many hockey players from the Charlotte Thrashers come in and out." He spins his wrist, acting like it's nothing. To be fair, the Thrashers take their name a little too literally at times, so seeing them around is probably like any other day. "Doesn't matter whether it's a baseball or puck, athletes are all the same. You'll be out like the other guys within a few hours because your teams don't want the PR disaster."

"I hope so." I crack my knuckles, wondering which guys he's met from the Thrashers to see if there's any way they might be willing to help me since I'm going to need someone with expertise in damage control, and I don't think Mary, our PR manager has had to deal with something like this before. Although Grayson does give her a run for her money at times.

"What'd you do?" He gestures to my eye, which I can only assume is a little black and bruised from when Simon landed his one punch, but since there aren't any mirrors in here, I haven't seen it.

"A guy was stalking my girl and her kid." That's when my fists tighten, because the mere thought of this dude getting anywhere near Mia or Jett again makes me want to punch a wall. The minute my fist connected with his jaw the first time; I realized something very important. Jett and Mia are mine now. Mine to protect. Mine to work hard for. Mine to build a life with, and I will do everything in my power to make sure that Simon doesn't get anywhere near them again, even if it means losing my career.

He raises his hand. "Say no more. I get it. If a guy touched my girl, I'd kill him."

"Glad someone understands," I mutter as I close my eyes, sighing because even in my angry haze, and no matter how good it felt in the moment, I knew while I was doing it I shouldn't have punched him. Acting like an immature college student in a bar fight only fuels the Frat Boy persona, and how am I ever going to get Mia to take me seriously if I don't start acting like a responsible adult?

I roll my neck to look at the guy again. "So, what are you in for? Bar fight or speeding ticket?" Because that seems to be the only two reasons people get stuck in here.

"Neither." He shakes his head, laughing sarcastically. "Sounds crazy, but I've been sitting around waiting for my trial for the last six months. Every time I think it's going to come around, they just keep pushing it back."

"Have they said why?"

He rolls his eyes. "The prosecutors keep hiring more expensive lawyers who say they are continuing to compile evidence. Every week they come up with something new that keeps me here just a little longer."

"So, wait. They haven't formally charged you with anything?" He shakes his head. "But they're forcing you to sit in here while they find something to pin on you?"

"Yeah, well, they seem to think I'm a 'flight risk,'" he mocks with air quotes. "I have a jet and a private island where I'm technically King since I'm the only permanent resident. Once I get there, I'm untouchable as we have no extradition treaty with the US."

"Wow. You own a private island? How does someone get that rich?"

"Oil, and a lot of dirty dealings," he replies with a straight face.

"Is that what you're in for? Fraud?"

"Nope," he pops out, waving his hand in front of himself. "It was a misunderstanding. They seem to think I killed my wife and her lover when I found them naked in my bed together." The smile he cracks doesn't make it sound like it was a misunderstanding. "The only evidence they have is the fact that I found them. There was a heck of a lot of blood all over the bedroom, but they'll never find the murder weapon, so there's nothing to pin on me." Still not helping. "Best bit, they can't use any DNA evidence against me anyway because it was my bed they were fucking in." He shrugs it off like it's nothing. "Talk about karmic justice."

I stare at him for a few minutes, hoping that he'll tell me he was joking, or something. He doesn't. He just leaves it at that. And waits for my reaction.

Act cool. Don't freak out because he knows my name. I could be next.

Leaning back, I scratch my hands across my legs. Well, this conversation has taken an unexpected turn and I don't know what to do. Sure, I punched a guy a few times, but do I really want to befriend a potential serial killer while I'm here? Wait, is he considered a serial killer? When does a serial killer become a serial killer? Is it after two or three kills? Either way, I don't want to be his next victim, so I act naturally.

"Karmic justice, indeed." I raise my brows, inwardly cursing myself.

Indeed? *Indeed?!* Really?

Before I make more of a fool out of myself, the entrance door swings open, and a guard comes strolling in. "Adams. Austin Adams."

My ears perk up because someone must be looking out for me. From my understanding, the only reason you get called up is you're released on bail, or your lawyer is here to talk. Since I haven't had my first phone call, or spoken to a lawyer, I'm assuming only Mia knows I'm here.

"You know what? That's me," I squeak out. "It was nice meeting you…." I stand before he gets too close.

"Dean," he drawls his name out as cool as a serial killer would and offers his hand. I guess I have to accept it. I'm quick with the limp, lackluster shake, but I'm unwilling to do anything that would make a fuss because I don't want to be that third dead body. "Good luck with your season. Hope to see you again."

I nod with a weak smile, then turn on my heel as fast as I can. "I hope not," I mumble, walking as fast as my big thighs will take me.

Please, please, please be someone with bail.

The correction officer watches me the whole way, offering me a curt nod as I walk in front of her. I hold out my wrists, fully expecting to be handcuffed, but she just stares down at my hands, nonplussed.

I drop my hands after she tilts her head in a gesture for me to move, and I scoot past her with a short, 'thank you' to try to appease her. What am I supposed to do in a situation like this? Do I try to talk to her? Maybe make a joke or two to lighten the mood, or would that be considered offensive?

"Where are we going?"

She looks over her shoulder with an eyebrow raise, and for some reason, the same mischievous smile that Caterina pulled on me so many nights ago comes flashing back. Not the right time to think about flogging equipment. "You'll find out soon enough."

Déjà vu hits me harder than I'd like to admit. Could this all be a joke set up by Griss? No. I've lost my V-Card and besides, this would be way too elaborate a scheme for him to pull off.

"In here." She opens the door to an interview room and jerks her head in its direction. I follow her orders, walking into the room and stop in relief when I see the two men standing in front of me.

Grayson inhales sharply before whistling. "Ouch. That looks like it had to hurt." He slaps an already wincing Tate on the shoulder. "Looks almost as bad as when Catty the Catfish humped your leg. Do you remember that?" He doesn't wait for Tate's answer, instead he walks past him straight to the prison guard with a grin.

"Louisa," he sings. She looks less than amused.

"Grayson Hawk. I was hoping I'd never have to see you again."

He raises his hands, letting out an amused chuckle. "Ah, I'm sorry I've stopped having bust ups with coaches. Blame my girlfriend. She keeps me on the straight and narrow." He winks. "Now, if you don't mind, we can take it from here."

"That's not how it works, and you know it. You get five minutes with him and then I'm back." She looks pointedly between us before shutting the door and locking it.

"I hate to say it, Rookie, but orange isn't your color."

"Gray," Tate warns. "At least he won't be in for long now that we're here."

"Are you here to bail me out?" Tate nods. "How the hell did you find me?"

"Mia." Just the mere mention of her name, and I can feel my mood perking up. "She called Cali. Apparently, she had her number from some teacher event, and I brought this guy." He points to Grayson with his thumb. "For moral support."

"Mia? You spoke to her? Is she alright?" I sound like a desperate puppy, but I don't give a shit. All I want to know is if Mia's okay.

"She's fine. Took a blow to the head, so they took her to the hospital as a precaution, but I believe she's at home with Cali right now."

"What about Jett?"

"Jett?" Tate raises a brow. "Oh, you mean her son?"

"Her nephew," Grayson corrects, which surprises me. I didn't think he was that observant. "Matt Grissom offered to take him to his house while Mia spoke to the police because he was freaking out."

"Griss was involved too?"

"The inning was postponed. Jett was taken out of the game, and Matt took him to calm down. We figured that you'd rather we pick you up instead of Coach." He lets out an awkward smile. "Plus, he's busy trying to figure out how to save your ass so you aren't suspended, and this is kept quiet. Your stats deserve at least a consideration for Rookie of the Year, and they want to make sure you get that chance."

"He's not mad?"

"No. Why would he be?"

I look around at the concrete walls, assuming the answer to that question is obvious. "Because I'm in jail?"

"Yeah." Grayson butts in. "You were arrested because the security guard saw you punch that idiot. Once the cameras were reviewed and they heard Mia's side of the story, it was obvious that little twerp provoked you." He laughs. "Although, when I faced a similar situation, I had enough control *not* to throttle the guy in the throat."

"That wasn't because you had restraint," Tate points out. "It was because you were knocked unconscious on the bar floor."

"Wait. I can go? I'm not being charged?" Grayson whips his head in my direction with a wry smile stretched across his face.

"Nope. You hit him in self-defense. He was ready to lunge at you if you hadn't turned around and punched him in the face first."

"What did they do with Simon?"

"That the guy you smoked?" Grayson laughs.

"He deserved it," I grit out.

"Not saying he didn't." He raises his hands in defense. "It's just that I've seen you hit a ball when you're in a good mood, and I wouldn't want to be on the back end of it when you're in a bad one."

Tate pushes in front of Grayson. "He ran out with a bloody nose before anyone could question him, but apparently Mia's been able to file for a restraining order and she has a protection officer at her house tonight."

"Did he make threats against her in front of security?"

"No. They reviewed the security footage and heard everything."

Grayson steps forward, pushing Tate out of the way. "Enough about that. Mia can talk him through everything when he gets to hers. What I'd really like to know is, did they search you?" His gaze drags up my orange jumpsuit, and his face has the kind of glee I've only ever seen from a child on Christmas.

"Yes, but why does that matter?"

He shrugs, his smile growing wider. "Just wondering if they accidentally took your virginity while checking for drugs up your -"

"Grayson!" Tate yells.

"What? It's prison rules now. Anything goes."

"Don't listen to him. I don't know why I brought him with me in the first place."

"Yes, you do. Just like the time I saved you with my tailor when you wanted to dress up as a Catfish to impress your girlfriend. I'm here because I've got a plan. One that can't be executed without me and *my* girlfriend. So really, you should be thanking me for gracing you with my presence."

As Tate rolls his eyes, my ears prickle with interest. "A plan? For what?"

"Mia and her nephew, but we can talk about it in the car." He glances at the door, noting Louisa, the guard, peering in. "You've got to get signed out of here first."

And with that, Louisa walks back into the room, stern as ever, but I don't care. My mind is reeling. Grayson has a plan for Mia and Jett, and I can't wait to hear it.

21.

CHAPTER TWENTY-FOUR

AUSTIN

Griss: Dude, are you out of jail yet? Because Rhode's pissed. She's sitting cursing the TV while her 'arch-nemesis' sleeps in her room. Selena may also be pissed that I used this whole incident as a reason to invite myself over.

Griss: Okay, I get he might be your future nephew in law, but I've got to be honest. Jett snores. Loudly. It's off-putting, and he's making it really hard to watch *Baseball Wives*.

Austin: What would you expect me to do about the snoring if I was still in jail?

Griss: You're out?! Damn. I was planning on flooding your phone with texts, just so you had something to look forward to after your stint.

Austin: Guess it's a good thing I got out then.

Griss: How? You broke a guy's nose! Not gonna lie, I wish I'd seen it. I always thought you were the shy, sensitive type.

Austin: I didn't break a nose, did I? Tate told me the guy got away before they could question him, let alone examine his injuries.

Griss: So you did punch someone! I knew it! Mia wouldn't give me the details, and Jett didn't know either, but now I need to know what the hell the guy did to deserve the wrath of quadzilla!

Austin: I'll call you in the morning. Right now, I'm exhausted, and I need to see Mia. Is Jett okay?

Griss: He's fine. A little shaken, but he'll be okay. I'll drop him by in the morning.

Austin: Thanks, G. I appreciate it.

Griss: Hey it's the least I could do considering all the times you helped me get out of trouble.

Griss: And Cat's Kitty Palace. I guess I'd still got some making up to do on that front.

Austin: Glad you finally admit the errors of your ways.

"Now, Austin." Grayson rolls his head to the side so he can see me in the back seat. I put my phone back in my pocket as I cut my gaze to his. "Remember, if you don't want to wind up back in jail, then you've got to stay at Mia's for the next forty-eight hours." Never in my life did I think I'd end up in the backseat of Grayson's G-Wagon after a four-hour stint in jail while he lectured me on my behavior, but here I am .

Crossing my brows, I look between him and Tate. "What are you talking about? I wasn't charged with anything."

"Yet," Tate adds, holding his finger up as though it makes a difference. "That guy could bring charges against you at any time."

"But he won't," Grayson interjects. "This is Austin Adams we're talking about. The guy didn't have sex until yesterday."

"Grayson!" Tate grits.

"What? It's true. Jailing Austin is like jailing Bambi. An over-reactive and unnecessary move. I am more than willing to bet when the security footage is released, Simon won't have a case, let alone any dignity left. Who pushes a woman around like that?" He says in disgust.

"Did you see him touch her?" And just like that, the anger I thought I had controlled comes straight to the forefront because all I can think about is Simon's hands on Mia, and the look on her face.

"Chill out, Rook." Grayson rolls to a halt in front of Mia's house. The lights are still on, and there's a giant black SUV sitting on the driveway. "Simon didn't touch your girl after security got there. We've also paid for her to have some extra security, as you can see. I just thought that this whole thing might be a good excuse for you to stay longer. Especially since we've got the weekend off, and Jett's not home." I ignore his wiggling eyebrows and wonder if the guy can ever be serious.

Opening the door, I say, "Thanks for the ride, and the offer for Mia. I know she'll appreciate it."

Grayson waves a hand. "Don't worry. Ivy is the best in the business. She'll get this figured out for Mia. I'm certain of it." He raises his brow toward the house. "Now, I believe Mia's been worried sick waiting for you. Might want to ease her mind."

As I open the door, Tate offers me a 'good luck,' and as if he was watching us, the security guard in the black SUV rolls his window up, allowing me to go to Mia's house.

I make my way to the door, feeling exhausted, but needing to see Mia is okay for myself. As I take the steps up the porch, the familiarity of the place is all-consuming. Somehow it already feels like home, and that's a scary thought when there's some guy trying to take it from me. Not that I'll let him get anywhere near them again.

Knocking on the door, I rub my hands together to ease some of the tension mounting inside my chest. When Mia opens the door, her mouth parts in surprise. "Austin," She wisps out, her eyes wide, but focused on me.

"Hey," I force out with a smile. How could four hours in jail make me forget just how beautiful she is? Big, soft eyes take me in, and she loses her breath.

That's all it takes.

Without a second thought, Mia's lips crash against mine, forcing me to take a few steps back onto the porch just to maintain my balance. Her hands grasp at the back of my hair, pulling as though she can't get enough of me. It's only been a few hours, yet she's kissing me like it's been weeks. But man, did I miss her taste.

"Mia," I manage to say between kisses. "Jett's at Griss's house."

Nipping down on my bottom lip, she pulls it before flashing me the sexiest smirk I have ever seen. "I know."

When I kiss her again, I grab her thighs, hauling her up my body until her legs clamp around my hips. She gyrates against me, and I can already feel myself getting hard from missing her so much. She pulls at the fabric of my shirt, and I know that if we don't go in the house soon, that security guard is going to come over and tell us to get inside. So I walk her through the door and shut it with my foot, barely aware of my surroundings because I'm too caught up with kissing Mia. I fumble around the room, hitting walls, countertops, tables, lamps... whatever, until I finally get to my intended destination.

The sofa.

Dropping her ass onto the arm, I take in the view. Mia's hair is a mess, her lipstick is smeared across her face, and her mascara looks like it's seen better days. She still looks hot as fuck. As I grapple at the edges of her shirt, she raises her arms so I can easily pull it off. Groaning, my hands immediately land on her bare breasts, and I roll her nipples, waiting for that breathy moan she does whenever I do that.

Sure enough, she lets out little pants of air as her head rolls back in pleasure. Her hands drag down my chest, and when she reaches my jeans, she rolls it back and looks at me, confused.

"Where's your belt?"

I chuckle, cupping her cheek in my hand and guiding her lips to me, kissing her again. "They lost it when I was arrested."

"Good, that makes it easier for me." She pushes my jeans, along with my boxers, down my legs and I kick them off before taking my place back between her legs.

Naked and hard, she stops for a minute, taking me in, and as much as I like watching her eyes go wide, I need more. She drops her hand, ready to take hold of my cock, but I grab it. "I can't wait. Turn around."

"Turn around?" She asks with hesitance.

Biting my lip, I nod, trying to hide my smile. "Turn around and lay your hips against the armrest, so I can see your beautiful ass and pussy laid out before me." She shivers at my words, but slowly, slowly, follows my orders. Bracing herself by smashing her hands into the pillows, she balances against the sofa. With her yoga-pant-covered ass fragrantly shaking in the air, I give it a little smack before smoothing my hand over her cheek and rubbing it better. The view is nice, but it could be better.

As I creep my hand up her spine, I feel her body take in a sharp inhale. Slowly, slowly, I track up her back until I get to the base of her neck. Threading my hands through her hair, I ask, "Can I try something?"

"Anything," She muffles.

"You re might regret saying that." Holding her hair tighter, I push her head down so her cheek is resting against the sofa cushion and her ass is high in the air. Then I let go of her, smoothing my hands over her body until I get to her yoga pants, and peel them off, leaving her in a blue thong. I ping her underwear, holding back the urge to bite her peachy ass and instead rub my hand across her left cheek. "You look so good like this, Boss Girl."

Holding onto my hardened cock, I give myself a few strokes, and stroke my dick across her slit, wetting my cock before I sit my cock at her entrance.

"Stop teasing me," she laments, and I smile, enjoying the effect I have on this woman.

Drawing my cock to her opening, I get about an inch in when I stop and pull out almost immediately.

"Why are you stopping?" She groans, looking up at me with hazy eyes.

"I don't have a condom." I admit, holding my dick in my hand because I have no idea where else to put it. "They took the emergency one I had in my wallet."

"I don't care." She waves her hand flippantly, I assume in an attempt to grab my dick, but I take a step back. "Please, just fuck me. I'm on the pill."

"You sure?"

"Austin, if you don't fuck me into the pillows in the next five seconds, I'm going to throw you out of this house, and you'll end up back in jail for indecent exposure."

Well, alright then. I'm going to ride my girlfriend bareback for the first time. I've heard it feels good, but I guess I'm about to find out.

With her ass wiggling in the air, I slowly guide myself inside her, and I wince.

I'm never leaving.

Skin against skin; it feels better than I could have ever imagined. She's so warm. So tight. So mine. I sink into her until I can't go any further and stand there for a moment, enjoying the feeling of being so connected to her. Although I'm only able to see half her face, I can tell by the blissful smile that she's enjoying it too.

With my hands on her hips, I slowly pull out a little before pushing back inside, building up my pace with every thrust. Her hands clutch at the pillows, scrunching the fabric, so I decide to move a little faster, and watch her facial expression with each move.

Every now and again, I can feel her pussy clench around me, which acts as a subtle indication to keep going. Bending forward, I reach down her back and grab her hair again, pulling her head off the coach and forcing her to look up to the ceiling.

She yelps in surprise, but wiggles her hips in approval. I didn't think I'd like being so dominant, but there's something so beautiful about her form stretched out like this with my cock moving in and out of her while she moans in pleasure. I push myself in as deep as I can, then pull out of her almost entirely before slamming back inside. I repeat it again. And then again.

It. Feels. So. Good.

This is just one of the things I've started to enjoy about sex. Pace. Knowing that if I speed up, I can make her come faster, and if I slow down, I'll keep her on the edge of an orgasm until I decide she's ready. The control gives me a little thrill, the mere thought making my cock throb inside her.

Maintaining my pace, I keep going. Watching the muscles of her back flex with pleasure. Then when I shift my hips, her shoulders contract, and she breathes out. Okay, she likes that. I keep my hips in the same position, pushing against her harder and harder, matching the pace of her pants.

"Oh, no." I barely hear her say it over our pounding flesh. "I think I'm coming," She cries, almost embarrassed, but I don't let her think on it for too long. Holding her hair, I fuck her harder, setting a deep, demanding pace. She's panting, trying to say something else, but can't get it out. Good. The next thing I want to hear from her is my name while she's coming.

The couch is creaking, moving ever forward with each punishing thrust. There's a very real possibility I'm going to fuck us into the wall, but I'm not stopping. Those little mewls and gasps are enough of a soundtrack to keep me at my pace.

Suddenly, all her noises stop and her back flexes. That's when I know I've done it.

"Austin," She screams, her body shaking with an orgasm. Her pussy clenches around me and I growl because that feeling alone sends me straight into my own climax.

With my eyes closed, I keep my hands on her hips, slowly thrusting into her in a hard, penetrating beat because I've lost control. The orgasm comes rushing through me, but I don't stop diving into her until it's subsided.

Breathing heavily, I fall onto her sweaty back and kiss the middle of her spine before resting my cheek against it. I close my eyes, taking in the moment, and the feeling of the aftershocks of her orgasms pulsing around me.

"That was something else."

"You're telling me," she says between breaths. "I've never been able to come with just penetration before."

"You haven't?" And just like that, my post-orgasmic haze has ended. Cut through like a hot knife through butter because she's just admitted that I've never gotten her off with sex before.

Still inside her, Mia grabs my arm and looks at me from the side. "Let me be clear. I've always come with you. You've watched, you've listened and, most importantly, you've played with my clit while we've had sex. But tonight. I didn't need that, and that's a first for me."

"Guess you missed me that much. Huh?"

Her fingers relax against my arm, and she laughs. "Could be. But having no separation between us and doing it in this position, just hit the right spot. That orgasm was so much deeper, and more intense than any orgasm I've ever experienced."

"We can do it again if you want?" I push myself up, still inside her, but that's when I feel it. We have a problem. Just as she's about to push herself off the sofa, I stop her.

"Don't move."

She laughs, ignoring me. "Yeah, I'm going to need a break before we do that again, Frat Boy."

"No. it's not that. It's just I didn't really think about the repercussions of taking you bareback on the couch." I wince, thinking about what's going to happen if I move.

Mia glances over her shoulder, still smiling. "Don't worry. There's a box of tissues on the table behind the couch. Just clean it up." She points her thumb at the white tissue popping out of a crocheted box. I pull a handful of them out and clean up as much as I can before carefully pulling myself out and wiping away as much as I can. Then I take care to wipe Mia down. Her eyes are closed, and she looks like she's in a blissful haze as I take care of her.

I drawl out an uneasy groan. "Yeah. I don't think a couple of tissues are going to clean this. I think we're going to need a shower."

She slowly slinks forward like a cat stretching and turns, relaxing her peachy ass on the seat before giving me a cool smile. "Is that a promise?"

Without another word, she takes my hand, and leads me to her bedroom. I don't say a thing because I'm more than ready for round two, three and four.

***

"I'll get it," Mia calls as she throws a shirt on, heading to the door. Her hair is still wet from her morning shower. Yes, another one because, to be frank, that shower we had last night left us filthier than when we started. Flashbacks of my cock in her mouth and fucking her into the wall come back to mind, and I smile lazily, looking forward to doing it all over again.

She skips past me, and I don't even try to hide the fact that I'm staring at her peachy ass in those jean shorts. Her thighs are a little pink from the spanking she asked for last night, and I'm already getting riled up thinking about it. "It's probably Jett," she sings over her shoulder, and that response immediately softens my dick. I guess I'll have to wait till later for that spanking.

"Doesn't he have a key?" I ask, but she's already down the hall and can't hear me. Sighing, I reach over and grab my jeans, shunting them on so I look presentable. For a guy that just got out of jail, I somehow got my dick sucked and had sex in seven different positions last night. That's got to be a record, right? I genuinely thought my dick would fall off if I had that much sex, but Mia was adamant that I'm in my sexual prime and wanted to push me to my limits.

By the time I've towel dried my hair and put a shirt on, I realize Mia still hasn't come back and it's been a while. I can't hear any voices either.

"Mia?" I call, but get no response, so I peer out of the room. There's no sign of her or Jett. Strange. Thrumming my fingers against the door frame, I stroll out of the room, listening out because I don't want to interrupt anything.

"Mia?" I say one more time before I get to the point in the hall where I can see the living room fully. Once I do, I rush over to her. Crumpled on the couch, Mia's silently sobbing, and I don't know what the hell is going on, but if Simon got past the security guard, I'll murder them both.

Cradling her in my arms, I push her hair back, seeing her bloodshot, swollen eyes. "What happened?"

She shows me some crumpled papers, and as much as I want to read them, I can't. "Mia, baby. What are these?"

"He's going to try to take him," she sobs silently into my chest.

"Who?"

"Simon." She finally passes me the papers. "It's another letter. He's taking me to court over Jett's custody."

I shuffle through the papers, and although I don't understand the lingo, I know this can't be possible.

"He can't. If he opens this up in court, they'll have your phone records and the video evidence of him harassing you. They might even potentially open up Hailey's case again. This is all a bluff to scare you." I'm almost one hundred percent certain of it, but the way Mia shakes her head makes me balk for a second.

"No. You don't get it. The phone records aren't traceable to him. They never have been. He's doing the same thing he did when he was pretending to be Joey. There's no way I can technically prove it's him, and a hunch isn't enough for the police to take my side. They need evidence, and they've got it. They already think I'm stalking him, and now I've left a money trail for human trafficking. Whatever he wants to push onto me, he can."

Clasping her shoulders, I dip my chin so I can look into her tear-soaked eyes. "Mia," I say slowly, hoping that gets her attention. "The security footage at the Stadium shows he was attacking you. He threatened me. Simon's on the run, and you have a security guard outside. There's a reason for it."

She swallows, looking no less comforted. "The only reason I have a security guard outside is because your very rich and generous friends got me one. I have no doubts that if they find him, he'll turn them against me, just like he did before. He does it every time, and I can't afford to fight him in court."

"I'll pay," I blurt out, but have no intention of taking it back.

"What?" She says with a disbelieving breath.

"Whatever you need, I will help." Sitting her on my lap, I kiss her forehead. "This isn't just your fight now. It's *our* fight, and I will do everything I can to protect you and Jett." Waffling our hands together, I kiss every single knuckle to emphasize just how important she and Jett have become to me.

"Austin. I can't ask you to do that."

"Good thing you didn't ask." Cupping her jaw with my other hand, I wipe away an errant tear with my thumb. "You know what? There's something I completely forgot to tell you last night that I really should have."

"Why didn't you?"

A goofy smile crosses my face before I can stop it. "We, uh, got a little distracted." She smiles for the first time since I found her on the floor, which is an improvement. "Tate and Grayson bailed me out."

"I figured after I saw that fancy car drive away."

"They didn't just bail me out, though. They also found out about your predicament, and they have a plan to stop Simon."

"What are they going to do? Beat him to death with a baseball bat, because I've already sent one ball player to jail. I'd rather not send another two. Especially one with the squeakiest reputation this side of Charlotte."

"No ball players will go to jail. At least not again. Grayson's girlfriend, Ivy, is a lawyer." That makes Mia's ears perk up. "Her specialty just so happens to be adoption. Apparently, she's taken on some of the hardest cases in the state of California and in North Carolina. Or at least. That's what Grayson says. He is sleeping with her, so he has a potential bias, but if Tate's behind it too, then I'm guessing she's good."

Mia's eyes dart as she processes the information before she looks up at me with sadness. "But I can't afford a lawyer, let alone one as fancy as Ivy sounds, and I don't feel comfortable asking you for help."

"Good thing she said she'd take on your case pro bono, then."

"What? Why?" She spits out with surprise.

I wave off her concern. "Grayson didn't go into it, but he said something about her having some personal experience that makes her want to take this on."

"Seriously?" I nod, and before I know it, her arms are clasped around me and she's sobbing into my arms, but this time it's with happiness. "Thank you." It comes out weak and I kiss her temple, holding her close.

"You aren't alone anymore, Mia. I've already said that I'll do whatever it takes to help you." And I will. Even if it means this arrest doesn't get cleared and I don't qualify for Rookie of the Year. Even losing my reputation doesn't matter because as Mia clutches onto me as though I'm her only life force, it doesn't feel like I'll be losing out on much at all.

In fact, it almost feels like it would all be worth it.

CHAPTER TWENTY-FIVE

AUSTIN

Reporters talk amongst themselves as we filter into the room, taking our respective seats in the Carolina Press Office. The minute I take my seat and look out into the sea of reporters, everyone goes silent. The clicking cameras is the only noise that fill the room. I adjust my collar, already feeling the heat of the situation when I haven't said anything.

I was expecting this reaction, and Mary, our PR manager, spent several hours going through the potential scenarios with me, but I still wasn't expecting the looks of disapproval. Even Sienna, our dugout broadcaster, is looking at me with less than stellar vibes, and she looks at everyone like they hung the moon. Everyone except for Max, of course. There's something going on between them. But neither one will talk.

I make myself comfortable on the chair and clear my throat before tapping my hand against the microphone to check it's working. It's all normal things I do before our press conferences, but today it feels like my every move is being scrutinized. Probably because it is. The rumors are rife. There have been a couple of speculative reports about my 'arrest,' but nothing concrete from anyone yet. The police aren't pressing charges against me, and the press conference is aimed at addressing the start of the series, so I shouldn't be as nervous as I feel.

When I hear the gentle tap of my hand, I adjust my cufflinks before folding my arms in front of me, feeling foolish. Formal shirts always make me look ridiculous. Unless they are tailored to fit my arms, I either look like I'm busting out of them, or I'm drowning in them. Luckily, Grayson had his tailor on hand to help, but it all still feels too formal for a pre-game interview. Mary catches my eye from the back of the room, giving me a double thumbs up, and mouths 'you got this.' I'm glad she has all that confidence in me, because I sure as hell don't.

I take another deep breath, and look into the crowd, as ready as I'll ever be to do this press conference.

"Good luck," Tate says under his breath, away from the mic, so they don't pick it up. I mumble a 'thank you,' back before looking at Grayson on his other side. He hasn't looked at me since we came in here, but it's not like I expected him to hold my hand. This is Grayson we're talking about, and he's got to pitch today, so he's not going to talk to any of us.

As I look around the room at all the reporters, strangely, I'm not nervous or worried about their questions. For myself, that is.

I am, however, worried for Mia.

She's sitting in the marketing department with Tate's girlfriend Cali right now, watching this whole thing. If anyone questions me, I've already got my pre-prepared answers, but I can only hope Mia's name doesn't come up.

"Okay, we're about ready to start," Mary says with a wide smile to the group of reporters. Holding a clipboard, she flips through a couple of pages before glancing back up to them. "We only have ten minutes today, so questions need to be short and concise." She lifts the paper on her clipboard, reading through it. "Sienna, you're first."

Sienna stands, looking between the players before her gaze falls to Max for a little longer than necessary. Max looks anywhere but her, which seems odd, but they've always been strange with each other. When she looks at me, I see the tiniest tinge of red in her cheeks, but she hides it well with pursed lips. "Austin, You're three quarters through the season now. There's only one other Rookie who is pushing out stats like you, and they're in the American League. Do you feel you can keep up with all the hype surrounding you?"

Well, Mary said she asked Sienna to go easy on me and avoid questions about the arrest, but this question just sounds like she's trying to suck up. "The only people that are making any discussions about it are you guys." She seems a little taken aback, and I try to relax because I'm coming in a little too hot today. Sienna didn't deserve that, and I'll apologize to her later. "Thank you for asking, but I'm here to focus on my game and help get our team to the playoffs. Nothing else matters to me."

Except Mia and Jett. But they don't have to know about that.

"And does visiting Charlotte County Jail constitute helping the team?" Dave, a reporter that I hate, coughs out. Mary is on the side, fuming, but doesn't stop the press conference because that will bring more attention to the question. When I look over to coach, he rolls his hand in a motion as if to say keep going. So, I do.

Leaning forward so I can get closer to the mic, I give the reporters a tight smile. "Figured you'd be the one to bring it up, Dave."

Dave sits back in his chair with a shit-eating grin. "Are you going to answer the question?"

"Yes. I am." This is it. I need to remember my pre-prepared statement, hoping I don't screw it up.

Just as I open my mouth to speak, Grayson's chair screeches across the floor.

"Austin was there visiting me," He pipes up, to everyone's surprise. Tate and I look at him with shock, but his only response is a side smirk and a wink.

What the hell is he doing?

Tate kicks my leg because he thinks I'm about to say something, but I'm lost for words, too confused over why Grayson is taking the fall for this, or how he'll explain it.

Grayson clears his throat, sitting up straighter, and leans towards his mic to address the press again. "It wasn't something I wanted to bring up on my start day, so thanks for that, Dave, but I'm happy to answer any questions you have because this will be the only time I discuss it with the media."

He won't look at me, so I turn my attention to Coach and Mary, who both look as equally perplexed as me. Apparently, Grayson's gone rogue.

"So, you weren't arrested?" Dave asks me.

"What part of he was visiting me doesn't make that clear, Dave?" Grayson asks before I have time to open my mouth and answer.

The room falls silent, and I can only assume it's because it's not the first time Grayson has had to address the media about an arrest. They know he's volatile at the best of times.

"So, *you* were arrested?"

"I prefer taken into custody since I wasn't charged. Austin picked me up. That's the only reason he was there. Our poor rookie was doing everything right, but you guys just want to make out that he's the bad guy because you want to ruin his stellar season."

"Why were you arrested?"

"Taken into custody," he sings, waving his hand. "It's nothing. Just the usual heated conversation with a fan." He shrugs it off because everyone knows his relationship with fans across the league. They love to hate him, and he gives it right back. "Oops."

"No one is being charged, and the fan is fine. Sent him a few signed balls, and he's happy." That's it. There are a few coughs from the reporters, but Grayson's admission has made this whole thing a non-story. "Now, if there are no more questions, I'd like to go back to my pre-game ritual or not talking."

Mary clears her throat to get the attention of the room. "Now that Mr. Hawk has cleared that up, can you stick to questions about the game, please? We don't like to discuss hearsay and rumors in these meetings." She gives the reporters a stern look before pointing at the crowd. "Dave, that stunt counts as your question for the day." He raises his hand in protest but doesn't do much else because he knows he's in the wrong. "Bobby, I believe you're next."

"Tate. I've got a question for you."

Tate perks up, his chair scratching against the floor as he eases his way to the microphone. "How do you feel about Holden Fox joining the team?" His eyebrows draw together in confusion, matching the rest of us.

"I have no idea what you're talking about. Holden isn't joining the team."

"There's a rumor going around that the Los Angeles Antelopes are trying to trade him for prospects before the signing deadline. The Catfish is one of those teams that have been mentioned as a potential landing spot for him."

"Bobby," Mary warns. "I said no questions about rumors. That is most certainly a rumor."

Bobby pinches his forehead. "Okay, well, *hypothetically*, if he were to join the team, how would you feel? A big player like him might take over as leader of the dugout."

"That's enough," Mary interrupts. "Please don't waste our valuable time on questions like this. Moving on." She looks at her clipboard and goes to the next reporter.

By the time the press conference ends, I'm in shock. No more questions about the arrest. In fact, there were no more questions addressed to me. As the reports file out of the room, I stay in my seat, flabbergasted that it all worked out so smoothly.

"Rookie, you're not going to make me talk some more today, are you?" Grayson is standing beside my chair, waiting for me to get out of my seat so he and Tate can leave the conference room.

Pulling myself to my feet, I hold my hand out. "Grayson. I don't know what to say."

He takes a quick glance at my hand and dismisses it by swiping my arm away. "Please don't get all sentimental over that. It was nothing."

"Sure felt a lot like something," I blow out in surprise. "Why'd you take the fall for me?"

I can tell he's already pissed that I've made him break his no talking rule again, but it doesn't stop him from answering. "Firstly, I wanted the press conference over as soon as possible. I've heard that if you sit in a room with Dave for too long, you'll lose your ability to throw a pitch." I roll my eyes because I should have known I'd never get a straight answer out of him. "Secondly," he adds. "I did it because you're a rookie. You've got your whole career ahead of you, and you don't need a rumor like that holding you back."

I raise a disbelieving brow. "So, you thought you'd take the fall for me?"

His lips turn into a lopsided grin. "Everyone already thinks I'm an asshole. Why not give them more ammunition?" I chuckle, because it's almost like Grayson enjoys being the bad guy on the team. "Since you're not leaving, I'm late for my warmup."

As he pushes past me, I slap him on the shoulder and say, "Thanks again."

"Yeah, just don't tell people I did that. I don't want them to think I'm going soft."

"Never."

"Now let's get out there and play some ball. I'm expecting some run support today."

"Always."

CHAPTER TWENTY-SIX
MIA

I look over at the large windows to see the crowd roaring because Grayson is on his ninth strikeout of the night and we're only in the fourth inning. How anyone gets any work done in a room like this is beyond me, but I guess if you're in marketing, you need to know your product intimately, and this boxed meeting room does just that.

As I read through the papers for the fifteenth time, I'm sure Ivy and her colleague are getting frustrated with me, but I need to be clear on what I'm signing. When I finish reading the last sentence on the final page, I glance up at Ivy, who's taking no notice of me as she reads some papers. Funny, I'm pretty sure she wrote those, so I'm guessing she's just doing it to pass the time.

Waving the papers so they slap against the table, I get her attention. She looks up with pressed lips and elbows Cody, her colleague, to get his attention.

"It can't be this simple, can it?"

Ivy gives me a tight, close-lipped smile, only emphasizing her deep-red lipstick. "It can. Jett's age, and the time he's lived with you, will benefit you in family court. He's a teenager now, which means he can choose which 'parent' he wants to live with, so all we need is for him to testify in front of a judge, and that should take away any parental rights Simon is seemingly holding over you. Although he's on pretty shaky ground, anyway."

I look around the room, noting that Tate's girlfriend Cali is peering into the meeting room. Sitting in the Carolina Catfish marketing department makes me feel wholly out of place, but something I'm finding hard to come to terms with is that all of these people want to help me. Even though they barely know me, they want to see Jett in my custody, and it's all because of Austin. That serious, sexy ballplayer that gets my panties wet from just thinking about him. But that's not all he's good for. He's kind, selfless, and his actions have only proven that he'll do anything to protect me. To protect *us*. It's crazy how quickly he's become my rock through this, and I have no idea how I can repay him.

Leaning in closer, I whisper, "But what about all those illegal things I did?"

Narrowing her eyes, she asks, "What illegal things? Housing and feeding your nephew while his father blackmailed you to fuel his drug habit isn't illegal. Foolish?" She clicks the top of her mouth. "Maybe, but not illegal. Unless there's something else that you haven't told me?"

Squirming in my seat, I think about how to phrase this. "Okay," Ivy quips. "If there's something you did, it's better I know about it now, then find out in the middle of court when I can't protect you."

"But what about the human trafficking allegations? I never legally went through courts to get custody of Jett, and Simon made up all this evidence to suggest that I was harassing him."

She raises one of her perfectly laminated brows. "Is that it?" I nod, and she pushes a glass of water in my direction. "I think you need to take a breath and have a drink."

Clutching the water, all I can think about is how much I've screwed this up. There's no way I can keep Jett, which means he's going to have to kiss his baseball career goodbye, and it will be all my fault.

As I take a tentative sip, I'm careful as I put it back on the table, my hands shaking with the uncomfortable truth that the world Jett and I built could easily go down.

Ivy is still looking at me with no emotion, and it's unnerving.

"I'm going to be honest with you, Mia." My stomach curls and I feel a little sick as I try to prepare myself for whatever she has to say. "Mr. Inwood has more chance of adopting a stick insect than getting Jett back." I whip my head toward her, and her lip curls. "Which is very unlikely, by the way."

"Oh?"

"Firstly, you've got me as your lawyer. I've read through the legal documents he sent you. If that's what you call them," she mumbles the last part under her breath. "And it looks like he copy and pasted them from a website. The firm that he's apparently represented by has no internet presence and I can't find that they are legally registered to practice law. I'm pretty sure Mr. Sheuster only sent you those documents because he wanted to scare you into giving him more money without the proper due diligence."

"You think?"

She nods. "I know, but from what Austin says, this has been going on for years, and I intend to close any loophole Mr. Sheuster thinks he has on you. By legally making you Jett's guardian, we can then use the video evidence to get a restraining order against Simon and clear you of any wrongdoing, too. He won't be able to come near either of you once I'm through with the paperwork."

My body starts to relax because as the words start to sink in. Is this what relief feels like? Because all of a sudden, I'm holding back a strong wave of emotions, hoping no one notices. Simon can't threaten me anymore. He'll be out of our lives forever.

As tears threaten to fall, Ivy clears her throat. "There's also something else."

"Something else?" I repeat. What more could there be?

"I was speaking to Detective Daniels about your situation." The name immediately sparks my interest. "You know him. He was the man that technically arrested Austin, but he also worked on your sister's case." I nod, swallowing the lump in my throat. "Well, I've actually worked with him a lot over the last couple of years, and he agreed to personally look into your claims of blackmail and harassment. That video from the game has brought enough evidence forward that they can search his home."

"What for?"

"Any evidence to suggest he has been harassing you. Whether it be bills for apartments under a different name, phones with messages, even his internet activity will be looked into."

As if my body can't control itself, panic sets in my stomach. "What if they don't find anything? He'll just be pissed off and try to make things worse for me."

Ivy offers me a placid smile. "That's where you're wrong. That video is enough to put a case forward for a restraining order. I'm just strengthening the case because I've got a feeling there's a lot more to this than Simon would want us to know." I nod my head, biting my bottom lip with concern. That's when she takes my hand. "Trust me. If we do this right. Legally, he'll be out of your life forever."

My mouth splits into a grin. "Okay, I trust you. Thank you."

She leans back and shrugs one of her shoulders before looking out onto the field where the Catfish are playing. She acts like this is nothing, but can't she see it means everything to me?

"I'm happy to help," she quips, tipping her head down at the field as she watches Grayson play with a small smile on her lips. "Kids deserve the best chance in life, and if I can be the person who helps them get that, then it's a no brainer. I will." Not one to talk emotions, she sits forward and taps her fingers against the table. "Now, if we're done here, I think we need to get out there and watch the end of the game because It looks like Grayson is on his way to a no-hitter."

She stands, dismissing her assistant. She walks over to the panoramic window with her arms crossed as she watches her boyfriend with quiet pride. "Were you into baseball before you met Austin?" She asks, the first sign of informality from her since we met.

"Yeah. Jett's a player and a fan. He's at an away game himself, otherwise he'd be here, amazed at the view." I stand next to her, and sure enough, Grayson is on his tenth strike out. He punches the air as he walks into the dugout, more pumped than I've ever seen him.

"It's funny. I knew nothing about the sport before meeting Grayson." She cuts a look at me. "Hell, I still only know the bare minimum. Ask me what a balk is, and I'll just laugh it off, but there's something about this game that just draws you in, isn't there?"

"I blame the tight pants," I say, watching Austin's thick ass jog off the field.

She throws her head back in a laugh. "I'll admit the pants are a draw, but do you know what really got me?" Even though we're the only two in the room, she leans over, almost ashamed to admit this out loud. "That finger licking thing the pitchers do before they handle a ball." She bites her bottom lip and fans her face. "Gets me every. Single. Time."

We both jump when the meeting room door opens, and Cali sticks her head in. "Hey guys," She sings, smiling as she takes a tentative step into the room. "Ivy, your assistant said you were finished, and I just wanted to check you had everything you needed."

Ivy turns, giving Cali a warm smile. "We are. Thank you so much for letting us use your meeting room."

Cali smiles, walking further in as she holds her pregnant belly. "It's no problem at all. I've got a couple of seats behind the dugout saved for you both. Would you like to follow me?"

"Can't wait," I say, looking forward to finally watching my boyfriend play without the worry of receiving a text from Simon.

***

"Congratulations," I shout, running into Austin's arms in the dugout. Austin cracks a smile before grabbing me into a dirty, sweaty hug and kisses me hard on the lips. Backing away, I laugh. "I can't believe that game."

He smiles, glances over his shoulder at Grayson, who's reluctantly giving the post-game interview while Ivy stands a few feet away out of view. "I don't think anyone can believe it." He shakes his head and looks back at me. The pure joy I see on his face is infectious and I end up giving him a small peck on the lips because I can't contain myself. "Apparently, taking responsibility for my arrest lit a fire in his ass, and he went for it. Although he'll be kicking himself in the ass for that walk in the ninth."

"A no hitter is still an impressive feat."

"You know Grayson. Perfection is his aim." As Grayson finishes the interview with Sienna, some of the other players sneak up behind him, throwing a bucket of ice water on his back. After the initial shock, he looks less than amused and narrows his eyes at Tate.

"I'll get you back, pretty boy."

Tate's already running off in another direction before Grayson can get to him.

With my arms still wrapped around his neck, I kiss the spot right next to his ear and whisper, "You did pretty awesome out there, too. In the press conference and on the field."

"As long as you're happy. I am too." With another kiss, he cuts his gaze to the rest of the team and a wry smile forms on his face. Dropping my feet to the ground, he whispers, "Come on. Follow me."

A spike of adrenaline sparks through me as he takes my hand and weaves us through the throngs of players. Everyone is too busy celebrating to notice that we're leaving. "Where are we going?" I giggle.

He doesn't answer. He just quickly heads through the clubhouse to his locker and pulls out some clothes. Taking his shirt off, I throw my hands up. "Woah, woah, wait. I'm all for a little playtime, but in here." I look around, and it's still quiet as everyone is on the field. "It's just way too risky."

He raises his brow, throwing a plain white shirt over his sweaty body. I hate that the mere sight of his expansive chest makes me want to lick the dirt off him. "Good, because I've got other plans. I turn around as he switches into his jeans, not wanting to be accused of drooling at the mere sight of his thighs, and when he's done, he slips his hand in mine. "Come on. There's something I want to show you."

Without another word, we've slipped out of the locker room and are on our way to an undisclosed location.

"This is where you wanted to take me?" I ask, my voice almost echoing. "The nosebleed seats?" Thank goodness I don't suffer from vertigo because these seats are crazy high.

He sits on the highest seat of the stadium, ushering me to join him. I sit on the seat next to him, our thighs knocking as we look at the field. The crowd filed out a few minutes ago and only die-hard fans are left trying to get an autograph from the team below. Way, way below. No one knows we're up here, and I'd be surprised if anyone checks.

"You call them nosebleed," Austin says, kissing my ear. "I call them the 'get lucky seats." His hand is already skating up my thigh, and when I try to swat him away, he comes right back.

"Austin. We can't do that here?"

He laughs into our kiss and twists his body, so his hand has a better angle. "Sure, we can. Security won't be coming up to check it's empty for another twenty minutes."

"But," I tip my chin, trying to get away from his dizzying kisses because he knows that's the way to get me to agree to do anything. "You've only just skated questions about being arrested, and now you want to add a potential indecent exposure charge to your list of crimes?"

"The only crime happening here is that skirt." He flicks his gaze to my short, ruffled, Catfish-themed skirt. The one when he asked me to wear it, I nearly cried with laughter because it makes me feel like I'm a teenager again. "No one is going to see a damn thing. That skirt is flouncy enough that it will hide my hand while I play with your tight little pussy. Come on. Make a Rookie's dream come true?"

Those words immediately make me wet as the memory of his thick fingers comes back to me. His hand pushes up the ruffles, and although I groan in disapproval, I open my legs wider anyway.

His hand pauses at my thigh. "I can stop if you really want me to. It's just since I've tasted your pussy, I can't stop thinking about all the places I want to take you. The 'get lucky' seats, the dugout, by the waterfall. The park is so big, the opportunities are endless, and it's getting mildly distracting. Especially after an adrenaline-filled win like the one today."

I take a sharp breath as his fingers tickle at my thigh. "I just figured if we actually played out some of these fantasies that maybe it would be a little easier to play without thinking about you every five minutes."

It all sounds logical, and the fact that Austin is having fantasies about me is hot. Fantasies that I definitely want to partake in. Even if it's just a little wrong. With his hand on my thigh, his fingers tickle under my skirt, waiting for the invite. I peer down at the field, and there are only groundskeepers there now. It's quiet enough that he's right. If we wanted to do this, we could.

"What do you say, Boss Girl? Make a player's fantasy come to life."

"Fine." I roll my eyes before kissing him on the lips. "What's your fantasy up here?"

"I think you can already guess," He says with a wicked grin. He kisses me again, his hand moving past the floaty hem of my skirt and dipping under the fabric.

"You picked this skirt on purpose, didn't you?" I say between kisses. "I wondered why you were so intent on this. "No," he laughs. "I knew you'd look cute in it, and it's a hot day. I'm sure you like the breeze." I roll my eyes. "However, I'm not going to deny it helps with access."

I have to bite down on my lip to avoid crying out in pleasure when his fingers slip past my panties and play with my folds. "So wet for me already, Boss Girl. Were you thinking about me while I was on the field?"

He drags his kisses down my jaw, to my collarbone just as his fingers enter me. "Yes," I groan, closing my eyes and gripping his thigh for dear life. It must be something about the setting that's got me worked up because I can't just be this insatiable all the time. His fingers dip inside me, and it's official; I've lost all sense of the world.

"That feels so good," I sigh out as he nips at my neck, moving his fingers at a slow, punishing pace, making my toes curl inside my sneakers. He's just so good at reading me. His thumb rolls over my clit, gently massaging, and I clasp onto his arm for stability. Falling out of one of these seats is a real possibility, and I'd rather not have to explain to the security guard why I'm panting like a dog in heat.

Austin ups his pace, knowing he's got me right where he wants me.

When I protest after he pulls his fingers out of me, he tuts. "Watch me." It's all he has to say. Eyes on eyes, he's the only thing I see. Austin draws his fingers to his mouth and licks my essence. I gulp, squirming because I so badly want to rub my thighs together to feel some friction. That was one of the hottest things I've ever seen. "I'm going to fuck you so hard when we get home."

Home? Did he just call my house home? Either way, I liked it.

He drops his hand between my thighs, and I bite my lip, unable to speak because his fingers are toying with me again. This time he's faster. More punishing, as though he knows how close I am and that we don't have much time.

My hips move to his rhythm, and with very little effort, I'm already on the precipice. "Come for me, BG." He bites down on my collarbone, and that pinch of pain is all it takes. I'm coming all over his fingers, and he's holding them in place, letting me take everything I need from him.

Thrust after thrust, the intensity of the orgasm fades, and when I finally open my eyes, I nearly fall forward because I forgot about the height.

Austin holds me against his body, keeping me stable as I calm down. With my hand on his thigh, I can feel his erection through his jeans, and I so badly want to return the favor, but I doubt Austin will let me. "That was the hottest thing I've ever seen," Austin breathes into my ear. "Next time we do this, I'm going to sit you on my lap, and you're going to ride me until you come all over my cock."

"Next time?" I say with wide eyes.

He cracks a smile before taking one final taste of his fingers. "Oh, Boss Girl, now that I've had a taste of that, I don't want it to stop."

Shutting my legs, I try to ignore the wet sensation between my thighs, because there's nothing I can do about it now and shuck his chin. "Have we just discovered a kink of yours? Outdoor sex?"

He pushes his lips out, contemplating. "Mhmm. I don't think it's outdoor sex, per se. I think it's ballpark sex. Maybe next time I can bang you in the dugout."

"The dugout?" I glance down at the little space, wondering how on earth we'd be able to do that in secret. "But there are eyes everywhere here. I don't think we could fool around in many places without getting caught."

Standing, he offers me his hand and guides me down the stairs to the concourse exit. "Oh, but that's part of the fun of it, Boss Girl. Getting caught with the hottest woman I've ever seen would be hot as fuck."

I smile, ribbing him in the side. "I can't believe I've fallen for a Frat Boy."

He clasps my hand, pulling me into him and gives me a long, slow kiss. "I can't believe you let me in your life."

"Always." It's a short, simple statement, but he knows the sentiment behind it. "Now let's get out of here. I've got so much to tell you about my meeting with Ivy."

"Of course. I can't wait."

Chapter Twenty-Seven

Mia

One Month Later

Holding the adoption papers in one hand, I clutch Austin's with the other. I want to laugh because this all feels so incredibly crazy. How did I get here? How did I manage to wheedle my way into this friendship group that has opened so many doors for Jett and me? Everything has been going our way for the last couple of months, and I couldn't be happier for Jett. We're finally getting a fresh start and putting all the bad stuff behind us.

"I can't believe it's that simple," I laugh, gazing at Austin in disbelief. He squeezes my hand as we walk - no skip - out of the courtroom.

Just as Austin's about to say something, Grayson pipes up behind him, "I take you doubting Ivy's abilities as a personal offense." Pushing between us, he forces our hands apart, and wraps his arms around our shoulders before looking between Austin and me. "It's a good day, isn't it?"

I give him a small smile because as I clutch the adoption papers, it's obvious how I'm feeling. Jett is officially *my* responsibility and Simon can't do anything about it. Not that he even bothered trying. He ignored all of my legal letters and didn't show up in court today. Although that probably has something to do with the fact that he's currently on trial for more severe charges.

"Ah, man, I love watching her in court." Grayson blows out a long breath, looking over his shoulder with admiration at where Ivy is standing. She's still talking to Detective Daniels, but I hope she finishes soon because I need to thank her.

"Don't you see it all the time?" Austin asks.

"Not as often as I'd like, but I can't complain. During the off-season, if I'm allowed, I sit in the back of the courtrooms and watch her work. It's magical." He looks at the sky and lets out a low chuckle. "Ah, I remember one time I watched her in court. She was working with a particularly brutal judge, and she was so worked up about it that she may have taken her frustration out on me that night."

"Things I didn't need to know for five-hundred, Alex," Austin says, motioning his head toward Jett.

Pulling away so we can walk down the stairs, Grayson lets us go first. "Did I ever tell you about the time I first met Ivy? She wanted nothing to do with me. Still not sure if she does." He shrugs it off with a bemused look on his face. "She had my balls in a vice then. Still does now, but I like it."

Cool as ice, Ivy breezes past Grayson and stands in front of Austin and me with a pleasant smile before she addresses Grayson. "I believe you're the one who's been begging to have his dick in a vice for the last few months, not me."

Grayson waves his hand, holding back his bemusement. "That's beside the point."

"He's right," she interrupts. "That *is* beside the point. The point right now is that you have legally adopted Jett, and Simon can't do a thing to stop it." I swallow a disbelieving breath because I never thought I'd get to this point. The relief is unlike anything I've ever experienced. "He can't blackmail you or contact you again. You have no reason to worry about him anymore."

"But what about if the other charges are dropped?"

She gives me a bemused smile. "The police aren't going to drop a fatal hit-and-run charge. I told you it was important to get his house searched."

And I can't deny she was right. They didn't just find evidence Simon had created a fake 'Joey' identity, but they found mountains of evidence for stalking, harassing and even the smoking gun. Hailey's phone was sitting on his coffee table like some kind of ornament. Unfortunately for him, he'd left it full of threatening texts. "The evidence found at his house, combined with Jett's testimony, and the fact that his car matches the description of the one that knocked her off the road makes it clear he was involved. Not to mention the string of other charges we could leverage against him."

She sounds so sure of herself, and through all of this, she's given me no reason to doubt her.

Without warning, I pull her into a bone-crushing hug. "Sorry about that," Austin says. "She's a hugger."

"I figured," Ivy says, unbothered.

"Thank you for helping me win this fight." I hold back the tears, knowing I need to be strong. I can cry in the comfort of my own home when I tell Jett all about it.

She lets out a grumble in disbelief as she pats me on the back. "Fight is a strong word. I've seen more fight in a dying fish than him. The only thing Simon had going for him was that he was on Jett's birth certificate, and I still suggest Jett get a DNA test." She pulls away, looking at me with meaning. I know she wants that for evidence, but Jett doesn't want to do it, and I respect his wishes. "Extortion, blackmail, harassment and stalking are just the tip of the iceberg when it comes to his charges. He's going away for a long time."

"Thank you." The words spill out again because no amount of them will show my true gratitude.

"I'm glad I could help," she whispers so only I can hear, and then pats me on the back. "Jett is lucky to have an aunt like you."

Grayson clears his throat and raises his hand to get our attention. "So, I have a question." Judging by the look on his face, I already know he's going to hate it. Pointing between Austin and me, he asks, "If Mia and Austin get married, will that make Austin a dad?"

Married? Again? How many people are going to push the marriage spiel on us? Not that I don't want to get married someday, but I've only just officially got Jett as my responsibility. I want to give myself some time before I add anymore men to that roster.

"Grayson," Austin replies sharply, putting his arm around my shoulder, offering me a reassuring smile. I'm sure he's thinking the same thing. He's too young to even contemplate marriage.

Grayson raises his hands, his mouth drops in disbelief, and then he leans in to whisper in his ear. "What? Why are you so angry? I'm just trying to help you out. You know you're not going to do better than her, right? Might as well lock it in."

"I know," he mumbles, knocking Grayson out of the way, and I feel my heart beating wildly because it makes it sound like he's been thinking about it.

"Well then, you're welcome," Grayson replies sarcastically. He wraps his arm around Ivy's waist, kissing her delicately on the cheek. "As much as I'd like to stay and celebrate. Austin and I have to be on a plane in four hours, and I'd like to spend a little time with my girlfriend."

Ivy rolls her eyes. "I'll be in contact with you over the next week to let you know if there are any developments on the harassment case I'm also raising."

"Great."

With that, Ivy and Grayson leave and as I turn to Austin, I crush him with a hug, holding him as tight as I can, knowing that I can't break him. "Thank you, Austin."

"For what?" He dips his finger under my chin, directing me to look up at him. I stand on my tiptoes to meet him with a kiss.

"For finding Ivy and making this all possible. Jett doesn't have to worry about Simon, and soon I won't either. I never thought this day would come."

"I didn't find Ivy. You've got Grayson to thank for that. However, I'll take the praise if it means you'll give me a blow job as good as the one I got in the shower this morning." He gives me a small, slow smile, waggling his eyebrows.

Shaking my head, I push against his chest. "Seriously? We've just saved my nephew from being stuck with his evil dad, and all you can think about is sex?"

He shrugs, smiling. "Hey, you knew what you were getting yourself into when you started dating a twenty-one-year-old."

I poke him in the ribs, making sure it hurts. "Twenty-two. You're twenty-two tomorrow."

"Ah, yes. And for a whole month, you will only be eight years older than me, not nine."

I drop my head onto his hard chest and groan. "Why must you always bring up my age?"

"Because it's by far one of the hottest things about you," he says, stroking my hair gently. "That and your resolve to do anything you put your mind to."

I breathe out and smile because for once; I feel calm and content, and it's all because of Austin.

"Thank you, Mia."

I pull my head back to look at his face. "For what?" I ask, trying to hold back my laughter. "Helping you lose your V? Because don't worry, you've well and truly ditched your Rookie status, both on and off the field."

"No. Although losing my virginity was important, you helped me with something more important than that."

"Oh, yeah?"

"Yeah. Before you, my life was heading in one direction. Baseball. It was all I ever thought about, and I genuinely thought I was happy. Hey, I got into the Major Leagues thinking like that, didn't I?" He raises his shoulders, looking sheepish.

"You did, and that's an absolutely incredible achievement."

"It is. But you know what? I didn't realize how empty it was until I found something that made me full."

My heart skips a little, and I try to hide my smile because I'm bursting with happiness. "And what makes you feel full?"

"You and Jett." It's short, simple and something I already knew because Austin's generous with his words, but that doesn't mean it makes me feel any less happy about it.

Austin takes my hand, kissing each knuckle in what feels like a promise. I check over my shoulder to make sure Grayson and Ivy aren't watching. No one is. It's just me and Austin outside this courtroom. "Whether you like it or not, the two of you have given me something to fight for. I want to be the best I can be for the two of you." I roll my eyes, dropping my forehead onto his chest. "I wouldn't have smoked so many homers, or batted in so many RBI's if it wasn't for you."

When I finally gain enough courage to look at him, he's just smiling, looking as content as I feel.

"Come on." I squeeze his hand, pulling him to the car. "Let's get home and celebrate before you have to get on that plane."

"That is the best thing I've heard all day."

EPILOGUE
MIA

Six Months Later

Heady and flustered, I push myself off the elevator wall, taking in my boyfriend. Wearing a tux, he looks just as gorgeous as the day I met him, and he's only getting better. With the side of my body against the wall, I lean into Austin's shoulder, toying with his little bow tie, and drag my finger down the buttons of his shirt to the buckle of his belt before toying with the thing I found there.

Looking down, I smile because I'm so proud of him. "Never thought I'd say this, but that is an impressive piece of wood you've got there." I giggle, stroking my thumb across the hard edges, unable to hide my excitement. Unfortunately for him, all of that free champagne has gone straight to my head, and I can only think about one thing. Thankfully, just like the Rookie ball, we skipped out early, so are the only ones in the elevator, otherwise we might get kicked out of the hotel for indecent exposure.

Grazing my fingers across the wood, I tickle against the hard ridges, waiting for a reaction from Austin.

Pecking me on the lips, all he does is give me a small smile and snuggle into me. "A piece of wood? Really? You never thought you'd say that? Because calling this," he raises the square award, "a piece of wood is like saying the World Series trophy is just a hunk of metal."

He raises a brow and kisses my nose in amusement. I pull back in shock, looking at him in disbelief.

"A hunk of metal? That's blasphemous. Who on earth would say that?"

Shaking his head, he laughs. "Doesn't matter. What matters is that you're all mine tonight." He cups my ass with both of his hands and kisses me ever so gently. I squeal when he squeezes, excited about what's coming tonight. We've got to celebrate his win after all.

Before I can enjoy it too much, the piece of wood - I mean trophy - pokes into my belly. "Ouch." I pull away from Austin's lips far enough for him to hear it. Tapping on the top of it, I say, "Can you put that down? It's getting in my way."

He shakes his head, and bites my bottom lip before popping it out. "I'm not putting it down until we're in the hotel room and it's safe and sound on the desk."

I roll my eyes, still toying with his belt buckle. "Come on. We're the only ones in here and even if it went missing, your name is on it. No one's going to take it because it'll be obvious it's stolen." As I raise his arm to admire his trophy, Austin tries to kiss me, but I turn my face, forcing him to kiss my cheek so I can look at his award for a few more seconds.

AUSTIN ADAMS
ROOKIE OF THE YEAR

He did it.

After this crazy, whirlwind time, Austin beat all the odds and actually managed to become Rookie of the Year. So many things could have gone wrong for him, but he did it. He worked his ass off each and every day and I couldn't be prouder of him.

He lets me take the trophy, and I re-read the plaque, stroking the little silver ball player in the center as I do. Austin growls, biting my earlobe, before he says, "What have I got to do to get that kind of treatment?"

I smirk and look at him with hooded eyes, while I suggestively rub the helmet of his trophy. "You don't have to do anything. You know you'll get it." I kiss him with just enough promise to keep him satiated for the rest of this elevator ride. "So, Mr. Adams. How does it feel to be Rookie of the Year?"

He grins, his eyes almost as bleary as mine from all the alcohol. "A whole lot better if I was celebrating inside you."

I roll my eyes, noting that we only have three more floors before we get to the penthouse suite. "Mhmm. And what's your plan after you finish celebrating? MVP? All-Star?"

He laughs, dropping his hips against mine so I can feel his erection growing. "What's with all the questions? Are you auditioning to be a broadcaster now? Because there might be an opening soon if Sienna takes a leave of absence." He winks, squeezing my hips before giving me a gentle thrust, and I throw my head back, not wanting him to see how good that makes me feel.

Sinking my teeth into my bottom lip, I focus on that spike of pleasure before shaking my head. "Nope. I'm just a curious fan worried you might get traded. What would the Caroline Catfish do without you?"

"I think that's the wrong question, Boss Girl." He kisses me on the lips, long and hard, before stroking my hips, and moving down to my ass cheeks. To say I want to celebrate with him would be an understatement. I *need* to.

"The real question is, what would I do without you?"

As the elevator dings open, I push him away, strutting out into the hall like I'm the hottest woman on earth, because that's how Austin makes me feel. Even though there were plenty of women at the event tonight who were younger, thinner, and prettier than me, he wasn't looking at anyone else.

Austin jogs behind me and, as he gets closer, he leans in. "Don't worry, BG. I'm already in talks with the Catfish over a long-term contract extension. I want to stay in North Carolina now that I've got something to keep me there." He winks because it was only just last week, I asked him to move in with me and he agreed. I obviously checked with Jett first, who was more than happy to have a throwing partner around twenty-four-seven.

Some people might think we're moving too fast, but with his crazy baseball schedule, he's not around for at least six months of the year. Having him move in with us only guaranteed that I'd get to see him at all.

And boy, do I *love* seeing him.

Austin stops at the penthouse door and pulls the keycard out of his pocket. I roll my head to the side, eyeing my boyfriend with skepticism.

"But what about Greg Harbor? Isn't he going to want his spot back?"

As the door flashes green, he pushes the handle down and opens it. "What about Greg? He's coming back from a play-altering injury and trying to negotiate an extra ten million a year in his contract extension."

"And that's bad because. ?"

"Because," He drawls out, resting his big paw on the bottom of my spine to lead me into the room. "He hasn't played since he broke his leg. Giving him such a huge sum of money when he's untested goods is a bad business move."

"Oh, and giving you that contract extension is a better one?" I say, elbowing him on the side.

He takes it in his stride. "Well, yeah. I'm a hell of a lot cheaper and they know I have a reason to want to stay in Charlotte."

"What's the reason?" I tease, pulling at the lapels of his jacket as I drag him further into the suite. Minimal light pools in from the floor to ceiling windows, but it offers just enough for us to get to the bedroom without turning a light on.

He lets me lead him down the hallway to the master. "If you don't know the reason, then I haven't been doing my job as your boyfriend correctly."

As I walk into the room, Austin takes my arm and forces me to turn so he can kiss me fully. He takes his time, languidly moving his lips against mine with a slow passion that tells me everything I need to know.

"Besides," he says. "As much as I hate to say this, but the Catfish are better off putting that money toward buying a superstar like Holden Fox than investing in another third basemen."

"Ouch," I suck in a hard breath, wincing. "Poor Greg. He gets injured and you take his spot."

"That's the game, baby."

Without another word, He places his hands on my hips, and lifts me to the king size bed. When he drops me down, I open my legs so he can sit his body in between.

As I look up at him, he smooths down my hair, taking me in from above. "I'll never get tired of this view," he says, looking straight at me before dropping down to give me another kiss. His hand skates across my back and he plucks at the zipper of my red dress.

"Don't you think we should close the blinds before we get up to anything?" I motion with my eyes to the beautiful skyline view we have of the city. Even though the lights are off, and we're high enough that I don't think anyone could easily see us, there's always the potential weirdo with a telescope on my mind.

"Nah. You know I like it when there's a little bit of danger involved."

He raises his eyebrow and gives me a slow smirk. I roll my eyes, pretending to hate it, but he knows I like the danger just as much as him. He pulls the zipper down, watching as the dress slowly falls off my shoulders to uncover my breasts.

As my chest is revealed, he leaves no time for anyone to see. He pushes me down so I'm lying on the bed, and lavishes my breasts with attention. Licking, nipping, sucking, he pulls at my nipples, knowing all the ways to turn me on.

Dragging my hands from his hair, I move to his shoulders, pushing down on them while lifting my knees as a subtle suggestion over what I want from him next. He listens, dragging my dress down just a little lower to kiss the newly revealed skin there.

"Patience, Mia," he bites, lightly scolding me. "I'll get there, don't worry."

He showers my stomach in kisses, dipping his tongue into my navel before flicking it over the skin like he would against my clit. I whine, wishing he'd go lower, but he refuses to be rushed.

The cold air skits across my stomach as he lowers the fabric further. I smile because I know what's coming. With my eyes closed, I focus on the cool feeling as more of my skin is exposed.

Then he stops.

His thumb rubs across the edges of my dress as he looks down, and then back up to me with a wicked grin on his face. "Oh, Boss girl."

Then he whips the dress off me, so I'm lying there in just my heels and underwear. A deep growl emanates from his chest as he takes me in. "You didn't tell me you were wearing this." He pulls at the black garter belt, letting it snap against my thigh as it falls back into place.

"Didn't want to ruin the surprise," I say with sass. He pats my hip in approval and, without another word, he drops to his knees and pushes the fabric of my underwear to the side. I feel the cool apartment air skate across my sensitive, already wet skin when he spreads my lips apart with his fingers. "Beautiful," he says, taking me in before lightly flicking his tongue across my clit. So lightly that I barely feel it.

One more flick, and it's a little stronger this time, but it's gone too soon.

Again.

I bite my lip. The stinging pain there makes the light touches from Austin more intense, and I hate it. I'm withering and squirming, wishing he'd just touch me the way he knows how.

"Austin," I breathe, bucking my hips to get closer to him, but he wraps his arms around my thighs, holding me in place.

I can't move. I'm under his complete control, and I can feel myself on the edge, annoyed that it takes so little effort from Austin to get me there.

When his tongue draws lazy circles across my clit, I thread my hands through his hair, enjoying the buildup of my orgasm. There's a small pinch of pain when he pushes two fingers into me at once, but then it quickly turns to something better. Something so much better. White hot heat strikes through my body and my back arches as the pleasure pulls me apart, ripping through me with more veracity than I expected, considering the amount of alcohol I've had tonight.

Austin devours me, feasting as though he didn't just have a four-course meal. He pulls the orgasm out of me until I'm lying spent on the bed. As my hands fall from his hair, he wastes no time. He quickly takes his clothes off and cages me under his hulking body.

I'm still withering and tingly from the orgasm, but Austin doesn't care. This is how he likes it. He positions his cock at my entrance, and then peppers me with kisses before slowly entering me. I feel every inch, and enjoy the feeling of him filling me without a condom.

As much as I like the intensity. I want it faster, so I drag my stiletto covered feet up the back of his legs and clamp them around his thighs, forcing him to push all the way in.

"Yes," I hiss, throwing my head back onto the pillows. "That's it."

"Shit," he groans. "I'll never get tired of how good you feel clenching around me like this."

He picks up the pace, rocking his hips into me with so much force that I've somehow made my way up the bed and am close to banging my head against the headboard. Faster, harder. He rocks into me over and over again. Having had no time to get over my initial orgasm, my body is worked up again. I'm so close to coming, it's ridiculous.

Just as I'm about to ask Austin to slow down so I can enjoy the moment, it happens. My body jerks and the pleasure cuts through me like a knife. Austin kisses me as he falls victim to his own orgasm, riding us until we're both spent.

He lies on top of me, catching his breath while I stare at the ceiling rose above. We're sticky, and exhausted, but that's exactly the way I like the first round. Then we can take our time.

Austin pulls his body up and kisses me on the forehead before rolling off me. "Remind me to rent us a hotel room every once in a while." He takes my hand and gives it a little squeeze.

"Why?"

"Because there's no way I'm having sex like that with Jett in the house."

Slapping him on the shoulder, I rest my head on his chest, relishing in the afterglow. "You haven't even moved in yet and you're already thinking about when we can have sex?" I roll my eyes, shaking my head. "Typical Frat Boy."

He brings my hand up, kissing my fingers. "I can't help it." He bites the tip of my index finger before saying, "I've got a MILF that I need to keep satisfied."

Shaking my head, I pull my hand away playfully. "Thought we already discussed this. I'm not a MILF. Maybe more of an AILF."

"AILF? Aunt I'd like to fuck?" He presses his lips together, a curve of a smile lighting up the edges of his mouth. "Doesn't really have the same ring to it. Guess we'll just have to go with my previous offer."

"And what was that?"

"*Making* you a MILF."

Before I can answer, Austin's on top of me, kissing my mouth shut, more than ready for round two.

THE END

Other Titles by Ana Shay
Covey U Series
Swipe Me (Devin's Book)
Miss Me (Adam's Book)
Hate Me (Aiden's Book)
Teach Me (Coming Soon)

Carolina Catfish Series
The Mascot (Tate's Story)
The Balk (Grayson's Story)
The Rookie (Austin's Story)

Standalones
The Quarterback Sneak
A Quarterback For Christmas

Join my newsletter Follow me on Instagram Hang out with me on Facebook

Printed by Amazon Italia Logistica S.r.l.
Torrazza Piemonte (TO), Italy